Ammon's Horn

by

G. Amati

Savant Books

Honolulu, HI, USA

2011

Published in the USA by Savant Books and Publications
2630 Kapiolani Blvd #1601
Honolulu, HI 96826
http: //www.savantbooksandpublications.com

Printed in the USA

Edited by Doris W. H. Chu
Cover Layup by Daniel S. Janik
Cover Images by Guerrino Amati

ISBN-13: 978-0-9841175-8-1
ISBN-10: 0-9841175-8-X

Dedication

For Mom

Special Disclaimer: Any resemblance between characters in this work of fiction and living persons is to be considered an act of love.

Acknowledgement

My thanks to Marlon Sampson without whose patience, kindness and technical skill this book would not have seen the light of day.

Ammon's Horn

BOOK ONE

Ammon's Horn

'Twixt the guile of the gods and the silliness of men,
chance spins its threads,
and necessity weaves the fabric of history.

—Epididymes

1. The Weather

Outhouse Express. Newcomb-in-the-Mountains, New York, 07.07.79:

Howdy, NetNerds. Maud Pritchet comin' at you from Newcomb-in-the-Mountains in what used t'be The Great State of New Yawk.

Up here at 2500 feet, it's a cool ninety-and-three effing degrees at 2:00 of the Aye-Emm and we got weather's gonna blow-your-mind, 'mongst other things. Tropical Storm Melissa comin' down from New-found-land up there in Canada. Weather Service says winds south-southwest up to and exceeding 175 miles per hour and comin' your way.

Folks in Long Island, Block Island Sound, Montauk, Sag Harbor, and the Rockaways are 'due for a bit of weh-thah,' as we say down East. But that won't be for couple, three hours, so y' got time for a mornin' latte. Hang in there—this just in: Satellite photos picking up on a wall of water out in the Atlantic. Fifty feet high, hundred miles east of Newfoundland. Be hittn' Nova Scotia in about a hour. Due t' be raisin' hell in Maine Massachusetts, New Hampshire, Ver-mont in a couple or three,

I'd say. At given rate of travel ought t' be hittn' Manhattan 'bout 4 PM, give or take ten minutes.

Sez here, residents are advised to evacuate to higher ground, like say, New Haven and Bridgeport. Fergit the Jersey Shore. Get your slickers 'n galoshes out the closet folks. Lotsa rain drops gonna come fallin' on y' head, so don't sweat the subways.

Checked it out this mornin' and the book says the Big Apple's only sittin' 55 feet over sea level. Somebody should've thought o' that long time ago. Ah-yuh. Hizzoner Mayor Hershel Petardi says he knows the Long Island levies will hold. He inspected them hisself. Hizzoner says he's gonna put word in the President's ear about maybe suing them Canadians.

This InterNet WeatherWatch brought to you courtesy of our various sponsors, but hey, what with the weather an' like that, skip the cookies, spams and promos and head for higher ground.

So, NetHounds, goose your Tee-Vees, prime your Pee-Cees, pack your iPods and iPads, buzz your bluberries and twit your twitters, your tweeters and your twatters, wag yur wifos and fiddle your fifos, and stay online for the latest. If you're still there, that is. Chow, now.

2. The Immortals

Chicago, high and dry at sea level 575.

Meanwhile, in the cool privacy of a dining room at Borgia's on North Michigan Avenue, world-class-financial-magnate Phoebus A. Belvedere switched off the WeatherWatch and partook of a light luncheon. He was aware of the surly maitre d' behind him. His super-powers picked up the bitching and carping of three quarreling chefs in the kitchen below. And little Connie Ocho sat opposite watching him consume his lunch: an antipasto of a quart of black olives, a platter of tiny imperial tomatoes and diced cucumbers, all delectably chilled in a blue-cheese dressing, a quarter libra of Feta cheese, and a loaf of fresh Italian bread.

"Yes," he says, wiping his bearded chops. " "Where were we?"

"Shi-kahgah," she says. "I'm pickin' up a museum. Sci-tech kinda thing," says she. "And we buyin' out the Shi-kahgah University. Yeah, and Subsume Consortium's takin' you over."

"Ah, I too am thrown into the hopper. Do I have a choice?"

"Hyperion Industries. That'll be last bead on Banque Toronto's Mid-West string. Can't run the show. I ain't got all the pieces."

Phoebus washed down the last of the antipasto with a litre of Merlo Toscana and it was time for the main course, an *ami meh rassa mahala*, a

3

saddle of lamb roasted with leeks in the style of the Roumeli mountaineers. This he graced with a half-libra of rice pilaf and a second bottle of Merlot. Mister B. eschewed dessert—this mortal bod he'd assumed threatened paunchy—except for a quarter libra of *baklava*, a sweet touch of home he couldn't resist.

"Ain't that a lotta chow t'be eat'n' this hour the morn'?" Connie queried.

"Not at all," Phoebus crooned into his wine. "Not when you consider I stand 6 foot 6 inches in my stockinged feet, that I weighed in at 257 lbs., that I boast a 52-inch chest, a 34-inch waist and that I am blessed with a twelve-inch instrument instantly ready for action and capable of ten repeat performances in short order, a fact which I will happily demonstrate if you will permit."

Connie demurred.

"This mortal form," he continued, "requires little if any sleep, but it does demand ample fuel to feed not only its physical requirements, but my prodigious mental powers as well, and these are central to our purpose, are they not?"

Connie Ocho arched a dubious eyebrow. She sipped at her glass of sauterne. Phoebus wiped his bronze-bearded chops and belched. "Just for the record," says he. "What am I costing you?"

"I'm suckin' you in for thirty-bil-seven in stocks, bonds, options and securities, and you got nutn' t' say about it 'cuz I got your debt sewed up." Connie Ocho consulted a roll of figures just now ticking script from her wrist-unit. "The phys. plant is good—total neighborhood of 3 bil., plus."

"Indeed! A nice neighborhood."

"Yup. Subsume's gonna make us all one big family."

"With little…pardon, big mammá at the top."

"That's right. We arready lookin' t' tap the European scene. Better get ready, big guy. Crunch is comin' real soon."

"Crunch?"

"US Corp.'s on the edge of broke. Southwest Fiscal District's talkin' about separate incorporation."

"Southwest—that would be Texas-Louisiana-Oklahoma-Arizona."

"Them. And keep it under your hat. Quebec is seceding."

"Quebec! Yes. There's been talk…"

"Referendum gives the new premier a mandate. Canadian army's mobilizin'. Catch it on UBC inna hour."

"Oh, ye gods! What next?"

"Oh, I can tell y' that too. We're ready. Me and Harry Barleycorn, Banco Venezuela. And Ian Caltrop in Switzerland…"

"Surely, Constancia, you haven't been consorting…"

"Consorting, hell! Hot money's what's left of the world's hard currency. And y' know what?" Connie grinned ear to ear. "Most of it's in my off-the-books pots."

"Constancia! I am shocked! I never thought you would stoop to dealing in dishonest money." P. A. leaned across the table. His affection for the little redhead breathed lust.

Connie Ocho whispered. "You're smooth, sweetheart. Real smooth. But you ain't showin' me a full hand. Matter of fact, I ain't always sure you're playin' with a full deck." Connie chuckled at her own wit. Heat rose in her, but a cool head prevailed. "Hey, Pheebee baby, grow up. Whose money d' you think it is? Ever since the ol' Yewnited States got privatized, electoral districts been cuttn' each other's throats and playin' off-the-books and mirror-partnerships. That's better'n seventy-five years. Likewise the UK, and the French and the Germans—everybody tryna run a 'free-market' in a tight-ass world economy. That's why the drug wars never got 'won.'"

"What are you saying?"

"I'm sayin' you ain't been paying attention, loverboy. The 'drug wars' been a phony from th' get-go. Company o' US Marines coulda wiped out them Colombian druggers in a week-end, if Washington ever gave the go-ahead. They been draggin' it out for damn near a hundred years 'cuz that's where the money is, Charlie."

Phoebus' hand cupped her knee and he drew his huge face close to her tiny one. His smile was absorbing. His big brown eyes were warm and supplicating. Connie suddenly felt his enormous hand engulf her thigh. She murmured. "I still don't figure you, Pheebee. What'sa big deal a classy hunk like you got the hots for little ol' me? I mean, I ain't exactly ugly, but there's lotsa younger chicks out there better lookin' and standin' in classier bods than mine."

"Ah, dear Constancia. Who can explain the mysteries of love?"

"Bullshit. Gotta be more to it 'n that."

"I've tried to tell you. I am one of the immortals. Without me, you would not have made it this far."

"Yeah? And I'm the queen o' Sheba. Shee-it! A gal makes it big and sure as hell there's some jock's stanin' behind'er takin' the credit. Well, big guy—stuff it!"

"When, Connie? I am dying for your love."

"Pheebee, I'm touched. And I 'preciate whatcha done for me. But if I give you whatchu want it's like too much gyros on the pitabread, you stuff your gut and lose in'trest. We been doin' good, you 'n me. Let's not fuckitup, hm? Now, getcher hand outta there, lover. I got places t' go and bidniss t' take care of."

"Til then, dear girl. *Au revoir*."

****

Connie Ocho took her leave. The immortal regarded his glass ruefully. He savored her image—cherubic, red-haired and most sumptuous-petit. For a few mental seconds he dwelled on her adorable breast, imagining...and on the ineluctable movements of her derriere. Then, he fell into sober and serious reflection on what he'd gotten himself into. The thought crossed his mind—his sister, the goddess Aphrodite. Could Didi possibly have stacked the deck? Her powers were, after all, equal to his own. But no. She wouldn't.

Or would she? Because:

That previous spring, Paris had produced a most beguiling atmosphere and on reflection Phoebus assumed Didi had had something to do with it. The tail-end of a slushy-wet English winter the night before had become a paradise of French spring a few hours later. When he met her at Orly on the 6 AM flight from Chicago, she had assumed the mortal form of Désirée des Dieux, Chancellor of the University and CEO of Xenon Institute, Fox River Institute, a university adjunct.

She strode across the terminal a smiling seduction at 6 foot 2 inches by the old Anglo-American measure, 187.96 centimeters metric, weighing in at 77.08 kilos, or 180 pounds avoirdupois—a big woman, needless to say, and, if not beautiful, at least artfully constructed.

But, her beauty aside, he knew his sister for a knowing subversion of anything the male of him might contemplate. She'd delivered him a sisterly kiss on the cheek and they'd settled in for coffee at a bistro off Boulevard St. Germaine.

This was just as the American firms took their coffee break and *la petit Americain* came bustling across the street to le Bistro Piquant and, quite innocently, became the focus of their altercation, and this at precisely the moment Phoebus opened his big mouth and stuck in his foot.

Didi set down her cup. "Any man?" she scoffed.

"Any man! Yes! By the gods, I will maintain that a man with his trousers down and in the throes of passion is yet and still in firm possession of his sense of self-preservation. You laugh?"

"I laugh! At your foolishness. Ha!" Didi crossed her magnificent legs and revealed a length of thigh from under the latest Parisian spring frock. "I laugh," she repeated. "The feminine principle precedes the male. Without her, there is no him. Without his object, he cannot be the subject. He might as well be a panting puppy for all he knows of what she seduces him to do, and to believe he is doing."

"Such gall!" A. Phoebus roared. He pounded the tiny table. Coffee

7

cups leaped and went shattering to the pavement. "Without my inspiration not one of a thousand-thousand loves would have flowered. Your pretty nymphs and milkmaids would have withered into virginal senility had I not touched some laddy's eyes, his heart—yea, his loins—to see her plainness as charm and her unprepossessing attributes as desirable beauty. Why, without my influence the most beautiful woman in creation is a drab."

"You say so?"

"I say so! Why, even the infamous Helen of Troy was a skinny, knock-kneed little frump, passable-plain at best, until I got Paris to see her otherwise."

"The Hades you did! It was I who inspired her to see that buck-toothed, bandy-legged schlemiel as a handsome hunk, without which delusion the Trojan fracas would never have happened."

"You will insist, will you?"

"I will do better. I will wager!" Didi bit her tongue before saying so, but she considered her brother, for all his beautifully masculine powers, to be the biggest post-pubescent of them all.

"Wager? Wager? What are we wagering?"

"Let's see…I'll bet, as say *les Americains*, the plainest slut on two feet will leave you hard and panting. Give her power and renown and she'll have no use for you."

"Oh, Didi. Come, now. You're not serious!"

"Further, I will wager that the most common of human females is faster and more conniving than any male. Yea, and that when the chips are down she is quicker, slicker and meaner than even a god amongst men."

"Oh, come now. Even you know better than that."

Didi veritably hissed. "Do it, then! Set your godly powers aside. Swear you won't turn the anguished maiden into a weeping willow, or a horny farmgirl into a desperate sow. As no more than a powerful man, in the best sense of that word, you will choose a protégé. Give her whatever she thinks comprises the best of the world, and then…"

"And then?"

"Savor her gratitude."

"Oh, but this is too easy. I am almost reluctant to take advantage. But, alright. If you insist. I will choose her. And as no more than A. Phoebus Belvedere, president of Such-and-Such Ltd., CEO of Whatever-Incorporated, I will raise her to whatever heights she aspires. And…"

"And?"

"I will bed her, and leave her broken of heart and spirit."

Didi grinned a smile that said she had mischief up her sleeve. "Dear brother, if I lose, I will spend a year at Bunny's Retreat."

"Bunny's?"

Didi aimed a rigid forefinger at the television monitor screen situated but three meters away. Habitues of the bistro who had been watching a replay of yesterday's *le ballon* had the soccer game interrupted and the scene shifted. There shown what at first glance appeared to be a hotel lobby— except that the guests were all men. And the personnel were all comely young women in various stages of undress.

"What's this? Looks like a brothel."

"Just so. In Hollywood. For well-heeled gentlemen with more money than taste and more leisure than sense. If you lose, you work in Bunny's Retreat."

"Work?"

"A minion. The clean-up boy."

"What? The god Apollo clean up after a bunch of…"

"Without your manhood!"

"You mean?"

"I mean you clean bathrooms and scour the bidets and wash the sheets and wait on the resident ladies as virile as a glass of stale beer, as rigid as boiled linguini. As…"

"All right! I get the picture!"

"Well? Do you commit to it? Or am I correct that you, the paragon of everything masculine, are all talk, and that your judgement of women is that of a virginal twelve year old?"

"Hah! Do I detect a fine feminine mind at work? It does constitute a fine instrument, dear sister, I admit. But over-rated. One of our playwrights said something to the effect: "What her wit won't garner, she sells her body for; and when that fails she's not above tantrums, thievery, and tears.'"

"That sure of yourself, are you?"

"I've had several thousand years to study the subject. The tune never varies."

"Good! Then put it on the line!"

"Bunny's Retreat!"

"In one year. For one year. Without your manhood! And none of your godly tricks."

"In one year. For one year. On your back! Yass. And I will be your procurer. I will scour the bowels of the city for the finest of scruffy denizens…"

"As your American friends say, 'You're on!'"

Which is precisely when Connie Ocho came bustling her pretty little bod across the avenue and across the pavement anent the Bistro. And hence, the wager.

Now then, to whatever other skills and attributes she claimed, Connie Ocho added a marvelous memory for detail—the *petit Americain* came to fetch fifteen cafes to-go, three black, no sugar, four sugar no cream, one cream light on the sugar, two cream no sugar, two cappuccino, one mocha *arlesienne* and two *cannelle*, plus three croissant, two *brioche*, five danish-prune. She would memorize and deliver each order proper to the party requesting with exact change. She was last girl on the totem, so to speak, most recently hired to Boudoin-Pochard, RESN, Real-Estate and Survey Network, International, on the books as an accountant and dizzy delirious with joy to be in Paris and only there because she had *la langue Francais* down as pat as her Shikahga accent permitted, and because she was a mistress of British idiom, and because she made her way admirably in Demotic Greek and held her own in Hochdeutsch which meant she did more email correspondence and phone work than data download and that she had in three short weeks taken the eye of higher ups looking to replace a liaison VP, so that given her near perfect mem-recall and her fascination with matters of real-estate, she sat with her nose up the financial world's bunghole, a position which might have been of enormous potential had she been other than a relative innocent, and wanting but a mentor, a guide, a subtle hand to steer her to the point of leverage from which she might have…but she didn't. She might have remained that innocent, we maintain, had she not by sheer chance come walking across the pavement cafe of the Bistro Piquant, and had she not been gifted by nature, for which read her *mammá's* genetic inheritance, with a perky derriere and a bosom attractive to the males of the species though the entire gestalt she presented added up to less than the parts promised. She was, in a few words. a pretty little thing and bright enough but she would have never constituted a threat had she not chanced to enter the bistro just then and had he not caught her eye.

"That one," says Phoebus. He half-thought to have made a random selection.

"She will do!" says Didi.

And it was not until the next mental milli-second that the twitchy-pretty little thing came to ring his memory bell and had him zipping through his mental catalogue under FF for Familiar Faces. Phoebus' eons of experience with mortals stirred a troubling thought—was it not perhaps *she* who had caught *his* eye? In any case, that's when he heard himself saying it, caught himself, almost, doing it again, banging the table and making a wager just as he'd done in that Trojan-Greek fracas and a hundred times before and since and as always thinking two steps behind his big mouth and knowing deep in the self-honest core of his immortal being that he most certainly would come to know chagrin and regret.

A jaded sun bleared up over Lake Michigan. Morning temp had cooled to 92 F. and a breeze struggled inland. In mem-image Didi's powerfully beautiful visage hovered. Phoebus strolled on past the Hancock Building.

Didi's mezzo voice challenged. "You're on!"

Phoebus Apollo spent eighteen months at Connie Ocho's elbow. He coached her in the ways of blood-and-fang international finance. She held out for real-estate. She quoted her uncle Miguel of Kastriotis-Ocho Real Estate, Chicago, as having said, "Money is liquid, it flows, and it don't care where it goes—yours today, his tomorrow. But, real estate! Ah, that's solid! Own the real estate under the rich man's feet," as he used to say, "and you got him fighting on your turf." For Connie it was almost a religion. And, in view of the global climate change in recent decades, a 25-x 25 foot lot went for a premium.

By the Spring of '75, The New York Times confirmed a tawdry little rumor suggesting an affair between the ChairLady of the SEC and an unbelievable blonde gentleman, because of which liaison, or in spite of it, an unknown by name C. Ocho assumed a seat on the board. Later in the year, the greasier tabloids had the chairman of the USC Senate Oversight Committee on Financial Finagling paying an undisclosed sum for certain prints and negatives. Connie was named Committee Field Liaison, a position without portfolio and a staff of twenty-five. Even the stodgy and understated Wall Street Journal commented on the overpowering femininity of that staff.

Infinite memory took him back to the Spring of...'73? Yes, 2073. He had had to answer an appeal from one of the very few mortals still faithful to the ancient ways. A woman, a Greek—actually. Irena Kastriotis was less Greek than Macedonian, and less that than an Albanian, but then that folk had scattered after the Federation of the Balkans in 2015 and this was, after all, the fourth quarter of the twenty-first century, as these mortals counted, and she was an American now, in East Chicago, in business, Ocho-Kastriotis Real Estate. In any case, from what her supplication to the ancient gods said, not only was Irena Kastriotis a believer in the old ways but a faithful mortal sorely in need. And so Phoebus had descended in innocuous mortal form, and assessed the situation.

In brief, Madame Kastriotis was in the real estate business with one Miguel Fuentes, and Miguel was uncle, brother of the mother, to young Constancia Ocho of Pilsen, the Fuentes-Ocho's rising in the Southside biz world and coming into their own. What Phoebus glommed was already bubbling and fizzing like bad beer because himself, Miguel, the one they called "*el Azteca*," was fortyish, tall, slender, with intense black eyes and a fine Roman nose, and intriguing to the ambiguous sexuality of fourteen year old Constancia, even if he was "so old."

In brief: memory will abide, and the child will be forgiven for coming away feeling cheated and confused as she must because beyond the room-dividing tapestry in that modest beach house, the other party sprawled naked on the daybed was Carmen, child of her mother's sister, a handsome girl in her own right and certainly enough to add jealousy to a younger cousin's gutful confusion. Of such confounding is motivation wrought, says Phoebus in a philosophic moment, because the child heard and she peeked and she saw and she fled and she took with confusion the beginning of a knowledge —not that Miguel should so do, that came as little surprise to a perceptive child—but that she, herself, Connie, should sift those same confusions and eventually come to realize and to admit just what it was she'd resented. And why.

From such might Aeschylus might write a tragedy. Or Verdi compose a melodrama. Perhaps those same confused motivations will suggest why Connie failed to do something as simple as convey a telephone message. Days later, she, on an errand, was in the office and uncle Miguel out to show a property and *la Kastriotis* was in the ladies room tending to menopausal metaphysics when the phone rang and there was only the child to answer. The message conveyed to the answering device said to tell Mister Ocho that the evening's meeting was off. She recognized the feminine voice, which may be why she didn't convey, why she deleted the message, and why that same late afternoon Uncle Miguel happened to be hurrying to an assignation that would not take place but—and here Phoebus might have intervened, one supposes, except such sticking of one's immortal finger into mortal affairs is frowned upon even when the subject is a banality and the consequence is, if you will, absurd-funny, as in ha-ha-ironic, but no less fatal.

In short, Miguel raced in pursuit of illicit passion, the object of which wouldn't be there even if he'd gotten there which he didn't because Engine Number Forty-Two honked, screamed and wailed its warning and caught the little Audi convertible amidships at the intersection of 103rd and Avenue "O".

Banalities, we say. And ironies. Even if Phoebus recognized them as such only after the fact—the fact that Kastriotis' supplications to Olympus had emanated from no more than menopausal anxieties; the fact that his peripheral reading had mis-read the child, and the fact that immortals are not much less subject to chance and necessity than are this lesser breed.

Pressed by family, she did attend, if briefly, services and then the wake. Later, that prosaic practicality that is the objective eye said they'd dressed him in his best blue-serge and, because of facial injuries, had him lying there wearing his over-sized sun specs so that he struck her as looking like what someone later described as a "myopic owl" and that would be her last lingering image of Uncle Miguel.

Perhaps Phoebus Apollo should have seen the extent to which he and Connie Ocho were ciphers in the game of probabilities and why she insisted on being so difficult.

The dining room at Borgia's closed in on Phoebus' anxieties. As CEO of Subsume Acquisitions, Connie didn't need him anymore. She'd gobbled up his own position in the market and was climbing to the top. What was "the top?" Would the world of financial chicaneries survive itself? If not, where would the gods be without mortals against whom to measure themselves. The proverbial fly on the wall might have heard him utter into the silence of that morning: "Ye gods, what have I done!" And then: "By Jupiter (*pardon, pappá*) I had best do something before she brings the human world down about their ears. But I cannot simply quit. There's Didi, and the wager. Damn me and my big mouth! Control, that's what I need. Let her think she's in charge. Let her have her head, as they say, but be ready to rein her in. Right? Well said, Phoebus, well said. But, I am going to need help. If I try any of my godly tricks, Didi will stick her foot in, for sure. Well, then, as these mortals have it 'set a thief to catch a thief.' What better ploy than enlist the aid of other mere men? And women. Of course!"

Ammon's Horn

3. And a Beautiful Woman

Island Upsala, Sweden.

"One weaves his fateful warp against the dubious woof of others, and so is the fabric of destiny woven." So says some poet or other, and so did Phoebus, in search of these 'others,' depart the urban majesties of Chicago and presume to become that very fly-on-the-wall in the bathing facilities of an apartment on the cooler edges of the world.

Always the connoisseur of things femininely delectable, he watched an inordinately beautiful young woman step from the bath. He followed her movements as she rubbed herself down with a large towel, appraised the movement of her supple breasts and the trembling of her incredible buns. She turned her back against the advantage of his field of view and appeared to make an application to her nether regions so that by the time he buzzed to the opposite wall the object, whatever it was, had vanished into her generous bush. To his regret, she donned a blue cotton robe. Bare of foot she strode into her study and she activated her PPC, the Psyche-Photonic Conceptor.

That would have been near midnight. She nibbled American cocktail crackers, a bit of lutefisk, and sipped a light sauterne. She placed on her brows the mind-to-conceptor band and prepared for an introspect-meditation. As an invisible presence, Phoebus followed the progress of her program.

****

In the dim light of her study, Kirsten Lagerquist booted up. Program Psyche Introspect Binswanger produced a near palpable presence in the middle of the room.

In an accented Icelandic, her photonic alter-ego suggested a diagnosis. There was, Binswanger suggested, an imbalance between Kirsten's assessment of her *eigenwelt*, the self seeing its-self as a unique being, and her *mitwelt*, her social being interacting with the world. Which is to say, the demands of Doctor Lagerquist were at odds with the desires of Kirsten. Her professional identity was forever faced with the problem of what other people saw when they encountered the incredible package that called herself Doctor K. G. Lagerquist, seeing as how that party occupied 193.04 plus centimeters (6-4) of an unutterably beautiful bod from which height she tended to look down on most of her colleagues and associates. The person in that bod was brilliant and accomplished—an M.D.specializing in internal medicine, a Ph.D. in Neuro-Psychiatry with a post-doc in neurology, and Chief of Pyscheneuronic Surgery at University Hospital, all at the tender age of thirty. She spoke fluently eight languages (three ancient, five modern) and could have opted for a career in music—piano, cello or bassoon. As for marriage, the Doctor abjured the very idea. Science had established beyond a doubt that the male of the species was an evolutionary aberration. The Y chromosome was a fragile spin-off of the female X. The male of the species was on its way out. Before long, the evolutionary process would complete itself and the male by-product would simply fade away. So, why bother?

Biographical record attests Kirsten Gundarsdottir Lagerquist was born January 1, 2052. She was conceived on her parents' honeymoon in a fisherman's cottage on the island of Breiðifjorðr at the edge of an Icelandic glacier on an inordinately warm day

18

and during a calving of the berg. It is said that Gundar Magnusson Lagerquist and his bride Helga Hamsun, being young folks of prodigious proportions, made love for three days and nights without stint and that their exertions produced a geological disturbance which in turn nudged Mt. Myrdalsjokull into belching its burden into the arctic spring and that this is what nudged the glacier into giving way. It was that, or some combination thereof. Details are not clear, but her *mammá* records that in those co-incident and crucial moments she herself shouted her passionate joy and Gundar Lagerquist bellowed in blasphemous triumph, that the ice beneath the cottage melted so that the structure fell a full meter. The earth shook and the shock registered in Reykjavik a full 5 on the Richter Scale.

Cause and effect notwithstanding, the fact of the matter is the child conceived was bound to be like no other. Helga sensed immediately the rooting of Gundar's seed in her own fertile womb and in one of her ascents to ecstasy she'd said her prayers like any good Lutheran, and having asked God for a healthy youngster she hedged her bets and also requested the blessings of the pagan goddess Hild because, as any good Icelandic woman will tell you, it is Hild of the faeries who looks over a girl when it's her first time. And seeing as how she was a hundred kilometers from her own *mammá* and feeling alone and lonely and the big bull they said she was married to was spread out over most of the bed with his mouth wide open and making the most gawdawful sinusoidal noises, she asked also the protection of Frigga, most matronly of Icelandic deities.

The lovely girl was born exactly nine months later in the maternity hospital at Reykjavik. The infant weighed in at an astonishing 33.069 kilograms, or 15 pounds—not too surprising as Gundar Lagerquist himself was a considerable hulk and Helga was no cowslip, but the request for an additional blanket and the complaint of high humidity was nigh incredible coming from a party two hours old. They named her Kirsten after Helga's own *mammá*.

In short, how was she to deal with the world except in impatient contempt if only because the world insisted on standing in awe of her, if not in fearful respect? A brief biographical sketch in the *Svenska Tageblatt* portrayed her as a young woman who had risen quickly to stand like a colossus, her two long and beautiful legs astride the equator of the world of neurophysiology. In archaic American idiom, her Alter-Ego Program Binswanger proclaimed her to be "just too damned much for her little world." Was she, now? Doctor Lagerquist reflected on Binswanger's sudden choice of vernacular expression. Her heretofore properly academic AEP was becoming downright common. "Something in the air," her dear mammá would have said.

Says Psyche-Photonic Conceptor Program Binswanger:

Problem 1: Doctor K. was a formidable presence. Added to her stunning beauty, her outspoken brilliance came across as arrogance and quite intimidated the best of the professionals in her field.

Problem 2: Co-extensive with problem 1, problem 2. said that in one's *Mitwelt*, her interaction with the social world, it was Doctor Lagerquist who proclaimed there wasn't a male of this human species she'd ever met who wasn't either a fogy, a fraud, a lecher and/or a silly twit.

Prescription: Kirsten, the woman, must get herself out into the larger world. She must abandon the shelter of her profession. It was Kirsten, the woman, who needed desperately the heat of interpersonal friction to shed light on her self-knowledge. She needed to grow!

"Well!" the Doctor well-nigh snorted, she was not of a mind to be rooting about in the common trough. Her professional training—yea her success and rise to the top!—told her that as a psycheneuronomist she'd more than enough knowledge than most concerning the human organism. No, she insisted, there was nothing for it but to suffer one's superiority in silence and with as much patient tolerance as possible.

So much for diagnosis. Binswanger's prescription went on:

100,000 mg. love daily.
To be taken all day and every day.
Preferably from a worthy male.

Bodily needs, Kirsten called it. *Spiritual sustenance.* Psyche's vital song. Doctor L. countered with work! And more work! Doctor L. must see to it that the anxiety-ridden ninny who was Kirsten remain productive She must not permit herself this silly schmaltz. She must lose herself exploring realms no scientist had ever broached before—the neurological laws defining the boundary between brain and mind.

No! counters the sentimental Kirsten, let Binswanger see what might be done to alleviate this *Einsamheitsproblem*—what Binswanger insisted on calling her "loneliness problem." And her *Geschlechtigsangst*—at this Germanically clunky mention of "sexual anxiety" Kirsten blushed. Her *eigenwelt* admitted to surrendering to occasional daydreams.

In Kirsten's sentimental imagination, "he" stood equal to her own 6-4. He was curly dark of hair and bronze of complexion and he spoke in a throaty baritone voice. And his eyes—ah, his big brown eyes—looked into her own icy-blues and knew, just simply knew, what stirred in her soul and in her body. In mind's periphery, Doctor L. knew Binswanger was playing strange games this early morning.

How else explain the "vision" (what else to call it?)

This holographic image emerged somewhere between her mind and the middle of the room. She was given to know that what she witnessed was immediate. It was happening in the right now!

A sun-darkened, big-muscled, broken-nosed animal straddled his sweaty musculature on some kind of noisy vehicle. His crudity suggested that combination of features termed "a cute brute" by one of her sillier colleagues. Her Kirsten-self allowed the adorable fellow was taking a motor-cycle machine across the desert. He was an ath-lete, if, indeed, that's what he was. But then the desert vanished. She stared into a future scenario, as it were, and it was she herself who drove an automobile into a narrow street. She stopped and looked into the pedestrian plaza of a small village. The same hairy brute emerged into the plaza on his motor-cycle machine. He roared and putted about as though looking for an exit. He approached the street down which she had come and her own machine blocked the way. For a moment it seemed they looked into one another's eyes. But then, a tiny automobile barged into the prohibited area. He turned abruptly to her left and the automobile appeared to pursue him. Kirsten stared into the scene with anxiety constricting her throat. The automobile hit the motorcycle from behind. The athlete fellow flew bodily in a wide arc and he hit the cobbles and lay, oh, so still.

"Benni!" she cried out to him. "Benni!"

Doctor L. shook herself free of this chimera. It was all nonsense, of course. She ought not to permit herself such sappy daydreams, and at the mention of loneliness and sexuality she might have shut down the conceptor, Binswanger and all. But then, how could she possibly know his name was Benni? If she hadn't known better she'd have sworn the conceptor chuckled. Kirsten Lagerquist was laughing up her own sleeve, so to speak.

In a huff, Doctor Lagerquist put Binswanger aside and pressed the search engine for publications in her own and related fields. On the Web menu she opted for Akademe, address NeuroBiblio.Int. She browsed: an article published University of Bangalong, Australia. Some twit or other was sticking wires in the brains of kangaroos looking for "decisional syntax in axonal arrays." At the College of Medicine, Chicoutimi University Hospital, Chicoutimi, Canada, another spoke of "Self-reflexive emissions per gnomonic excitations in the hippocampal-cortical architecture." It was all so banal. So elementary. At which point she'd have given it up and gone on to her morning gymnastics if she hadn't seen on the mind-transcript screen, hadn't heard through the cerebro-audio transmit, saw—heard—someone calling her name. "Kirsten. Please. Doctor Lagerquist!" Int.Web menu vanished. A private channel accessed a "news" program for her exclusive perusal.

The summary whispered through her EarPod and into her acutely attentive psyche. Something about "gods." Two of them. About scientists, neurotypes like herself. And physicists. Specifically, one Anatoli Polichuk. Doctor Lagerquist knew him only as a name, and by global reputation the world's pre-eminent physicist. It said freelance "psyche-surgeons." Really? It said thieves, both public and private.

What Binswanger prompted next suggested a future connection and a rehash of recent events. Was this possible? Technology must have its limits. Or was someone, something manipulating the conceptor? And her own mind! Whichever it might be, there it was! Her mind-conceptor menu offered an image of herself scanning supervisory screens of the *hospetalen* command center. *Uff dah!* This was memory rehearsal! That previous May she'd been alerted to goings on in Organs and Tissues 3a. and 5b. But why the alert? She'd seen nothing more alarming than one Med.Tech on 3a. doing routine psyche-probe and another party on 5b. doing "poke and fiddle," as Lagerquist derided. Lab. 5b: that was the little gnome of a fellow, Gregorian, excising brain tissue and mucking about with hormone and steroid enhanced preservatives, zapping gyri and lobes and corticoid sub-systems with energy beams of one psy-frequency or another. Mind's eye recreated the squat little Gregorian fellow. He stood no more than 5-10, a dark and swarthy little man —her dear *mammá* would have said trollish—flitting about the lab and amongst the huge flasks and stepping over cables, and himself once or twice arse-end scorched of a laser cannon. In Doctor L.'s opinion the man didn't really know what he was looking for and she doubted he'd recognize it if he found it. What's more, contravening the rules, Gregorian had permitted an unauthorized party access to the lab. Official inquiry identified him as a "telecom-repair man." From the report one might assume there was a monitor to repair, or perhaps a photonic transmitter in the lab needed mending. Standard procedure said farm it out, not invite it in. What in the name of a flaming haddock was he doing there?

Conferring with Binswanger at two AM in naught but a skimpy robe, she saw her then-self in the Control Center, tall, erect, imperious in her stiff-starched white tunic. "Binswanger," says she aloud. "What are you doing?"

The answer came as a whisper into the chamber of her mind, as Doctor L. might have phrased it. The voice said, "We integrate the meaning parameters inherent in incidents heretofore unconnected but potentially predicated on a future-event becoming a parametric activator of pastwards incidents." Kirsten's common sense translated—put together unconnected events from the past so that they make sense in the future and so, existentially, the future makes the past happen in a "meaningful" way. Kirsten scoffed. What convoluted nonsense! Nevertheless, Binswanger insisted: Kirsten went into a retro time-trance: August 7, 2077, a scant year before, seeking an incident-connection between activities simultaneous in labs on 5b and 3a.

Specifics: MedTech Gerda Olafsson does a Positron Emission Topography scan, or PET, and records p300 consciousness waves. Through CmSr Monitor she records possible mind-thought patterns. Report says:

Janson, Helga, age 37, trauma, head injuries, comatose. Prognosis: subject's chances of survival stand between 5 % and zilch. Informal history says the silly twit had gone to Iceland for the skiing, the slopes of Iceland's Oraefajökull being of the few left about the EarthGlobe and so quite the rage these days. Play-back of subject's own mem-scan says she'd been hit by the falling limb of a mahogany tree.

Doctor Lagerquist noted there were no trees in Iceland, mahogany or otherwise. This being so, how could Jansen, Helga possibly remember it? Secondly: a sub-level sifting of subject's experiential inventory said she'd never been off the Island and had never seen one—a tree that is—in her entire life, other than in photo-illustrations. Which might or might not be germane except it left the fact—she died of head injuries. Question: What bashed Janson's head? Well, then, the med-tech must have somehow projected and so tainted the subject's mem-scan.

Med-Tech Olafsson herself was adamant in laying the tree-mem to subject Jansen's concussive hallucinations. As a good Med-Tech should, she had disconnected the leads from the subject's cortex. Her log records, and, yes, Olafsson's own mem-scan verifies, the monitor kept right on registering Jansen's consciousness frequencies and that would have been totally unremarkable except for the fact there shouldn't have been any frequency registration, or any response at all because for a full five minutes there wasn't any cardio registration, no respiratory response, the patient, Janson, Helga being total-physio dead! Mem scan records Olafsson cursing the crazy machine and offing the switch.

It was the Kirsten persona, rather than Lagerquist, who reduced the situation to its probable cause-effect. Radio frequencies are scatterable. A bit of atmospheric turbulence will interrupt the televisionary reception of one's favorite detergent melodrama (something Kirsten sneaked into her hour of refuge from duties). Given this possibility, there was but one other party in all fifteen labs doing any neuro-consciousness research at that hour. Logico-probability said—Gregorian! Doctor L. needed no photonic machine to do this remembering:

From over the lab bench Gregorian had looked up at her through his watery brown eyes. He was saying: "...indeed, to take an organ, a sub-unit, out of the brain and to seek out the "mind" within the tissue, this is generally regarded as the stuff of fantasy, is it not?"

Gregorian ventured as much as a purely rhetorical statement. Lagerquist had read the eagerness in his eyes. The man thought he knew what he was talking about. He actually expected a hypothetical confirmation but she wouldn't have it. She took up the contradiction, literally. "Yes," she agreed. "An absurd proposition, to be sure," she said. They drew close. He to one side, and she to the other. The meter-wide glass bubble between them revealed through the cloudy fluid the *giri sui-conscientiae* hovering there, three tiny pieces of convoluted tissue the size of a table-tennis ball. Photonic energies hummed softly and caused the estrogenic fluid to glow. Aram Gregorian's own voice on the audio-disk enunciated carefully, in academic English, the report he was crafting as a guide to repeat examination:

> Ruiz Evangelista Alejandro, born on the Golfo de Mosquitos, Nicaragua, age 52. Admitted, comatose. Severe cranial trauma caused by a blow to the cranium by the falling limb of a mahogany tree. Subject deceased 3:17 AM. Subject's psychic energy systems maintained uninterrupted by immediate activation of the Gregorian-Takahashi psyche sustainer system. Subject's brain continues production p300 waves. Strong emission CmSr consciousness frequencies...

The recorded voice droned on. Doctor Lagerquist wasn't fully listening. Subject was struck by a limb from a tropical tree on an island on the arctic circle? Not merely absurd, but stupid!

Gregorian: "I am trying to explain. He is in there!"

Lagerquist: "Who? Who is where?"

Gregorian: "Ruiz, Evangelista Alejandro. He is in there, in the specimen!"

Lagerquist: "What kind of tree?"

Gregorian: "The psychic essence…tree? Mahogany, I think. But, What has the species of tree to do…"

Lagerquist had reached over and punched the recording off. "There are no mahogany trees in Greenland, now are there? So your venture is an interesting speculation, Gregorian, but hardly conclusive, is it?"

Gregorian insisted: "Indeed, we have isolated and 'preserved,' if you will, his consciousness. Yes, his 'mind'! We are proving it is possible to down-load the human mind and to perpetuate its function indefinitely."

"Really, Gregorian. I have little time to waste. If you insist on pursuing fantasies, I'm afraid…"

"Not fantasies, Doctor! Pederson and I…"

"Pederson? New to the staff, is she?"

"Pederson, he is…electronics…"

"What are you saying, Gregorian? We have no department of electronics here at UP."

"He runs a shop…television repair…"

"A television-apparatus repair man?"

"Yes…but…"

"Enough, Doctor! I have duties to attend."

Gregorian had resigned his position at the Institute shortly thereafter. Free-wheeling association gave Lagerquist in memory what she'd overheard literally one late morning in staff dining hall—that the little gnome of a fellow had been "in love" with her. This was preposterous, of course, even if true. But why should she be remembering this now? Well, one did have to deal with inferiors.

The pendulum clock in the dining room behind her struck three. The retro time-trance was broken. Kirsten stared through her mental screen in wonder. What was Binswanger up to? This must be her doing. Or was she herself going bonkers? All right! Let it fall as it would! She knew her own voice to shout into the morning darkness: "Access! What have I to do with 'gods'? Or thieves? Or athletes? We'll bite. Who is the athlete? Synthesizer! Access!"

"Access Granted: Please Consider, A persona's Eigenwelt is a lonely place, is it not?"

"You're saying my 'un-conscious-ness' creates this?"

"Events did take place. Personages are vivo-extant."

"Really. I repeat—what have they to do with me?"

"Consider as possibility: Kirsten Lagerquist has inter-acted. The effects of her interactions upon others may be contributory to their decisions and actions. So will the pattern of events be affected. So will she be prompted to respond. As do the ripples of a pond."

"What's this nonsense about 'gods'? And thieves?"

"Observe scan of events now ensuing."

Binswanger took Kirsten Lagerquist's mindscape gently as in cupped hands. Her cognizance slipped the routine of time-present and time-to-come. She became an invisible witness to events transpiring in a place far away, in a place of pitiless sun and an endless vista of scorched earth, and the sounds were the strangled bass-baritone of motor-cycle machines. Lagerquist raised a brow and sneered. It was Kirsten who stared wide-eyed at the hairy fellow on the motor-cycle machine, and she who drew sharp breath at the "cute-brute" grimacing into the pitiless sun.

As a fly on the ceiling, Phoebus left her there. But not before one last fine *focus* of his compound eyes determined the nature of the cylindrical object this near-goddess of a woman had let all but slip from its pubic nest. Yes, he had chosen well.

4. Of Athletes...

Somali Overland Desert Rally, Berbera to Mogadishu.

That same July morning, a gull winging inland from the Indian Ocean might have spotted ribbons of dust churned up into the still desert air. On descending, that same gull made them out to be caused by cyclists, four of them, struggling against sand and sun and near intolerable heat. The sun torched their faces and sweat stung their eyes. The roar of the Harleys and merciless light framed their world. At Bahado, Team 4, SparaFulmine (which is to say, LightningBolt sparkplugs) had left the dry bed of the Jubeh and struck out into open country. Two of the teams were somewhere behind them and one team lay ahead. On their second day into the sand they'd lost Moresby to engine trouble. The remaining three bikes did a pit stop at al Hamurre and half way to Callis they were about to lose Benni Pistone to a bum fuel injector. Pistone told Blaisdel and Schneider to go on to Las Anode. He would side-track it to Iddan and catch up, or he'd call for the chopper. The whine of their cycles died quickly.

Light and heat poured down like rain. Benni urinated into the sand and the silence. He was near the end of his steroid cycle. The need for replenishment stirred within him and with the need came the beginning of depression and self-deprecation. Simple self-examination blistered him.

What was he? A rat in a maze. A name and an image in a video ad. A simple schmuck making big money for nameless, faceless shakers and movers. The little bottle was empty. The label on the little bottle read: *Farmacia Atletica...* Pistone, Bennino...one by mouth every twenty-four hours.

"A man dies in this place," he mused, "he's piss in the sand." Benni's memory framed an image of a Lo Sport magazine cover. It depicted "*il Benni*" in the saddle, all jaw, pectorals and biceps. Vivid recall gave him the publisher's office in Milano. An agent shimmied her fluid buns across the office. She muttered something about the body of Adonis and the *acutezza* of a brick. She'd laughed. He'd had to look that one up in Paco's dictionary. Paco was his manager. His friend. But he sensed even Paco acknowledged Bennino Pistone was no mental giant. Benni raised a median finger to them all. "Awright, so I ain't the sharpest knife inna drawer. Go piss inna sand! Tell lo Sport 'at's what Benni Pistone said."

From the edge of his mind he measured the distance between the kid on a second-hand bike in the mountains of Italy's Abruzzi and, as a young man growing up in Brooklyn. Mind-mem measured the manufactured icon he'd become in Milano and other sports capitals of the world. Paco's voice came to him like a reassurance and a reaffirmation. "To climb Everest is the yesterday news, eh?" Paco said. "Last year, Bugaroff and that Australian climb the North Peak inne underwear and sneakers. Anna sonic-speed racing is for the Saturday afternoon they interrupt the commercials. Now the world makes the peace—everbody got a full belly anna guarantee you gonna live hundred-fifty year. So nobody cares who pulls the strings. Politics is for yesterday, anna screw-balls make trouble we shoot 'em or we put 'em inna jail. Money! At's what counts. Money for the beegeh-shot. And sport is to make happy *i scostumati*, the slobs, like you anna me, ah?" Memory's rehearsal had the diminutive Paco pacing the garage-office with his thumbs in his vest, and he lectured. "Anna for us there is the steroids, all nice an' safe an' legal. They got guys playing games bottom the Pacific Ocean. I mean, c'mon Benni, only thing ain't been done somebody takes a cycle 'cross the desert. I mean, it's gotta pull in a buck, you don' think?"

So, Benni risked his sweaty hide in the Somali desert with a mil. in corporate backing and hype. For what? So's he wouldn't have to work for a living? *Come on!* But, enough of self deprecation. Paco was the brains here. Orders said detour to Bahado. See the Frenchman, Castigné. Drop off a small package, and get back into the race. Benni removed three wing-nuts from the injector cover. His fingernails removed the punched American dime from the injector throat. He replaced the cover and remounted. The Harley snarled and droned over the rutted track, due south. Bahado oasis was a bump in the sand, tents and goat turds. "Go west," Paco had said. "Five kilometers. Take the track. You can't miss it. A garage. Cinderblock." And there it was.

In the 30's the place had been a wireless station in the Mussolini war with Ethiopia. In the '90's the Americans put in the pumps to fuel their 'copters chasing Somali gangsters. The patched-up wall to the west was *souvenier* of mortar fire out of the Ethiopian incursion of 2007. Benni cut his engine. The silence hissed like steam. The pumps were sand scoured cylinders; the garage, a cinderblock shack set on a tarmac apron under a tin roof. And like an anomaly from a future age a slender antenna of light metal struts climbed the cinderblocks. Against the late sun, Benni squinted up at it. The antenna was seven meters of aluminum struts and, atop this, a meter-wide affair of three intersecting, counter-rotating hoops. The hoops sat atop a black box the size of a small valise. Not like any broadband transceiver he'd ever seen.

The garage smelled of petrol and stale oil. A German three-quarter-ton hiked its rear on a jack. In the little office, atop an antique digital computer, a phosphor-screen monitor stared at him. A little man slumped in a swivel chair before the desk. The computer hummed. The little man stared unseeing at the ceiling.

"Ei. I'm here to drop off a package. Wut's goin' on?" The sun-browned little man didn't stir. "*Ma, che fai? Dormi?*" You 'sleep? No response. The thought pushed its way through his mind. "You dead?" Benni put his fingers to the side of the man's throat as he'd seen done on his videocom. Supposed to be a pulse, or something. Nothing. There were no signs of violence. No blood. Ugly little fart. Still warm. Stank of sweat and whiskey. His uncle 'Mando, that's what this reminded him. Armando Pistone had gone the same way. Sitting under the arbor, a glass of grappa in his hand. Died, of a heart attack. Never spilled a drop. Apprehension roiled Benni's gut. On the desk, a SatCom phone and a few sheets of paper. Benni summoned his grit. If the man was dead, what to do with the package? Just leave it here? Who was to pick it up? If it got lost, or stolen, he'd not collect his money. Best judgement spoke to him in the voice of his *pappá*—"Ei, jackass. Check the desk drawers!" Benni examined the drawers. Nothing of consequence. An hour shot and he was fifteen kilometers off course. Screw this scene. The SatCom phone buzzed. It buzzed again. "Allo."

"Hello, Castigné." A woman's voice.

"Naw. Castigné…he went out."

"Out? That's not possible. Who are you?"

"I'm Pistone. The messenger. You understand? I come to drop a package. The old man, I think he 's dead."

"Oh, shit!"

"Yeah? What I'm s'posed to do? I want my money."

A long silence. The woman came back on the line: "Listen, Pistone, you have a computer working?"

"Yeah. A computer."

"What does it say?"

"Says: Kolditz-Probisch Freight. And lotsa numbers."

Another long silence. The woman came back on. "Listen carefully, my friend. You have the package? "

"Yeah. I got it."

"Good. Open it." Benni unwrapped the package carefully.

Four old fashioned computer "floppies" fell out onto the desk

"You have the discs? Good. Put the red one into the D7-drive. Know how to do that, do you?"

"Yeah. I'm not stupid."

"Type in Siphon UWB and hit Control-Power."

Okay, siphon UWB, Control Power. Now what?"

"The antenna is not responding. Hit it again."

"Yeah. Okay. Nothing happens."

"Goddammit! Something's wrong with the disc. Or the PC's screwing up. Better move fast before the whole thing crashes. Listen, friend, I'm going to have to read it off to you, hear? You copy and program the antenna from there."

"Z'at what it is? Okay, I can do that."

"Good! You do this for me, I guarantee you double what you were promised. Okay?"

"Double?"

"Double."

"Jussa a minute." Castigné occupied the only chair. Benni ventured a tug at the left arm. The little man slipped forward. The chair rolled out from under him and he slid to the floor. Benni took him under the 'pits and pulled him to one side. He slid the chair to the desk and sat. "OK. Go."

"How's your typing?"

"Not so good. Two fingers."

"It will do. Take your time. Type as follows: A. Test selection signal frequency. Divert per optical antenna frequency parameter 28 to 30 GHz. Target Cell Tb75 at frequency 29.73 MHz. per ATT Broadband at 1500 kps. Got it?"

"Yeah. I think so. But you gotta talk slow."

"Slow as you please. Just hope the PC doesn't crash. Okay. Next line: B. Test reception point Bank Colombo. Sri Lanka via SatCom relay IndOcean recept 29.73 MHz. Got it?"

What followed was an hour of recitation, Benni to whoever this was, and she, from what Benni could fathom, was selectively feeding on-going transmission through this antique machine and the green floppy disc and thence to the strange hoop on the tower out there. He mused: whoever this was, and whatever the program might be, it had to be shady. "They must be crooks!" He astonished himself with his own perception.

He'd been intent on the scripted screen when it happened. Even later he couldn't be sure he'd actually seen her, or whether it was the insufferable heat pushing him to delusions. Yet he would have sworn...She appeared, slowly at first. Her face and figure widened 'til she filled the monitor. Pale, she was, and very blonde and wearing no more than a skimpy white bathrobe. In the span of a mind's moment he forgot the programming and the matter of funds and banks because this beautiful apparition seemed to be appealing to him, calling his name soundlessly. Benni squeezed shut his eyes. He shook his head, and when he looked again, she was gone. The screen read SatCom relay IndOcean recept 29.73 MHz.'

Got it? The voice on the phone insisted.

"Yuh," he grunted. "I got it."

Kirsten. That was her name. But how could he know that?

Benni rolled the screen gingerly, one line at a time, his big fingers unused to the little keys. The woman was talking to someone else, and she came back with a chuckle. "It will do!" she almost laughed. "Now attend very carefully. Press the key says Matrix. Keep your finger on it. And hit a hyphen 5 once more."

Benni did as he was told, slowly. Screen director lower right-hand corner said: Chanticleer Directory Override Siphon Yes? No?

"Okay. I done that. Now what?"

"Does it give a total?"

"Total. Says, "47,523,244.32 Euro dep, Override Siphon."

"Good! Press I for Insert."

"Okay."

"Listen carefully. Next to the computer find a small apparatus, looks like a black, plastic pencil case."

"Okay. I got it."

"There are two little buttons on it. One red. One green. D'accord?"

"Okay."

"When I give the word, in fifteen seconds—that will be at 12:00 your time—you do have a watch…"

"Yeah. I gotta watch."

"Good! Let us synchronize. I have reset my watch to your time. I have 11:58. Ready?"

"Ah, 11:58. Okay. What I gotta do?"

"At exactly 12:00 hours, noon, press the green button. And counting… 58…59…"

Benni punched the button. The blue screen produced:

Directory Chanticleer.

Parallel-Read, program Select-Infect inserted. Operator this program will now remove disc. Operator will proceed per protocol.

The telephone line went dead. Computer screen went blank. "Allo? Allo?" Had the woman hung up on him? Benni stared dumbly at the black screen and he felt used, and foolish. His mouth tasted dry and sour. His wits said he'd been conned. His watch said he'd lost the race. And he was out the money promised. But he had the discs. He read idly the labels inscribed on each:

OP. Siphon: 1. Op. Siphon 2. Op, Siphon.3. Op. Siphon 4. Activate.

Maybe big money involved. They owed him, yes? Benni shoved the discs into his shirt pocket. Paco would know what to do.

By quarter to ten he was back on the sand and on his way to Iddan. He mind-drifted back to the office in Milano. The agent shimmied her buns and insulted him. He remembered sweating under studio lights in a wet tee-shirt and in painfully tight jeans. The photographer grinned at him from behind the camera and she gave him the tongue and lips gesture. Maybe he wasn't big horsepower in the brains department, but there were lotsa women. And the money was good. But then the Harley's engine coughed. The injector was clogging for real.

The sign read: Iddan, population 100,000. Benni eased the big machine down-slope into the main street. Neat white buildings, commercial establishments. Garage Caruso was a low, white box set back of petrol pumps and a concrete apron. A mechanic took the bike. Benni doused himself in cool water from a hose and found the john. The scrawny mechanic slipped in a new injector, fastened, twisted, closed and tested.

Ada Caruso was tall and heavy-set like an Italian peasant of his own stock but dark of skin and fine of feature, like a good-looking Somali. Benni mused—her *pappá*, or her grandpappá, had to be a *Napoletano*. In grease stained jeans and shirt she toweled her hands and stared at him. Her big breasts strained at the work-shirt. She smiled at him and her nipples had come erect. He and she came to stand nose to nose. He looked down into her great brown eyes, she up into his own. In good Neapolitan dialect she murmured, "*Ei, paesan*'. What's your name?"

"Benni Pistone."

"That's not what your *pappa* gave you."

"Pee-sto-neh Been-neen-oh."

"Yeah." She gave a devouring grin. "That's more like it. Well, Bennino, your bike is ready."

"You do nice work."

She drew closer and she said, "We aim to please."

And he said, "Pays to have good equipment."

And she said, "And to know how to use it."

"And he said, "I'd like to try it sometime."

And she said, "You know where I live."

Benni took a last swallow of bottled water, spat onto the concrete and remounted his Harley. In a thousand meters he'd left Iddan behind and the road unwound due-south, an interminable ribbon of concrete down the Somali coast. To his left, the sun scattered diamonds on the Indian Ocean. To his right, sand and seared earth vanished against a sterile sky. The mem-image in the monitor flooded his seeing…She called his name softly…

Benn-neee…She was so very byoo-tee-fool…Kirsten was her name. The image faded. The monitor screen had reverted to symbols and figures. Yes, he had to be going flaky. Six hundred kilometers to go. Last stop, Mogadishu.

****

Kirsten shut her eyes against what she'd seen. The man…Benni…he had hit the pavement so hard! He might be dead. But it was Lagerquist regained control. At what was she recoiling? She didn't know the figures on the screen as anything other than mind's fictions. Had this really happened? Or…At which point the thought descended like cold water poured down her back. Or was that yet to be? Benni, Kirsten murmured. Desire rose warm in her big body. At which point, to her own amazement, her mind screen brightened once more and she looked into another alien scene.

Ammon's Horn

5. Thieves

Into the winter months of '79-'80, global warming continued to be unpredictable. A rise in Pacific currents pushed an Arctic front east and down onto the great City of Toronto and by the ninth of December it came down as sleet and rain. A few hours later the temperature dropped into the teens and the City of Toronto was a windy waste of new snow frosting old sludge and ice. In mind-screen, Kirsten saw a frowsy little woman stop just inside the rear Service-Personnel entrance to FirstBank Toronto.

She removed her hood and shook the crust of rime from her coat and from her tote-bag. She hung up the coat and made for the security desk. The guard regarded the mousy middle-aged frump. She placed her feet in the proper "X" marks on the floor and the camera picked up the name on her blue lettered I.D. tag: "M. Brewer. FBT TH 1370652: Restricted 4-5." Invisible fingers swept her body. A retinal reading and a configuration sweep verified her physical identity. The guard at the desk noted Visual Recognition in his log. He motioned her on.

Floor Five. International Matrix. The elevator doors swished shut behind her. No surveillance cameras beyond the elevator. Widely spaced cubicles to her left and glass fronted offices to her right. Brewer rolled her bagrack purposefully down corridor. Midway down she extracted a denim roll from the bagrack and deployed a pre-select-frequency scanner of Cray's devising. It narrowed Brewer's recept of Bank Toronto's UBADS beam to fourteen discrete transmission bands. Of the fourteen, one frequency width would command precedence. It would be receivable only through a cerebro-conceptor chip implant, and it would bear Ocho's output "fingerprint." Cray and Brewer knew that "print" like the sound of the woman's voice. At the entry to CyberSpace Cubicle 17, Brewer's scanner signaled a hit. The operative's name announced itself in black letters on white: Quentyn, Beryl and Control Matrix Central. Brewer narrowed her search. Quentyn, Beryl had to be the bearer of a cerebro-chip-implant entrusted to a Matrix Control.

Brewer sat herself at the conceptor console. She adjusted Quentyn, Beryl's CCI band to fit her own brows. The cerebro-chip implant in her brain responded immediately and, in effect, she sat in Beryl, Quentin's "mental space."

At Brewer's behest, the Conceptor proffered program Penumbra Chimera. Examination proceeded from this cover-all to a second encrypted program. Program Two implied a further descent. And Three suggested one still further. From here Brewer inferred Operative Programs to employ a nested-eggs configuration. In twenty minutes she peeled six successive eggs and she sat staring into Chanticleer whose page forbade further inquiry.

Brewer called up a ten-day history. It said that a week before, in a routine safety scan, Quentyn, B. had run a Simulated Intrusion exercise. The simulation had examined Penumbra-Chimera's seven eggs for evidence of infection. Brewer clipped a MemChip-reader into the circuitry and re-accessed that Mem-File as a Clear-All Exercise. The CAE copied to the MemChip reader and the reader relayed to Brewer's own cerebral implant. The SI exercise in Quentin's directory was now accessible to Brewer anytime she chose to "re-mem" it, and with it the ideographic alphabet system of the encryption code. As Cray was to pontificate, Brewer had "brought home the eggs." Once they'd broken the code, the yolk was theirs to "poach," and he would laugh at his own punning wit. Left to solve—the problem of selection-diversion of Chanticleer's frequencies from the UBADS beam.

From her refuse bag, Brewer produced a cell phone. She inserted one lead from the phone into the conceptor transmit port and punched in a number. The phone-screen signaled recept-alert. Contents of the MemChip were transmitted to Dover in a matter of seconds. The transmission's buzz ceased. A man's voice announced. "Reception complete. Out." Brewer punched out, and the Mind-Conceptor interface went blank.

Brewer's near photo memory saw the cubicle exactly as she'd found it. She rolled up her tools in the blue denim and continued with her humble duties. Custodian's storage crib was equipped with an annihilator column. It reduced refuse to a harmless molecular dust. Brewer emptied her sack. The column made hardly a burp at the inclusion of a frequency scanner, a cell phone and a MemChip access microdot.The rest of the evening she dusted shelves and polished fourteen conceptor desks. She power-mopped one-thousand square feet of hardwood floor. She relieved fourteen baskets of their innocuous refuse and fourteen shredders of their paper noodles. At 10 PM she took coffee in the lounge and gossiped with three other clean-up ladies and a surly super. By 10:45 she was at the commodes in the Exec. Lounge. Midnight, she logged out. Security guard grunted good-night and M. Brewer ducked into the wind and snow.

****

Doctor Lagerquist drew a cup of coffee and gave herself to a profound musing. Someone was usurping Binswanger. That much was clear. Someone was infiltrating her alter-ego program to use her. Who, and by what extraordinary means, constituted a mystery bordering on fantasy. To what ends remained to be seen. A large fly buzzed past her ear. Wasn't it late in the season for flies? She replaced the Cerebral Access Band about her brow and it was on with the show. Retro-Scene Three gave her Chicago. 12.24.83:

****

The van wasn't supposed to be in the Metro Drive Underground at two in the morning on Christmas Eve. The police were supposed to see to that as a matter of routine. But they didn't, and it was there. And seeing as how Charles Endicotte was recently out of the State Pen he should have been minding his p's and his q's. But he wasn't. He was stone-sober, focused and at his technical best in the maintenance tunnel beneath the city, a well-lit, antiseptic place, air-conditioned and humidity-controlled, a place devoted to efficiency and directed purpose, the kind of place that appealed to him because it said surety, certainty, and control. Everything his self of selves sought and missed within himself, the technician in him found in the transistors, and the modems, and the circuitry of the empire of the conceptor.

The panels succeeded one another down the walls of the tunnel like mute sentinels, numbered and labeled cryptically. One by one the numbers declined: UBM FTWFC 146790MW-35-C. Reference chart said he stood directly beneath Chicago Center, fortress Chicago-One, First Trans-World Financial Commission. What lay behind this panel was as one finger of the two photo-optic hands connecting Chicago to all of the eastern US, Inc. and Canada and Central America and by sat-link to the rest of the world. If one understood Cray's oblique way of getting to a point, their quarry had unknowingly given them her commo profile. The upshot was that she could not enter the Trans-World system without alerting them in Dover, or in London, or in Geneva; that they had belled the cat and were now watching her move through Inix conceptor system across the world, depositing funds, opening, closing, diverting accounts of questionable money for highly dubious and anonymous people. Her moves alerted Cray in Geneva, or Brewer in London, or Endicotte in Chicago, or wherever photo-optic-cables to broadband-wireless to satellite-links might carry the arcane dialogues conducted between financial institutions big and small. What they said was that this anonymously encrypted party was preparing to scatter tens of millions or more across North America and Europe and Asia, preparing to hide the total in shells, in dormant trusts and dummy corporations. It suggested that Cray might have been in on something big at the beginning, whatever that was, and had gotten cut out. Cray had said little, but then other folk's melodramas were best left in the closet, at least for now.

The metal panel came away easily. The alarm system was a nuisance to one who had studied its circuitry. The critical seven points of connection followed the diagram on his clip board. Nothing to cut. Merely connect to the digital circuitry in proper sequence, a slipping in of the dime-sized chip he'd painstakingly designed in his sojourn at Menard Prison. The genius of it said that UBM's own frequencies would activate and simultaneously nullify any interference pattern. As did the best of viruses, this program became integrally part of the bank's own system.

He was back in the access column at two minutes to three. One minute to wait. The signal in his earphone clicked three times. Endicotte lifted the manhole lid and the aperture in the van's undercarriage appeared above him. He grasped the edges and pulled his lanky frame up and replaced the lid. Cray's bearded face appeared to him even before he was fully in. "Well?"

"Well what? Piece o' cake. I told y' that."

****

With the absurd ease of a television drama, the scene shifted once more. Kirsten was given to know this was Dover, England. Three conceptor screens stared from the sitting room wall of the small cottage. The ancient parlor table sported a multi-line telephone and a SatCom phone unit. At right angles, the surface of a mirrored bureau hosted a laser printer. From a workstation, electronic cables connected to the Universal Broadband Access Distribution System which beamed its signals along housetops and on to satellite relays across the world. To this end, a tower of light metal struts rose along one side of the ancient stone building almost hidden in the enthusiastic green profusion of an English garden. At the roof, the struts rose another three meters and a meter-wide antenna of three intersecting hoops peered out as something precise and alien. Its unspoken language attested indifference to the silent struggle of vines and creepers below.

A slight turn of her head gave Peg Brewer her own image reflected in the mirror, that of a nondescript, alcoholic "wash-out," as Cray described her. It also gave her the tall, round, speckled-bearded figure of Sebastian Cray approaching. "Who was that?" he inquired.

"The delivery boy."

"What's happened to Castigné?"

"His heart, probably…"

"The discs? What's happened to the discs?"

"The PC crashed before I had a chance…"

The big man was fairly shouting now. "Whoever he is, he's got the activator!"

"Don't take it out on me, goddamit!" she shouted back. "Something cut our UBADS broadband-to-satellite link."

A nasal, flat man's voice came through the SatCom speaker, London-Geneva. "What's happening, folks?"

"We've done it, Charles!" Cray boomed, affecting cheer. "Select-Infect is established. The glitch took place at our diversion point—Somalia to Colombo. The old PC, it's crashed."

"Figures. Got what you asked for. A one-time inject. One hour, one cable, one message and cut the line. Safe!" The voice was snide and ironic. "What's with the discs?"

"Calm yourself, Charles. The virus is inserted. I'll fill you in when we meet in Geneva."

"Peg," Cray spoke aside to Brewer. "Can you raise Paco?"

"Ungaroni?" she said. "He's on circuit. Mogadishu until tomorrow. Then a video shoot just outside Geneva."

"The cyclist. His name. . ?"

"Calls himself Pistone."

"Yeah. All right, Cray," Charles voice blew resignedly. "I'm off to Colombo?"

"Indeed, my boy. See to it The People's Depository is well prepared, will you? Pipeline's all set up for re-direct of funds to that account. Don't want any glitches on their end."

Peg Brewer turned to regard Cray with a worried look. "Perfect time for a screw-up. I've got the Siphon virus ready for dry run."

"Yes, my dear," Cray crooned. "Begin."

Brewer's big screen displayed a graphic of symbols and figures imposed upon a rotating representation of the Western Hemisphere, North and Central America, the Atlantic, and then the west coast of Africa. A tracer followed the UBADS data signal stream across the continent from Algeria to Libya to Niger. It veered south and east to Chad and the Sudan, thence to Ethiopia and the flat expanse of Somalia.

"There my dear," Cray crooned. "The Somali desert. Place called Iddan. Our diversion sticks a finger in. Chanticleer's frequencies shift ninety degrees—ninety degrees, mind you, across the Arabian Sea to Colombo, Sri Lanka! Ocho's Chanticleer will have proliferated into a dozen anonymous accounts scattered 'round half the Earth. Ninety degrees, and they drop! One-hundred-thirty-million Euros." On an adjacent screen to Brewer's left, new data appeared. Brewer scrolled up:

FirstBank Toronto, account Directory Chanticleer, S. A. number 561.906 CP. Credit to Account Furbe-Oblique, Genevre, S. A. no. 996.007 BB: 350,000 Euro.

Peg Brewer mused aloud. "Furbe-Oblique…"

"A new one," Cray smirked. "Connie Ocho has stuck a spiggot into KhazakGroupe PetroChem12."

Peg chuckled. "How do they get away with it?"

"'They' are the government, my dear. Just as Constancia Ocho is FirstBank Toronto. Her bank controls North America. She has them so deep into shell companies and tax-havens that the NorAm financial complex simply cannot pull out. And investigation is impossible: The investigators are themselves part of the system.

"Not that Toronto went in kicking a screaming, mind. As Liaison for Foreign Accounts, Ocho has long opened accounts for the less-than-respectables, cash up front. In a month, they're an old and honored name and their funds are legitimate-looking accounts around the world." Cray's countenance went grey. Brewer might have said somber, if not frightened. "She's going to conquer the world, my dear. Not with a phalanx of hoplites, nor a regiment of foot, no air-force or armored brigade, and she doesn't need an atom bomb." He chuckled. "Bombs would ruin her real estate. No, dear, she'll conquer with the weapon everyone respects—money!" Cray's face reverted to a cheery, rubicund mischief. "Yes, and our Siphon will be right there noting the transaction, ready to scoop up her eggs." He gave forth with a mock sigh. "It's dirty work, but then, someone must see to other people's filthy lucre, wouldn't you say? It won't be long now, we'll settle the score." He mused now in mock seriousness. "I'd like it to be a hundred billion. I do so love the very sound of it, hum?" Cray broke into a belly-jiggling guffaw. "One hundred billion in other people's illegal money. Oh, the delicious irony of it all. It won't do any good her trying to back-track. There won't be anybody there." Cray chuckled. "And if dear Charles does his task properly."

Charles' voice crackled through the room. "You keep screwin' up like you just did and our ass'll be hangin' right out there."

"Never fear, Charles. The gods are with us."

"That a fact?"

"Where are you Charles?"

"My man just met his courier at the British Museum. Got a suitcase big enough to carry a month's laundry."

"Charles? Are you there?" Commo between Dover and London hissed silence. Ten minutes later, the green connect-light lit up. Charles Endicotte's voice came through loud and clear.

"I'm at FirstBank London...service desk, three meters behind. Cashier's beeping me the high sign."

In Sebastian Cray's imagining, tall, lanky Charles Endicotte is dressed as a conservative English businessman. In the bank lobby he makes his way through the light crowd and opens his attache case on the service table, its leading edge aimed to the left of the cashier's window. The party at the cashier's window presents his card-encoded credentials. Cashier swipes the card and accesses the appropriate record on his conceptor. Across the three meters of the lobby a receptor program in Charlie 's attache case is activated. Cashier counts mounds of paper money and entries are made in the conceptor record. Funds have been deposited-transferred. The party departs. Charlie E. carries off a replication of that transaction, account numbers, amounts received and transferred to FirstBank Toronto, account coded Chanticleer.

An email message awaits Endicotte in his rooms at the Chalfont, London. "Charles. Change of plans. Best meet us Geneva."

****

Doctor Lagerquist mused. Where was the pattern to all this? The connections? To the motorcyclist, or whatever he was? To the Financial Commission in Chicago? And Polichuk? Someone named Ocho was buying out the world. What possible bearing could this have on Polichuk's work in SpaceTime Dimensional physics? And what could it possibly have to do with her? Kirsten requested, "Bioscan: Polichuk."

Digest said:

Polichuk, Anatoli, born 2002, Minsk, Ukraine; educated St. Petersburg Akademi of Sciences, Ph.D., 2026; post-doctorals Cambridge, and the

Institute for Advanced Physics, Manitoba…Nobel Prize for field-state resonances ("force-field physics") 2033…

Shared Nobel Prize with Babette Halevy (2040) for establishing the mass of the photon.

2042, paper on collateral dimensions posits the existence of parallel universes co-extensive with our own…shared a second Nobel with Herman Takahashi of the U. of New South Wales. Currently, Dr. Polichuk heads a team investigating trans-dimensional-interface physics at the *Institute Pour l'Etude de la Science Physique*, Geneva, Switzerland.

On Correlative Search, Kirsten's NewsNet revealed that the world renowned physicist had vanished from the main boulevard in Geneva in broad daylight. This made the nets, the teevee and print media from Kokomo to Khazakstan. So, Binswanger, how was this relevant to her? Give it a focus, dammit, or she would shut it all down! And what was this nonsense about 'gods'? Her dear *mammá* might still believe in elves and gnomes, but she, Doctor K. Lagerquist, M.D., Ph.D. twice over was a scientist and certainly far above such mythology.

But then the screen gave her what might have been an old-fashioned commercial interruption. A powerfully handsome fellow in a bronze beard grinned at her. His white, stylishly nautical tunic bore the logo Spa Apollinaire, San Tropez in red letters across the breast pocket. In a mellifluent baritone voice he hawked the pleasure of sun and water at this French resort. A ten second peep gave her hundreds of teen-agers frolicking on a beach, all totally nude and seemingly glorying in the fact. The baritone voice-over seemed to be addressing her directly. The fellow all but mentioned her name, She needed a vacation, he said. These youngsters were having such fun! Why didn't she join them? His face floated over the beach scene. He winked at her, salaciously, she thought. And vanished.

Kirsten Lagerquist sat back and let the light of a bleary dawn bathe her face. She'd been at the conceptor some seven hours and her body was weary. What she'd witnessed bordered on indulgence in fantasy. "What are you telling me, Binswanger?"

The voice in her mental chamber responded. "Existence of the 'I am' presupposes existence of the 'other' predicated on a simple polarity of complementaries."

"Polarity? Complementaries? Talk plain, dammit!"

"Plain. Kirsten is incomplete. She creates from her considerable intelligence this dialogue. She as *Eigenwelt* addresses herself as *Umwelt*, which is to say the 'I' consults the 'me' and the 'she'."

"Yes."

"Of which Binswanger is merely an objectification."

"Yes. I must know this or concede I have gone bonkers. But that doesn't explain. Who are these people? And 'gods'? I must be over the edge."

"Consider, Doctor. From a world of infinite possibilities, you have but to select, combine and create. It is called 'experience.' Or, does one fear to risk?"

"Risk?"

"There is always, in a system of many variables, the risk of a loss of control. The governing parameters may not hold. Initial conditions must be selected to ten decimals. But if the parameters include want, and need, and desire…"

"Who, then?"

"He may not yet exist. Kirsten may yet have to create him."

She lost herself in formless thoughts. When she roused, first sunlight streamed through the window of her study and she had a painful kink in the small of her back. The blank screen before her wheezed its photonic annoyance. Had she really seen athletes in the desert? Gods in Paris? And the great Polichuk himself! "Oh, come now," says the Doctor to herself. "Does a scientist permit herself the silliness of fantasy. But wasn't he adorable!" In her EarPod, NewsNet intruded once more. After five minutes of bite-sized local and international news, our news-gnat promised and camera cut away to a sage and ponderous sci-type pontificating.

...and so Earth's climate has continued to warm and our arctic and antarctic ice sheets have decreased drastically. Melting of the Greenland ice sheet has resulted in a sea level rise far in excess of the worst estimates of five decades ago. Sea-level is up 15 meters, or 48 feet so that forty percent of the North American population is impacted, the major effects being felt on the populations and infrastructures of the gulf and East Coast states.

Moving south from the Canadian border down what what once the coast of Maine, the town of Pond Island, suitably named, is now exactly that, a pond of water, as are Gouldsboro, Bar Harbor, Belfast and Camden. Goodbye to Boothbay Harbor, Brunswick and Falmouth. And scratch your plans for a visit to beautiful downtown Portsmouth New Hampshire: it is no longer there. Nor are Gloucester, Mass., and Salem, and US Geological Survey says the great city of Boston, good old 'Sandbags on the Bay,' is just a matter of weeks from packing it in for higher ground.

In pique and annoyance Doctor Lagerquist tore out her EarPod and hastened off to a cold morning shower.

****

In Mogadishu, Gigi Mirabeau and the Orpheon HydroChem team came in first on the 12th June at 1:17. Two of Fischietti's team, Electro Pastiche, made a second two hours later. Blaisdel and Schneider of SparaFulmine Sparkplugs, trailed a distant third. Benni coasted into the garage late that evening. Paco looked up from his racing sheet. His monkey-like face came up all creases and grimace. "Where the hell you been?"

"In the desert. Where the hell you think? Your friends, they fucked us! Me, I'm suckered both ways."

"Whatta you saying? Castigné…"

"Croaked. He must'a had a bad heart, I think."

"*Managgia! Chi se lo aspettava?* And the discs?"

"Here, you keep 'em. Wanna fill me in, maybe?"

Ungaroni shoved the discs into the pocket of his red zipper jacket. "You don't wanna know too much," he said. "It's dangerous."

"Ei, I'm out thirty-thou Euro! You wanna know about dangerous? I'm gonna tell you about dangerous!"

"Keep your voice down! I'll tell you what I can. This *Inglese*, Cray. Got a thing going. Worth a billion. Today is twelve June," Ungaroni mumbled. "They transmit—a week, ten days."

"Whatta you talkin'?"

"Benni?" Something like a smile cracked the manager's homely face. "I think maybe you should go back inna desert."

"Yeah? What for?"

"Was no conceptor crash. I think the Cray he cuts me out. Like before. Go take a shower. Get something to eat. We gonna talk."

"Yeah. About what?"

Ungaroni smiled. "When you was at the Bahado, you see the tower?"

"Tower. You mean the antenna thing? Yeah."

"The hoop thing on top. You better go get it."

Ammon's Horn

6. Send in the Clown

Back in Chicago, commercialization of the Christian holy day beeped, jangled and hooted from every corner of the city.

Phoebus sought escape from the noisy deprecation. He sank himself in thought mid the comforts of the Chicago Club. His mind went to the parallel and abstract. Any problem was fundamentally reducible to geometric principles. Pythagoras had said so.

Mathematically imaged on the screen of his contemplation, Connie Ocho (O) was the prime factor. Her rowboat strove to cross the schematic stream (Fundamentals of Mathematics for Secondary Schools, Scotch-Oarsmen, Evanston Illinois, 2063) to cast her trajectory as the vector of prime magnitude moving at a right angle to Polichuk (X), her prime objective. Then he introduced Pistone (P) and Lagerquist (L) as counterforces. If strong enough, they should cause deviation of O from point X by a factor of...ah, but there lay the rub. Constancia Ocho was not a rowboat crossing a stream. And Pistone and Lagerquist were not impersonal counter-currents of water.

No, this was a human equation. It required a human variant. A skew. If the Lagerquist woman was to serve as a trump card, then what was needed was what Las Vegas gamblers called "a wild card." In meta-humanicalspacetime, Phoebus searched a near infinite catalogue of referents. His interaction with mortals having been extensive, the immediate-timeframe took him across the great City of Chicago to the Southside. Historically speaking, one might say, he eavesdropped on the ebulliently unprepossessing likes of one Mackenzie van Horn and his variegated problems.

****

For van Horn, realities converged around morning coffee. They said December rent on the studio apartment was due last week, and the morning mail said the IRS was threatening him for back taxes because it said right there in merciless figures they had earned over three-hundred-thou for the year 2080, which put him—them—in the 36 percent bracket which brought the total up to—allowing for deductions, taxes withheld and including penalties for non-payment and interest on it all—to five-thou-three-something. He'd tried to tell the man at the audit *she* had earned it. Shawnah made the money as a physical therapist at the University of Chicago Hospital before she walked out on him. Before walking out, she published, right there in the Chicago Tribune, his name, big as lights: "van Horn, Shawnah Ogilvey —Statement of Disclaimer of Debts," just before she'd withdrawn their last dime and took saved-up vacation time to join her mamma in beautiful, sun-drenched Jamaica. She'd left him with the monthly statements and rent due, saying she was fed up with his "periods of retrenchment" as he called it, with his "opting for a mid-career course correction," all seven years of them. His shrink said he could call it a mid-life crisis if he chose, but for the fact that at age forty-three this was Mackenzie's crisis number eight or nine—ten?—something. That put mid-life back to his early twenties, a notion Mackenzie found self-deprecatingly funny. But what the hell, he had a job interview scheduled in the morning and the credit card in Shawnah's name was still good for seven hundred. It wouldn't be the first time he'd faked her scrawl and seven hundred was enough for a new suit, shoes, a shave and a haircut, enough to get looking mmmmmm gooooood! At 10 AM, he would interview with the man or lady, as the case might turn out to be...

The figure in the bar room mirror gave him back as five inches shorter than he'd have liked to be, pleasingly ruddy of face, handsome, almost, and pleasingly round. "Good looking," Martha had admitted—broad brow, strong jaw, "cute" nose she'd said. But that was on the honeymoon, and even if he was now 25 pounds over the limit, a dark three-piece with a tight vest gave him an air of sober maturity, that and the bit of grey in the dark curls about his temples. He could drop his voice down three octaves and make his blue eyes glitter steely-like and come out serious-substantial. There was all that and the fact he was quick to pick up the rhetoric and ad-lib the details of any problem so that those who knew him most intimately, Shawnah, and before her, Martha—his first wife Federika didn't count as she'd been much too quick and impatient to really give him a chance—as we say, those who knew him for any time, especially those who loved him, might see one Mackenzie come in the door and another one go out. It got to be a recycled joke—the van Horn was either "on a roll" again and like the rose in the privy would come up smelling mmmmmm gooooood. Or he was out of a job, down and depressed and deserving of tolerance and patience and a little lovin' til things picked up.

Phoebus mused: This was not to say Mackenzie wasn't bright. He did have a quick grasp of detail, what his shrink called an overly-developed gestalt, so he could see the picture, seize the over-all design of a project in minutes. He'd once tried being an actor, what with the great voice and all. But he got between the sheets with a member of the supporting cast and her young husband didn't like it, and how was van Horn to explain to the man his unutterable weakness for strong Afro-American women and their weakness for his line, whatever it might be at the time. So he got a busted lip, the young husband did ten days for assault, and the young lady disappeared as did a promising acting career.

But the gestalt thing, it was Shelly Korshack's view—Sheldon was

Mackenzie's shrink—that Mackenzie was potentially brilliant but that his Jewish mamma had smothered it, the necessary discipline, the kind of stick-to-it a man needs to go from insight to a patiently worked out, verified conclusion. That aside, Shelly said, Mackenzie van Horn might have been a bloody genius—this over lox and bagels and a beer at Kupferman's on State and 43rd on Chicago's south side.

Shelly Korshack was to write Mackenzie up in a book of case histories, later, much later. The description made van Horn to be a man whose knowledge of himself was a gratifying image, whose memory was an on-going video, and whose life was a script rewritten to suit the hero of the day. Which is how, moxie to the fore and in new Brooks Brothers threads, he got to see the Brunhildee in Personnel at the University's Xenon Institute Labs in posh Fox River Valley forty-some miles west of Chicago and to be working on the Mandlebrot Project where they were charting "the whole fokn' universe," no less, making a road map of SpaceTime, they said, in 4dim. configuration projections. You had to be a mathematician, damned near, a bloody physicist just to run the cerebro-transcript DMC, Direct-Mind-to-Conceptor, for crying out loud! and here he was, with barely two years in the junior college, starting near middle of the ladder, pushing twelve-five-plus a month, one-twenty-five thou a year, before taxes, proofing-editing-styling "messin' with biiiig stuff, real intel-lek-choo-all," he clowned because he was on a roll and somehow, in three days time he would learn what he needed to know about running a DMC or enough to fake it 'til he got good at it, and if he didn't, well, what was to lose?

If, indeed, as they say, the Judeo-Christian God takes care of fools, drunks and little children, Van Horn averred, then Mack van H. had to be a bit of each because it was that same Friday after his interview at Xenon when he took his last twenty dollars to the Switzer Brauhaus on Lincoln Avenue for a long slow drink and some deep thinking and the one person who could help him in his hour of much needed counseling sat there at the bar at one of the PM preparing for a descent into inebriate meditation.

Endicotte and van Horn. Or, van Horn and Endicotte. Buddies. Perhaps because complementaries. Mack van Horn mulled the matter to no firm conclusion, but there it was: a fuzzy kind of perception. Where he himself was impetuous, exuberant and trusting, Endicotte kept a reserve of skeptical judgement. In the Naval-Coast Guard, they'd played fast and loose with Service rules and hit-and-run with the girls in and around the base at the new Newport News, Port Appalachia in the Vee-Ay. Their attitudes, if Mack had been open to it, also complemented. He himself wanted, trusted, needed, loved and would have given away whatever he might have for the thin warmth and vapid promises of an hour. Charlie Endicotte gave away nothing.

Mackenzie van Horn almost concluded Charlie really didn't like woman. They were to use, to enjoy, to discard, and he kept as much remembrance of any one of them as he did the martini glass he left behind on the bar. Shelly Korshack might have described Charlie's disposition as denying his past and ignoring his future, as finding the eternal present in the depths of his 1 PM martini.

But, it was the cold eye of immediate demands which commanded. It said Charlie had no roof and that Mack awaited his first paycheck. As Mack put it poetically, fate and necessity had dictated they should find one another once again like the inevitable crossing of the braids of a rope.

"Charlie! Good Kee-ryst, it is you!"

"Ah-yuh. Whatcha been up to?"

"Not much. Working?"

"Nope."

"You're just the man I gotta talk to."

"Why 'zat?"

Mackenzie's rubicund face joined the gaunt, sallow face in the bar room mirror. The bartender queried. "Indeed! my good man. In-deeed!" said Mack in bubbly good spirits. "Why don't you distill for us two of your finest martinis."

"What? What?" Endicotte clowned.

"Charles, friend of my heart, companion of my soul, ol' buddy. I have a job!"

"You have a job?" The spare, tow-headed Endicotte grinned from over his martini through bad teeth and glazed eyes.

"A po-zi-shun type job, wouldja believe?" says Mackenzie. "DMC tech. The for-mid-able Xenon Labs."

"Di-rect-Mind-to-Conceptor. Wow! When d'you start?"

"Monday. At 12-05 the month! buddy mine. That's seventy-five thou a year—count 'em—seventy-five-thou a year! Hey, that's just for openers, and that's three,-yup, from what I was making at the magazine." Mackenzie made with his low-in-the-throat chuckle and preened in the mirror.

"Christ!" says Endicotte. "Who'd you blow?"

"Ah, well, Miz Phillips of personnel was impressed with my variegated resume, you see. We had lunch, wood-ja-bee-leeve. And I got to meet, all much too briefly, the big honcho who runs the Institute, all 6-2 of her, the FOR-mid-ah-bull Désirée des Dieux!"

"Hadda be. DMC. Whatta ya know?"

"From nothing, Charles. From nothing. I thought you might teach me."

"When d'you start?"

"Monday."

"What's the program?"

Van Horn went weighty and portentous. "Got to do with fiz-ziks, my man. Fiz-ziks. I'm gonna be a fiz -ziss-sist."

Endicotte set down his empty martini glass and beckoned for another. The look in his eyes was shrewd under the glaze, and the grin mischievous. "Whatta you know 'bout fiz -ziks?"

Mackenzie grinned into his martini. "Diddly-squat. Except for what I maybe remember from junior college. But, you teach me the one and I'll learn the other, bubbie. I'll learn—real fast."

"Wal…" Endicotte summoned clear thought. "First off, they're gonna put a chip in your head."

"Yeah. I know."

"Then they gotta tune you to a conceptor. Nothing painful, just…wall, some guys find it easier than others, if y' know what I mean."

"Gotcha. So, Charles, buddy o my heart, where you staying?"

"Funny you should ask."

So, van Horn spent a week-end at Billings Hospital, courtesy of the University, and that is how they inserted the Conceptoral Chip into the *cornu ammonis* of his hippocampus. And that is how two old friends came to share a tiny dig at the State Street Commons on 42nd and State Street on Chicago's Southside. And that is also how, in a hiatus between part-time, night-time and day-labor jobs to which he fled, that same Charles E., being an avid reader, happened early one morning to pick up from the communal coffee table a library book checked out to one M. van Horn who never read a book past the tenth page. Endicotte happened to shift the bookmark, causing an innocuous item to grab his attention. It consisted of a conceptor-generated bank deposit receipt made out to that same M. van Horn. Seeing as the aforenamed gentleman was, for several years past, indebted to him to the tune of several hundred dollars, and how, being an avid devourer of things coded and encrypted, Charlie E.'s mind automatically went on the alert for any peculiarities. In his usual trusting and voluble way, van Horn had, he remembered, referred to entering into the "BIG-time!" In fact, van Horn had an account with the UnivChicagoBank, the University's financial instrument, which was in turn the chief depository and dispenser of funds for no less than Xenon Institute, which was, as we have seen, the employer of one M. van Horn, associate DMC editor for the Journal of AstroPhys. All of this information was grist to the mill for one adept in matters electronic, and as tempting as filet mignon to a hungry man whose pockets had of late had produced little more than lint.

Trust, van Horn would have said, is a wonderful thing. An observation to which Charlie E. would have readily concurred. It is what friendships are built on. It extends to one giving no thought to where one may toss his trousers at night, or leave his EBank AccessCard. Said card lay on the bureau they shared, the bearer thereof lying asleep after having spent an arduous day laboring as an editor. Not so for Charlie, who, having pursued a night of undemanding menial labor and having partaken of several cups of strong coffee, was wide-awake and given to mischief. Charlie examined the EBank AccessCard very carefully. From training per US Naval-CoastGuard Intelligence EncryptSchool, he knew a microchip when he didn't see one. But it had to be there and it had to be keyed to an access program in the bearer's conceptor.

The rest was a simple matter for one adept. The bank receipt gave him a bar code. The card gave him the microchip. No great task for Charlie to scan the bar code with a handy-dandy Ultra-V. "pen" filched from Navy-CG Encrypt School. The "pen" was easily coupled to van Horn's modest PC which got hyped with an encrypt-decrypt program Charlie E. carried en-disc in his shirt-pocket along with dry-cleaning receipts and the like. The combination transfigured the simple conceptor into a veritable devourer of financial code. It all came out in EngScript and ArabNums. It said that funds for Xenon were held by the University in an account in UnivChicagoBank. In turn, UCB derived its funds from various sources. With a few deft additions to the code, one could persuade the Bank in question to augment the account by an amount equal to that by which said account was depleted, the difference being debited to an account whose ponderous code identity said USDEPTSCITECH, the FedGov itself, no less. The lean and ever-hungry Endicotte mused. Not only would van Horn be able to feed the wolves at his door, but he'd be in a good position to extend a loan. A job well done, he crooned. But then, what's a friend for?

In the succeeding three weeks, employee-depositor van Horn, Mackenzie, was, to say the least, surprised and delighted at the stability of his bottom line. No matter how great his withdrawals, funds were deposited and his balance kept pace. Luck having fallen his way of late, and he being "on a roll," who was he to question fate? Van Horn should have asked. He should have suspected something to be amiss. He wasn't stupid—five hundred in pocket money subtracted from thirty-five hundred deposited leaves a balance of three thousand—not thirty-five hundred. Yet there it was, a deposit for the said amount made within twenty-four hours of withdrawal. Where did these deposits come from? Ah, but didn't somebody up-there love him? Don't ask. Gift horses have bad breath. He off-put himself with a jibe and a joke until three months later during the summer of '82. He'd been able to pay Charlie what he owed him and Charlie took off to California to visit his sister. Shortly after, van Horn received a summons to appear in the State's Attorney's office. He was questioned, threatened, and made to swear and sign a deposition which if he didn't he would be indicted as a co-conspirator and guilty as Endicotte. He would be tried and convicted of fraud and conceptor-driven theft of the funds of UnivChicagoBank to the tune of some seven-thousand-three-hundred-forty-eight-dollars and fifty-seven cents, enough money to have covered the rent and back debts, including the IRS problem, plus the beer and skittles he and Charlie had enjoyed.

Ah, but fate is not only fickle, van Horn mused, she's also got a mean median finger. Whatever Charlie had done, he supposed, he'd meant well. And, hey, didn't they have a ball with that free-flow geld! Now Charlie was off to the calaboose once more, whilst he, a van Horn of the Chicago van Horns, was poised to rise, to climb the editorial ladder, and, perhaps as in his more lurid dreams, take that climb right into the bosom of that fan-tasy in human form, the incredible Chancellor Didi des Dieux.

Van Horn went west, to Fox Lake, Illinois. Charlie went east, to the Federal Facilities in Pennsylvania, and though each may have nursed the thought that they would meet once again, it was for neither to surmise how portentous a role each was to play in the unfolding of the history of the world.

Which leaves us with the question: How does it happen that little more than two years later the likes of Charlie E. comes to be doing what it is he is doing in veddy British Saville-Row three-piece and bowler replete with brolly in a stylish pub for up-and-coming accountants in Hyde Park, London, the latter being a long way from Hyde Park, Chicago. But those are distances measured in kilometers, or miles, and ignores the proximity of interests to be found between kindred spirits, especially when one is lean of pocket and has never been able to spit away the acrid taste of two years spent in the Army Penal Compound at Leavenworth in the late fifties, and another twelve months at Menard Penitentiary in Joliet, Illinois.

The Federal Government had been good enough to put one-hundred dollars into Endicotte's pocket before they loosed him into the streets once more, a free man. He went back to Chicago. Aimless as always, he sought work and remuneration. He scanned the classifieds of the Tribune and of the New York Times before a Classified Personals ad in the Times seized his attention. Someone required the assistance of a party well-versed in conceptor encryption. The ad promised, if vaguely, considerable reward for minimal time expended, in return for an email address, vital stats and a brief bio including, of course, Social Security Number and Armed Service Registration Number. Charlie E. pressed his nose to the window of necessity whose other side promised goodies. Through the Chicago Public Library conceptor service he punched the button. Sunday A.M. he counted what remained of his resources and headed to O'Hare Field for a flight to New York.

At the stodgy but respectable Knickerbocker hotel on Seventh Avenue, the other party greeted him under subdued lights, his broad expanse swathed in a silk smoking jacket. The man motioned Charlie to a comfy lounger before the fire and returned with a pitcher of martinis in hand. Charlie felt scruffy in the other's presence. Introducing himself as Sebastian Cray, Colonel, British Army, Intelligence Service, retired, a portly, polished, sophisticated gentleman of the old school, aristocratic in a trim salt and pepper beard, affable in bearing, under the exterior polish Charlie sensed a dangerous reserve.

After his second martini Charlie mellowed and went a little careless. though in his mind, he felt he was listening well enough. "My rap sheet? How do you know about that?"

"I, like you, have a way with conceptors. You infiltrated the Defense Department's private accounts."

"Wasn't hard."

"Embarrassed a few sensitive people, did you?" his inquisitor asked.

Charlie sniggered. "They'd spent five years and untold dollars to set up the screen and I cracked it in a week."

The alcohol began insidiously permeating his mind and system, and Endicotte, ever the serious clown, rose to the occasion. "The Navy did teach me well," he managed to blurt out.

"More recently, you did a year in the Illinois State Penitentiary for a similar escapade, not so?"

"Aye, guv-nor. Caught with me fingers in the cookie jar, I was."

Cray ignored Charlie's clowning. "You are a very enterprising fellow, Charles."

"Thank you, sir. Thank you." From where he sat, Charlie threw the man a mock salute.

"However, you do exhibit a penchant for being caught."

Charlie smiled self deprecatingly. "There is, of course, that."

"How would you like to repeat the performance. For, say, in the vicinity of a million dollars?"

Charlie sank back in the lounger. He regarded the portly, bearded fellow on the divan. The martini was dry, of an admirable gin. The furnishings in the room surrounded and enclosed an air of comfortable elegance. Charlie closed his eyes and drew a very deep breath. He exhaled and regarded the intent gaze of the other man. He smiled. He clowned. "Whom do we gotta shnooker, milord?"

Cray rose. He waved the pitcher. Charlie proffered his glass. Cray drew up a cassock so that he sat conspiratorially close to Charlie's knees.

Charlie leaned forward the better to hear the man's low, husky voice.

"Charles...I may, may I not?"

"That's me."

"In your estimation, what constitutes the 'perfect crime'?"

"The per-fect crime." Charlie rolled across his thickened tongue, thinking hard. "Means you get away with it and nobody knows, right?"

"A step further, Charles. A step further. Try—a theft no one dare admit has been committed."

"Um, I like that better!"

"By parties who cannot be apprehended."

"You have piqued my int'rest, guv'nor. Go! Go!"

"And funds which the loser cares not to trace."

Charlie had grinned from ear to ear. "Like I say, sir. Whom do we shnooker?"

Cray stood. He smiled a wry and noble smile. "Schnooker? Why, Charles. Would we so stoop? Of course we would. If the prize were worth... say a billion?".

"So," Charlie snorted laughter. "Let's get on with it, man."

"What we have in mind, Charles, is a subtle siphoning of data. We've already availed ourselves of the party's encryption. And our piggy-back virus puts us in on both ends of her transmission-receptions. She can't send or receive without our being in on it.

Charlie E. sobered. "I am, sir, indeed impressed. But, please, back up a sec. You said 'siphon.' Meaning you figure to tap the financial InterNet."

"Something like that."

"I take it your target's coming through on UBADS broadband—open-air, transmit-tower to satcom."

"Precisely."

Charlie E. gave it a long minute's hard thought. He reasoned aloud in a hoarse whisper. "If I read you right, trick is to pick your customer's cell signal out of the UBADS data stream—select one out of thousands coming through the broadband." Charlie raised a dramatic finger. "But you'd have to do it without interrupting the flow. UBADS transmission is delicate, y'know. Rooftop to transceiver-tower to SatComs and back down again. Rain'll affect the signal stream. Snow. Trees are a brick wall. You did say Chicago?"

"I didn't say. Matter of fact, it's Toronto."

"Big game!"

"The biggest. Our quarry is one Constancia Ocho, President, and creator of what the trade refers to as 'unorthodox accounts.' Without going into a bio-history of details, let us observe that my colleagues and I have a long-simmering score to settle with this same Constancia Ocho."

"Diddled you, did she?"

"Left us flayed and skewered."

"Dirty money!"

"Exactly. FirstBank Toronto's near one-up on Zurich in that department. And our girl is playing a private hand in a public game. If I know her well, and I daresay I do, she'll own Toronto and the North American continent before she's through."

Charlie whistled softly through his teeth. "My dear sir," he said grinning. "You don't play for pennies."

Cray grinned back. "Hanged for a wealthy sheep as for an impoverished goat. Question is, can it be done?"

"Humm. You're not asking for much." Charlie E. savored another excellent martini. He frowned. Then he looked up, narrow-eyed and grinning. "You said you're already 'in' on the encryption. So, you've got access…" For long seconds, Endicotte's face went blank, his eyes intent on a distant mote. "Ummm…but the select-divert…that's tough. Like I say, UBADS bandwidth is delicate as a virgin's button." A heavy silence descended on the room. Charlie E. seemed to daydream, his gaze seeking the silent counsel of the shadows. At length he set down his empty glass and regarded Cray with a look that was near boyish and mischievous. "How about we use a PC."

"How's that?"

"PC. As in 'personal conceptor'. As in keyboard and phosphor-tube monitor, and the like."

"The advantage?"

"Obsolete technology. Nobody uses digital, hard-drive systems anymore. But the digital's still good for a tap. Use it to hacker the Broadbeam. If, like you say, you're already inside the firewall and you haven't stirred a ripple, you're half way there. Nice thing about floppy-hard-drive is it's portable. Take a peek once a week or so and your piggyback virus records the data ready for the pickin'. Put the discs in your pocket, walk away. Target's own on-board calendar keeps you up-to-date." Endicotte snickered. Every time she punches her button, our peek-a-boo downloads, writes it down against payday. And nobody knows we're there 'cause like we're singin' the same tune right along with her. BUT, dear sir, we haven't taken a dime—yet. So we don't set off no alarums, 'n like that."

Endicotte fell silent once more. He brightened. "Pick a strategic spot along the UBADS channel—like in Bungle-dash, or some fuckn' place. When the cash drawer's full—bingo!—intercept the signal profile. Stick in your floppie and your PC shoots your diversion program to pre-selected depositories. Whole operation—fifteen seconds to a minute. Shut down and walk away. Ditch the PC, burn the discs. No-body home on this end for the NetWork Police to backtrack."

"Brilliant! But, I repeat. Can it be done?"

"The diversion. For that y'need hardware to filter-divert the one signal you want without interfering with the rest of that UBADS beam. And that, sir, is a very tall order."

"Can it be done?" Cray repeated.

"Oh, well," Charlie mused. "With good technique and the right equipment. The thing is getting in without setting off the bells."

"And you know how to do that?"

"Nope," Charlie admitted. "But lemme talk to a friend o' mine in

Connecticut. Man's a real genius with photo optics. And he owes me a favor."

"May one assume you are aboard, as it were?"

"Sir," says Endicotte with a mock salute. "Midshipman Charles Endicotte reporting. I am your man!"

"Capital!" Cray chortled. "Ah, but I see your glass is empty."

****

On that same day in July, Aram Gregorian rued the wages of love. He lay hospitalized with a broken femur and splintered humerus (left leg and arm), several broken ribs, a fractured clavicle and three fingers of the left hand. He had been admitted to the emergency room of Copenhagen General at 3:47 PM of the 17th of March, 2083 suffering from the aforementioned injuries during whose recuperation the patient must have suffered injury to the head sufficient to produce a delirium as he was given to whooping and shouting and bouts of crying and a repetition of the name 'Kristal.' Or 'Kristen.' Attending staff was not certain, and the name went down in the medical report as 'Crystal.'

He did survive. He ran a gauntlet of regrets and fears, of hopes and despairs, a carnival of delirium that took him through fantasy by way of memory to the harbor district of Copenhagen. He remembered quitting his position at the Institute in Upsala in a hurtful rage. He had had enough of that damned woman's effrontery, enough of her ego, enough of her high-handed ways. He was going to go home. Back to Armenia. To the little village of Pola Aragac. He planned on insulating himself from the world for the length of an Armenian winter, just himself and twelve or fourteen cases of vodka. His plan said that if he survived the winter and the vodka, spring would blow fresh from the Caucasus and revive him, purged of despair and disappointment and cleansed of any thoughts of her. The plan took him as far as Copenhagen station. He'd bought a ticket and with an hour or three to kill before flight-time he permitted the weight of anger and resentment to simmer. He kept seeing her, the look of disdain and superiority, yea of contempt in that beautiful *viságe*. It was an image he needed desperately to erase. So, he made his way out of the station, bag in hand, and 'round the corner to a pub handy to the thirsty traveler. He had an akvavit. And then another. Later, he would dimly recall standing a round for someone, recall struggling through his adequate Swedish to meet on the Scandinavian bridge to her Danish, and then their shared surprise at a mutual ease in English. She was pleasingly plump, ruddy of face, most engaging. Spoke in a whiskey baritone, stood them a round and he another. Time of the mind meandered and he missed his flight.

Hours spent in recuperation lend themselves to an etiology of the fortuitous and accidental, to an examination of the depths of one's capacity for folly. "Precisely, and by what carefully contrived stupidity did I screw-up so very brilliantly? Oh, pain of acknowledgement. Am I really the fool I remember myself to have been? And is this really me? Then, who was that?" Experience revisited two or three days before yesterday. It said she was bushel-basket broad with enormous breasts and a head of close shorn blonde-grey hair and that she snored like a demented trombone. By the clock beside the bed they shared it was 10:30.

The intrusion of light said this was at least one morning after. He wasn't going to Armenia. Not today, and judging from the drums in his head, he wasn't going tomorrow, either. Besides, there were a few things he had to take care of before he yielded to the demands of the immediate world—all requiring a trip to the facilities. After, one, immersing his head in cold water until he risked drowning, Doctor Gregorian, two, prescribed for Aram G. three aspirin with plenty of cold water for the dehydration. Item three was to satisfy his immediate need for some strong coffee.

She sat across the table from him in the incredibly cluttered one-roomer in a loft above a warehouse overlooking the Copenhagen docks. Only now in the self-pitying debility that is one's hanging-over did he take full measure of his hostess. And she of him. The drink did not seem to have affected her.

To him, she was most appealingly homely, rubicund, and sardonically merry. Gregorian had the feeling he'd said things the night before he shouldn't have. Where words left off, she seemed to sense what the sufferer thought to hide, and by the bottom of a second pot of astonishing coffee laced with something good it was she who prescribed for the doctor.

"To truly love someone, you see," she was saying, "is to decide that one has been authentic with himself."

"Authentic?"

"But of course. Kirkegaard—he was a Dane, you know."

"Indeed."

"Says that to love is to transform the object of one's love."

"Yes?"

"And one's self."

"Are you always so profound in the morning?"

Over a belly-rumbling, breast-shaking chortle: "Making love is my profession. So, you see, I know what is. And what is not."

Gregorian stared down into the black depths of his coffee. "I have a feeling I talked too much."

"Love and vodka. Anguish and a big mouth. Best therapy there is. If you listen to what it is you say."

"If I listen?"

"Of course. Who knows better than you?"

"What do I know?"

"You love her."

"Is that what I said?"

"Oh, yes. You've got a bruised self, you see. As says the poet, a broken heart."

"Pardon, but what are you? A psychoanalyst?"

"Sure. Why not? I am…what is it the *Amerikans* call it…the psychic band-aid?"

"What else did I tell you—tell myself."

"What else? Ah, yes. You don't like you."

"I don't like myself."

"Because as you see yourself you are not loved by her."

"Makes a certain kind of sense, I suppose."

"As says the philosopher, when a person loves he becomes the true individual. Kirkegaard says 'the solitary one.' "

"Kierkegaard."

"Says, to love the other one must be sufficient unto himself."

"I see. And since she doesn't love me, I am not sufficient?"

"Ask yourself."

"Ask myself. What if I don't like the answer?"

"Then, that is the answer."

"Hah! Indeed. Have you ever been 'sufficient?'"

"Oh, yes. My true love, he, too, was a man of science. Anatoli, is his name. Polichuk."

"You jest!"

"You didn't know the world's greatest scientist is also a lover? Ah, yes. We were students. University Krakov. Many years ago. We have been lovers on and off again many years now. Last time I saw him was…"

Her name was Beatrice "Berti" Huffding and though she never said so explicitly, Gregorian made her out to be a kind of wandering salver of bruised souls, a provider of psychic palliatives, an existential bandage. Later, when he'd come to terms with his own insufficiencies, he would recall the searing heat of her body and the penetration of her loving care into his pain. He had need, and she had provided. She demanded and he had admitted to the presumption behind his self-inflicted pain.

Gregorian stayed with Berti for two days. They drank, smoked and talked. He had never smoked before. The tobacco, with something added, allayed to some extent the anxiety that gnawed within. She took him to bed again. Alcohol, tobacco, and the great dissociator that is intercourse, they drew him out, stretched him, allayed the fear in him. He could, after two days, agree that he was "not sufficient." So then, while she was out replenishing supplies, he re-packed his bag and left her some money. He had made his decision. Nothing to do but put an end to the insufficiency by eliminating the man. Which is what he tried to do by stepping in front of a bus. The Express on St Jörgens Sö Boulevard came fast and he was perhaps too quick because he stepped in front of a sedan coming the other way. It hit him hard and he knew hardly any pain. Until he woke up. After alcohol, tobacco and sex, and now with a broken leg, cracked ribs and the rest, he was still insufficient.

Ammon's Horn

7. The Scientists

2080 blew in from the Alps in complete defiance of global warming.

In the lovely country house Ocho had procured for him in the suburbs of Geneva, an aging Anatoli Polichuk was roused from dreamless sleep. His nurse-housekeeper helped him out of his pajamas and into the shower. Half-past the hour she had his breakfast on the table. She dropped a capsule into his tea and watched it fizzle and dissolve. At a proper interval she presumed to enter the bathroom. He stood dripping wet with a towel around his modesty and a look of faraway dreaming in his eyes. "Doctor Polichuk?" she ventured. The tiny old man's grey eyes focused on her. Slowly, the huge, scruffy beard-mustache parted and a smile spread across his homely features. "Goot morning," he said softly. "My, you are a pretty one. What is your name?"

"My name is Gudrun. Same as it was yesterday and the day before. Now, Doctor, let's get dressed shall we? You're due to lecture at the University at eight."

"Yes. I lecture. Today is…"

"Monday, the third of July. "

"July 3. The earth approaches aphelion. That is, ladies and gentlemen, deh farthest point of distance from the sun at 2.5×10^6 kilometers farther than the mean distance of 149.6 x 10^6..."

"Later, Doctor. Breakfast first."

He ate an egg, scrambled, a piece of wheat toast and a small piece of cantaloupe. He drank his tea, black. In the next hour, he'd mentally calculated three necessary variations in the texture of spatial intervals between hyper-dimensional vertices. His abstract thinking was given to vivid, child-like imagery. Metaphorically speaking, the universe, to him, was a bubble. Adjacent to it was another bubble and the shape of the mating surfaces determined arbitrary hyperspace. "Kissing," he said, "like to say a triangle on deh flat chalkboard is a different geometry if deh chalkboard is a cylinder. Yes? So, deh Riemannian geodesic determines deh shape and texture of our piece of deh SpaceTime jigsaw puzzle as is expressed by deh tensor equation." He scribbled both sides of the table napkin with a pen. He hadn't focused on the small conceptor amongst his breakfast things. An edge of his mind noted a largish brown ant crawling slowly across the white tablecloth. It paused as though regarding him and then skittered off to hide under the rim of a saucer.

"More tea, doctor?"

Someone was there. Gilda! No, Hilda. Or was it Frieda, the one before. Hilda was wife number...three? Yes. He drained his cup and gloried in the warm sunlight breaking across the frozen Alpine horizon.

His eighty-three years sat lightly on him this morning. He felt confident. Mischievous. He wiped his mouth on the sleeve of his shirt. He sucked his teeth. He farted loudly and smiled. Hilda would not have permitted such behavior. Hilda. Or was that...what was her name? Berta! Ah, Berta. Number one. She frightened him."

"Almost time to go, doctor."

"Yes?" Polichuk smiled beatifically. "Where we are going? Let us go to deh zoo, yes? I would like to go to the zoo. I love deh monkeys. Darwin says that in deh evolution of the pongids there is no sinus, you know. So for a monkey to catch cold..."

74

"No, doctor. You're lecturing at the institute."

The grizzled face went sober and serious. "Ah, yes. But you see…" He spoke to her as to everyone and to no one, "…deh tensors describing deh curvature of spacetime…" he announced slowly and carefully in his accented English, "…are expressible by deh 5-dim. geometry of hypersurface homogeneity. One visualizes deh 3-dimensions of our physical universe as an embed in a four dimensional Riemannian space, deh fifth being…"

Gudrun got him into his suit coat and adjusted the snappy little borsellino on his head. Huge stoney-faced Hauptman the chauffeur took him by the elbow and escorted him to the sedan waiting outside.

"Young man," Polichuk announced. "We are to go to *Ecole pour l'Etude de la Science Physique, Parc Tremble*. You know how to go there?"

"Yessir," Hauptman answered patiently. The old man was seated and belted into the back seat and the sedan moved smoothly through the tree-lined suburb. Within twenty minutes they had passed through the open countryside and moved over the Ports de l'Isle, Rue des Moulins, and into the Rive Gauche of the City of Geneva.

Meanwhile, back at the villa, Gudrun cleared the dishes. In twenty minutes she had photo-copied the napkin and emailed it to its destination. The voice on the telephone expressed irritation. "I'm sorry, Miz Ocho," Gudrun responded. "I can't always get him to use the conceptor. On a napkin…Yes, ma'am. I'm emailing it now. Yes, ma'am, Hauptman knows where to take him."

****

Had Polichuk noticed, he would have counted seven classroom students, three grey-beards like himself, two post-acne grads, two nondescript women. But he didn't. He lectured, talking aloud to the chalk board, to the figures and symbols he scribbled. And they, in turn, talked back to him, the recursive dialogue growing upon itself, reinforcing itself until the inevitable post-quantumn co-relativity conclusions emerged.

Then, he had to go back and explain, as a mamma to a child, the phonics of *a*, *b* and *c,* and how one must square the modulus of the quantum to approach classical probability. Hence, one might be tempted to think of the SpaceTime manifold as a deterministic structure (Polichuk used the sample of a solid brick) whose manifold vanished below on the sub-level of the quark, yes, and even smaller on the Plank length because there the universe-brick undergoes violent fluctuations in geometry. Doctor Polichuk seized his lower lip twixt the thumb and forefinger of his left hand. With his right he chalked slowly, methodically. "And so, you see," he muttered, "where $(2.998 \times 10^{10}$ cm/sec$)^{3/2} = 1.616 \times 10^{-33}$ cm. And of such is conjecture made," his voice trailed off as he stared into the distant air.

Somewhere in the ancient building someone had the temerity to jingle a bell. Doctor Polichuk stopped in mid sentence. His brows rose and then he turned with a warm smile and for the first time addressed those seated before him. "Thank you, ladies and gentlemen." Anatoli's stomach said it was time for lunch.

The lady who had sat at the back of the classroom approached him at the Cafe Berghoff. She took the chair opposite him without ceremony. Reluctantly, Anatoli Polichuk relinquished his pursuit of the calculus expressing the 3-dim. motion of a hypothetical point posited on the derrier of the waitress moving before him. The young woman sitting at the table before him spoke, but he didn't quite catch…

Puzzled, he protested. "But, I do not want to go back to Baltimore."

"We're not goin' there."

"You are not Berta?"

"No, Doctor. I'm Ocho. Constancia Ocho."

"When did I marry…? I don't know…"

"We ain't married, Doctor. I'm…"

"Ah, good." He chuckled as at himself. "You are so pretty. Will you marry me?"

"Listen, Doctor." Madame Ocho placed a tiny audio-recorder on the table. Anantoli Polichuk heard his own voice. It was a slow, low, methodical mumble, as given his habit of speaking out loud to himself, anticipating a morning's lecture:

...produces a quantum bearing on deh scalar magnitude determining deh interface of deh respective branes, expressed as deh absolute ω/TS, deh ω an immediate variant whose value is arbitrarily expressed as product of deh Candrabindu ritenow (rn) deriving as product of deh ritehere (rh) as a linear transform of deh aw (afterwile). Hence we derive deh metric tensor whose points are events (x1 thru x4) expressing deh SpaceTime, and i, j k denoting deh components of deh 3-vector. But when ω gets in dehre is deh infinity factor, *oi gewalt*, comes deh "kissing," you see, deh branes come togedehr, like to say two bobbles, or like you back up into someobdy in deh shower, buns to buns, and deh infinity got no timespace to move in for linear but is going to split, you see, so deh (x1—x4) etc. goes one way and deh (i,j,k) etc. is going deh odehr way (we ain't figured yet which way is deh odehr way) and what you get is split in deh SpaceTime.

Polichuk studied her soberly. "This formulation...just this morning I was thinking. *Oi vey*, my thinking got a big mouth. I have not published, have I?"

"No, Doctor. You ain't published. But we..."

"We? Who is we? Who are you?"

"I'm Constancia, don'cha remember? We're partners. We're gonna 'open the gate.' Your experiments..."

"Experiments?"

"In SpaceTime. You do remember Doctor Waltari, don'cha? And Doctor Marczali? The lab'rah-tree at Montreux?"

An image rose to the old man's mind. The effects of the tranquilizer in his morning tea diminished and he remembered Waltari clearly.

In his mem-scene Wanda stood against the light in the chaotic pattern of lasers and condensors, the accumulators and high-energy apparat of a dimensional-physics laboratory. In his mem-scenario she turned and the light caught the sheen in her close-cropped peroxide hair and a smile lighted her plain-pretty face. She put down her calculator and approached him smiling. Her arms encircled him and she pulled him into her squat-square body. She stooped and kissed him warmly. "Darling, man. How are you?" Her bosom pressed against his chest, her thighs against his and he would have responded, but this same woman whose name was Ocho had spoken and broken his reveries. "Come on, Doc. We got work t' do. Meantime, I got a few documents f' you t' sign."

Wanda was shortish and squarish and plump and to Anatoli's adoring eyes, she was beautiful. And was there anything more beautiful than a beautiful woman? But, this morning he would do his best to set aside the youthful urgings in his aging bod. In the huge laboratory, the Ocho woman had built for him in the old winery at Montreux, across Lake Geneva and east of Lausanne, the good doctor calculated mentally the quantum unification scale. At odd moments he imagined he could actually see the stasis wall of quarkian vapor before him. And hear it! At times it brought back the male voices, gentle tenor to rough basso, in the chorus of the Temple Beth'el near his boyhood home in Minsk. In exactly 15.37 seconds the superconductor would convert electromagnetic waves into gravitational radiation. The baritone of infrared would join in. Electronic altos would sing the first melodic line and the tenors and counter-tenors of visible light and of ultraviolet would complete the first of the two lyric themes.

His theory said that at Planck plus 10^{139} the TimeSpace through which the G-field moved would shear. Space would be isolated and the Time it occupied would "revert" by a factor inverse to the frequency of the TimeSpace from which the diversion began. The result—his own brilliant

78

deduction, and if he didn't say so it was because he was an unassuming fellow and he blushed so easily—the result would be a generation of negative energy. The Casimir effect. It would access the 5-dim. It wasn't really the 'fifth-dimension,' you see. That was a misnomer. It was actually the next set of dimensions comprising the universe "next door," adjacent to our perceived three-plus-SpaceTime. It would eventually absorb our own and make a total, his theory said, of four plus seven. A universe of eleven dimensions. Such was beyond what human imagination could conceive. That is what the mathematics described. But, how "real" was mathematics? And then, how "real" was "real"? Perhaps this was to be seen. In any case, the dimensions would "open-up" to one another. "Fifth dimension." That was a mis-reading, a terrible metaphor concocted by that mouthy woman writing for The New York Times. He was supposed to be interviewed but the woman kept putting words in his mouth and mis-anticipating what he meant to say and so she wrote what she wished which had precious little to do with what he, Polichuk, might have said—that the adjacent universe would, how to say it— emerge? No, join! That was better. His own explanation to the school children in Harlem was better and the kiddies loved it. For them, he likened the event to a nest of bubbles. Yes, that was nice. One could picture a lot of bubbles, as in his bathtub, and one bubble got too close and pushy to the next one and poof! two became one! The pretty woman from Geodesic Magazine, she dubbed it QBT—Quantum Bubble Theory. Yes, that was nice.

Despite his best efforts, the warm glow rose in him once more. In love again. Two ex-wives, Federika and Marta. Better sense threatened. Hadn't he had enough of women? Of love? Of romance and all that schmaltzy nonsense? He chastised himself. Ah, but Wanda. She was brilliant. Especially in devising instrumentation. Where he himself was numb-thumbed and ambi-clumsy, she was so quick to grasp what he haltingly described in theory, so quick to make the "gadgets," as she called them, she and the other one, the Hungarian neanderthal, Laszlo. Such wonderful instruments they made to exist from the vague diagrams and pictures in his foggy mind. But he had her keep her distance because, as he phrased it, she "made for him deh concentration to be difficult." But then if she hadn't been there to encourage him, to stimulate his imagination—it was amazing the way she stayed a step ahead of what he was preparing to say, the way she anticipated the TimeSpace—the 'shoehorn,' she called it, that adorable creature—and, *borjhe moi!* (which is to say, "my goodness!") she and Laszlo were making what he had only imagined. Georgi Shmolka, the one in Prague who called himself a psychometrician—an old fashioned Freudian fraud—said Wanda was his mother, and that she satisfied Anatoli's Oedipal desires. What a lot of—bool-sheet? Was that the word? Yes. His *mammá* dead these forty years didn't look anything like Wanda.

And so they had held preliminary field trials without drum-rolls or razzle-dazzle publicity. TimeSpace boundary *a* reached quantum state, right on cue; quantum gravity chimed in nicely and established consonant harmony in the key of G-major. A wall of dimensional tension rose and its quantum frequencies sang "like a tin pot in a wind storm," as a journalistic wag was to put it later. Wanda increased gravitational input and co-relative TimeSpace *b* chimed in. The dimensional branes conjoined. They "kissed." Had the adjacent "bubbles" conjoined to form a hole? An opening at the dimensional interface? Call it what one wished, our witnesses peered as through a door into another universe for all of the three seconds before the plutonium transformer blew its stack and everything shut down. The effect was recorded in the instruments.

How does one apologize to the reality one has irrevocably altered? Like saying to God: Forgive me, I have broken some of your divine crockery and there is no putting it back together. So, while the two young people whooped and shouted and celebrated, Anatoli Polichuk bowed his head in a silent prayer and felt like a penitent little boy, even as part of his mind raced ahead into descriptive formulations defining what this thing was that they had done. It would require something on the order of a quadratic equation expressed as a tensor, a Lorentz transformation coordinating six frames of reference including their relative SpaceTime interstices. In the midst of one of his best moments of formulation, he spotted her standing at the back of the laboratory. He didn't like her. She was too pushy. She had a way of ordering him about, and now she was speaking to him in that authoritative manner he could not avoid…

"Madame Ocho," says Doctor P. "Did you see…"

"Yeah. Real nice. Gonna be a big winner, you bet…them SpaceTime things…your shoe-horn…call a press conference and of course the US Prez, himself and the Prez. of Switzerland and the Prez. of France and the Prime Minister…on the twelfth in New York to discuss real estate implications…"

"Real estate?"

"…corner the market. Right off make the US Corp.'s budget look like pocket change." She was laughing, he thought, like a mischievous child, a greedy, mischievous child, and she was telling him what he would do, what he would say, admonishing him. He smiled, nodded and tuned her out because in the brilliant light of the Alpine sun streaming in the window and with the tranquilizer wearing thin he had latitude to wonder how in the world Madame Ocho could have known about the TimeSpace boundary. The "shoehorn." Doctor Polichuk fished in his trouser, then coat pockets as Ocho had said something about incorporation. Incorporation? That was not possible, unless one accepted the outdated premise, the nucleon hypothesis which incorporates the isospin vector $T = $ to Et and the orientation Tz as equal to E Tz but with the proton excess exceeding Z T—but this was an insight he had had that very morning and he remembered writing it down, somewhere, what had he done with…

"Polichuk Enterprizes, Ltd," she was saying, "No need to include my name on the letterhead, I'll take CEO and, of course, treasury-accounting…"

"Ah, that kind of incorporation!"

" 'Course. Wha'dja think I meant…you lose something?"

"No. Nothing. A piece of paper. Not important."

Wanda had stood right beside the Ocho woman, smiling warmly.

Wanda was so proud of him. Young Laszlo, too, attempting a smile, saying something about what they had accomplished in trans-dim instrumentation and how the plutonium transformer was already under repair and they'd be ready for the big public demonstration in a week or ten days, and something about tele-bijin and public relations. They were smiling at him, all three. Wanda, too. When he'd been little more than a *boychick* in the Ukraine his *mammá* had smiled at him that way, when he had been a gooood boy, smiled when he had won first prize in mathematics at the Kiev Polytechnic. And Federika smiled when she cashed his university paycheck and they bought the house in Bamberg. And Marta smiled like that when she appeared with him in Stockholm wearing mink in the summer. She was smiling when she got him up at seven to make a nine o'clock class, and smiled and whisked away the plates when she said he was day-dreaming and it was time to get moving, and she undid his bib napkin and tied his four-in-hand and tucked-in his shirt and zipped his fly and made him shine his shoes and she called him childish, and what would he do if he didn't have her to look after him? The doors to the office annex slammed shut and echoed through the cavern of the lab. Ah, here was Wanda, here and now, and she, too, was smiling.

Anatoli emerged to himself on the laboratory-annex stage. He woke blinking into the brilliance of lights and at the multiple cyclopses that were cameras. He stood amazed at how quickly it had all happened. Or had time contracted? Was that possible? Standing clear of the numbing fog of the tranquilizer, a morning's woolly theorizing had become, in swift order, empirical tests, published results, engineered instrumentation. And now, on one screen before him hovered a huge graphic portrayal of the Bibbity Bau configurations of IsoSpace extension into seven adjacent dimensions of what might very well constitute the "universe next-door." On a second screen there shimmered an enhanced snap-shot, as it were, of the 3-second peek they had had through local SpaceTime into that adjoining universe. He was shocked to recognize himself up there and to his left, an enormous floating head investing a real-time television projection. Voices came shouting at him from beyond the lights, from out of the jam of people hidden in the dark auditorium:

"…an opening into a whole 'nother world?"

"Well, young man, what we see here is describable in functions of hypersurface…"

"Break that down for the layman, sir. What you mean by distribution of simultaneous worlds?"

"…the idea of Feinman, The sum-over-histories' possibility, quantum of projections to make realities…"

"Would we be able to step into what you have called 'the next bubble' in the 'bubblebath' of adjacent universes'?"

Time vanished. The world smothered him in a roar of voices, a shroud of lights, then pressure and a threat. His heart fluttered and he grew dizzy. His last clearly conscious memory was of Wanda's face close to his own and her look of concern, and Madame Ocho's voice yammering on the perimeter of things saying something about 'Feinman's reality states.' Or was it 'real estate?' Before the world went away, Anatoli Polichuk had to ask himself a question and to frame the beginning of an answer—what was nurse Gudrun doing here?

He woke. This was the university infirmary? Yes.

"How I am feeing?" he asked.

"You are tired," Nurse Gudrun informed him.

"I see. May I work a little?" says he.

"Don't exert yourself," says she. "Here you are."

She placed the little teleconceptor in his lap. Anatoli sat up in his bedclothes and pillows. She placed the MC band about his brows. His thoughts touched on and then produced a mem-image of a large, grey-blond woman. She spoke to him in a heavy Danish-English accent. He knew her apartment in Brussels. The memories were very warm. Anatoli tapped the keys.

Her address was luvyoubibi@heggewish.dansk.

****

Geneva. Clinique General Beaulieu:

In jig-time, Anatoli Polichuk settled into a level-one-induced somni-state and looked to be holding his own. Which is where van Horn found him. He didn't so much "find" him as fall over him in a satellite-linkage sense of the term because he, van Horn, hadn't left Xenon and Anatoli Polichuk hadn't so much as made it across his private room to the loo, bed-bound as he was, neurologically sedated, the whole package of him inserted into a stasis chamber like a tiny hotdog into an enormous bun. "Patient # 3670011 ASXenon Gen. Polichuk, A." had his upper Cortico-Cerebral linkage calibrated at level b2 hype-3; a prompt-tape whispered questions into his mental ear, a sure-fire and proven way to keep upper cerebral frequencies active. The above-mentioned CC linkage was in turn conveyed to the Institute's data matrix at the labs in Montreux, some hundred miles over the curve of the lake by way of SatCom Suisse, and the point of convergence, mind-to-conceptor-to satellite is where they "met," and then only because:

Gerry Queen was an old buddy from their Naval-Coast Guard days in the two-oh-sixties and her "Queen on Line" video program—what one critic called, her "chatter-splatter, piss'n-tell" program—was losing ground in the ratings. He/she (?) and van Horn happened to meet over a drink at a posh pub on Michigan Avenue, a watering hole for denizens of the media spotlight. Queen was a good listener and van Horn's jaw was ever-so-smoothly lubricated with Tangueray—very dry, very straight up, one olive, please. Thus, as fertile imagination will do when coupled with a hungry ego and an agile imagination, van Horn said something in confidence to this mavin of videodrivel and got an invite to appear on the show. But that gets ahead of the actual sequence of events, because, first:

On mental screen, it had begun on that last day of September with Melodía Upshaw-Pzybiliski, chief copywriter, Journal of Astro-Phys, fifth

84

floor, doing a slave-galley whip-cracking on her crew of DMC schlemiels laboring on the fourth floor with the copy to be emerging as "page-text" [per WebNet Xenon.compub]. And one particular style-and-edit man, she observed, was having the off day. Van Horn's mind-and-matter coupling drifted, the "mind" end being on other matters, he having, the evening before, sought comfort and succor, if not a warm and sympathetic body (feminine) with which to temporarily assuage his bruised spirits. Begin with the fact his wages were again garnished to force-pay debts he'd completely put out of mind, and that his rent was overdue and the landlord threatening eviction. A precise rendering of the evening yielded the image of an anomalous, middle-aged van Horn at a table at Jimmy's Woodlawn Tap with his last fifty-bucks in pocket and some eight or ten University denizens, the oldest being all of twenty-three, of precociously nubile proportions enhanced by careless attention to the state of her apparel. The result was an arousal of the mature gentleman by the powerfully attractive, if fecklessly, reckless youngster so that apropos, many drinks later (he on gin, she on beer), he "took her home" to his place on State and Forty-Second. The Commons. The same tiny apartment, Charlie E. had long-since departed.

Smooth-talking lecher that he was, Van Horn got the young lady all the way into his bed and was pawing open her bosoms's restrictive undergarms, when, given fatigue and alcohol—and the female of the species being what it sometimes is—she elected to object, smacked him, cursed him, expostulated on her virginal innocence and on his own miserable lechery and—she didn't really have to as he'd never have harmed her—screamed. long and loud enough that van Horn did a night in the can on van Buren Ave. which may help explain why he was so morose on that critical morning.

He'd sat suspended in the time of the mind which duty-wise ought to have been preoccupied with a swatch of space centered on the system Furculum Inguinalis covering about forty billion cubic light years of space, give or take a bil. Melodía Upshaw-Pzybilski over-rode van Horn's own text. She was droning: "…the conventional approach to redshift survey is the two-point-correlation Brié-Griffith survey utilized in clusterings in excess of 10 parsecs, whereas in a Camembert distribution the Benson function = 0 for volumetric studies..."

Van Horn corrected for a sentence-paragraph over-ride, punctuating at the 'however.' Mind-to-machine he inserted commas and crafted a legible, comprehensive paragraph, whereupon he opted for appropriate graphics as Upshaw-Pzybilski's voice was saying, "...the brightness of the galactic aura is better discerned from the Sagan telescopic complex on the Jovian moon, Ganymede from which perspective..."

It was two in the afternoon, the room was overly warm, he was still hung-over, and he was bored with the meaningless drone of words humming through his audio cortex. He was thirsty. And peckish. Thinking on the lovely, pleasurable, young body he'd assayed the night before, and angry—horny—"pissed," as Endicotte would have put it—at the way the evening had ended, he fumed. As he groused, the hum of words went past him, even as his fingers plied the board controls and he fantasized himself victorious—yea, vindicated!—in a court of law, lovingly forgiven by his wife and his two ex's and by the lovely lovely, triumphant over his sea of troubles. It took him ten long seconds to realize something had actually changed.

History places the cosmic storm as occurring April 1, 2084. His own, after-the-fact analysis of the affair discloses that while he was fighting off sleep, up in the unchartable geography that is Earth's exosphere some 460 miles above the Atlantic, a solar flare poked an errant finger into the vicinity of the Earths magnetic field. To a properly-equipped eye, it might be said to have bathed the sky in color. Such an eye would have witnessed the coronal belch nudge the HermesSatCom, mediator of commo for most of the Western World. As a result, the WorldWideWeb stuttered. USOL.Org choked. WorldNews.Org and WWW. UniversalInfo.Org alternatively sneezed and barfed, and in Earthwide electronic commo there was a great jostling and shoving. Channels got jammed and photo-optic lines were forced to blink. Televisionary melodramas got scrambled and commercial announcements got put on hold. Included amongst those communicatively discombobulated circuitries was the University's Mid-Atlantic ComSys Network bridging exclusively XenonLabs at Fox River, Illinois, with universities, institutes, foundations and laboratries scattered across the broad belly of Europe and Eurasia. Communications were for some forty-five seconds engulfed in misdirected chatter, jabber, spew and sputter. The result was that some very odd people got to talk to some other, equally odd people.

Through the warm fog into which he sought refuge, van Horn knew the voice was no longer that of Melodía Upshaw-Pzybilski. It was, instead, a man's voice. The accent wasn't Hispanic. It was Polish. Maybe Russki. And the subject matter wasn't red-shift survey, it was…quantum? Van Horn raised his left hand, poised to punch "panic." He paused. This wasn't copy. The tone was too conversational. As though the speaker were answering questions. Or responding to suggestions thusly: "…because, you see, a particle, which is having zero dimension, it sweeps out a one-dim trace, or, as you say, it evolves in SpaceTime a world line, so a line, which is having one-dim length, sweeps out a two-dim world-sheet, and a membrane which is having two dims, length and breadth, it sweeps out a three-dim volume."

Van Horn puzzled and held back his panic. "Who the bloody hell is this? Hey! You!" The voice persisted: "…and dimensional membrane—what they call a B-brane—it sweeps out a world-volume of p + 1 dims. Of course, you got to have enough room for p-brane to move in SpaceTime. So, B + 1 this must not exceed $(2.998 \times 10^{10} \text{ cm/sec})^{3/2} = 1.616 \times 10^{-33}$ cm the over number of ST dims. convergent, you see…"

There was a long pause. Van Horn imagined he heard someone, off-stage as it were, intervening with a question. Sure enough the voice came back.

"It is Dirac. You see, he postulates that the electron. it is not a point, but a bubble—like a 2 dim. membrane that closes on itself because centripetal energy is isotropic. You see…"

There was a long pause. The Russki voice came back. "Like I say in paper of '26, we, too, are bubble, a membrane in three physical dimensions and SpaceTime. What we see in experiment yesterday iss like to say deh bubble next-door, you see."

La Pzybilski suddenly yammered in his ear. "Van Horn, this isn't standard copy...to whom are you talking?"

"I don't know! Bee-lieve me. I'm just as confused as you are. Hullo, out there! Can you hear me?"

"Da. You come in loud and clear."

"Who'm I talking to? How'd you get in on..."

Judging from the conversational tone, this other party was probably on a Discourse-Webstrand direct to a publication matrix parallel to the one van Horn was employing even now. Undismayed, the other party continued: "... it is Breen, he speculates if superconductor con-verts EM waves into G. rad., then we reach absolute ω/TS and deh infinitely compressed-polarized G. wave: it will produce EM energy reducible to minus frequency at Plank level. At t level and frequency ω, you see, TimeSpace has no place to go in and deh no time it iss moving through will shear. Space, it will be isolated, and the Time will 'revert' by a factor inverse to frequency of TimeSpace from which the diversion begins, you see? 'Allo? Who iss, please?"

"Who is? You got to be puttn' me on! This is van Horn of Xenon Institute, Fox River, Illinois and I am picking you up on our DMC editorial interface. Who is this? Identify, please."

"Van Horn? That iss your name?"

"That's right, van Horn. Who..."

"I am Anatoli and I am pleased to meet you."

"Okay. So tell me, Anatol, how you're doing this."

"They got me, pal, lemme I should tell you!"

"Who? Who's got you?"

"Deh Ocho woman. Now it iss for me to understand every-t'ing. From me, she steals data. Like a rat wid deh cheese from a trap, she got me. With drugs, yet, dehy make me like a bunny rabbit, yes? So I don't even know what iss time of day. And Wanda. Oi, Wanda, beautiful Jezebel! Such love, she says, and does dis to me. Listen, pal…"

"I'm listening!"

"Five level. You understand?"

"Five levels. Okay…"

"Through program dehy are placing on my head, I am giving physics, because I cannot stop mind from talking—a big mouth it has, lemme I should tell you. But to you I say, help me. Dis woman, she iss a mon-stehr! From physics deh alternative dimension she is making real-estate! *Oi gevahlt!*

"Whaaaaat?"

"She iss selling, how you say it? Neh-brahsh-kah."

"Somebody's selling Nebraska? Okay chum. You got it. They're picking your brains and somebody is selling Nebraska. Well, you just stay with that, Anatol. I'm sure everything's gonna work out…"

"Van Horn! Pzybilski here, just what do you think…"

"It's all right, ma'am. Some clown from outside got in on the DMC frequencies. These hackers got a sense of humor, I guess. Yes, Ma'am. I got it all straightened out. Errant copy deleted."

Which is how Van Horn stuck his other foot into it, because, as noted, three nights later, he bumped into Gerry Queen, and over drinks and tall stories, got himself invited to be a guest on the show. He was hyped on a pre-view of the Wednesday-show-to-come (8-EST-UBC50) as Xenon's roving authority on things in general. He got a pretty big spot-light, as such things go, and as an actor, raconteur and crafter of tall tales, van Horn gave a good rendition of the Russki hacker replete with accent. A good time was had by all, guest, host, and the global TV viewing audience.

Ammon's Horn

8. Ruminations

On a warmish morning March, Kirsten Lagerquist sipped morning *kaffee*. From the little balcony of her apartment, she looked out over the flooded valleys and the mountaintop islands of what had once been her beloved Sweden, and she mused. That night, she had dreamed. Binswanger said dreams were an attempt to accommodate conflict. Be that as it may, Doctor Kirsten Lagerquist had never had a dream that made any sense whatsoever. Such things were a waste of time, and she certainly wasn't putting any credence into the Freudian business of wish-fulfillment, or whatever. Which didn't explain why she saw him in the dream. She might have put him out of her thoughts completely having but glimpsed him in the conceptor mindscreen for no more than a minute—except for the magazine.

She had held her March first meeting of department heads and afterwards Heinrich Schrekenhaus of radiology insisted he had matters of importance to toss around, as he put it, and wouldn't lunch be a good time-place? Doctor Lagerquist made one of her rare appearances in the Institute cafeteria and Schreckenhaus expostulated on the merits of the latest model in PET scan equip, a holographic projector—the whole of the brain in 3-D., sectional and/or holistic, digital animation of activated neuronal functions projected in real time. He was droning on and hammering at the details when he became aware that she had become aware that he was taken with her and that couldn't take his eyes off her breasts, because for a few seconds there, she'd lost track of his sputter-mumble presentation, engrossed as she was with the picture in the magazine some twit had left on the table—a gaudy colored full page depiction of the man in her dream. The athlete. What was his name? In the few seconds following, she managed to read enough of the caption to infer her dream-athlete had been injured. Unaccountably, she'd caught her breath and felt herself go feverish. She was further put out by her inability to explain why the photograph of an homely, hairy, oversized Italian anthropoid on a motorcycle should so unsettle her. In the few seconds it took to regain control, she realized Schreckenhaus was grinning—drooling to be more exact—and she had no recourse but to throw an arm over her bosom and stalk angrily out of the cafeteria, the old fool having seen evidence of the fact she'd been silly enough to permit a mere photograph to arouse her.

What she'd taken with her, of course, was what she'd absorbed of the text accompanying the photograph: the name, Pistone, aka "*il Benni*." The tone of the exposition was so endearingly sentimental, it forced writer and the reader to share sympathies, almost love, for the sweaty hero.

Connections, Binswanger had said. She must make connections. In the chaos of psyche-configuration she could "make-sense" of her behavior only if she identified the emotional content within the parameters of her psyche. Kirsten drained her *kaffee* and immersed herself once more in her conceptoral screen. Consider, says Binswanger, such had occurred in September, a month before, the motorcycle in the desert and all that. And the magazine article, it was dated…what? She hadn't noticed! It might be months old! She had to know! Which explained the titter and gossip amongst cafeteria staff over the sudden re-appearance of la mighty Lagerquist late that evening looking for something on and under the tables so that if it hadn't been for the busboy having scooped up the magazine Kirsten might not have permitted her emotional state to override her more rational self. She might have never gotten her own photo in the tabloids—a furtive woman was reported to have caused a disturbance in the print-media kiosk at PressCity anent the Public Library, corner Sankt Olofsgatan and Svartbacksgatan Avenues at 10 PM on the evening of the 17th. And it was sheer chance that determined that a paparazzo with camera got curious concerning the very tall, leggy, blond and gor-geous woman poking 'mongst the sports and porno mags that time of night. It was sheer chance that he got one good pic before she ripped the camera out of his hand and decked him.

Next morning's International Transom screamed a headline: *Uff dah! Who Was That Fem?* and ran a gaudily touched-up pic made to present a gaunt, overly-painted wench masquerading in the latest glamour-clinique style. Kirsten thanked her dear mammá's gods and elfin creatures that the rendition bore little resemblance to the subject the ill-fated camera caught behind the magazine rack.

Doctor L. was furious over the Transom's foto-pic. Kirsten, on the other hand, was alarmed at the article's suggestion her athlete might have been injured. Kirsten Lagerquist pulled herself together, so to speak. She cursed herself for having gone hot and silly. Calmly, methodically, late next morning, she permitted the Internet to reproduce the article for her. Under "Cycle-Motor-Competition," the news item dated the month before revealed the details of the incident. Dakar in Senegal. The athlete's motorbike was damaged in a race in the mountains. The crash had cost him three cracked ribs and a championship.

Meanwhile, there were professional matters to attend. There was the mess Gregorian had left behind, including the meter-wide flask replete with brain-tissue. What to do with it? She vaguely recalled later she'd dismissed it all, told the lab people to chuck it all down the drain, and she might have forgotten it all, except that the Pederson fellow sat outside her office for near a week before she relented and saw him.

"Pederson? Do I know you?"

"No, Ma'am." Pederson stood, hat in hand, a diffident little fellow with a wispy mustache and unruly blond hair. He had difficulty maintaining eye-contact. "I worked with Doctor Gregorian."

"You're the television fellow!"

"Yes, Ma'am. I did some transmit work for Doctor Gregorian."

Lagerquist waited.

"Gotta do with people's brains!" he hushed. "Not so much transmit, lotsa recept."

"I see. And was there?"

"Ma'am?"

"Did you transceive anything from the 'brain'?"

"Oh, yes Ma'am! Liked to scare me witless, lemme tell you! Y'see, I did like the Doctor said. I mean he wires it up—the brain that is—sets it up for photon-recept. All's I did was rig an audio-oscilloscope through the selenium rectifier so's we could sweep the different frequencies, like in any AM-FM radio, or a telebision, y' know. 'N'en the doc, he feeds the signal tru this digital audio ghizzy he made, y' see, an' it happened."

"What happened?"

"She was suddenly talkin', least that's what the Doctor said. I wouldn't know. All's I know is we got signals from in that jug o' brain stuff."

"Signals?"

"Yes Ma'am. Real clear. At about 21 cm."

"Isn't 21 cm. the frequency of hydrogen?"

"Yes, Ma'am."

"Well, then. There's your explanation."

"Yes Ma'am. But this hydrogen was talkin' to us."

"I'll look into the matter, Mister Pederson. Send us a statement. Goodbye, now."

To Doctor Magda Johansson-Gunderhagen, top admin-honcho of the Institute, Gregorian's resignation had yet to be justified and explained.

And the Transom had identified the mysterious lady of the kiosk as one K. G. Lagerquist of the Institute, and the Institute could not have its Chief of Neurology in the scandal sheets, Gunderhagen confided in the younger woman. From time to time, one came into need of relaxation.

Kirsten heard the message: *Relax. Go get laid!*

Doctor Lagerquist took a leave of absence.

****

Phoebus Apollo consulted his analeptic library. He flipped back through the pages of mem-time, as it were, and, being a bit lazy when an easier recourse was at hand, pressed his telecom unit into a kind of service its inventor could never have anticipated. "Research!" he commanded, and the humble contrivance complied. "Photo-optics," he specified, and the facts were revealed.

Time: Previous year, July, 2084.

Place: Bristol, Connecticut. The ad-hoc engineering facilities of one Harry Servo, designer-engineer extraordinaire, unrecognized.

The incident: a meeting of Servo and one Charles Endicotte.

The item: detailed schematics per conceptor screen of what Servo called an ElectroMagnetic lens, which is to say a "lens" consisting, not of glass, but of infinitely-variable electro-magnetic waves such as the ones that had powered that same humble television set. Harry Servo was at pains to describe the lens. It was perfectly transparent and infinitely variable. It would let pass unhindered any and all the EM waves of a broadband signal stream, except for those pre-selected. With this device, Servo emphasized, one might listen in on thousands of digital conversations and redirect any one to a pre-selected receiver. All one needed was point of origin and destination-address. What the graphics displayed to a highly pleased and astonished Endicotte was a box the size of a small valise, atop which sat three intersecting hoops within whose infinitely-variable circumferences sat the invisible lens.

"Say the multipoint bandwidth signals come in north to south," Harry Servo was saying. "Program lens one to your pre-select signal, set lens-two on frequency-receipt, and then swivel hoop-three to re-direct the signal, say, east."

Phoebus fine-tuned his powers of inference. He knew Harry Servo to be letting his imagination play with the possible uses to which this wonder-toy might be put, but then, having been Charlie E.'s Leavenworth cell-mate, he had enough sense to keep shut his mouth. Phoebus time-scrolled ahead. In the weeks following, Servo had built the device. He had shipped it to an import-export outfit in Hamburg. He did what he was bid, then did his best to clear his mind of it and, presumably, the cash was good. Phoebus scrolled on.

Time: February, 2082.

Place: Bahado, Somalia.

Item: The antenna tower at Bahado.

Castigné had had the tower built, struts and braces courtesy of an outfit in Marseilles. From his vantage in retro-time, Phoebus watched the little Corsican sweat profusely under Africa's noon sun while two local rascals climbed the rickety scaffolding's 20 meters to affix the hoop-lenses to the top and position them just-so to intercept the line-of-sight broadband signal. Castigné let his imagination go geographic as his credulity strained— conceptors and broadbands and the like lying on the other side of his comprehension. Phoebus upped the audio and his retro-inquiry tossed him into a video conference call, Castigné to Sebastian Cray. Cray spoke to Castigné as would an adult to an ignorant child. He was assuring the Coriscan that, indeed, the pre-selected signals originating in Toronto, Canada, would be picked up by a satellite 650 kilometers in space, re-directed across the ocean and then over continents, and that they would arrive in the Somali desert on their way to Capetown, and here, at Bahado Oasis, the signals of interest would be netted. The ones selected would do a right-angle turn and be scooped by PacSatCom 650 miles over the Pacific Ocean to be directed and received at the True and Faithful Repository of the Depositors' Monies (TFRDM) of Colombo, Sri Lanka, 45 degrees equatorial latitude, and some 2500 miles across the Indian Ocean. The remaining stream of thousands of signals would proceed unimpeded to the coastal towns of Meregh, and on to Mogadishu and to Capetown. How did the affair diverge from Servo's carefully engineered scheme to the spatchcocked affair in process? Phoebus pressed on. Fine-focusing the time, place and event took him back to the tawdry, sweaty banalities of the previous summer:

Castigné had lost his cellphone on a bleary-boozy trek back from town. In his mind, somebody could have lifted it in the tavern, or he'd equally-likely dropped in the sand. Without it, he'd sweated himself to near cardiac arrest, running back and forth from garage-office to tarmac and back, shouting to the rascals on the roof the telephone instructions from the Englishman in Geneva while lobbing near-burst curses at the idiot Brit chuckling at how wonderful modern technology could be.

When it was over, Castigné had taken a shower-bath using a ten-gallon drum with a perforated bottom and all fifty gallons of precious water. He cooled. He relaxed with a quick meal of sausage and bread, and the better part of a litre of Bordeaux. Then, he'd sat and slept. The messenger with the magnetic discs was due next morning. The little Frenchman woke in the middle of the night, famished and needing to relieve his bladder. He peed under an African sky overwhelmingly beautiful to anyone receptive to its breadth and to a plentitude of stars. Castigné, however, had seen it all before. Dawn shattered the sky and Castigné dozed, this time, in his desk chair, physically relaxed, to the point of gentle, cardiac insufficiency.

****

So, Phoebus muttered. That is where Benni Pistone found him, in the same desk chair looking at first glance like nothing so much as a scruffy little man burrowed into a most enjoyable snooze.

Phoebus scrolled on. Castigné wouldn't be there when Benni Pistone returned two days later with a small truck. Phoebus slowed the re-play. He followed Pistone's arrival at six in the morning. In this retro-scene, Benni collected wrenches from about the garage and proceeded to undo the fastenings on the roof and loose the guy-wires, carefully easing the whole thing down. Servo's ingenious EM lenses came away easily enough by which time the morning was getting on and the sun was already hot. Benni left the antenna sections there on the ground. He wrapped the lens affair in a soft cotton blanket the Caruso woman had given him, and then in a canvas tarp as Paco had told him to do. He'd pulled the little truck around the shack to re-take the track back north when he saw a little fellow standing a few meters off next to a donkey, a black wraith in a white singlet and sawed off dungarees. The little fellow caught Benni's eye and smiled a great, wide smile of gleaming teeth and an overshadowing, opaque look of one who might know everything or absolutely nothing. Benni gunned the engine and headed back into the desert. The desert scene faded slowly. The last thing Phoebus saw was the gleaming smile adorning the face of one Ishaak Briccone tucking a camera back into his shirt.

9. Commission

April of '80 drizzled on indifferent to the discomforts of men and beasts, and Mack van Horn had fallen in love again. Inevitably, she was tall. Perhaps it was because he was short that he liked them tall. She was unutterably beautiful. He adored beautiful women because they were…well, they were beautiful. She was strong, and dominant, and decisive, traits he found irresistible "—oooow take me, baby, take meeee!" And, she was Afro. "Not as in American, but as in Ah-free-kah, the real thing, baby, the genuine ar-tick-ul." She was his boss, the boss of the bosses, which was more than enough to set a man dreaming, especially considering he hadn't been laid in three months which made a fella apt to get out of sorts. Besides, if he took a break, sneaked a cigarette (he was permitted three a day), stood in the doorway to the cafeteria off the lobby during lunchtime, he could see her lever those magnificent legs, pivot those incredible hips, sway her beautiful self off to the executive dining room. The sight of her ruined him for the rest of the day. After such enchantment what relevance was the arcane world of astrophysics? What did it matter that the Universe was fractal-planar, open, closed. saddle-shaped, multi-dimensional, a bubble-bath, or the cat's ass stuck on end-of a spent wad of chewing gum?

But, work he must, and so van Horn put on his cerebral headband and, albeit half-heartedly, stepped between the spaces between endless outer worlds. Copy got read, and his mind edited. Copy was revised and corrected. The mind expanded and fitted. Latest theoretical assertions measured against standard database and, "hey baby, nothing wrinkles below third level parameters because we are swinging this Pee-Emmm." Graphics emerged in van Horn's mind-screen, imposed a telescopic image via Sandage 5-Very Large Array (twenty five astro-tele-em dishes), at Lunar north pole. Senior in-house writer's psyche guided his own, droned like a voice in his mind and text enlarged: "…galaxy distributions for southern section of El Puchido red-shift survey combines the third section of GfB3 catalog in the northern hemisphere…" Van Horn prompted and the conceptor went to cut-and-paste, combined paragraphs, punctuated, capitalized, and corrected all "with the left hand," as Charlie E, would put it, and all "in the foreskin of the afternoon." Van Horn chuckled with satisfaction. "Ah, such is to be merely brilliant. All in a morning's work."

****

The stone in Didi's shoe was the shaky financial status of the University of Chicago Corporation, trustees, provost and financial whizzes having permitted the venerable establishment to tatter and tear, totter and damned near go insolvent. Ah, for the good old congress of the U.S. Government to come to the rescue as in days of yore. Call your congressman and plead a case, and *voila!*

Didi had come in as executive prez. only to find the gothic honeycomb on the green Plaisance along 57th Street empty as an abandoned hive—no lectures, no classes, the libraries moldering and the labs all in crash and clutter. What had been the pride of American learning was a storefront outlet in Mandel Hall hawking tapes, discs and a few tattered books—classics to physics and art to zoology. The great University, originator of the Great Books, site of the world's first atomic chain-reaction, was a page on the

WebWorks and a giveaway of academic treasures most of which had long since become artifactoids and curiosities. The only viable organ left was in Fox River, the Xenon Institute, and that, too, so dispersed of assets and personnel as to court its own disaster. Now, Phoebus' own Connie-the-Ocho fem-threatened both University and Institute with buy-out and dismemberment. Subsume Unlimited was assuming the University's staggering debt, but having a Hades-of-a-time just getting a handle on its mismanaged and ill-defined assets. Which was just as well. For the nonce, the facade held fast. Like the gargoyles on Rockefeller Chapel, the University Corporation's PR front grinned and grimaced, gripped the stones and put on a good front.

Meanwhile, the chancellor kept abreast of developments abroad.

The U of C's Swiss extension in Geneva was still operating. Polichuk was on the verge of a breakthrough into alter-dimensional physics, perhaps into lebensraum for a sorely over-populated Earth whose resources were all but depleted, a prior claim on which alter-dimensional real-estate stood pending and worth a few billion toward Chicago's salvation. If the old man didn't croak on her first. And if Constancia Ocho didn't over-reach herself and ruin the prospects. Meanwhile, the ten-thousand square kilometer telescopic array on the moon's north pole went on producing great-volume images of galaxy-strewn worlds for night-time television entertainment, and a binding contract with DigiCrisp Corporation assured moon-shots and Mars missions and the like at astronomical expense (and scientific-educational tax write-off) all of which was presented to a vanishingly small audience because U. of C. video ratings were down in single-digits since the re-intro of prime-time-live sex and of snuff competitions. What had the sage of Baltimore said? "No one had ever gone broke underestimating the taste and intelligence of the mass audience." Ah, well, says Didi to her musing self, *Chacun à son goofy*.

At The Oriental Institute, Chancellor des Dieux kicked off her shoes and put her feet up on the twelve-foot Babylonian obelisk serving her as a desk. The air-conditioning was down, the air was thick, and she hadn't had lunch. Later, she would admit to the fumble—she'd groped for the cater-service button and she hit the video button which may have been fortunate, she admitted, or it might have gotten past her—a talking head, a commercial transmission advertising geriatric diapers, or some such, an anchor person carved out of cosmetics and held together with hairspray was nasal-garbling something about bubbles and baths, or some such, and Didi reached to switch off except the apparition said something about real-estate. And dimensions. Didi back-tracked her mind and the sense of it began to emerge. "Doctor Polly-chuck," the specter was saying. And something about a "dy-mention-all bubblebath." And something to do with someone having had a heart attack.

Didi shouted into her commo console, "Get me Geneva!"

She made a dash for the exit door on her way to the University Commo Center and her EarPod picked up the switch to a snide nasal cum-facetious commentaror interupting with:

...bulletin from the former West Coast. Remember Ba-ha-California? Kind of hung off California, as in state-of. Well, throw away your maps, folks, 'cause it just ain't there no more. Just a lotta little islands now, like Santa Clara and them, had sense enough to grab the high ground. This has kinda got Californians worried. I mean, like the song says, water's rising, and how long can the levees at our own San Diego hold out? Are y' list'nin', los An-jah-lees?

****

The same Tuesday morning of the Chancellor's anxieties, and a mere forty miles away at Xenon Institute on the Fox River, van Horn spilled a cup of coffee and shorted out his control board. He was still wearing his cerebroband and the shock of the shorted circuit smacked him hard. In the brain. The cerebrum. In the gyrus ideo-conscientius. Had he been able to articulate those three seconds, he'd have said he knew himself as his-self. As two entities who were one. One to know and one to be. But it lasted no more than three seconds and there was no time for any judgmental observation. The two-ness which was a one-guy closed down. He shouted mock imprecations, laughed at himself, and joshed with his patient, barely sympathetic colleagues. Shortly after 1 PM, having lunched, he found a message in his email: "Report to the Chancellor's office soonest."

"The Chancellor? Wants to see me? Well, I can always get another job, I suppose. Hmmm. Since when's it take a chancellor to fire a schlemiel?"

Two security units like out of a video game—homburgs, opaque eye-shades, black suits and white gloves yet—whisked him by limo the forty-some miles from Xenon in Fox River to the Plaisance in Chicago. "In a limmo, yet! Never been fired so fancy." Van Horn chuckled and feared. At the Oriental Institute, he was body-searched in the foyer and two unit-types escorted him fore and up.

Ten after four in the afternoon. The sun streamed through the gothic windows and framed Chancellor des Dieux in a glory of light. (*"My gawd, but she's perfect! Like a fuckn' goddess!"*) Van Horn forced himself to concentrate on what she was saying:

"Van Horn, I am putting you on special assignment."

"Ma'am?"

Standing up close, she was even taller than he'd thought her to be, and more beautifully forbidding. Van Horn was terrified and elated, intimidated and aroused. The Chancellor had opted for nude-nylons that morning, and a short skirt, three-button blouse and no bra. Van Horn's throat constricted. Heartbeat went to 120. ("Oh, be still my pacemaker!") He drew a short breath and his mouth went dry because she was looking him directly in the eye, hard, impersonal and mean. "Tiger: pussy that eats a man!" The scatological phrase popped into his mind and he was sure afterwards he'd giggled even as he stammered and sweat whle she was speaking to him. He had her arm twisted behind her back—not too hard, mind—and had drawn her panties to her knees and was elbowing the pesky garment out of the way because at the same time he was down and…ready to…

She was saying something about her brother and other fools, if van Horn heard aright, and something about a tizzy-buns and a bum-blaster coming in from left field and getting into the act. Afterwards, van Horn retained and re-played her having said something to the effect, "You realize of course, that the calculation of function-specific factors as constants in a sum of arbitrary variables cannot account for the shifting of the ante-programmatic parameters."

"Um, yes. Of course…"

"I know I promised not to interfere, but my brother's already stuck his foot in and the game goes too far. For a bit of "noo-kie," Phoebus has put the entire mortal world in jeopardy. Financially, and…yes, physically! Wager or no wager, it is time to throw in a joker and scramble the eggs."

"Joker? Eggs? If you say so, ma'am."

"But without my dear brother knowing. My means have got to be innocuous. Improbable. That's where you come into it."

"Yes, ma'am."

"You will be my joker. My wild card. You will go to Geneva."

"We got an office in Wisconsin?"

"Switzerland. You will contact Polichuk. You have established rapport."

"Don't know the man."

"You spoke to him."

"I did? Oh! The Russki! Sure. Be delighted to meet…"

"Learn what you can about the 5-dim."

"The what?"

"And I want you to meet…her!"

A monitor on the Chancellor's desk lit up. Van Horn followed the movements of a petit little redhead in a too-tight skirt. A pretty if hard-nosed little broad, he would have said.

"Who?"

"Constancia Ocho. President-CEO of forty of the world's biggest banks and corporations."

"No joke?"

"Your mission, should you choose to accept it, is to seduce and destroy."

"It is?"

"And learn what you can about Chanticleer."

"Chanticleer. Yes, ma'am."

"And the 5-dim. bubble. What does she plan for it?"

"The five and dime *whaaat?*"

"She's planning a complete financial take-over of the world. And she'll succeed. With my silly brother's help. As though that were not bad enough, now throw in whatever the good Doctor's got in mind for TimeSpace…"

"Time. And Space. Yes Ma'am."

"Your mission is to discover."

"Discover."

"You won't be alone. I will be there to cover your back."

"My back. Yes Ma'am."

The Chancellor stood close. If he'd ducked his head a trifle he'd have nose-nuzzled her nipples. He resisted. He looked up, she looked down. She smiled. "Bring home the bacon, van Horn. You will be well rewarded."

"The bacon. Rewarded. Yes, Ma'am."

He'd been dismissed. Back in the corridor he struggled to recap what she'd said. Under a tight-security contingent he got taken over by a sour-looking tech in clinical whites. Anxiety-ridden memory suggested the Chancellor had not fired him. It said she'd assigned him to Billings Hospital's PsycheSurgical Clinic. Psyche? What the hell for? He wasn't having psyche probs, was he? Or maybe he did and it showed up in his MC edit projections.

Possible? "Van Horn, what'd you get yourself into now?"

At Psyche-Surge-Clinic he was strapped to a table, his head stuffed crown to chin into an evil-looking helmet and a stone-serious tech glowered at him. In deference to the overheated lab, she wasn't wearing anything under her loose smock. So much was obvious when she crouched over him to adjust the helmet. If she'd smiled, maybe done something with her hair, a little makeup...

She attempted a smile. "Heff you effer been tru a mem-probe, Mester van Horn?"

"Huh? Ah, no. I've never..."

"You will zleep, you see. Venn you vake, you will heff tolt us..."

In a manner of speaking, he slept. Surface consciousness was extinguished. Just as one might see in a dream, he relived scenes from recent experience. Gerry Queen. His/her impossibly pretty face, the real one visible from under makeup to his know-better. The voice, a put-on. Other media-celebrity types at the studio table and the heat of the lights. Himself seeing himself in a monitor over there and lookin' gooood!

The clinician did something with the controls. Van Horn dreamed he was back at his workstation at Xenon. Through an extra-terrestrial static the Russki accent whispered in his commo: "...steals from me the data...and the Hungarian, he instruments, you see...*hoooshshooooshooooosh* to make of the fifth dimension real estate...she conquers the world! *hooooooshhoooooshhooooosh*...from spatial dimensions she is making shopping malls."

Van Horn came up groggy, looking into a cup of coffee and sitting on a lump in his left cheek. Then the campus shuttle car zipped him back to the Oriental Institute. The Security types all but lifted and carried him back to the Exec Center on Ellis Avenue.

The zombie was no more than five-eight, his own height, but his face looked like something hammered out of metal. "All right Samborn. We give you a crash course. Ever use one of these?"

Van Horn examined the weapon. His eyes went to cold steel and his voice dropped two octaves. "An SW semi-auto. sidearm. Fires a 9-millimeter cartridge at 1500 feet per sec. I'm an aficionado. you see. I have an older model in my collection."

"Know how to use it?"

"Never miss a Sunday at the range."

"You may have occasion to use this."

Van Horn put on ear protectors and stepped up to the firing stage. He held the weapon. Proper stance. Two hands, feet apart, sighted down the short barrel, squeezed…and fired! He put six shots in the center eye and two in the inner ring." The air in the range rang with aftershock. Van Horn gave his best sneer and handed the smoking weapon to the zombie. Zombie mumbled. "Master of arms on your way out."

Back in the street, van Horn thought back on the last hours' events. He was now lethally armed. The thought made him queasy.

It was now going on six of the PM and he requested home. By the time they'd whisked him back to his digs on State and 14th, he felt sick to his stomach.

On Saturday, May 10, 2085, AireSuisse GravityWalker 706 hovered at 161 kilometers, ten miles over Geneva. Passenger shuttle carrying 114 descended swiftly in its antigrav chute and set down gently in the landing dock. Van Horn paused in the entryway to the concourse wearing the latest in the traveling gentleman's trencher (so said Gentleman's Weekly), a very fine set of American boots (setting the trend) and a pair of Givenchy shades for that distinctive touch. In the camera of his fantasy, for the adoring crowds of his imagination, his handsome face broke into that gentle acceptance, the openness that was the essence of Mackenzie van Horn. Reality descended. Anxiety said he'd stepped onto the threshold of destiny. The visage of Chancellor des Dieux peered in his mem-image…(*"Oh, Didi! Didi, I could… hmmmmm-AAAAH!"*) Imagination permitted him to seize her by the bra. He drew her close and he looked down at her from his six-four, but a surge in the crowd behind him prompted him to step aside. Banal reality re-asserted and at module 49 a uniformed chauffeur greeted him stiffly, took the bag and said, in effect, "Follow me."

****

In a private room at the Rigshospitalet, the National Hospital of Copenhagen, Aram Gregorian woke to the sounding of his name.

"*Le docteur* Gregorian?"

"Indeed."

"Tisibon, Claude. Of Bombaste-Tisibon Fraternite Scientifique Independent, S.A, an independent entity we are, you see."

Propped against pillows and imprisoned in plaster, Gregorian saw the fellow squarely framed in the light of the window. The effects of sedation had the creature floating, like a mayfly in a beam of sunlight, a small, near cadaverous creature wearing an over-sized, wide-brimmed fedora, enveloped in a huge black cloak from whose depths peered his huge bespectacled eyes and whose near transparent tissue revealed the bone beneath the skin. With his one good hand, Gregorian rubbed his eyes and looked again.

From behind a pair of enormous, horn-rimmed spectacles the creature smiled the sweet avidity of a wicked child. "A letter I write," the creature said. "On paper. With stamp. The conceptor I cannot abide, you see. So it is a liberty I take."

"When?" says Gregorian. "When did you write?"

"The seventeen February, the Universal Calendar twenty-eighty."

"Good gawd, man. That was nearly four years ago. Do you expect me to remember?"

"*Mais oui!* Remember you?"

"Indeed, I do! By George, I do! Don't get that many pieces of old-fashioned mail. Refresh my memory."

"The Horn of Ammon, monsieur. The *giri sui-cognoscenti* of the infra-temporal complex—We have recorded. A digital process…"

"You have recorded what?"

"The neuronal syntax of the telencephalic vesicles in the ventricular zone. It employs the pregnane X receptor, PXR, as you say in your article, Journal of PsychoNeuronics, January 2081, volume seven, number 17. Yes, the neuronal syntax of thinking, if you will. And we think several cogniphrinic variations, though we've not been able to identify them. But unmistakable is the result. *Les emanations ante-verbal de le syntaxe neuronal sont manifest*, you see, e make the mind-record, Bombast, he devises…"

"Please. Begin again. What are you babbling about?"

"The recording sir. Cognitional activity. Bombast and I, we read everything you write, especially the article 'On isolation of molecular constellations as derived from the action of estrogen β and of androstene-3,17-dione as an amplifier of cognitional acuity,' which you regard as…"

"Get to the point! What have you recorded?"

"The syntax, sir…"

"Begin again."

"…it is established of an underlying grammar."

"A grammar."

"Yes, doctor. Bombaste, he attempts to establish an auditory organ-complex link so we may speak to it."

"Speak to?"

"The mind, *Monsieur docteur*, we've isolated the mind!" The little man lost himself in thought for a moment, and then he giggled. "Bombaste says we have—how you say?—*mariné*."

"*Mariné?* Pickled!"

"Ah, *oui*. Just so."

"'Pickled.' Pickled what?"

"So far we are able to take it. The physiology, you see. We would need a body. A brain into which to transfer."

"I'm not sure I understand what you're getting at. But how can I be of any help. As you can see...*je suis invalide."*

The little man chuckled at the pun. *"Oui, Monsieur.* But such infirmities are not permanent. With help, it would be possible to remove one's self."

"Remove? Where to?"

"Genevre, Monsieur."

"Genevre? What's in Genevre?"

The pale little face went sober and intense. The eyes widened behind the huge lenses. "The advance of your brilliant work. And..." Here Tisibon's intensity broke once again into that diffident smile. "And our subject, perhaps?"

"Our subject. I see. And what would that be?"

"Not 'what,' sir. Rather 'who?'"

"All right, then. Who?"

The smile broadened. *"Se c'est possible, monsieur,* the greatest scientific mind of the century? Yes?"

"Scientific...Polichuk?"

"Mais, oui, Monsieur. Consider, your theory—'The Transmissibility Activity of the Cerebrum,' Journal PyscheNeuronics, March 2081.' Bombaste and I, we have devised a means to make this possible." The tiny fellow drew closer, his eyes enormous behind his lenses, and his demeanor, Gregorian would have said, was near maniacal. "Will you help us, *Docteur?* Will you participate in the vindication of your brilliant theory?"

Gregorian lay back in his pillows feeling himself to be a man stunned. If what this clown said was anywhere near true...He felt the despair, the weeks of ignomiry, and yea, the insult heaped upon him. His mem-image was of Kirsten Lagerquist's face, her words, the implicit threat "...if you persist in pursuing fantasies..." But reality said it was this creature Tisibon whose face had drawn nose-close.

"Let me understand this clearly," Gregorian rasped. "You mean to transfer a mind, a consciousness, from one body to another."

Tisibon drew closer. The little man's breath had grown short. He perspired in his enthusiasm. "*Mais, oui.* We have a psyche-subject…most suitable. What we lack is a suitable body."

"My theories…" Gregorian gasped.

"*Mais oui!* Your life's work, sir!"

"A mind…transferred." Gregorian focused his gaze. He was looking into the near hypnotic power of the mayfly's eyes. "Indeed! Tisibon, can you get me out of here?"

Ammon's Horn

10. Hyperion

Hyperion Industries. Merchandise Mart, Chicago.

Indifferent fate had put van Horn in the stratosphere even as A. Phoebus Belvedere gaveled HI's final meeting to a close. Hyperion Industries had ceased to be as of May 1, 2080.

The board of directors met for a wrap-up session and then dissolved into a straggling group of thirteen exec-types muttering shock and dismay, making their way through the great mahogany doors. Only Didi remained. She smiled at him from down table.

"Well, big fellow? Now what?"

"Subsume, Unlimited assumes control of Hyperion Industries and that wasn't in the script. Last week, it was Danubian Technologies Consortium. She owns Eastern Europe, you know. And the week before, CentRes Jerusalem got tucked into her purse. I mean, dammit, she nearly had the Arabs and Israelis at each others throats again 'til they woke up to who'd done the leveraging."

"Let me see now," Didi stared wickedly at the ceiling and ticked off on her fingers. "Day one, British Hydroxide Energies rolled over. Day-two, it was DeutschesFotronishe Commo who kissed her rosy behind and paid dearly for the privilege. Mid-week, her buxom soldiers engineered the takeover of Euro-Alliance d'Espace, Helsinki. And that, plus SudAm Space and AeroEspacion Brazil puts that game and most of South America into her purse, fiscal and real. You have taught her well, Phoebus. Another year and the little bitch will own the world."

"I give her beauty—at least that's what others perceive—and more power than any single woman has ever had. And yet ... "

"She hasn't the time of day for you. Is that it?"

"She rebuffs me as she would a knock-kneed hayseed. Didi, have you been meddling?"

"Not in the least, dear brother. I haven't so much as breathed on her. No, it's all your own doing. As always you under-estimate the power of the human female. You choose to see her as little more than a bundle of emotions wrapped 'round a clitoris. You and your hairy-chested minions can't stomach the thought of an intelligent woman with craft and, yes, the guts and wits to prevail in the masculine world. And when she does carry the day you stamp your feet and whine like little boys. A woman's just not supposed to beat you at your own game."

"Nonsense. We're perfectly capable of tolerance and largesse. Always willing to give a girl a chance. Nevertheless, I begin to wonder if we haven't created a monster!"

"'We?' Oh, no Phoebus. She's all yours. But, you just won't learn. There is no monster more deadly than a powerful female."

"I begin to believe it. Nor, apparently, more single minded. Not even I, the paragon of manly beauty, virtue and sexual prowess can make her blink! Now if you would just let me..."

"No godly tricks now, remember? As I was saying, power and gratitude are mutually contradictory—Helen should have taught you that much."

"By Jove! That little fracas might have gone my way if you hadn't interfered."

"I didn't have to! Though I don't expect you will ever believe me.

There was no more magic in Helen of Troy than nature herself provided. I merely taught her to do what comes naturally, but more…expertly?"

"Do what, by Jupiter!?"

"Oh, please, Phoebus. Let's not get *Pappá* into it or there's no telling what might happen. But, I must say, you're playing a complicated game, this round. What's with the nest of thieves?"

"Cray and company? They're my parametric variables. I need to exert some control before she's completely out of control. In the interests of which control I am marshaling pertinent sociological forces."

"Sociological?" Didi chuckled. "As in Professor Phoebus Apollinaire of the University…"

"…Allepo. Women's College of Social Dynamics"

"Yas, I remember now. As Professor P. Apolliniare, you seduced the entire feminine faculty and half the student body and left under a cloud."

"Nonsense. Nowhere near half. In any case, though we are immortals, we remain less than omnipotent or omniscient, public opinion to the contrary."

"You're losing control."

"Damned near. And since you won't permit me to employ my supernatural powers—I mean even a peek into the future would help—I have decided we'd best marshal the variables already potent in the situation. What are you smirking at now?"

"Is there anything more dangerous then a sociologist who thinks his choice of things to study constitutes physics?"

"Since you limit my means, Didi, have I any choice? I'm stuck with connections already made. I like to think in terms of powers of triangulation. Take the Cray-Ocho-Ungaroni triangle. Through the Ungaroni connection, the Pistone fellow and…"

"And? Lagerquist?"

"Oh, come now, Didi. I've got to light a fire under the lad somehow. And you've got to admit, the combination, hulking athlete and brilliant doctor, is ingenious. And no, I haven't touched her. For the nonce, she's sweating out her hormones and waiting for her hirsute friend to find her. When the silly twit gets off his motorcycle there's no telling where this comedy will lead. Last peek I had at him he'd broken a leg."

"His ribs, dear. His ribs. And the physicist?"

"Polichuk? Ah, he's Ocho's instrument. He was supposed to provide her with 'Trans-dimensional real estate,' or something."

"Don't look now, but I think he's had a heart attack."

"Damn it all, Didi! How's a fellow to win this game if you keep peeking into his cards?"

"Not peeking, dear. Just outplaying you. Which reminds me, haven't you lost one of your connections?"

"Lost?"

"The other doctor. The neurophys."

"Ah, Gregorian. No. Haven't really lost him. Though I must say he's been a disappointment."

"This is as odd an ensemble of clowns as you're mustered in an eon. Just what have you got up your sleeve," Didi crooned, "sociologically or otherwise?"

A. Phoebus Belvedere smiled. He helped himself to a carafe and poured an excellent coffee. Didi considered him from across the breadth of shiny mahogany. She lit a mentholated cigarette and regarded him through the smoke. "I don't trust you when you're quiet," she said.

A. Phoebus regarded the coffered ceiling, and when he looked back at her he was positively beaming. "As you say, dear Didi, one has but to work with the human potential provided, ungovernable variables and all. And then, perhaps, enhance them."

"Well, play on, little brother. We are now in the first week in August. There are eight months remaining and you're winning this wager for me all by yourself."

"Ah, yes. Our wager. I do remember some such silliness. But, come now. You're not serious about that silly wager. Are you?"

"Indeed I am! As serious as Constancia Ocho is about ruling the financial world. As serious as you are to bed her. She may well become the chief honcho she dreams to be, and you may well ruin the mortal world on the way to bedding her. That, or there's a job waiting for you at Bunny's Retreat."

"A minion, you said. To wash sheets and undies for a regiment of whores. Well, alright, then. Never let it be said the god Phoebus Apollo walked away from a wager. Before this circus of unpredictabilities closes its tent, I'll have la Ocho spread-eagled and begging for more. And I'll see you warming a set of Bunny's sheets."

Didi chuckled with relish. "Dearest brother, the game waits to be played. Meanwhile, shall we look in on your friends?"

Didi pointed a finger. The telecom unit lit up.

****

Aram Gregorian had prepared himself for he knew not what. If it had struck him that Claude Tisibon was awfully efficient for a diffident and absent-minded scientist, he said nothing. Gregorian had been cleared to leave Copenhagen General. Flight for two was already booked, ScandinAire, Copenhagen to Geneva. Up one handicap ramp and down another, they made the shuttle flight swiftly and in Geneva they breezed through customs without a hitch. A cab stood waiting and reservations at the Hotel St. Germaine were all made out in the name of and charged to the account of Gregorian, A. It was 1 PM when they were shown to Gregorian's rooms and a waiter brought lunch. Tisibon never ceased from smiling from behind his glasses, and it was this smile that gave Gregorian passing concern as the tiny fellow looked like the proverbial cat that had eaten the neighbor's canary.

Next morning, on a warm, lovely day in Spring, an especially equipped van came for him. It took him and wheelchair aboard and in jig time and they were off to the Clinique General Beaulieu. Evidently, Tisibon had arranged everything.

At Clinique General, a pale and wizened face crowned in profuse grey hair peered at them from the white pillow. The brown eyes warmed, and the homely face creased into a broad smile.

"Doctor Polichuk?"

"Da. I am Polichuk."

"Aram Gregorian, sir. Indeed, this is a pleasure."

"Gregorian? Gregorian? You are one in fusion-stasis? The one who measures the mass-time-particle, the temporon."

"Ah, no, Sir. I am a lowly physiologist. Neurology, actually."

"Neurology? Ah, I am afraid there is nothing you can do for me, doctor. It is my heart, you see…"

"No, sir. You mistake me. I come out of professional courtesy and because I consider it an honor…"

"You are injured?"

"A broken humerus is all. An accident…"

"Please, Sir. Talk to me. You may be last person in whom I am able to confide."

"Come, Doctor. Surely you will be up and about in no time."

"Listen, young man. She steals my work! Two years now. Everything. What I think, what I write. They keep me, how you say, tranquil…" The old man was crying.

"Indeed, sir? Who's stealing your work?"

"Good morning, gentlemen." Gregorian didn't see him immediately, having the wheelchair to contend with. He turned it about in the narrow space and there was Tisibon. In whites. With a stethoscope dangling from his neck. With efficient dispatch Tisibon scanned the cardiac monitor, read the chart, and excused himself as he pushed past Gregorian and did a quick examination of the man in the bed.

"Tisibon!" Gregorian gasped. "You're?"

"What sir? Oh, yes. Didn't I mention? I am Professor Polichuk's private physician."

"You sneaky rascal. Why didn't you tell me?"

"What is there to tell? I am the physician. You, the neurologist. He is the patient. Together we shall…"

"Yes? What? Together we shall what?"

"We will save the world's greatest mind."

"Indeed! And put it into the body of another?" Gregorian could not have explained why it all struck him with such force, why he should see it as both absurd and utterly monstrous.

"The mind, doctor." Tisibon was near giggling. "Bombaste says with your help we can 'down-load' it,' as say *les Americains*."

"Something is wrong, Doctor?" Polichuk regarded Gregorian with alarm."

"Yes, sir. Indeed, it does appear to be possible…"

"Possible?"

"To do what he says. To…'down-load' it. The mind, that is. 'Pickle' it…"

"Pickles? What's with pickles?"

"It has been possible to preserve tissues against future use," Tisibon interjected, speaking directly to Polichuk.

"Da? And so?"

"And to clone whole organs."

"And so?"

"And so, it now appears we may be able to do so with a mind."

The old man's smile faded to somber amazement. "My work…and now? *Ach!* Tisibon. You can do this? This is how you 'save me?'" Polichuk's eyes widened in wonder and fear. "The woman, Ocho, she wants the fifth dimension, for real estate…something. Hours of the day, she steals from me. The work of my mind. The time of my life!"

Gregorian spoke softly out of a weight of dread. His nose was an inch from the old man's. "Listen, Doctor Polichuk. We may be in grave danger."

"You think?"

"We must get you out away from here."

"Away? *Ach*, how to do this? You with a broken leg. Me, I die to sneeze."

"Help. We need help."

The smiling face of Claude Tisibon inserted itself at this juncture. *"Messieurs,"* says he. "Not to worry. Salvation is at hand. The psycho-synthesis will be generated. The transference will be effected. We will, *comme en dit an englais*, 'down-load,' yes?"

Tisibon stepped back into the full light of the window. One could not see his eyes for the opaque glare in his spectacles. He assumed a thoughtful stance, arms behind his back, head slightly bowed. Then he began, as though he were addressing a class at university. "Your mind, *Docteur*, is as fine an instrument as the species has produced. It will be preserved independent of the frail biological system it inhabits, *n'est pas*?"

Gregorian regarded Tisibon in derisive alarm, and not without anger. "More of your 'pickles' is it?"

"Gregorian, *attendez vous*." Tisibon never ceased from smiling. "We have acquired an adequate body."

"Oh, have you now? Listen, we've got to get this man to a safe place. And for this, we need help."

"Allo?" says Tisibon.

"What . . ?" Claude Tisibon was looking back over Gregorian's head toward the door. Polichuk had sat up with a shocked and fearful look in his homely face. Gregorian pivoted about in his chair and someone shoved past him. A big woman. A nurse, by the looks of her. She approached Polichuk's bed and stood reading the monitor and the charts. Polichuk appeared to be trying to vanish into the bedclothes.

"Go a-way! Leaf-me-a-lone!"

"Now, now, Professor. Relax. Everything's going to be all right. We are going to make a little journey."

"Excuse me, but just who are you?"

The nurse scowled at Gregorian. "I am private nurse for the Doctor Professor Anatoli Polichuk. I am in the employ of Madame Ocho. Madame Ocho is owner of this hospital. And who are you?"

"She is the one!" Polichuk peeked from out the bedclothes. "She steals from me...my theory...my work . . my mind!"

Gregorian collected his wits. "I am Aram Gregorian, professor neurophysiology, and I am as well an M.D., and I say this man is not fit to be moved."

"Are you the professor's physician?"

"Ah, no. I am not. But..."

"Then, butt out, booby!"

"'Butt out booby?' See here...Tisibon! Do something!" But Tisibon merely stepped aside and resumed that opaque demeanor which nothing was likely to penetrate. A gurney came rolling in attended on one end by an orderly. Gregorian was amazed to see the huge nurse rip the sensors off Polichuk's body. She whipped back the coverlet and with both arms lifted the frail little man from the bed as though she were attending a baby. Expertly, she placed him on the gurney and covered him head to foot in the white sheet. "Go!" she commanded, and the gurney backed toward the door.

"Woman! What are you doing? You are jeopardizing this man's life!" Gregorian shouted.

"Stand aside, sir. I have my orders."

"May I see them?" The intruder stood in the doorway, attache case in one hand and his other hand in the pocket of his coat. He spoke with a voice of authority, deep and resonant and assured. There was stone in the man's jaw and iron in his eyes.

"And just who are you?" Gudrun demanded.

"I am called van Horn. I am an emissary from the Chancellor. And I, too, have my orders. In writing."

"Ah, have you, now?

The stout little man moved into the room. With a deft hand he pulled back the sheet. Anatoli Polichuk looked up at him with fearful eyes. The man's basso rolled out gently. "Doctor Polichuk, I presume? Van Horn, here. We spoke, you and I. Do you remember?" Anatoli Polichuk managed a weak and grateful smile.

"What d'you want?" The nurse fairly shouted.

"There is a special flight waiting at Cointrin. Medical facilities are installed. Professor Polichuk comes with me, to Chicago. The Center for Advanced PsycheNeuronomy. You will accompany us to the terminal, nurse, and see to it the Professor is made comfortable. Well? Come along! We haven't much time."

****

In those same minutes, on a lower level in that same Clinique General Beaulieu de Genevre, Paco Ungaroni was striding across the admittance lobby. Before the Centre d' Admissions he cleared his throat and stood his tallest five-five. "*Perdoni. Sono il dottore Ungaroni. Il Pistone, Bennino, il mio paziente, dove?*" I am Doctor Ungaroni...my patient...

"Ah, *oui, docteur. Un moment.*" The chubby attendant at the service desk did something to her conceptor. She turned and smiled at him sweetly. "*Piston, B. Salle quattre B., deuxiéme etage.*"

"*Merci.*" Doctor Ungaroni headed for the elevators.

Second floor, around a bend, he met a tall, dissipated fellow with bad teeth wearing orderly's greens. The man broke into a sour grin. "Well, I'll be damned. You got to be Paco Unga-roni."

Paco stared up at Endicotte. "Angh...I think I know who you are. Where is Benni?"

"Oh, he's here all right. But, he's not going anyplace in a big hurry." Endicotte snickered, and strode down corridor. Paco hurried to follow.

"Benni? *Ei, Pistone!*" Paco croaked. Benni lay in a narrow bed covered chin to shins with a sterile sheet. That he was alive was attested to by the rise and fall of the diaphragm in the inhalator and by the beep-beep of the cardio monitor. He stared at the ceiling seeing nothing.

"He can't hear you," says Endicotte.

"What'sa matter with him?" says Paco.

"Coma."

"Coma?"

"T's right.

"Ah, I see. So, when?"

"Any minute. Maybe tomorrow. Maybe never."

"Capito."

"So, he can't tell us what we wanna know."

"Ah. Yes. You wanna know where is the antenna."

"Something like that. And the discs."

"He knows?"

"He's the one took 'em. And you told him…"

"I told him take down the antenna. Was supposed to meet me in Le Brassus. We would sell to you the discs. Ei, whatta you think, ah? Baruch, or whatever he calls himself, he owes me. For tree years inna cage, he owes me. But Benni, he does the video witte motorcycle and then somebody hits him. Was you?"

"What'd he do with the discs?"

"I don' know."

"C'mon, Macaroni. There's couple billion dollars ridin' on this."

"Yeah? You think I wanna bury it with him? Use-a-you head."

"I think maybe we better go see the man."

"*Ma, frégati!* I'm not going noplace." Paco saw for the first time the tiny little weapon the Endicotte fellow produced from the waistband of his greens. "Whatta you gonna do with that?"

"You be a good boy, and I won't do anything."

Another party intruded, a round and serious fellow in surgical whites with a snood pulled low on his brow and a respirator mask about his chin. Charlie Endicotte stared hard at this fellow. His face and demeanor rang a bell. "Come, *mes amis*," says the Roly-Poly. "We have work to do." Paco and Charlie E. placed Benni Pistone on a gurney. Roly-Poly snapped his fingers at Endicotte and shot a gun-patter of French at him. Endicotte fastened the IV-glucose to the side of a gurney. Paco helped mount the respirator to a transport stand. In minutes they had all in preparation to move the body of Benni Pistone. "What the hell're you doing?" says Charlie E.

"We prepare this patient for transport."

"Yeah? Where to?"

"Ah, that is none of your affair."

"Yes it is." Charlie displayed his little pistol.

The roly-poly screwed up his piggy features. He pursed his lips and flared his nostrils. His brows rose and his eyes widened. He regarded Endicotte and his little gun and he laughed. "*E bien?* You will shoot me? Ah, no. It is this fellow you want, eh? But alive. Awake. Able to speak. This he cannot do. If you shoot me, zut! he speaks no more."

"You can wake him up?" says Paco.

"This buffoon, he puts away the cannon, we will see."

Endicotte produced a cell-phone and spoke rapidly in English. Roly-poly busied himself with a cylinder of breathing gas and attended the patient's various tubes. He snapped his fingers. Paco jumped to and guided the gurney with Benni aboard toward the broad far-end doors, onto an elevator and into the morgue. Roly-poly said something to Paco in a French-Italian *patois* and he busied himself at the laboratory bench. It appeared he was preparing a hypo syringe. Endicotte tucked away his cell-phone. "Okay guys. Orders from headquarters says the bod is ours. Let's get it ready, shall we? And then we roll…" At which point Paco swore the American had gone completely daft. Endicotte threw his hands high in the air and he shrieked. Slowly, he lowered his arms and the look on his face was soft and stupid.

Roly-poly caught him from behind and Paco hurried to lend a hand. They put Charlie E. on a slab. "*Il dormirá, j'pense. Vien!*" says Roly-Poly."

Paco stared at the surgically precise Bombaste with uncertain curiosity. "Our colleagues await," says Bombaste (for that is who roly-poly actually was). With this they left Endicotte to sleep things off on a mortuary slab. Paco pushed the gurney with the comatose Benni P. aboard. He followed Bombaste out into the brilliant afternoon. They crossed the wide drive to where there awaited a clutch of individuals apparently in some altercation having to do with the idling ambulance, a patient on a gurney, and another in a wheelchair.

****

To the end of his days Aram Gregorian would re-live the next hour. What would ring again and again in his remembering would be the inner voice that kept asking how in the name of sanity he had ever gotten himself involved in this terrifying grand guignol. They'd made a not uncommon safari down the fifth floor corridor of the Clinique—a nurse pushing a patient on a gurney, a man in a wheelchair, a doctor in whites and a gentleman in mufti. The gentleman in the trenchcoat showed papers at the admittance desk. Doctor Tisibon signed the necessary documents and the patient was cleared for discharge. An ambulance awaited them. Nurse Gudrun strode to the center of the drive and, fingers to her lips, emitted a piercing whistle. Seemingly from nowhere, a sedan roared up and came to a screeching halt in front of the ambulance as though to prevent its passage. A huge Teutonic type in chauffeur's uniform came bounding out of the sedan. The emissary stepped forward. "Just a moment there, my good man," says he.

"Ja? Who the hell are you?"

"I am the emissary. From Chicago."

"From Chicago? Who sends you?"

"She sends me."

"Ocho?"

The emissary smiled a wicked smile. His eyes twinkled with triumphant scorn. "The Chancellor."

"Really?" The other loomed over. "Our orders are from the Ocho, she who owns and guides everything, including your University. So, step aside, little man, or I will step on you!"

Gregorian observed all this from his wheelchair. But his attention was diverted to a pair emerging from the double doors marked *mortuaire*, the bigger, stouter of whom pushed a gurney.

A diminutive fellow in a powder-blue suit and too-big a fedora scampered to keep pace. They approached across the drive. A neutral observer might have remarked at the eight people clustered there on the Clinique driveway, three in clinical garb, two on gurneys, and one in a wheelchair, the others in various mufti. Of the pair-plus-gurney emerging from the *mortuaire*, the bigger fellow introduced himself as *Docteur* Bombaste, Chief of Pathology and co-founder of Fraternite Scientifique Independent, S. A. To everyone's amazement, he seized van Horn in a great bear hug. He kissed that startled fellow on the left cheek and on the right. He looked most earnestly into van Horn's eyes and said, "Do not be overly concerned. All will be well." With that, he turned to face Hauptman, raising in his clenched hands a firearm.

"Hey! That's my..." van Horn shouted. The driver, Hauptman, backed off with his hands raised. Bombaste spoke to him in a rapid and incomprehensible Franco-Germanic *patois*, but it had to be a statement of no uncertain semantic. The big nurse stood there stammering, but Bombaste only smiled. "*Messieurs. Madame.* Whatever you may have had in mind, the program has been altered."

Gregorian observed their movements with some dismay. The surly and threatening Hauptman turned timid and deferential. He and the nurse lifted the collapsible gurney with Polichuk aboard into the van of the ambulance and saw him appropriately fitted with life-support. To Polichuk's parallel-left lay another gurney, similarly occupied and similarly fitted. The down-load body, Gregorian assumed. These buffoons had, indeed, prepared for everything. At Bombaste's suggestion, Hauptman lifted Gregorian bodily whilst nurse Gudrun collapsed the wheelchair. Rider and chair were tucked into the van between the gurneys as neatly as possible. Paco buried his little self amongst the items of medical apparat as best he could and the doors were slammed shut. Tisibon mounted into the passenger seat of the ambulance and sat between Bombaste and van Horn. Hauptman removed the sedan. Bombaste took the wheel of the ambulance. "Oh, yes," says he. "This belongs to you?" He held the weapon, barrel down, and van Horn meekly, ruefully accepted it. The ambulance moved swiftly away onto the main street. He turned to van Horn. We shall report to Madame *la chancelier* that we have done well, *n'est pas, Monsieur l'emissairé?*" and he laughed a good, long, phlegmy wheeze.

Van Horn roared a good guffaw. "We're a team! man. A team!"

"*Mais oui, Monsieur. Vraiment un' attelage.* We now possess the item to be transferred. And the proper receptacle. Soon we will place one into the other, *n'est pa?*"

Ammon's Horn

11. Assault

Through Sweden's mountain air, early May smiled most benignly. As for Kirsten's inner weather, "disconnected" is how a friend once described it. To be without work, or a positive anticipation, was to be "weatherless," she'd said, describing the response-behavior of the psycho-neurotic who is removed from familiar surroundings. But despite the austere indifference of that soggy winter of '84, Kirsten Lagerquist had had Binswanger. She might not like what her alter ego had to say, but at least the irritation was familiar which was more than she could say for this strange woman whom she hardly recognized, even in a mirror.

"What is your problem, Kirsten Lagerquist?"

"I thought you might tell me."

"I shall. Now, begin."

"My problem may be described as a disorientation, an alienation of habitual norms of self-appraisal from existential authenticity…"

"Begin again."

"I am…disaffected from…"

"Begin again."

"I am…lonely. I am in need…deprived of…"

"Yes?"

"Love. I am in need of…"

"Yes?"

"I need a drink!"

There was aquavit in the pantry. For holidays and such. Hardly touched. Kirsten half-filled a drinking glass and downed a goodly belt. It burned, and it fumed and it made her stomach sizzle and her eyes water. In her skimpy terrycloth robe she sat on her haunches at the edge of the kitchen table and summoned courage. She downed the rest and once more half-filled the glass.

"What are you doing?"

"I am getting drunk. To get drunk is to become intoxicated. Intoxication is defined as that process of escape from one's problems, from one's self, through the use of intoxicant or narcotic substances. *Sköll!* Down the hatch! Now then, Binswanger, what have you got to say? Where were we?"

"You were saying, 'I am in need of a good…' "

"A good…"

"Yes?"

"A good…loving? Yes. And a good…fucking!"

"*Brava, cara mia.*"

"Oh? Really? Since when do you speak Italian?"

"Ever since you began using that kind of English.

Now, consider…"

"Yes. Looking up at thirty, I am a virgin. And…"

"And?"

"Can you explain to me—why him?"

"Of course I can. Consider…"

On a day in that same August, in the dialogue mediated between "I" and "me," she was "I" once more, moving with a purpose which remained wordless under an urgency she dared not explain. Who was this person who packed her bags and who strode unseeing through the Upsala Lenna Station.

A first-class railway carriage, Upsala to Stockholm, left her with the compartment to herself. One can lose oneself in the inanity of a photo magazine.

The face of her athlete looked up at her from the centerfold page of Lo Sport. Kirsten would have said the face of a peasant. A son of the Mediterranean. A fleshly scion of olive oil, hot sun, pasta, garlic, wine and coarse ignorance. A "pop" figure. A semiotic icon for the masses. A gross summation *sans* word or thought. A caricature contrived for the beastly sensibilities of the crowd. Muscle. Brawn. Brute strength. A symbolic nosh for the those too young, too stupid, for those unable or unwilling to examine or select what to feed their appetites. An animal counterpart to the crude beings who championed him, and to make matters worse, he was made even uglier than necessary by a broken nose badly healed. The scar on his left cheek appealed to the animal in his fans, as did an abundant crop of body hair, the need of a shave, and a glistening mantel of sweat. The human animal, she mused. Packaged cheap and sold as the best at his worst. The lavishly illustrated article promised more to come next issue downline. Photo-shoot would be at Le Brassus in the Jura Mountains bordering France and Switzerland, just south and west of Lake Geneva. Projected, a motorcycle competition in the mountains. Daring Adventure! The sensible person that was K. Lagerquist questioned the sanity of what she was doing.

She changed trains at Stockholm, south and east to Malmó. The ferry took her to Copenhagen, at which point she grew impatient with the snail-crawl of boats and trains and with herself for stalling because, she admitted, that's what she was doing. In Copenhagen she booked a flight. An hour later her plane set down in Geneva. The air-conditioned terminal whooshed shut behind her and she stood in a brilliant Alpine spring.

Photo and publicity staff of Lo Sport had pretty well taken over the Alpenstock Inn at the edge of the village of Le Brassus. Kirsten had to settle for a B&B in town, but next morning she saw the lo SPORT logo on bright red zipper jackets wherever she went. The evening of her arrival, someone at the B&B left just such a crimson jacket draped over the back of a chair in the dining hall. Kirsten took it, though with what intention she had no clear idea.

Dawn broke over the mountains in a shattered splendor. At the Hotel Le Brassus, magazine staff filled the dining hall and scattered themselves out into the brilliant morning. There was rude chatter and the roar of motor vehicles and from where she stood at the edge of the melee Kirsten thought she caught sight of him but he was almost as quickly lost in the press of the crowd. She took up the red jacket and hastened into the dining hall for a cup of coffee. From the window, she saw the last of the small four-wheeler utility wagons prepare to leave. Someone hailed her red jacket and she hurried out and obediently clambered up into a press of bodies and video equipment. She did the climb into the foothills crammed in with four others who shouted and laughed and chattered amongst themselves.

"You got to be one of the models. My name is…"

Kirsten didn't catch the name. She looked up from where she sat on the bed of the truck and smiled, and acknowledged.

The magazine staff burst into the shallow cup of the valley like so many red insects swarming into light. They hooted and shouted orders, directions, set up tents, cranked generators and unlimbered equipment. Like a ragtag army they quickly established operations before the imposing flank of a broad rise. From where she stood back of the video cameras and a crew of some fifteen she saw Benni Pistone astride a monstrously big motorcycle and suffering the ministrations of the makeup man.

Kirsten succumbed to the conclusion—in the flesh he was, indeed, more cute than brute. Up close, she saw the gentleness in him, the vulnerability, she would have said, behind that coarsened visage and she laughed at herself. He sweated under the anomaly of electric lights and looked to be feeling foolish in skin-tight black trousers and a distinctly feminine jacket of white acrylic engineered to accentuate his torso. There was a good deal of shouting back and forth across the open expanse. Someone wanted a girl in the picture with "…lots of tit and thigh."

"Okay, lets have a take!"

Benni Pistone fired up his cycle and puttered off and up the rise and out of sight. "Ready when you are, Mister D," the director called from his control panel.

Benni emerged on his big machine. He came down the slope, slowly. The cameras either side of the video truck framed him and shot their digital images into standing monitors. At near bottom level. Pistone paused. A plump young blonde in briefest shorts and halter emerged from the blind. She and he engaged in what passed for flirtatious dialogue. Cameras zoomed in. The director shouted. Benni doffed his absurd little cap and the girl mounted behind him and she took on a look of stupid languor. Or perhaps, Kirsten thought, of passionate stupidity. Such was what passed for "sexy."

A disembodied voice croaked through the speakers. "That's a take. Run those for edit. Whattayou think Mister Cray?"

Kirsten noticed for the first time the stout gentleman in a salt-and-pepper beard, a light jacket of silk poplin, summer togs and opaque shades. He stepped from the shadows. "The girl is too short! You're losing her! Get someone taller!"

"You!" an ugly androgyne in poplin seized Kirsten by the elbow. "Come on, sweetheart, we haven't got all day." Kirsten came to stand under the brilliant lights, speechless. "*C'est bon*. She's tall enough to make the scene. Makeup!"

She might have protested. but they sat her down and put something on her face. Benni Pistone stood but a few meters away looking at her and mumbling to the party behind him. The very tall *cafe-au-lait* Afro he spoke to appreciated Kirsten from under an enormous mass of black curls. So Kirsten sat and let them paint her face and take her blouse and her bra and they squeezed her into a push-up bra and a low-cut zipper jacket two sizes too small. It was all over very quickly. One minute she was in the shadows behind the blind, then the cycle moved slowly past her and stopped.

She was looking down on Benni Pistone's curly head and then into his brown eyes, and he was looking up at her from the cycle and muttering. "Okay. We talk five seconds. Now you smile. You know how to mount . . ?"

Someone shouted at her from over the speakers. She mounted. They moved slowly downslope and someone shouted, "Put your arms around his waist!" They did the rest of the downslope with her chin resting on his right shoulder. Doctor K. felt contrivedly stupid. For a few seconds, Kirsten closed her eyes.

Back at the video truck someone unzipped the jacket from behind and whisked it off her. Kirsten stood fastening her bra and looking for her blouse in a milling crowd of people when Pistone moved past her without so much as a second look.

The Afro from the photo-shoot, minus outrageous curls, gave her name as Didi Baguette, but Kirsten could call her Margo and, really, they should do lunch which is how Kirsten came to snack in Le Brassus's outdoor cafe listening to this creature's incessant chatter. From where she sat, Kirsten could see into the restaurant interior, but whatever Margo might have promised, il Benni didn't show. The stout gentleman in summer togs and dark glasses sat off to one side, talking into a cell-phone. Margo was saying something about how she was with the agency in Paris and they had her name and number. Models zipping in and out of town could usually find a bed and stow-it at Chez Bienvenu on Parnasse, but she had a cousin with her own apartment and she was going to be in Paris for several days and they could meet? The phone number was…Kirsten didn't remember what she ate or drank.

The one calling herself Margo leaned across the table, her face up close to Kirsten's. "Listen," she said, and her voice seemed to penetrate Kirsten's very being. "Listen, I will be with you. Always. You may not see me, but I will be there, with you and for you. Do you understand?"

Kirsten did recall her shock at being kissed on the mouth by another woman, and whatever it was she meant, Kirsten understood.

Then, Margo was gone before Kirsten's eyes. As though she had never been. A waiter hovered. Kirsten sat another minute staring into space. She felt curiously elated, and dismayed.

Chance will manipulate. It determined she should walk the several blocks to the auto-lease. Her rental came whizzing up and the fellow held out his hand. Kirsten slid in behind the wheel and eased her vehicle into a narrow village street. Something the Baguette woman had said teased Kirsten's mind. "Take care of one's own," she said. And something about "looking after one's sisters." Something about "acolytes." There was something about the woman's garish appearance and her outrageous behavior—to kiss another woman—on the mouth! But Kirsten dismissed the mental image. In Geneva she would connect with Upsala. Quiet panic in her belly said she had to talk to Binswanger. There was more to this escapade than the silly absurdity of it all and she needed to "get a rational foot on solid ground." Such ruminations having taken her attention, she sat confused.

Instead of facing the auto route and its impenetrable stream of automobiles she'd gone to the right, down a near empty street, the wrong way on a one-way and she sat facing a *Debut Prohibite* sign with its red slash prohibiting entry. She looked into a small *carré* whose pedestrians glowered and gestured at her. She would have somehow turned in the narrow passageway and made her way out, except she didn't because she saw him in a car parked directly across the narrow street, the same stout fellow who was the video director (she thought she'd caught his name as Craig, or something like that) he of the grey-speckled beard, the silk poplin and shades. He was parked the other side of the narrow street and absorbed in talking into his cell-phone. Across the few meters separating them he looked directly at her with no sign of recognition.

The police would ask her afterwards, and she was to tell them, she being not only a witness but a doctor, that, yes, she had been there, having gone the wrong way, had stood looking into the pedestrian square and like a theater devotee fourth-row-front she'd stared into a re-play of a previous hallucination, had almost anticipated the motorcycle bursting from the street diametrically opposite, had seen the pedestrians scatter and the 'cycle sweep wide about the perimeter. She had seen the tiny Petit Géant auto emerge directly after, had sat horrified to realize they were not racing but that one was in pursuit of the other, that it was her vehicle blocking the narrow street that kept the cyclist from escaping because she saw him, and she would have sworn that for a brief instant she'd met Benni Pistone's eyes before he swerved to her right and the auto cut short across the plaza and caught him. She would describe in graphic terms the impact, how the motorbike lifted and sailed. She would see again his body make a low parabola before he hit the cobblestones and lay still.

She'd run and knelt over the injured man, shouted to the gawking pedestrians to call an ambulance. He opened his eyes and tried to speak but then the glaze of concussion took and a crowd was pushing and shoving about her and a short, rather ugly little fellow pushed his way through and knelt the other side of the injured man. He called out, "Benni! Bennino!" and she was shouting at him to stand away because that one had his hands in the injured man's clothes. Kirsten shouted at him in French and later under prompting she would recall the ambulance, and the paramedics and a very tall, bronze-bearded fellow in medical whites introduced himself as Doctor Belvedere and seemed to know that she was Doctor Lagerquist and together they entered the van of the ambulance, one on either side of the unconscious man.

They did the 65 kilometers between Le Brassus and Geneva in less than an hour. She saw the injured man whisked off to emergency at the Clinique General. A police inspector was there. Yes, Kirsten assured him, she would remain in Geneva in case she was needed…in case the investigators… if there should be an inquest because given the extent of cranial injuries, he might die. A day later her baggage arrived from Le Brassus. She inquired at the Clinique. Doctor Belvedere met her. The stricken man, Bennino Pistone, was still in a coma. Given his remarkable physiology the chances were he would live. As to his waking from coma, that was another question altogether.

The very next day, Wednesday the nineteenth, Doctor Kirsten Lagerquist was summoned to the Prefecture of Police, Schtroumph, Rue de la Servette. He introduced himself as inspector Philippe Apollon. Kirsten sat before his desk and responded largely to the top of his head, or to his left ear.

"You don't know the man."

"No."

"You were filmed…together. For a magazine."

"Yes."

"You're a model."

"A doctor. I told you. I head the department…"

"In Sweden. Yes. We're checking. A doctor who models for sports magazines. Who comes all the way from Sweden to Switzerland to ride the motor-cycle with a man whom she's never met. Is that accurate, doctor?"

"Yes. I suppose."

"A doctor who sits and watches that same man, whom she has never met, being run down by a car, and whom she then attends medically."

"That's correct."

"Who was the man in the other car, doctor?"

"I told you. I don't know."

"But you had seen him before?"

"At the video session. Yes."

"Is this the man?" A screen was made to light up the far wall. The perspective gave out across a narrow street, and down. A man had alighted from a car and a zoom lens had closed in on him. Kirsten saw what might have been the portly man in shades at the video-shoot, the same man in the car at the scene of the run-down.

"I can't be sure."

"Try this one." Another shot. This one closer. He wore the same kind of dark glasses, but now the silk-poplin was a cotton twill and the jaunty cap a porkpie hat. His head was inclined toward the camera, turned so that he addressed someone to his left."

"It looks like the same man."

"And the one driving the car? You didn't see him?"

"As I have already told you, no. It all happened very quickly...no more a few seconds."

"And, of course, you will tell me you have no idea what's happened to his body."

"His body?"

"He was mistakenly pronounced dead on arrival. Some fool didn't bother to read the report. Or doesn't know what comatose means. They took him to the morgue, and before we could get to him, he'd vanished."

"Amazing! But, no. I don't know."

"Thank you, doctor. We will have no further need of you. The sergeant at the front desk has your credentials."

It was Doctor L. nudged Kirsten into an afterthought: The inspector looked much like *Docktor* Appolon. They could have been brothers.

12. Leverage

Presidential Towers, Chicago.

Constancia Ocho kept reserved a suite of twelve rooms at her Presidential Towers on Lakeshore Drive. On this lovely Spring evening, she lay back in the big lounger in comfy robe and slippers. She read the day's reports, but out of the corner of her eye was aware of her maid picking up her undergarms, shoes and blouse from the salon floor.

In the dining hall, furniture to the walls, Pammy, Debby, Mimi, Flori and several other of auxiliaries whose names escaped her were doing calisthenics to a vigorous aye-bee-cee and hup! Connie caught the pink-glow highlights of rosy posteriors and the quiver of bare breasts. She sank herself into her reports.

A maid moved silently across the floor with a tray of light dinner—slivers of Peking duck *en brioche* in a mild Szechwan sauce, sauteed shiitaki-and-snow peas and a salad of greens and pearl tomatoes. Yes, and a small glass of sauterne.

Relaxation at the end of fatigue and the awareness of Kari's delectable derriere set la Ocho to drifting. Kari. And Tari. Were there any two anywhere near like them? Anywhere? The big fella—Phoebus, or whatever he called himself—Kari was his doing. Always one to check out a gift horse's dentures, Connie Ocho had done some snooping.

Tari and Kari were identical twins. By age twenty one they stood tall and long-legged, ash blonde, blue-eyed and of a dusky-rose complexion that said their recent Greek origins had been kissed with an African connection in the near genetic past. By twenty-first century standards, they were optimally endowed physically, intellectually formidable, and exceptionally pretty.

Tari was the older by two minutes and named Tarimina Agapé, pronounced properly in the Greek, tehr-rim-ME-na aga-PAY, but she, being a good American girl, said Tari ah-GAPE. As in open. And willing. If the guy was worth it. Because—here she chuckled at her own naughty puns—there wasn't any percentage in just giving it away and a girl had best make good on what she had while the having and the giving were good.

She'd taken a first in MR at Vanderhype University, and at the U. of Chicago she'd studied Public Manipulation under A. Fevre Chaud, visiting professor from Matabele University. *La Docteur* Fevre Chaud was the world renowned authority on intersex warfare psychology. To this day, there persist rumors that Tari and the prof might have been an item for a time, but never mind that. Tari began her working career as an intern to news anchors Sam Foresight and Kookie Robbins on the News Cabaret Hour, UBC, and she herself had done a ten-minute stint for OnBeam 98 The PM-Report when Robbins was called away to cover the Evangelical riots in 2052. During her stint at OnBeam, she met the CEO of TeleVista-Hyperion of which Universal Broadcasting Corp. was a subsidiary.

Mister A. Phoebus Belvedere was quite taken with the young lady's journalistic talents and word has it he gave her a personal interview which included a week-end in Monte Carlo, a leisurely tour of the Greek Isles and ten days in Paris. Tari had an EarPod surgically implanted and her genius at media relations and public manipulation, plus daddy's pull, got the young lady a prestigious position on the President's Media Staff.

So it comes as no surprise that Tari should rise professionally as quickly as she did. Congressman Theodore "Teddy" Agapé, was rep. of the composite congressional district comprising seven counties of the state's of Nebraska, nine in Iowa, and four in South Dakota, a demographic potpourri made necessary by the population decline after the ABETS epidemic of the 50's. The Congressman was also a major stockholder in UBC Communications, Inc., also chairman of the Federal Commo Commission, and a close friend of A. Phoebus Belvedere. So, when Aristotle "Telly" Malakas, President of Amalgamated Unions, Inc., got elected President of US Inc. the Congressman called in a few IOU's and Tari became the nation's first Secretary of the Media.

Kari was no less beautiful than her sister, and no less brilliant. At the tender age of nineteen she assumed the position of VP for Pivotte & Twiste, one of the nation's more prestigious PR entities, a subsidiary of Hyperion Industries. Following interviews in the Rockies, Acapulco and the Cote d'Azure, A. Phoebus Belvedere introduced Kari to Constancia Ocho. Ocho, never one to let toadstools gather under her *chaussons*, had scooped up the young beauty and put her in charge of organizing Ocho's Troupe.

Phoebus looked on his new protégé with great satisfaction. He had coached her well, *ad rationem* and *sub conscientius*. As Ocho's right-hand gal, she would serve as his "ace in the hole" (Phoebus loved coining brilliant new metaphors). Coaching Ocho's Troupe one at a time, all forty of them, was a time-consuming task. Even as an immortal he could only be one place at a time. There would come a point, the immortal knew, when it would be necessary to step in and thwart his protégé's march to ultimate domination. His best projection said keep the bitch from her feed, rein her short, and keep her hungry. With scent of the ultimate *rosbif* up her nose, he would demand, and claim, his reward. He knew he could count on Kari to "blow the whistle" at the critical moment. She called him "Pheebee" and she agreed that his metaphors were nothing short of original and brilliant. And, oh my goodness, yes, she would keep an eye on the boss and keep him posted. Phoebus grunted a silent satisfaction at the avidity with which this mortal Venus descended to her tasks.

Meanwhile, Teddy Agapé looked after his darling girls. Not to suggest he used undue influence, but Tari took to dividing her time between Chicago and Washington DC II. Within a few weeks, the new president proposed and Congress approved creation of the Office of Secretary of the Media with a staff of fifty seven, first secretary, one Tari Agapé, of Chicago, Illinois. Immediately she began a campaign to burnish the new Pres.'s image and to downplay the general impression that "Telly" Malakas was a "well-meaning, good-hearted asshole," as one print pundit had it, when the truth of it was he was merely inarticulate and a trifle slow. Tari's motherly instincts made her feel positively protective of the amiable jerk. She did most of his talking and kept his public exposure to a bare minimum.

The new cabinet position included InterNet wiretap authority which is how she came to sift the beltway rumor on the prospect of a cabinet for religious affairs. The other rumor ping-ponging around the beltway said a secret, off-the-cuff group was to meet somewhere out of the beltway, except Tari had already established belly-to-belly rapport with three senate staff members and two congressional secretaries and somewhere in the warm-sheets-and-pillow-talk it slipped out. Senator Carly Snarl of Oklahoma had already told her to stick her nose into somebody else's bush, but Tari was most adept in use of legalistic extortion. Besides, whatever they were cooking would need the Executive branch behind it and she herself wielded big clout with the Oval Office and they'd not get to first base without media support. So, deal her in. Snarl had no choice.

Add to Senator Snarl, R. of Oklahoma, Senator Sally Prybar, D. of California; Congressman A. Fulcrum Lever of Nevada and Senator Claude Hammer, D. of Utah. No recording equip permitted. Tari didn't need it. She had an instant-total-recall memory and if push came to shove she could always submit to a mem-scan—she'd been through that before in her vetting, courtesy the FBI, Department of Interrogation.

The meeting was held at 11 AM in a suite in a nondescript hotel in Adirondac Station some twenty miles south and east of the Sciatica beltway,

Washington DC II. Participants registered under assumed names. When they'd had the room swept for bugs, the two sides regarded one another from opposite sides of the table.

In an unassuming blue-green Italian silk jumpsuit stood the Reverend Mordecai GaryBob Bloodworthy, officially High Counsellor and Inspired TV and radio Voice of the Affiliated Churches of the Christian Resurrection, Baptist, Evangelical and Otherwise. Tari's mental camera and subliminal commentary pegged him a big, raw-boned Alabama cotton chopper for whom the act of smiling caused smarts and winces on both sides.

Tari recognized the party to his right from his photos in the Times. Representing His Holiness, Pope Fervent the First of the Roman Catholic Church Ecumenical, his Eminence Vincent Cardinal Vendetta. "Mean little *daigo*," Tari's mental copy said, "In Cardinal's robes he'll be a walking a fire hydrant."

To the Cardinal's left, in simple cashmere gabardine caftan, shot cuffs and a Rollex of unassuming platinum, Rabbi Morri Kogan of the Hebrew United Congregation, Temple Jehosaphat, Orthodox Reformed, Jerusalem, Pa.

Each took up his share of beating about the hollybush, in the midst of which Tari gathered there was nothing less in the works than the establishment of a cabinet position, the Secretary of Religion, the position to rotate amongst reps. of the three major constituents, details to be worked out later at Synergical HQ in Witchita. Back of the haggling over details there had to be an unspoken buy and sell. Cardinal Vendetta, especially, seemed to relish his grip on Snarl, and maybe on Hammer. There had to be a trade-off or Snarl would never have sat for it. And how were they going to get this past the Congressional Committee on Surreptitious Negotiations? Another trade off? Another lever?

That week-end Tari took a plane, New Reagan Field, Pa., to Richard M. Daly, Chicago. From a suite in Shalimar Towers and on a secure SAT-link, encrypted and scrambled, she took a call from Paris, European HQ of

Subsume Unlimited. Tari listened attentively. She had a memory stick taking notes."Ma'am Ocho? What's up?" Tari said.

"Kamper-Buckett plan. What're the payoffs? Who's payin'. Who's collectin' and how much? You got a pipeline?"

"Not yet, I haven't. But soon. Real soon."

That night, that ineffably lovely young thing lay back in her huge four-poster. Her image in the ceiling mirror gazed down at herself most lovingly. It blew her a moist kiss. It slipped down the bottoms to her two-piece jammies. She composed an orgasmic sonata in squeezeful-oozies. Melody rose and counterpoint supplemented. In her hyped mem-image there emerged the uncompromising visage of the Reverend Mordecai GaryBob Bloodworthy.

Bio research said:

Bloodworthy, Mordecai GaryBob. Born Tuskegee, Alabama, September 1, 2048. Educated, public schools; University of Alabama Evangelical Seminary; honorary doctorate, Bob Jones University. Married Thelma Rae Chancy, 2049; widowed 2078, the Reverend Mrs. B. having died of cancer.

The Reverend was moderately well off—no hint anywhere he lived on anything but the modest salary the Apostolic and Canonical Christian Media Network paid him.

Tari's agents went south to dig around in the Rev.'s native stomping grounds and they uncovered:

Files at the Mobile Gazette going back twelve years connected the Rev. and his Gospel Hall of the Holy Good News with Covington Savings and Loan. The Rev. had sat on the B. of D. The bubble of the 20-sixties burst and the S&L went belly up. An IRS probe said it had been gutted from the inside. Four of the S&L officers were indicted, two of them tried and one convicted, but the Reverend M. G. Bloodworthy came out clean. Near thirty mil-five-hundred K. was never accounted for.

Months 3 through 7, 2065, The Montgomery Herald ran knee-deep in reports of sexual hanky-panky in the Gospel Hall of the Apostle Witnesses involving members of the Reverend's staff and under-age boys and girls of the choir, but the Reverend fired the offenders and came out of the privy smelling like no more than a slightly smudged rosebud. Suit and scandal, however, closed down his Gospel Hall and the Reverend had moved on. Shaking old bushes produced nothing further. Time for Tari to take a direct hand.

Cudgel Falls, Alabama, pop. 5400: Early on a Thursday morning, the Reverend Bloodworthy was surprised to learn that his faithful secretary Myrna Oldgrass had taken sick. That stalwart horse had been in harness twelve years. She had followed the Reverend in his missionary journeying and served him most unobtrusively and well. Now without warning there was a new face behind the desk in the rectory of the Affiliated Temples of the Apostolic Resurrection, Inc., G. M. Bloodworthy, D.D., & Pres.

This was a younger face which smiled sweetly from under a low crown of dark curls and drawled on about the temp. agency having sent her and how she just knew they were going to get along "fay-muss-lee."

The Rev. was caught off guard—this tall, leggy youngster had his Sunday sermon notes edited, polished, and printed in double space, large caps just the way he wanted, and all this by noon the same day. And he was surely alarmed—she'd gone through seven years worth of the Church's files in less than a forenoon, read, organized, filed and cross-indexed and saved to conceptor mem. and back-up hard copy. She explained file and access to him, all this on the Thursday before his Saturday presentation originating WWOL, the Weekly Word of the Lord Broadcasting Company, Channel 1. and his Sunday God's Hour featuring the Apostolic Revival Choir originating in Mobile and transmitted by cable and Sat-Link to 37 local channels in and about the old South all the way north to Ohio. Anything else she could do for him? The Reverend looked down at her cherubic face, stepped away from her fervent presence, his face creased into a painful smile. He thanked her, declined, and retreated perspiring.

Cudgel Falls is only 50 miles from the bitty little town of Nesbitt (pop, 741) over the Cumberland County line, and that's where they had to go that following Sunday seeing as how the Reverend Doctor Bloodworthy owed a favor, a kind of return courtesy to Reverend Billy Jo Stark, and so Miz. Tari Grape—or was it Sherry Grape?—the Reverend couldn't seem to pin down the woman's name—she hustled on over to Nesbitt and made necessary arrangements, including where the Rev. was to stay-over that Saturday night because Nesbitt being so bitty couldn't offer the amenities of a hotel. The Reverend would stay in the home of the Widow Mrs. Carstairs, the widow having been left by her late husband a handsome big house and she let rooms to bachelor-type gentlemen.

Well, now, the schedule called for a prayer meeting of the steering committee of Cudgel Falls' Apostolic Assembly at the home of the Reverend and Mrs. Stark, this on a late Friday morning. Then, lunch was served, biscuits and gravy, bacon and grits and lots of Mrs. Stark's excellent peach marmalade. Fourteen of the more prominent faithful had also been invited and the Reverend Stark stood at the head of the table and called for a brief prayer of thanks to the Lord for His blessings and that's when it happened.

Some say she was thin and young, and some say she was middle-aged and fat, but most everybody agrees she wasn't anybody anybody had ever seen before. General agreement says she stood at the far end of the table and just when the Reverend Bloodworthy raised his voice to ask the Lord to forgive our trespasses, the woman in the flowered muumuu (orange marigolds and yellow daisies on a lime-green background) appeared as out of nowhere and commenced to wail and moan, and, to the general consternation of all she pointed her finger, index, right-hand, at the Reverend Bloodworthy and she hollered something about sinners coming in the guise of the righteous. Then she whooped like a cow with the colic and lit out across the dining room where she tripped on the carpet, grabbed the table cloth to right herself and pulled down a cup, one of a set of Mrs. Stark's best china so's it fell to the floor and got smashed.

The Reverend Bloodworthy went red in the face. The parties assembled did their best to look the other way, though the Reverend himself would have been at some pains to explain why he felt so embarrassed seeing as how he'd never laid eyes on the woman before and in light of the fact he hadn't any more idea what particular sin or sins she might have been referring to if indeed she meant to finger him! The whole incident didn't cover more than a minute by the end of which the Reverend Bloodworthy recovered his composure and he asked for a minute of silent prayer in which those assembled might request of the Lord his guidance and charity for the poor deluded creature who had so intruded upon them. This was done and everybody felt a little better.

Saturday afternoon came the Annual Bible Institute Picnic. There were hot-dogs, potato chips and Pepsi Cola. Towards evening, the Reverend held a prayer service at the local High-School. Television people brought a truckful of equipment so the Reverend drew things out to accommodate them, seeing as how the video would be shown the following week on WWOL, channel 1. Then, Mrs. Carstairs served a light supper and the Reverend retired early.

If it hadn't been for the widow Carstairs' brother Clarence sitting up late with Billy Cootch out there on the porch having a late night cig-gar and a nip or two, they would never have seen what they did see coming out of the room occupied by the Reverend. Then, the police would not have been advised of it and it would have all passed unnoticed. But they did, and they were, and it didn't. Afterwards, the Reverend concluded whoever she was she knew the lay of the land before she got there.

Conveniently, the Carstairs' house sat on the very edge of the village. It was built with a wide porch running along three sides. These old houses featured large windows and summer weather prompted folks to leave them open. Any able bodied person, male, female or active child would have found the room occupied by the Reverend very easy to access. Fact of the matter is that somewhere around three of the AM the Reverend woke from a light sleep with the feeling he was not alone. She stood over him, close, nose to nose and whispered something he couldn't quite make out. In alarm, the Reverend managed to push her away and to half sit and to reach for the lamp on the nightstand. She was kissing him! On the mouth! Lecherously! And all the while she emitted a kind of sniggering giggle, and she'd slid her hand beneath the coverlet and she was fondling him! The Reverend writhed and twisted and the lamp went on, and there she was, the same lady, except now, in place of the marigolds and daisies she wore what, he supposed, amounted to a cloak of sack cloth, a threadbare thing that fell in one piece from shoulders, up over her ample bosom and down to her ankles. Her hair which she'd worn in a chignon now fell about her face. The Rev. attempted to rise but she pushed him back against the headboard and, to his horror, she let fall the simple garment and she bestrode his body and assaulted him with a pair of enormous breasts. *She was trying to get into the bed with him!*

Afterwards, he could not be sure what happened, but he would remember he'd come to stand in the middle of the room with the shadeless lamp in his hand, raised, as though to strike, which he might have done but for catching sight of her generous rump as it vanished though the window. Booted feet thumped on the porch outside. There were cries of alarm and interspersed with whoops and laughs. Someone eventually called out, "You alright in there, Reverend?" The Reverend slammed the window shut, drew the blind, righted the lamp and waited. It grew quiet. But, there was now someone else in the room, leaning against the door. She came forward, smiling. The Reverend protested, "You gotta believe me. I never seen…"

"Of course not. But, it couldn't have been all that bad." Miz Shelly grinned wickedly. The Reverend would liked to have died of mortification. His flesh had responded.

He sobered. "Who are you?" To his amazement, she came to stand up close. She was almost as tall as he. Her hand fell, and he gasped. Then the dark hairpiece came away and he was looking at close-cropped ash-blonde curls. "You…you're…"

"Washington. The Spillway." She stroked him, and her robe fell. She stood in her bra and underpants.

"I see. What d' y'want?"

"Call it a trade." Off came the underpants.

"Blackmail?"

"Trade. The woman won't say more than she must."

"What we tradin'?"

"I know about Chancellor Trust. A million dollars worth of names buried there." Sans bra or panties she pushed him down onto the bed and slid her hand up under his night shirt.

"Ummm," he said.

"Like that?"

"What're you after?"

"What is Kamper-Buckett?"

"Ah! So that's it! Um, yessss…but you don't really have to, you know."

"Your pleasure is my pleasure, sir."

"Aaaaah…been so long. All-mose forgot…"

"Good, huh? Now, tell me about Kamper-Buckett."

"Can't tell y' much, 'cept, yew wanna make a li'l ol' bundle, yew buy land. Real estate.

"Real Estate? Where?"

Airee-zonah, and New Meck-see-koh. Price on a piece o' scrub's goin' threw the ceilin' reeal soon, and don't say yew heard it here."

As for Kari: Madame Ocho put her in charge of Ocho's Brigade. They were to be Ocho's field soldiers and, as one may imagine, every one of them was a beaut. They were thirty-six tall, short, plump, svelte, blondes, redheads, brunettes, ivories and ebonies, coffees and teas. They were lawyers and auditors, systems analysts and consultants, managers, directors and marketeers and PR's and journalists and entrepreneurs and every one of them a graduate CPAMBA, with a couple of Ph.D.'s thrown in. In short, Ocho's

Brigade was fully capable of meeting the tastes and requirements, of exploiting the weaknesses and whatever sinful appetites the forty chosen captains of Earth's governance and industry might harbor behind their conservative paunches. With which in mind, in a bright April sun in the Bois de Boulogne adjacent to the Cité de Paris, A. Phoebus reviewed his recruits. They stood breasts to the light and tresses to the breeze. He reviewed, we say, as in appraised, admired and approved.

The Parisian media, electronic and print, were to speculate for weeks to come on the parties responsible for the emergence of a company of forty young and astonishingly beautiful young women marching down the Rue Héliodor, "…nipples erect and adorable derrieres given to the light," says the Paris tabloid le Loucher (English edition, Squint) marching hup, two, three, four into the hotel Delphique where they remained inaccessible to the slavering inquiries of press and public.

Fact of the matter is they retired to the suite Athéne, top floor where, furniture to the walls, A. Phoebus outlined the campaign, instilled in them the spirit of battle and encouraged where it may have been latent and unexpressed, that willingness, that wordless because so very—carnal?—yea, carnal—willingness to stoop, if you will, to extremes. And it worked. In the following months, the recruits threw themselves into a most intense training, with A. Phoebus acting as Company Commander, lecturer, coach, and hands-on trainer. Who better to understand the feckless foibles and callow weaknesses to which his own sex is liable? In the last week of training, A. Phoebus examined privately, closely and thoroughly each of the forty in turn, after which examination he pronounced each ready for battle.

Each recruit was to acquit herself admirably. Assignments were given, a captain of industry, finance or public service as the target, and in thirty-nine of the forty cases the target-victim succumbed and capitulated. One entrepreneurial holdout was of an alternative persuasion for whom a special recruit was hustled up and he performed most eagerly and capably when pressed into battle.

None of which was lost on Didi des Dieux. She had no doubts concerning the more immediate outcome. Phoebus' troops were, after all, the finest, *id est*, the most ruthless creatures of their kind. Nor did she fear she'd mis-read la Ocho. That one never confused means and ends, and, what, after all, was the feminine body for? Set aside the procreative agency for which it was designed and which it shared with mere cats and cows, that masterpiece of natural engineering was certainly not to be confused with the merely athletic end to which it was most pleasurably suited with ten seconds' hyperventilation after the act. No, the question at the back of Didi's mind: with such instruments at her command, how far would Constancia Ocho go? And, would Phoebus reign her in? Or was he too busy with examinations to mind the store?

But, the Telecom switched itself on. Trumpets. Drums. Sam Foresight summoned urgency. The persona of Telecom USCCanada announced the PM National Report, BiteSize Edition July, 2085:

On the Econ Front: The GNP has fallen by another 13 percent. The National Debt is up to forty trillion. Department of Finance won't release figures on budget deficit—Report suggests this is to prevent riots in the streets and a Wall Street implode.

Item: Unemployment stands at 15 percent and rising. The Fed has raised Interest rate to 18 percent. Inflation is at 18 percent and rising. Export of American jobs is a veritable flight, nineteen more corps reported closing homeland plants and moving to Greenland, Spitsbergen and points Arctic in the last fourteen months. Says one wag: "Hey, it's cooler up there."

Item: Congressional proposal backs return to the gold standard or tie the USI dollar to the Scandinavian Kroner.

Rumors: plan afoot to rescue the US Inc. by a) union with Canada and Mexico to form a continental protection barrier, and/ or b) selling off western US to Asian concerns. Last item most interesting: begins as blatant satire in the LA Bayou Clarion and gets the journalist a visit from the FBI and 48 hours detention.

And on the weather front: Bulletin: Nome, Alaska: Tsunami-high waves have battered beaches from the Kodiak Islands to Bering Beach and the Hot Springs and Spa at Yukon. Forty two people have been swept out to sea, last count. Authorities are considering banning swimming at Montague Island and at Chugach, Anchorage, and Cordova. At this very moment swimmers are being plucked from the waters off Kayak Island by boats and helicopters.

Meanwhile, at Tucson Harbor Project: Authorities anticipate opening of facilities to deep-water shipping by April '90 at latest.

Ocho hit the key for Transmit SatCom; encrypt, scramble and expedite:

To Kari Agapé, Subsume Liaison, Toronto:
Kari, baby: TeleCom Canada is shooting off his mouth. Stuff a rag in it. And find out who's tapping the crypts on Kamper-Buckett. Hang his hide real privately!

To A. P. Belvedere, Chicago Investment Exchange:
There's sand in the gears, honey-child. I hope you don't have any in your shoes. Tap me soonest.

News droned to conclusion with odds and ends. The London Economist for September 7 reported the arrest of one Sebastian Cray reputed international thief and money launderer for questioning in the PoreCon scam of '76-'80. Cray was held questioned and released on bond. He had since disappeared.

Cray! Ocho fairly shouted the name. According to this revelation, he was back in circulation after almost five years and probably up to his old tricks. Knowing him as she did, he was maneuvering to get back at her. But in five years she had risen too far for the likes of his grubby paws.

In the late '70's, Cray had been her money supply. His Porcelain Reclamation Corporation, or whatever he called it, had been a front and—she had to concede his nerve and his skill—he'd had none less than the US Corp. as his guarantor, though how he'd managed that one was still not clear to her. There was big money out of Eastern Europe and Asia to launder, and it got laundered. Before it was over, Connie Ocho had funneled a hundred mil through her office at FirstFed, New York with top management looking the other way, this in the early days before she'd taken over Toronto.

The operation effectively compromised the Swiss Banks and pulled them into her network. She sat in a position to buy them out. The go-between bank in Zurich had asked no questions and FFNY shut one eye and couldn't have cared less. The operation went sweet and slick for almost three years until a lowly minion at Créance Suisse blew the public whistle and woke the treasury of US Inc. to the fact its name was being used in a scam. This operation was a tad too public and the roof caved in. Her own cut-outs kept her name out of it, and they missed grabbing Cray by a hair. The little Italian got burned and did time in San Gall. Five years later, Cray was back in the flow and from the looks of it looking to get even and to get rich at her expense.

Connie Ocho returned from her memory-sojourn, and the troops were winding down—"aye-bee-cee-hup!" So much for yesterday's accomplishment. Now for the bills, glitches, kinks and other nuisances. Top of the stack of paper-print mail—CES, the *Consortium Electrifisation de la Suisse* had the gall to send her a bill. Didn't she own...

A quick check through her conceptor said no, she did not. The Swiss sat in the middle of Europe like a lump in one's drawers. They remained the perfect amalgam of private enterprise and public ownership. And they defied her. What's more, their leverage was of a sort she dared not challenge. They called it *electrifisation*. Some spelled it e-n-e-r-g-y. But whatever label one put on it, it spelled hands-off. No stock to buy there, no debt to collar and assets stood free and clear because a) they had never gone public. They had remained a private consortium of seven families in a two-centuries old cozy cuddle with the central government in Bern, and b) the secret of their success was a secret process by which they generated electrical power whose plants supplied Europe from the Aegean to the Baltic and from the Orkneys to the Siberian Pacific. Their plants produced no waste other than a great deal of hot air and water-vapor. The details of design were kept in a vault in a bank in Zurich in the name of the *Republique Suisse* which acted as CES's guarantor. Now these smug independents dared send her a bill...no, not to her. The bill was intended for the *Institute pour l'Etude de la Science Physique*, Geneva. The labs. A bill for EU: 153,347.57—one hundred fifty three thousand, and that only covered the six week period from July to mid August. What kind of parties was Waltari throwing over there?

Ocho shoved the invoice in with other items to be posted to the Institute. Let Wanda handle it.

The phone rang. Priority call. Geneva. The Institute people. Wanda herself. The woman was fairly shouting over the phone. Something about the cat being out of the bag, and did she have on her TV?—the Queen program? Re-run of a recent show. Cable Service Omnivore 7.

From Connie's wall-wide screen the smarmy-benign face of Gerry Queen looked like nothing so much as a cross between a hungry cat and a prettified mannequin gone to seed. Pull-back—a table, several people seated around. A rotund, middle-aged youngster in a close-crop of iron-grey curls regaled the others with a tall tale he obviously relished exaggerating: "...so I says to him, I says, Anatol, ol' buddy, my first wife's name was Federika, too! Can it be we're married to the same broad? He says to me, I mean he's got the Russki accent down damned-near perfect, says, '*Niet*, I don tink so onless you are married to deh president deh ook-raine."

Laughter all around.

Says the cadaverous cutie in the enormous wig: "How'd he ever get into your program?"

Curlytop: "Well that's the giveaway. I mean it hadda be some joker in-house, or some hacker's made it past Xenon's firewall 'cause this clown's claiming he's in Switzer-land, wouldja believe! says they got his head wired for sound and he's looking for the way out. And get this: Somebody's cornering real estate in the fifth dimension and building condos, right out of sci-fi…"

At Presidential Towers Madame Ocho was shouting. As though she'd suddenly gone over the edge. On the commo. "Gimme Geneva, right NOW! And contact the Tee Vee, on Seven. We gotta have somebody in there. Gimme the name o' that clown in the grey curls. Get my PI agency on him I wanna know everything right down to his jockey-short size and put a tail on 'im!"

The mention of the Cray's name was enough to set gnats of anxiety buzzing and the re-worked cinema of memory spun a reel of imagery in Ocho's mind. The little Italian. Paco something or other. Sharper than he looked. Started with the postage stamps on the packages he couriered and by back-tracking the money transfers he'd almost fingered her for the CaspianGroupe money funnel.

If Connie Ocho had sifted the matter to its nit-grit she'd have learned that before he became a sports promoter, Pasquale "Paco" Ungaroni had been many things, but always he was a student of human nature, a reader of other men. In the early two-sixties, Paco had funneled bad paper between Switzerland, Monaco, and New York, a safe operation because, inter-dependent as they were. None of the three principles, the brokerage thief, the courier or the banker, could identify the others except by pseudonym. It was a variation on the old open-triangle cell set up by the French resistance in World War Two. You couldn't finger a man you didn't know. And he couldn't finger you. But the American Securities people caught the inside man at the brokerage and the Feds got into it and pressured the Swiss. The banker got spooked and Paco was nearly collared. As courier, Paco would have gone under, too, except for a late-night phone call from "cousin Bertrand" just landed in town and why didn't they meet for a drink? The police missed him by an hour. But the gesture surprised him. The other guy was in the clear. He didn't have to do that. Obviously, the man wanted something from him. Paco left Lausanne and sat tight in Nice for a week.

On a beautiful Saturday morning he was out on the terrace of the second-string Hotel Rococo having coffee when a big bearded fellow—round, thick, and very British—took the other chair at his table and carried on as though they'd known one another for years. Paco took in the salt and pepper beard, the granny glasses perched on the end of the nose and the thinning black hair pulled tight along the scalp. Paco had known him as a voice on the telephone. Now, he became Colonel Sebastian Cray.

Cray was what Paco called *uno che si pulisce il naso alla distanza*, which is to say, he picked his nose long-distance. A meticulous planner, careful not to get his hands dirty, or as the English said, "his tit in the wringer." There was always someone to put up front. Cray spoke Italian well enough, and French. And German. And Hebrew. This morning's conversation was in Italian, and mostly one way, and light, and fast, and you had to listen twice to catch the drift of what this one was saying, that the Swiss operation was good for having been short-lived. Too long on one frequency, he said, and wasn't it time two old colleagues ventured out into more fertile fields? Paco Ungaroni sipped his caffe-Amaretto and waited. US Government contract, is what Cray said. Specifically a sub-contract with the Army. Inexpensive to operate. Most profitable."

"Legal?"

"Of course. You don't think I would suggest something shady, do you?" Cray studied the pastries offered on the waiter's wagon. When he looked back and took Ungaroni's eye once more he was smiling most ingenuously and munching a cream Danish. "Mmm, delicious," he mumbled.

"You ought to try these. Yes, more coffee, please."

****

Ocho accessed the conceptor's Search-Memory: item Porcon Industries, history thereof:

In an indescribably beautiful Alpine spring in 2071, Sebastian Cray had morphed his image and his name into the persona of one Peter Paul Baruch. That sophisticated gentleman had presented himself to the offices of Confiance Suisse in Lausanne on the north shore of beautiful Lake Geneva. He gave his business address as a suite of offices in Ben Gurion Plaza, Tel Aviv. He presented himself to the bank as president of Société PoreCon, buyers, sellers, recyclers of industrial goods. He was contracted procurement agent for the US Inc Army Corp of Engineers, Division of Reclamation. He presented a letter of credit from the Porter-Hazleton Bank of Chicago, subsidiary of FirstBank New York. A brief telephonic commo with Chicago's VP in charge of liaison, one C. Ocho, confirmed the guarantee of thirty-million dollars. Confiance Suisse was most happy to accommodate *Mssr.* Baruch.

As a purported contractor to the US, Inc., gov., Mssr. Baruch was in a position to discount US paper. Standard procedure: When a company invoices the US Inc. for a million dollars, and the government acknowledges the debt, promising to pay in 60 to 90 days, a businessman can take the invoice to any bank and draw a million right away, minus the bank's commission. With a US Inc. imprimatur on the invoice, any bank in the world would welcome Baruch and his paper.

To Lausanne's top-skim society, Doctor Baruch was a cultivated gentleman, a collector of ancient books and manuscripts. He spoke excellent French, Italian, German, English and Hebrew. His Rolls Phaeton was commandeered by an ugly little Italian—or Frenchman—no one was ever sure. Shortly after his arrival, he had purchased the Villa Faubourg Paradis,

10 acres on the outskirts of town, and another forty acres near *Eglis de deux Pigeons*, the site of a long-closed factory once producing porcelain and ceramic goods. The million dollar guarantee was adequate collateral for the purchase of the properties, as was his position as a contractor for the government of the United States Inc.

Reclamation—in this case *les vase de toilette*—ceramics manufactured by a Kamcon Industries, Teeterboro, New Jersey, were sold to the United States Army Corps of Engineers for use in their portable facilities. Two additional details rendered this finely spun mythology plausible: The first—Cray explained to Paco over excellent Scotch in the clubroom Association Diomédée—being the Corps' reputation for demanding perfection in its procurements. An item met their rigid specifications or it was rejected. The second being that those standards of excellence were nigh impossible to meet using a mass-production schedule such as Kamcon pursued. A percentage of the bowls would have been written off as a loss. Porcelain, as everyone knows, is a most recalcitrant material. Like diamond, it is of the highest order of frictional strength, but of a low order on any tensile scale. A bad porcelain bowl can not be salvaged or remade once fired.

Or, at least, one could not until development of the Schiegle-Hubsche process. As Mssr. Baruch had explained to Confiance Suisse, Hermann Schiegle, was a wholesaler of scrap looking for an easy goldmine—this in '57 in the days immediately following the Israeli-Palestinian buy-out of Groupe Arabique—and Adolf Huebsch was an itinerant industrial chemist apparently of great chemical savvy but little common sense or imagination. Shiegle could be checked out against the Commercial Registry, if one liked. Huebsch on the other hand, remained something of a non-entity, brilliant as he may have been. In Baruch's narration, Huebsch found a way to refashion porcelain and Schiegle sank their limited capital looking for a market. Baruch's own Société PoreCon bought license to the process, Baruch said, then arranged to purchase from the corps the imperfect bowls for pennies on the dollar. The bowls were then refashioned to specification. The Corps got its quota of vases and PoreCon made a fortune selling back the reworked merchandise. Construction industry and the commercial world of sports opened the market even further.

Monsieur Baruch was a very private person. Other than generalities he said little about himself to his acquaintances at the Club except to offer, when he could, opportunities—an investment in Kazakhi oil; a million might get one in on the development of NorskSpa or the latest Libyan venture in Lake Tripoli. And then, most hush-hush and not quite ready to go public, Control Metereologique…If anyone lost money on such ventures he would have been embarrassed to complain. Baruch was a solid and conservative citizen —though of what country no one was sure. He was, to be sure, a gentleman whose sole passion was his rare books and manuscripts.

It was rumored he was married. Or divorced. Or estranged. It was something he could not keep under wraps. She was in the mental institute in Zurich. Or was it the alcoholic ward in Luzerne? Lausanne is a small place and word did get around concerning Doctor Baruch's weekly journey from Lausanne to Zurich. He took the train. He departed promptly on Monday morning, and he arrived back at the station promptly on Tuesday afternoon where he was met in the Rolls by the French chauffeur fellow, French, or Italian, or whatever he was.

Paco, calling himself, Pascal, was the chauffeur, and the mechanic and the Master's valet. He was chief cook and bottle washer, so to speak, and also foreman and chief engineer at the porcelain works. The Schiegle-Huebshe process was highly secret so the grounds were fenced and locked and guarded. Paco was also a kind of delivery man. Once a week he drove the company car to Grenoble in la France. At Grenoble, he went to the post office and mailed a parcel, a large paper-wrapped box-and-tape affair. The mailing address was always the same: *Livres Anciennes de Amsterdamm*. And always from: *Bibliotheque Antiquarienee*, Lausanne. Paco would not have been above peeking into the parcel to see what it was he was mailing but the tape and paper were such as to preclude tampering. Having so mailed, he then took an empty suitcase to an apartment building. He left the suitcase inside the foyer. The purpose for this wasn't spoken of and Paco didn't ask. Once or twice he met the concierge in the foyer who took the suitcase from his hand. She gave him a grunt and a steely eye. He always departed for Grenoble early on Thursday A.M. stayed over, and returned by Friday afternoon. Monsieur B., as he was called amongst the servants, made his Zurich foray by rail on Monday-Tuesday. He always returned with the suitcase.

Other than his quarrels with the housekeeper, Paco had few complaints. Funds deposited in his personal account over a year were more than he'd made in ten. He was comfortable. He ate well, slept well and in that first year had put on nearly ten kilos. Whatever the scam might be it had to do with the parcels he delivered, and with the suitcase. If Paco was given to surmise. he said nothing.

It might have gone indefinitely had it not been for something in the established scheme of things must needs, inevitably, go awry. Or, perhaps, it was two some-things. The third winter of their stay in Lausanne, the situation blew up.

Late on a Monday morning in January, Paco had returned to the house from his inspection of the porcelain works. Under his supervision, the 134 *vases de toilette* were "recycled" for the thirty-seventh time—shipped to Macon, Georgia, in the U.S., re-packaged and shipped back again. Paco saw them on their circuit once more and returned to the house. The housekeeper said there was someone in the library looking for Monsieur B: A lady, she said. And from the look on the old woman's face, there was something amiss.

Paco pegged her at about thirty five. She was auburn haired, slim to gaunt, and well dressed. She gave Paco a forced smile. "Where is he?"

"Mister B.? Gone to Zurich. "

"Shit! I've missed him."

"What's wrong?"

She regarded Paco through a lens of oblique misalignment. He caught a minor smear in her lipstick and the slight dishabille about her clothes and hair. He would have laid this to the effects of travel, except for the slight slur in her speech which, he inferred from experience, she'd spent years bringing under control.

"Feds are onto us." She managed to look at him directly for ten seconds before her gaze wandered again, and she assayed a smile. "You must be Paco. I'm Peg Brewer. The Missus. Mrs. Basil Pertwie. Or is he using Baruch? I'm the skeleton in his closet." She laughed a small self deprecating laugh. "Well, you better get hold of him real fast, Paco, 'cause somebody punched the button on us. They're waiting for him in Zurich and the banks are real mad at him."

"Banks?"

"And federal types. You better make tracks, too, booby, 'cause soon's they collar him they'll be here. I'd bet on it." The library clock said 10:45 AM. Mister B. would be half way between Bern and Zurich. He could alight at any one of five stops and make a good escape. Paco made a quick, incisive call via cell-phone and dashed from the library. Her car was just leaving the drive. He'd have to run with what he had in his pockets. He'd take the sedan as far as Le Brassus and then the train to Nice. That is what he would have done except for the two men waiting for him in the garage.

Made public, the charges said conspiracy to defraud, passing bad paper and half a dozen other Swiss laws. Paco was a courier, the prosecutor contended, an accomplice to a scheme whereby the one calling himself Baruch deceived Confiance Suisse and Banque de Commerce Zurich. The USICanadian Feds were investigating Porter-Hazelton, Chicago and Baruch's claim to be a procurement agent for the U.S. Government. In good faith, Swiss banks had lent him upwards of forty million dollars over three years. In point of fact, the prosecutor said, and he appeared to be miffed at this, there was no Division of Reclamation in the US Inc. Corps of Engineers! As for the invoices, they were printed in one of the finest, if not the last, letterpress houses right there in Innsbruck. It was a minor minion in Bern who'd caught the first scent of something wrong. The invoices had been rushed and the ink had smeared. It was enough to initiate an investigation, and like the thread in a sleeve, it unravelled quickly.

But, said the prosecutor, this was a mere whiff of *le garbáge*. It was an entry, a wedge into a greater scheme—securities! And the laundering of misbegotten money. Oil money from Russia! From Bulgaria! From Iraq and Iran and Rumania! From all over the world. Money hidden from a proper taxation. Money earned in a dozen illicit and nefarious ways, funneled through a series of small banks and brokerages in Eastern Europe into Switzerland. Money carried in suitcases as large amounts of cash and out again as legitimate Swiss accounts to purchase US Inc. securities, to be cashed and deposited in Luxembourg, in Liechtenstein, in Rep. San Marino, in the Orkneys, in the Caymans, in a hundred hidden accounts in the names of hundreds of shell companies, from which procedures Monsieur Peter Paul Baruch, or whatever his name might be, grew enormously rich. That is what the prosecutor said. That such a one was dangerous to the financial community. That such a one and his minions belonged behind bars, permanently, but that such a one had been warned with minutes to spare—the Geneva to Zurich express had arrived without him. Effectively, the authorities admitted, they knew little of the man behind the masquerade.

Paco was impressed, proud to be part of such a grand operation, except for looking at five years in the facilities at San Gall of which he did three and got deported back to Italy. Which is where, if Constancia Ocho was to believe, he'd got religion, became an honest man and a sports promoter. USICanadian Feds sniffed around Porter-Hazelton's Office of Foreign Liaison, Constancia Ocho VP in charge, but she'd covered her tracks exceptionally well. Over the next four years, the gentleman who had called himself Peter Paul Baruch searched assiduously for the seven-hundred-fifty-million she had surely tucked away. In so doing, he uncovered the edge of something called Chanticleer.

13. Where's Benni?

The incident with the motorbike had shaken him. Charlie hadn't intended to kill anyone. Persistent image of the guy sailing across half the plaza…and the way he hit! He woke nights in a sweat dreaming the police were at the door. Theft was one thing. World would be no place without skillful crooks. But killing a guy! Shee-it, man, they still took that *seriousa!* He could get five years!

Cray said it might be best were he to go back to Paris, advice which Charlie seized eagerly. He took refuge at the American Bar. He got drunk that first week in September and he intended to stay that way. He lost track of time and he was aware of little except that the concierge gave him a sour face and an iron eye. Somewhere around the end of June, Cray called, left a message for Charlie to call back, and when he did they argued, and Charlie cussed the man out. He wasn't ready to travel. He was too drunk to manage it. It would have to wait. He said later he'd been sleeping it off and Brewer showed up in broad daylight. She snided he'd been sleeping it off for damned close to a month and it was time to rise and shine. Endicotte told himself he didn't like the broad when he was sober and he sure wasn't gonna fall in love when he was drunk. She showed up with some hired hunk and together they stripped Charlie naked and shoved him into a cold shower and forced coffee and food on him. In two days he was, as he himself expressed it, "sober and pissed as a wet fuck-king cat!" Peg Brewer suffered the insults, the bad temper, and the man's filthy habits—she was an arrested alky herself so none of this was new. Day three, Charlie was nearly reasonable and merely weak-sober. She dismissed the hunk and faced Endicotte across a cluttered breakfast table. Cray had called. The comatose Pistone was in Geneva. Ungaroni had surfaced. There was work to do.

****

Van Horn mused on how well things had gone. The Chancellor had prepared him well. But then, he'd always had the knack for the con and was a genius at working off the cuff, as it were. From his creative imagination he conjured a scene in which he was being de-briefed: "So, I says to the Chancellor, yes, *Madame ma Commandante*, I had to revert to brute force, but then those two baboons backed off quick enough. And the French brothers, they proved…useful?…that was the word. Yaas, quite useful." His mind drifted back to a day in his relative youth, to the Wagon Wheel Club. In Detroit it was, when he was agent and manager for the Post Modern Jazz Quintet and he'd conned the management out of accommodations for himself and the six members of the combo. And then there was the time Charlie E.'s big mouth had gotten them into deep feco for…But he snapped to. They were out in the country. The mountains were behind them and to the right. "Excuse me, but aren't we going the wrong way? Terminal is south of the city. We're going north."

"*Oui*," says Bombaste. "We go north."

They drove through the Parcours Viticole, a magnificent trail of terraced Chasselas vineyards above Lake Geneva. They headed north and west. Van Horn ventured into in his high-school French. "Would you mind telling me where we are going?" "Ah," says the roly-poly Bombaste. "We go to val Bourgette You know val Bourgette?"

"Van Horn bit down on his impatience. "Not really. But why do we go to val Bourgette?"

"Because," says Bombaste. "in val Bourgette, la Suisse, there is the laboratory. There, we will preserve the brilliant mind of *le physicien*. The one who is called Polichuk. To preserve something," says Bombaste, "be it an olive or an onion, one must have a place in which to place the item, *non*?"

Van Horn fell silent. He didn't understand what this buffoon was up to. It didn't sound good. Nevertheless, he felt the presence of Benni Pistone behind him like an ominous weight, he who was neither dead, nor alive. And Polichuk. Who might croak at any minute. Bombaste guided the ambulance north and, when they'd cleared the western edge of the lake, back east toward the mountains. After two hours of twisting mountain roads Bombaste slowed the huge vehicle to a crawl. It seemed they burrowed into a thick green place heavy with low slung trees and every meter smothered in flower-bearing shrubbery. To his right, van Horn made out a cultivated field. "This is a villa?" van Horn snorted.

"Ah, no," says Bombaste, "The Villa Bonchance is there! *En la France!* He pointed to the rise of the mountain flank to the west. Discernible across a narrow valley, a stately manor house hugged the slope. "The valley is *val Bourgette*. That side is *la France*. This side is *la Suisse*. One can say of Tisibon and me that we live in one country and that we work in another. Villa Bonchance in Pontarlier is my family home. My ancestor, Maurice Etienne Bombaste marched with Francois le Premier. For this he was made Duc de val Bourgette. We will go there. But first..." Bombaste paused before a wooden gate and a gaunt fellow in cover-alls and boots swung open the gate.

They stopped before what appeared to be a dairy storage barn. Bombaste swung the ambulance around and reversed, the van doors facing the wide double doors of the barn. The ambulance backed in and they went from sharp sunlight into soft shadow. The doors closed before them. Van Horn sat in near darkness for a full minute. When the lights went on he dismounted with some disbelief. Here were no cows, buckets, hay or dung,

165

the general fetidness of things bovine, but surgical lights and three operating tables. He stood in an atmosphere of clinical antisepsis and the vague feeling of dread he'd generated in Geneva knotted his gut.

The tiny Italian fellow was first to jump down from the ambulance van. He was shorter than even van Horn himself. Van Horn extended his hand and introduced himself. He plunged into a flood of chatter in American English, most of which went over Paco's head. "We're gonna make hiss-tree, man!" the other was saying, "Hiss-tree, never been done before."

"I don't…"

"Mind transfer. BumBlast been explaining it to me. Take it outta the old man's bod, put it in the hunk." Ungaroni digested slowly the import of those words. The *Americano* chattered on as though it were a matter of football scores. Apprehension tied a knot in Paco Ungaroni's gorge.

Paco woke late next morning to a late October rain and in a narrow cot in what he took to be an ancient farmhouse. A sour-faced old woman served them breakfast. Paco ate well—sausage and eggs, strong coffee and good crusty bread. Late that afternoon he sat perched on a lab stool to one side of the barn-cum-laboratory.

Benni's inert figure lay under the surgical flood light. Life-support equipment hummed, buzzed and beeped. The respiratory apparat chuffed and sighed, and about Benni's shoulders a webwork of wires and sensors pierced his skull and fed into a column of wicked-looking electronics that flickered little lights.

Head to head with Benni lay another party, similarly festooned. This was Anatoli Polichuk, Paco was informed, the one whose psyche was to be preserved. Forming the first leg of the X to the left of Pistone lay the anesthetized figure of the one identified as Aram Gregorian. A similar web of equipment all but obscured his head. And completing the X-configuration lay van Horn, similarly senseless and obscured in equipment.

Over this scene of the scientifically arcane fluttered Tisibon like an anxious butterfly, except that this butterfly spoke. Aloud. He addressed himself to the over-hanging microphone, and to Paco, the latter sitting in a far corner of the laboratory wide-eyed in helpless amazement, Tisibon having prepared for himself a near-perfect captive audience.

"*Voilà*," says he:

Le Benni Pistónne, yes? We seek to resume in him once more *le procédé psychique-cinematografique*—the cinema of the thinking mind—as says the great Portugais-Americain. But, in le Pistón the circuitry is interrupted. The body it is alive, but how to 'knock on the door,' eh? *Oooo la!* We attempt many times to persuade him to speak to us, but there is no *personnalité* to respond. *Com'en dit en englais*, there is 'nobody home.'

So. We have also as our guest *le Docteur* Anatoli Polichuk. Ah, this brain, this 'mind,' functions *tres brilliant*. It is the body that fails, the heart, the kidneys, the animal organism in which *la nature* chooses to put this 'mind.' We, my colleague and I, we are prejudicially selective. We will attempt to save the better of each of the two, yes? And, if we succeed, the mind of Polichuk will waken in the body of an athlete!

Understand, please, we are not assured of success. Our invention *merveillieux* is not proven. We proceed, *comme on dit en Anglais*, with the *le cheval arriere l'èquipage*, yes? This to take advantage of an opportunity that comes upon us too soon, perhaps. *Ei, zut!* What to do?

Now, you ask. What of these other two? This Gregorian, a brilliant scientist, and, like ourself, he is *psycheNeuronomist*. He lends himself to the cause. Also, it is most fortunate he is of high-*cognifrine* frequency.

And this one? He is emissary from *le Chi-ca-gó*. Examination reveals this gentleman to transmit very high frequencies. In his brain is the *pes hippocampal* very large, you see. Very powerful it transmits the frequencies. The 'Horn of Ammon,' it is called. And he is called *le van Horn*. Peculiar, yes?

Tisibon giggled, then he continued:

When the psy frequencies of the Poilchuk are transmitted through the "horn" of this one it will be like a loud trombone, you see. Also, this van Horn he is a peculiar specimen. Of bilaterally cerebral access. Like to say he should be born two. Twins. But he is one. With two minds, almost. One through which to be, and one made for to see. This is advantage. He will be as a valve, a channel. From the transmitter, to the recipient. Yes?

So, the van Horn, to serve as channel, and the Gregorian, to be the transformer, to 'step up,' the cognitional frequencies of the Polichuk, to the brain of *le Pistón*. When *le bon docteur*, he inhabits a new body, we have saved a brilliant mind. The others will suffer no ill effects. We hope.

Tisibon called out, "We are ready, *mon ami*."

The one called Bombaste remained in the shadows of the lab. On a signal he did something, and the electronic apparati increased the intensity of their humming and blinking. A minute passed. Another. Tisibon stood with his hands to his face looking to be as anxiety ridden as a cat bearing kittens. The apparatus emitted a high piercing whistle and the inert form that was Bennino Pistone moved! He turned his head.

Paco, even at some distance, saw the light of consciousness in the lad's eyes. "Bennino!" he cried and it was in that moment that Tisibon's delicate balance between achievement and disaster slipped. It may have been Paco's doing, or it may have been a technical oversight but what is beyond dispute is that Paco leapt from his perch and lunged forward, that he tripped over a cable and seeking to keep from falling he barged into a bank of instruments, that something in the photonic-cerebral process got interrupted, or re-channeled because, as Tisibon himself would testify to his utter amazement, Benni Pistone did make one attempt to sit up, and he might have but for the wires and tubes restraining him. He may have heard Paco call out his name, may have seen him in the instant before the little man fell forward on his face. The whistle went from a G above high-C, moaned itself down scale, and ceased. Benni Pistone lay back, and was still.

"Claude! *Qu'est que vous faites*?" Bombaste shouted.

Claude Tisibon plied an ophthalmic light into Benni Pistone's eyes. "Well?" says Paco. "Does he live?"

Bombaste emerged into the light. "Try a Babinski!" Tisibon raked a steel probe up the sole of Pistone's foot. "Nothing? Try the knee-response." Tisibon tapped the body's knee with a rubber hammer. "Nothing," says Bombaste in a throaty rasp. "We must hurry. Adrenaline!"

Tisibon raised a vein on Pistone's right arm and plunged. The cardio monitor gave a jump in frequency, but the body lay inert.

"Ah, *mon ami*," says Bombaste sadly. "We have failed."

"Perhaps not," whispered Tisibon. "The heart continues to beat. But the reflex responses are not stimulus enough."

Bombaste could have sworn his little friend was smiling. "Remember, *mon ami*, this is the body of an athlete. It is very strong. It therefore requires strong stimulus. *Voilà!*" With this he yanked loose a lead from the electronic column which he then jammed into the scrotum of the body. He turned up the current. The body jumped!

"Hey, what the hell y' doin' t' me?" the subject murmured.

"He lives!" Bombaste shouted.

"*Docteur* Polichuk. How do feel?" Tisibon put his nose but an inch from the other's.

The subject hesitated a moment, then smiled. He chuckled, then muttered in a confidentially-hushed bass-baritone, "Hi, doc. What's going

169

down? "

"'What goes down? *Mon dieu*! Who are you?"

"I'm Mackenzie van Horn. Why? We got a problem?"

Tisibon had ceased to smile. "*Eu*, Claude," he whispered. "I believe we have an error," he said.

****

At 2:37 A.M. that morning, a witness might have seen Benni Pistone rise from the surgical table on which he lay. But for the light on a corner desk, the lab was dark and quiet. Only the monitors beeped and hummed. The witness would have seen him remove the sensor patches from his chest and arms. He searched about for his clothes. Having found them, he did twenty-knee bends and fifty push-ups and took one last look about the lab. "There's tree guys laid out like some kinda zombies. Like y' see inna movies, wit wires innair heads. What the hell is 'iss place, ennyhow?"

Having assayed the question, the answer came in a different, a more cultivated voice. "Indeed. One might conclude he finds himself in a *psycheNeuronomic* laboratory."

"Yeah? Where's Paco?"

"He'll be about somewhere, I'm sure. I say, gentlemen, aren't we hungry?"

"Da. The mind it is a wonderful instrument, yes? But always it is in need of the animal body."

"Yeah, man. Gotta be somethin' t' eat 'round here someplace."

"Indeed, gentlemen. If I recall, there is an all-night diner in the village."

A brilliant moon lit what looked like a farmyard. Beside the ambulance sat a battered Citroen four-banger. The keys were in the ignition. The Citroen cleared the drive just as lights came on in the house.

14. Human Voices Wake Us

On a sultry day in late July, on the noisy, crowded gravity-walker bus to Nouveau San Tropez, Kirsten swallowed hard against apprehension. Doctor K. said she was being inordinately silly, but Kirsten's feeling persisted. She was probably responding to some subliminal key Binswanger had implanted in her psyche. Whatever it was prompted her, she knew for a certainty she was going to find her athlete.

In Nouveau San Tropez, Kirsten found the coastal city steaming under an aberrant sun and overrun by an army of tourists. She spent her first day confined to her room—she'd settled for a *pension* at the edge of town, avoiding the gaggles and flocks of outrageously young students. On her second night, she consulted with Binswanger, not so much in dialogue as in the generation of an understanding. There was something she would do. It would resolve everything. When she thought upon it afterwards, she recognized the extent of the distraction through which she had moved. In her subject-patients, she'd termed it depression. In herself, it was an obsessive determination.

The beach was impossibly crowded. Chagrin would recall afterwards the sign on the fence dividing and concealing the beach. It read in French and in English:

Costume de Bain Laisse aux Choix
Bathing Dress Optional

It was not optional. She hadn't brought a bathing suit. Well, then, *allors!* Shit, as said the English. Considering what she had in mind, what mattered one nude body amongst hundreds. Kirsten rented space in the communal locker room. Then, feeling ever-so-slightly self-conscious, she walked amongst a crowd of scampering, shouting, gleefully naked youngsters. She was grateful for the indifference of the crowd about her. There was that which must be done. She continued her long-legged stride parallel to the water and toward the late-morning sun. Some fifty meters down she was well away from the crowd and approaching the barrier. Signs warned of rocks and undertow. She kept walking.

As on a silent signal, Kirsten turned and entered the water. The conviction of her quest grew stronger. She was completely aware of the cool waters of the Mediterranean climbing her body. It reached her loins and then her waist, and she welcomed it, she urged herself on. It reached her breast and she felt with her feet the sand grow finer, less littered with stone and shell. The water rose to her throat. Another dozen paces and she closed her eyes.

Whatever it was, it stabbed the heel of her right foot and near caused her to fall. Kirsten uttered a mild imprecation and in the immediacy that is mind and sensation she weighed the pain against the irony. It had caused her to stumble and so to submerge for a few seconds and to inhale water. Pharynx and sinuses rebelled. She would remember choking and being suddenly desperate for air and that she panicked because she couldn't find bottom and the blind moment had her flailing and then something or someone had her by the waist, embraced her, buoyed her up, up so that once more she stood in the brilliance of the sun, in the largesse of the sea rasping and coughing and, she admitted later, inwardly laughing at herself for being so silly, and when she'd cleared the water from her eyes, it was his head of dense curls she noted, his shoulder she coughed over and he was standing there looking up at her with something like amazement in his face. She was still coughing and sputtering and fighting the glare, and the emergence of anyone at that moment startled her. Recasting reality. she later told herself she might have ignored him and simply walked around him. She hadn't wanted to meet anyone and this stranger was a nuisance. She might have except his arms encircled her buttocks and his chin engaged her navel and in a dizzy moment image and knowledge came together. It was he! The athlete, the man of the motorcycle, her patient in the street at Le Brassus. For an eternal minute they stood so, her buttocks on his forearms, her elbows on his shoulders. He smiled up at her, openly, happily while she coughed, while she resented the light and the air and whoever this was had embraced her, resented because before she was capable of words she was already formulating her explanation, how she'd been bitten, or cut, but he spoke first and he startled her as she struggled to clear her throat and her eyes to affirm who this was and he was saying, "Indeed! Doctor Kirsten Lagerquist! Is it really you?"

He'd carried her. Conventional person that she was, she cast an analytical eye on the image of herself and of him as others might have seen them. He carried her as he might have a small infant, back to the beach the fifty meters or so out of the water and down the Plage de Pampelonne. She couldn't erase from memory her being carried, the fact she'd an arm about his thick neck and that he walked looking intently and continuously into her eyes and she into his and there must have been a thousand young people on that beach every bit as naked as they and yet neither of them was aware of anyone else being about. In the classification of things amazing, if not impossible, she knew he was in physio the motorcyclist, but out there in the water he had addressed her in the voice of Aram Gregorian, the incongruence of which set her back on her heels, so to speak. Now, he spoke to her in a voice she had heard but once, a very few words mid the intense confusion of a small army of technicians intent on making a video.

It was the same voice which had spoken and it was the same face had leered at her from under the rim of his motor cycle helmet, had inquired of her even as she was being dressed—or undressed, she was not longer sure—except that the words had suggested to her a banal lechery—"You got plans, eh, mebee later on?"—the same voice she had heard making its way through the din of the televideo crowd. His speech had been broken and coarse and uncouth while this beautiful creature, for that is what she had to admit even wordlessly that he was, had addressed her in a soft and cultivated manner, inquiring as to the injury she'd sustained to her foot, which brought two questions paramount for her to consider: If this man was the motorcyclist, how did he know her? They had never exchanged names. Memory laid him on the cobbles of a street with the unmistakable opacity of concussion glazing his eyes. He had lain there promising a likelihood of coma, or that he might not survive, and then but four days later to have been familiar enough to address her by her professional name in a voice that so strongly reminded her of Gregorian. Not that she minded, and that may have been another surprise, that under the shock of near drowning she should in retrospect permit herself to be profoundly pleased, yea, excited, that he had scooped her up this way.

The entire experience brought back her buried memories of faerie tales, of elves and goblins and the "little folk" from her native Iceland so that for a moment in their long walk down the beach the Kirsten part of her psyche played with the notion he might not be real, a notion the conventional and the professional Doctor Lagerquist immediately dismissed. "But, the facts, please," she insisted. "Who? How?"

He…one of them…binding her foot. She thought she remembered that it was the Pistone portion of this amazing schizoid chimera that had squeezed from the wound what venom might have entered, had applied antiseptic and finally bound it with white gauze, expertly, swiftly, there in the locker room. He was down on one knee before her, talking to her, speaking, muttering, the words mumbled before he stood up and bid her wordlessly to stand. She stood. She was the taller. He took her elbows. She put weight on her injured foot, stumbled at the stab of pain and fell forwards a trifle. He took her by the waist, drew her close, and she assented to, invited his kiss. "You was gonna drown yourself," he said. "Me, too. I'm drownin'. I don' unnerstand what's happenin' here. I ain't all me."

"Yes, But it's going to be alright."

"I'm hearin' voices. Udder guys. Like inside my head. Like mebee I'm goin' crazy, hearin' voices…"

"Bennie. It's all right," she sought to assure him. "It's going to be all right."

"When I seen you, out there, inna water…it's like I knew who you was right away. Like I knew you so good…from way back, but I mean, we never…"

"I understand, Benni…May I call you…"

"Oh, sure, I'm Benni. You, you're?"

"Kirsten."

"Kir-sten," he repeated softly. "But I'm gonna get this straightened out. I'm gonna be all me. Listen, kid, they tryna tell em I'm stupid, but I ain't so stupid I don' know somebody's messin' with my brains, y' know?"

"No, you're not stupid," she said, and she drew him close once more and it was she who kissed him.

"Beautiful lady," he said in his boyish gutteral. "I'm gonna get straight…you be there, hear? Like I fished you outta the water, you gonna fish me outta this…whatever y' call it…like drownin'…"

In town, over lunch, it was Gregorian to the fore. He explained briefly how it was four psyches had come to invest the Pistone body, how it was but one at a time could "surface" and regard the world.

Lagerquist did her best to understand the outrageous thing he proposed as a matter of fact. And to his own question, what was she doing there?

"Pursuing a dream, if you will," she said. "I gave in to a kind of infantile...madness. What else to call it?"

"You would have ended your life," he said most clinically. "Instead, you fell in love."

"But I don't know the man! We met once. We hardly spoke."

"Kirsten, Kirsten," Gregorian chuckled. For all his explanations about psyche-transfers she was nevertheless amazed to the point of disbelief that this hairy-homely, hirsute and fascinating creature was Aram Gregorian, that they were sitting at a small table in a bistro on the shore of the sea. He was laughing at her sympathetically, and then confessing. "I, too."

"In love? With me?"

"Indeed! It was so...painful. You were my superior. I was...in my own body certainly nothing to boast of."

"I was cruel. Will you ever forgive?"

He regarded her through Benni Pistone's eyes, but with the gentle wisdom she understood to be that of Gregorian. "Please," he said. "It is futile to speak of pain that is passed, or of forgiveness. This incredible affair, it isn't over. There are many things to resolve. Besides," he continued ruefully, "my companions may have their own agendum. Hah! And here they are now."

At which point a tubby individual wearing an English bowler and thick glasses had joined them. He introduced himself as Armand Bombaste, Chief of Pathological Neurology, Clinique General, Genevre, The droll Bombaste said he was honored and delighted to meet Doctor Lagerquist. He'd read everything she'd published, but, he said, subject should never have run off. It was dangerous. No telling what sort of relapse he might suffer, his major d', that big fellow, had been of enormous help, yet and still he and Tisibon had had the devil's own time and trouble tracking him down. Fortunately, the Pistone visage was internationally known. Through this peroration, all delivered in an admirably fluent, if accented English, the Gregorian who inhabited the physique of the Pistone had sat in rapt attention. Now he fairly hissed his anger. "This is madness! Good Lord, what have we done?"

"Done? Why, the doing of it should be obvious on several points,

Monsieur. First, we have saved the psychic entity which calls itself Polichuk. Ah, yes. It is there, in the psychic space of the infra-temporal cortices of the Pistone brain. Intact. And it shall be retrieved, you will see. All will be put to rights. But enough sojourn in the sun. We must now return to the laboratory as our patient—or..." he paused in mid sentence to consider—"shall we refer to this gentleman as our patients, in the plural?" Doctor Bombaste raised his brows and emitted a chuckle as at a private joke. In any case, the subject was still under recuperative psychotherapy.

In the course of this meeting it was agreed Doctor Lagerquist would join them and bring to bear on the case her considerable expertise. She looked into Benni's eyes and agreed. Oh, yes, she would join them.

Ammon's Horn

15. Anabasis

If April be the cruelest month, as one poet has it, then July must be the grittiest. A good time for venting the last of summer's grudges. It wasn't the first time he'd been spurned. There had been others going back into time before clocks and calendars, and always, he, Phoebus Apollo, had shown his pique, or as Didi put it, had permitted his ego to get the best of his judgement, and always the poor creature desired took the brunt of his childish temper. No, he wouldn't turn Ocho into a weeping tree, nor transform her into a doe in hopeless rut, or whatever, if only because, given his flexible proclivities, Phoebus had access to other sources for solace. He found the banker, Adonis Perikardis, to be adorable, and Adonis being quite perceptive took the big fellow by the shorthair so to speak. But that gets ahead of the story.

Over that summer, anyone following the WorldNet Stock Exchange for the Southern European Bourse might have used a set crayolas to color the takeover a shade of livid green. Ocho needed Thesaurus Athenaios, the key investment bankers in Hellas (which the Anglos call "Greece") and financial key to the whole Balkan lockbox from Zagreb to Bucharest and from Athens to Istanbul. This is where history says Connie's troops had run into an intractable obstacle.

Connie ran this theater of operations from her Med. HQ in Torino. Fondo ZuppaForte of Milano was known derisively on the Anglo financial circuit as Strong Soup, or as The FrigginZip. FZF were investment pirates, bond bandits, market manipulators and stock squeezers for damned near all the Mediterranean theater from Lyons to Palermo, Brittany to Budapest. Field Marshall for this operation was a little financial fascist named Marcantonio Grappacoglioni—his name translating in the common tongue as 'ball-grabber'—and that is what he was before Connie leveraged him, bought him, stripped him, and re-made him and his mercantile mercenaries into her own sniper-scope. This gunsight she now zeroed in on parts south. Connie said later she had expected it to be like stopping a rabbit with a tank.

For his new commander, Grappacoglioni played an old game. Before he made so much as whisper of a public announcement, he'd obtained 4 billion from his old network of bond pirates while Subsume (covered by a Milanese brokerage) circulated confidence letters of tender offer to acquire. The quarry being solicited by anonymous parties were by this maneuver prohibited from trading their own stock. The maneuver also shut their mouths and kept the stock price from going through the roof. Nor were Kari's troops above plying a little sex, sleaze, squeeze and blackmail to see it all remained mum 'til the deal was done. And it did get done. But not before the rabbit fought back.

Thesaurus Athenaios' president was young Adonis Perikardis. Perhaps because he was so young he had the temerity to go public with his problems. He elicited his stockholder's sympathies and got a majority approval to water the company's stock. Almost overnight he parked the biggest percentage of his assets with anonymous parties in a blatant buy-back scheme and made it known there was a white-knight prepared to counter any attempt to play his debt over equity. A good rap on that same woodwork brought all sorts of things into the light, including Thesaurus having hired counter-artillery of dubious reputation. They were given in the metro directory as Hephaestus-Persekurion and, in the book of popular savvy, as specialists in dirty infighting. Arrangements were made. Telephone calls ensued, one man to another. George, "Gigi" Persekurion, he of several brilliantly ominous reputations, would visit Adonis Perikardis, President of Thesaurus Athenaiios, in his office on the tenth of May.

But first: A letter had arrived on Perikardis' desk from Arlington Virginia with a US Inc letterhead. It announced the imminent demise of one Aristotle Apostopoulos. If to be believed, it had been dictated by that good man from his deathbed in the interests of his only heirs, his grand-nieces Tarimina and Karimina Agapé, daughters of his nephew, Theodore, the American congressman. As a stockholder and member of the board of Thesaurus Athenaios, A. Apostopoulos advised bank president Perikardis of his impending end and of the provisions of his will which left his considerable fortune, plus properties in Greece and 15 percent of the bank's stock, to the twins. The letter exhorted Adonis Perikardis to take the ladies in hand and to see to an equitable settlement of their affairs. Now then, a 15 percent stockholder was certainly not to be sneezed at.

That Apostopoulos had living relatives came as something of a surprise to the folks at Thesaurus Athenaios, and that the old man should express love and charity for his grand-nieces flew in the face of his lifelong rep as a nickel-squeezing tyrant. Adonis' people did a sweep of InterNet International for biographical data going back twenty years but neither the media nor official records mentioned living relatives. Verification came via Washington DC II, an address in Sciatica Heights and over the signature of Theodoro Agapé. Confirmed: the American congressman was, indeed, a nephew of Aristotle Apostopoulos, the son of the old man's only sister, the missive hinting ever-so-subtly at some smudge of illegitimacy.

That settled, young Perikardis set aside his business affairs. That afternoon he would tend to the arrival of Karmina Agapé. On the 27th of June his chauffeured limo took him to New Piraeus, Port of Athens and at 9:15 AM Adonis stood at the foot of the gangway in a crowd of some three hundred people awaiting the disembarking of the passengers of the cruise liner Peloponessus. For whatever reason shapes a person's imaginative impressions, he fully expected to greet a self-possessed dowager of middle years. Little wonder his surprise at the descent of a very tall, full-figured young woman, certainly not over thirty, with naturally curly ash-blonde hair and a pair of the most brilliantly blue eyes by which he had ever been threatened.

The young lady saw a dark-haired and fearsomely handsome little fellow, short by most standards, at five-seven, and slender, one might have even said, spare of frame, weighing surely no more than 65 kilos—160 pounds American. A reserved gentleman of her own age. He would have seen her comfortably ensconced at the Ilisia, but she demurred having arranged to stay with cousin Gigi at a condo in Apollon.

Then, they had lunch, a private dining room at the Anavisos. That afternoon they were to see the ruins of Athens—wasn't he awfully young to be the president of a major bank? By which time she'd quick bathed and changed and they ducked the armies of tourists and had a drink. No, he wasn't married and the unseasonably warm weather had Miss Agapé fluttering about the Agora in a see-through blouse and the skimpiest of underwear by which time she was Kari and he was Adonis and she'd taken to holding his hand quite tightly while she favored him with her incredible eyes, her devouring smile, and the music of her tittering laughter.

Fact of the matter was her grasp of Greek was more than adequate and he permitted himself to be imposed upon if only by her own effusive innocence. Her business matters were, of course, his business, but business was not all facts and figures—it was people! Perikardis phoned his office— he would not be in for another day.

There is an implicit rhythm to such matters. The tempo insists to the degree the participants attune to a common beat, and for all his reserve Adonis was not insensitive. No son of the Aegean could have mistaken the sparkle in her eyes, the sudden flashes of color in her cheeks, her stammers, titters and giggles at his most banal utterances for anything other than what they were. He assessed, as a banker should, her assets and her liabilities, and his staff began the disposition of her financial endowments after which dreary business he took her on a tour of the Agora, and of the Parthenon. "Parthenon...parthenos...virgin...temple of the virgin, with reference to Athena..."

Next day, they flew in his private shuttle grav-walker to the temple at Eleusis, and on up the Corinthian coast they went under sail, and lunched on splendid beaches—she was near overwhelmingly desirable in a string bikini. They went over land by donkey to the Temple of Delphi by which time they had drawn close, almost ventured to a kiss and he to an intimate word which did not get uttered because a peasant with figs for sale barged in on them.

Before the Temple, huge masculine figures bowed their heads in deference, quite indifferent to their own genital displays before which Kari fell into titters and giggles all over again until the reserved Perikardis held her close against her silly embarrassment and he ventured a smile and despite himself savored for the first time in his young life the lift and swoon produced by the pressing of a woman's body against one's masculine own, and the power of her kiss. Much contrary to what he would have anticipated, his anatomy responded. Something to ponder. But, duty will call. The following day was the ninth.

Adonis' appointments had stacked up and bank matters awaited tending to. He and the young lady flew back to Athens with murmured protests of agony over their parting and fervent promises to meet again soonest.

****

Gigi Persekurion arrived in a chauffeur driven limo and was preceded across the lobby by an officious baboon who opened doors and tended his master's needs. Adonis was taken aback by the man's unrelieved ugliness and by his charm—overwhelming and nauseating by turns. Georges Persekurion was broad, bald and hook-nosed, dressed like a throw-back to a cinema cliche—striped blue serge, black shirt, white tie and the inevitable pearl-grey *borsellino.*

Adonis wondered at the man's reputation with the ladies. He was said to be a sure-fire seducer of young women, a notion difficult to believe if predicated solely on his appearance. The ugly fellow crossed his knees the better to show off his patent-leather perforated-wing-tip shoes. He assured Perikardis his firm was underwritten by *de la force formidable*—he affected an execrable French—and that Thesaurus Athenaios would be surrounded by an unbreachable envelope. They would swallow up—"devour," is the word he used—anyone posing the slightest threat, personal or institutional.

****

These were stalling tactics, to be sure. The predator had all the ammunition needed for take-over and more time to wait him out than the prey had money to fight with. But, Ocho had to wonder, who was the white knight? Someone with mucho geld and moxie was holding off her takeover and she couldn't imagine who that might be. Says she, speaking figuratively, "Who's he in bed with?"

Came the week-end, a long sojourne in holiday. Karimina and Adonis had a chaste three days of early breakfasts and knew the exhilaration of mountains and sun and sea, the intoxicating drug of youth laughing aloud in the ruins of antiquity. Perikardis sensed those ruins as he had never before and weighed his ambivalent sexuality in the scales of her joyful being. They flew back to Athens where after concerts and after sunsets, after brilliant company and talk of novels, after cocktails and talk of you and me came an evening, an hour delayed that hung heavy as a messenger of portent waiting without the door. He'd gone so far as to reserve rooms at the Oikoseroumenon, a hospice catering to the erotically romantic. In subdued lights and subtle music he might have been prepared to utter commitment.

And it was probably she who prepared to broach that most dangerous word, she who was willing to give it breath and a passion's commitment should he falter.

There are details in description of those few hours that do not make it into her final report on the affair. Like the fact she succeeded in undressing him. Like the look of unbelieving amazement on his face upon seeing her nude. And her own sense of imminent victory, her interpretation of his amazement to be a response to the power of her sex. Perhaps. But if she was prepared to consummate, he effectively sealed her lips. Not with a kiss, but with a raising of reserve, a drawing back. Before they proceeded, he said, they must talk further. He must explain. She must know. About him. What he was. That she was avid, almost adamant, that she ventured to rouse him with means as old as is the species, and that she failed, is no surprise. He begged her forgiveness and they parted, she to her condo in suburb Apollon, he to his apartment in downtown Attiki; she sullen and angry, and he as a very troubled young man.

How to explain to her, this young woman so brilliantly feminine, that what the world saw of him was what it insisted it wanted to see, and that its prejudice preconditioned his image. In unforgiving daylight the pragmatic aspect of the Adonis psyche saw itself in banal reality. The fortunes of peace had raised him from lowly teller in the branch bank in Thessalonika to president of the combine in Athens, all in a few short years and all by dint of his savvy, his unerring judgement, his uncanny assessments of the market, and, truth told, by virtue of his encounter with the extraordinary gentleman who called himself A. Phoebus Koronaris—Niki, to his friends. Wasn't it Niki who had elicited young Adonis' first ventures into…into…the young man was reluctant to name it…into love? And Niki again who fostered in him the courage to embrace his ambivalence? Yea, and Niki again who warned him against the possible duplicities inherent in emotional adventures? One aspect of his double nature may have yearned to love that beautiful creature who called herself Karimina. But his second self gave that the lie in that it would not deny itself.

Love may indeed conquer all, as some silly wag has said, but by and large the workaday world remains indifferent to that sentimental commodity. From Torino, C.E.O. Ocho kept a finger on the pulse of matters Aegean. She had worms ensconced in Thesaurus' woodwork. Names were revealed and the parked stock was revealed. Monday morning's papers trumpeted the news —Thesaurus' stock got played over equity. As it was a private institution, Athens' central Securities Commission was loath to step in and, as such governing bodies will do in a crisis such as this, they dithered.

Adonis Perikardis arrived at his beloved bank early that morning to find a police cordon denying him access. He was given to know his offices were locked, his records sealed and his position as officer of the bank (and by tenuous extension the state) suspended. But, all was not lost—not yet. A loose confederation of interests calling itself the Confederation Peloponnesus had immediately filed suit. The State's Attorney, to the extent he wielded any influence, sided with the victim and for a few hours the battle settled into stalemate.

Given the tensions of the day, Adonis, like any hero of history or mythology, sought solace. Or at least a respite. Nikki. Where was Nikki? A shoulder to cry on, a friend to offer small comfort if only in his reaffirmation of friendship. He called the Kolnaki Hilton, but Nikki was abroad. Karimina? Did he dare? His resilience of spirit flexed its muscles.

A leering sun set slowly over the Aegean. As often he did in hours of crisis, Adonis woke to the fact he had driven his Maserati aimlessly in and about the suburban countryside. The willy-nilly of subconscious choice had taken him to the suburbs of Neo-Apollon. Wasn't that where Kari resided? He found the Andromeda, a complex of condominiums catering to the nouveau riche in search of garish affirmation. Well, then, as he was in the neighborhood, he would surprise her.

The name on the roster (pasted over an original) said K. Agapé. He rang. She queried. He answered and she admitted him. On the elevator going up, he mulled it tentatively. This was her cousin Gigi's condo, the said cousin currently visiting relatives in Thessalía. In a periphery of attention, Adonis might have raised a brow at this, preliminary search of the family Apostopulos-Agapé had given no data on cousins, first, second, or otherwise. But in the impending heat of the evening he let it pass. Kari answered the door in a bathrobe. He saw her adorably disheveled. She bid him comfort and disappeared to put on something appropriate.

On the terrace, she wore an appealing negligé. There came a quiet hour for the baring of naked selves and for revelations. She blushed in a tale of her childhood's foibles and all the while their knees met beneath the table and her incredible bosom flushed all dusky pink and beautiful and a tale unfolded, part report, part prophecy foretelling, a tale told by a…Sibyl! Yes. Kari's *mammá* protested her credence, but she paid the woman a silver coin for her foreseeing. The woman said that the child would journey to the land of her ancestors. She would meet the man of her destiny. She would know power, the Sibyl had said, and riches to make Croesus a piker to compare. Kari's voice had fallen to a low whisper. Her demeanor became one of shy deference.

For his part, he confessed to finding himself at the cusp of fortune. Tomorrow would tell what the fates decided. And by tomorrow he would have decided who, or what, constituted the confused fellow calling himself Adonis Perikardis.

Kari vanished some minutes to do whatever it is women do under these circumstances. A digital recording suffused the rooms with American song, "I'm in the Mood for Love." Conflicting truths hovered just beyond Adonis' resolution. He wandered the condo apartment. With an unseeing eye he noted articles of feminine clothing tossed here and there. There were English-language magazines and journals. On the desk—though one would not accuse him of prying—he could not help but notice young Karimina employed a conceptor-SatCom link of a weight and sophistication equal to that which he himself employed in his office. Nor was his reading eye capable of ignoring stacks of print, in French, in English, in Italian—the young lady apparently communicated widely. And then—roses! A bouquet of red American Beauties in their delivery tissue from whose delicate red petals peeked a card. He would not have read it had it been in English. She was a beautiful young woman, certainly desirable to many men. But the card, he could not help notice, was inscribed in Greek! Whom did she know in Athens might send roses? She'd never been to Ellas before, she said. Adonis savored an appetizer called anxiety. He could not help its progression into an *entre* of suspicion. A thousand and one little incidents, phrases uttered, minor contradictions and re-takes exchanged over the previous ten days came to mind now. It had all happened so quickly. Native to the Greek is his wiliness —so says the cliche. But, if so, with it, too, must come a wariness of the guiles of the other party. Add to this a smidge of potential jealousy that another might be courting his *innamorata* and he was prepared to be abashed, to let suspicion and jealousy rise as a bitter taste in his mouth. He had wandered over to the inside wall of the apartment. He stood before a set of wall-to-wall bifold doors. A closet, no doubt. Except that the doors had not closed completely. They stood open to the extent of permitting an item to protrude slightly, a sleeve, a piece of organdy, or perhaps of taffeta—one of those things women will wear. It was almost crushed in the aperture which was at one and the same time a pity considering its fragility. All in all, it was an affront to Adonis' unbending sense of order. He would replace the sleeve properly and restore the doors and the wall to their pristine order. To which end, he pushed open the door a mere fifteen centimeters—some six inches— and gently replaced the sleeve as it should have been. He would have re-closed the door, except it would not move. There was obviously an obstacle. Yes. A shoe. A man's shoe! An elaborately patterned, black, wing-tipped, patent-leather shoe. Adonis tore open the doors. There were suits! Dark blue serge suits, three piece, double breasted, with pin-stripes! And pearl-grey *borsellino* hats.

Adonis resumed his seat on the divan. Kari came toward him across the room, a vision in something diaphanous. Her breath was labored and her eyes lidded with desire. Through the wiles of her gown and the clever light of the chamber her body stood revealed, breasts, belly, flanks. She was so big! So…gross?

His imagination conjured up the ineluctable pocket into which love is thrust and from which no man retreats the same man he went in. For critical seconds, he remained sitting. She stood. In a scene he was to replay into eternity he would have risen but in the same instant she stooped as she would have had to do being some five inches taller than he and, for some reason he would afterwards define as having been salvational, there popped into his mind, even as her devouringly beautiful mouth drew near, a phrase attributed to another if more intensely short fellow, a French painter, he of the genetically dwarfed legs who is said to have said something to the effect that "all men are the same height in bed." In that fragile moment, it came enunciated in his mind. It struck him as ludicrous, the fact of it, the truth of it, the ironic manner in which it applied to him—he'd always been critically self-conscious of his diminutive stature—so that he conjured an image of himself crouched in that most awkward of positions to which two human bodies are subjected in the act of…love? And then, there was his own sexual ambiguity. Was it really an anomaly to be able to love both a man and a woman? He'd never resolved the question. He'd only smarted under an inference of the conventional world's misapprobation. His graphic imagination—to which he seldom gave reign—saw himself, and herself as a mouse fucking a sow!—the whole proposition ludicrous and obscene. She descended to devour but her arms came to enclose nothing but the cashmere of his empty coat.

That would have been the evening of the tenth day of Kari's assignment to Athens. Around midnight Madame Ocho came up on the CommoNet. News of the imminent collapse of Thesaurus Athnaios was all over Europe. But there was still someone sticking his foot in the works. Kari had fudged. For the first time in their association she was playing less than square with the boss. What had she come up with? On the Net, Kari ran down the roster of things not learned—where the rest of the stock was parked, who held the bonds, names on extended indentures. Every conceivable nook and cranny had been sealed against Ocho's corporate invasion, says Kari, and did the boss know of a P. A. Koronaris? On her end of things Madame O. did a quick bio check and came up blank. Kari had found the name in Adonis' calendar of appointments in the inner pocket of the abandoned coat and, yes, she would look into it right away. That little son-of-a-bitch wasn't going to get away from her!

The aforementioned commo took place September twenty-first at 11:30 PM, Athens time, 10:30 Milano. By midnight Kari, bathed, dressed, coffee'd and smoke-and-steam furious, had punched the panic button and roused her platoon, seven of the troupe stationed about the precincts of Athens Metropolitan. A quick bio check of the Metro Direktory gave three parties under Koronaris, two improbable and one more likely, an A. P. Koronaris staying at the Kolnaki Hilton. An hour later came a call from agent Perspikakis. There was action at the Athens Holiday Inn, the license number on the Mercedes parked outside said it belonged to a Perikardis, P. A. The automobile didn't move until 3 AM; then it was tailed to a palatial home in Palateia Monastirakiou. Next morning, it was parked outside the Club Bio-Bio where the owner-driver breakfasted. It showed up next at Thesaurus Athenaios on V. Georgiu, for two hours, then back at the Kolnaki Hilton. Street agent Melina Perspikakis needed no high-volume instructions. She'd had the apartment suite lensed for video, wired for sound and sat.-linked to a private channel Athens to Torino.

Kari had direct-scope to the suite in question. That was little Perikardis, all right. But who was the great big guy with the bronzy beard? The image in a silken robe turned facing the lens.

Kari commo'ed the boss right away. Through the lens, photonic miracles configured object to light patterns to electronic emissions and at near the speed of light re-configured these as an image on-the screen in a condo in Torino a near straight-line thousand miles away.

"Ma'am," says Kari to the boss. "Get a load of who's in bed with whom. This you ain't gonna want to bee-leeve!"

****

A. Phoebus Belvedere ground the situation most finely through the mill of his wisdom. That they were lovers the world must never know. He was an immortal. Surely, his private life, if anyone's, was…well…private. But it was absolutely essential that he calm this lovely fellow, cool his anxieties and resolve the impossibly romantic, if sexually confused, dilemma he himself had created for Adonis…and for the lady…and for himself! Adonis, dear fellow, was in love. Even now, the little fellow sat up in their bed and expostulated on the pain his torn psyche was causing him. Phoebus would have turned back once more to offer balm and succor, except that the NetCom signaled a message coming through demanding audio connection.

"I don't believe it," says the voice on the E.Com.

"I beg your pardon? Who…"

"Smile, Pheebee. You're on Candid Video."

"Didi?"

"All yours, sweetheart."

"What are you…"

"You do make a charming couple."

"Ah! I understand that..."

"Your secret's out."

"I see. And there's a price attached to all this, I suppose?"

"Oh, sure. Your little friend knows what I want."

Phoebus knew a fury rising in him he had not known since Didi outfoxed him in that Trojan fracas in Asia Minor. What was Constancia keeping from him? She'd already swallowed most of Europe, and now she stooped to this petty little blackmail to add to her loot. Well, then. It was time for A. Phoebus Belvedere to retire, and the god Phoebus Apollo to muster his mighty powers. He would show this mere mortal woman what could be done when a god summoned his anger!

From behind him, a plea. "Niki?"

"Yes, dear boy."

"What am I to do?"

"Relax, sweet child. Everything will be all right."

"Come to bed, darling."

"I'm coming sweetness. I'm coming."

Once more the NetCom insisted. Phoebus peered into the office of the Chancellor of the University of Chicago. Had the gentleman been capable of a smidge of humor about himself he'd have admitted Didi had indeed, up to this point, enjoyed the upper laugh and that the derision heaped mercilessly upon him was well earned.

"Enough!" A. Phoebus roared. His aspect abruptly went melodramatic. "'The liquid laughter trickling from your lips becomes as dry sand in my throat.'"

"Archilochus," said Didi. Her on-screen grin was wise and derisive.

"That's not Archilochus," Phoebus objected. "That's Sappho, the sonnet begins 'Love disdained…' "

"You're wrong," Didi retorted. "Check it out for yourself. The Great Books says…"

"Damn it. I ought to know whom it is I quote," Phoebus snarled. "I'm the one inspired him."

"You're getting old. Phoebus."

"Nonsense. Gods don't get old."

"You're right. Then maybe it's time you grew up."

"Didi, will you stop that damned snickering?"

"I can't help it, dear brother. I keep remembering what you looked like sitting up in that bed when the video caught you. Though I must admit he is very sweet. Lend him to me some week-end, will you? Perhaps I can make a man of him."

"Didi! Have you no mercy?"

"Are you prepared to concede the wager?"

"Wager? Concede? I don't…"

"Let me remind you…Bunny's Retreat?"

"Damn that nonsense! Ocho is about to leverage the whole of Europe!"

"With your able, or unwitting, assistance."

"She already owns damned near all the money there is! Mankind will wear the shackles of her avarice!"

"You did teach her well."

"That little twit of a female will rule the world!"

"She said it herself…something about an aphrodisiac. Have you had any yet, Phoebus? Well?"

"Aphrodisiac. Didi, you've been eavesdropping!"

"Just keeping an eye on things, dear brother. Well? Ready to concede?"

"No! I have one last card to play."

"Calendar says July 06. 80. Couple hours and the year is up. You have until midnight, dear brother. Ta, now. And do enjoy yourself, dear. You do look to be in need of some relaxation."

A few seconds later, on the wings of whatever means gods use to move about, Phoebus emerged in Torino, the Hotel Agnelli. He asked for la signorina Ocho. Would the clerk please phone and say A. Phoebus Belvedere was on his way up. The supercilious fellow allowed as how Ms. Ocho was not receiving visitors this evening. Did he care to leave his card? In a rage of exhausted patience, Phoebus turned the insolent twit into a bowl of pasta Milanese and stormed toward the elevators.

At the penthouse he used his godly powers against the unyielding door and let himself in. No maid came to greet him. The salon was dark. Phoebus made his way to the bedroom. He stood in the doorway looking into the small pool of light given by a bedside lamp. Constancia sat up in bed. She was quite nude. She read aloud from a large book. Her voice was soft and hushed, as though she read to someone:

> …thus do you unfold yourself
> to me,
> as do the tender petals
> of a sleeping flower
> to warm winds and the loving light,
> to me,
> oh my other, my little sister, my love.

Phoebus focused his super-sight and from across the room and read the large lettered title of the book she held: Lyrics of Lesbia.

Connie Ocho caught sight of him in the five-meter wide mirror over her vanity table. She smiled at him. "Well, good evening, big fella. How it goes?"

"You were supposed to keep me posted, were you not? That was our agreement."

"Posted? Posted?"

"You've leveraged the continent of Europe and I knew nothing about it!"

"Oh. Well, y' know how it is. A girl gets busy…"

"And besides…Connie…you promised…"

"What's 'at, honey? What'd I promise?"

Phoebus stepped from the shadows of the door into the light. "Yourself. That's what you promised." He doffed his suitcoat. "And now that you have acquired what I have made possible, I intend to see you make good…" He'd kicked off his loafers. He unsnapped the buckle to the belt at his trousers. He let trousers and briefs drop. His manhood stood erect and ready when the coverlet next to Ocho stirred.

A feminine loveliness sat up. She was bare, dusky-pink and oh-so pretty squinting into the light. "Oh, hi, Pheebee. How are ya?"

"Karamina!"

Constancia Ocho smiled fit to crack her jaw. Kari drew the sheet up over her lovely breasts and managed to look a trifle abashed. She even contrived a blush. An info'tainment channel on the teleconceptor snapped on and was yammering about the newly-named G.W. Bush Dockyards at Houston Harbor and something about a threat of war. Phoebus knew only the hammering at his monumental ego. He examined the meaning of the word 'chagrin,' in English and in the original French. At the edge of the soft light of the vanity, and repeated in the merciless mirror, his enormous member wilted. Connie Ocho smirked, and Kari giggled.

****

Ada Caruso recalls that beautiful African morning in the first week of a blisteringly hot May. A stout, gentleman in a salt and pepper beard and sporty-conservative whites and calling himself Major Cyprian Moore appeared in the office of the garage. English, by the looks of him. "I am looking for someone," he said. "Or rather, I am trying to determine if he's come this way. Have you ever seen this chap?"

Ada examined the photograph. "Never seen this one."

"You're sure."

"We don' get very many Europeans come this way."

"Of course. Well, then, I shall require a vehicle. Something suitable for desert travel. And a driver."

"For how long you want this?"

"Oh, a few hours at most."

Ada had the English LandRover prepared. The gentleman signed lease papers and paid in advance. She fetched Ishaak and watched the Englishman mount and the vehicle vanish in the dust of the street. In the garage, she resumed her repair work. The visage in the photograph hovered in memory and imagination. The Italian. Bennino. *Il Pistone*. The motorbike rally. He'd made his pit stop and she remembered a minute's flirtation and things suggested. According to the local paper, such as it was, he'd lost the race. That had been six months back. He had returned a week later to rent the little truck. He was gone a few hours. Despite the difference in their years—she had to have ten on him, at least—they had made love and he was most gentle and most engaging. She raised her head over the edge of the vehicle hood. The item he'd asked her to keep safe lay where she had put it, wrapped in a tarp.

Ishaak's street friend Yakob Hatari had had the little digital camera from the fat Frenchman who was the capo at the field of the little grav-walker flying machines. The Frenchman had paid Yakob to take pictures through the window of the hotel the better to incriminate his fat wife and her current diversion. Yakob Hatari took many interesting photographs and was paid well for them. He in turn sold the little camera to Ishaak. Ishaak loved to peruse photography in the picture magazines, the men on horses, and the men on motor cycle machines and the men who played *jai jalai*, and the men and the women who swam near naked in the sea and who were called *too-reesti* and who stayed at the great white hotel in Obbía. That is how he had come to recognize the man as the one who rode the motor cycle machine when he came to Garage Caruso. A few days later, Ishaak had borrowed the mule belonged to Moishe Habash the Jew and he went into the desert to the place of the petrol pumps to take fresh bread and fruit to the Frenchman whose name was Castigné and that is when he again saw the big fellow of the motor cycle machine. That one drove a truck and he took down the antenna in the heat of the noon sun. My, how the white Europeans did perspire!

Every day at noon when people with a fig-seed of sense take the little sleep, Ishaak climbed the storage shelves of the Garage Caruso, way at the back, and way up high in the dark where it was cool. The storage shelves sat above the wall partitions and if one wished one could traverse the entire garage from one end to the other and look down and see sometimes what he should not see—like the Italian, the big fellow from the motor cycle machine. He was there when Ishaak returned late in the afternoon and he and la signora were in the little bed where la signora took her noon sleep and from his perch in the eaves Ihsaak saw things he should not see and he took a few more pictures. A week later, the fat European, he of the salt-and-pepper beard, the one who dressed in white—everything, his hat, his coat, his trousers, his shoes all white—he came to Iddan in a little grav-walker *aeroplano* and he asked la Signora Caruso about the petrol pumps and she gave him a truck, and Ishaak it was who drove back to the petrol pumps with the fat European in white but there was no one there. Ishaak tried to tell him. Not today. Not yesterday. "When?" says the fat European in white.

"Seven days ago." says Ishaak.

"Who?" says the fat European in white.

"Ah," says Ishaak. "Memory of a stupid Somali is not very good. But *fotografie*, they are of good memory."

An hour and a half of impossible heat and jouncing over desert terrain took them to two petrol pumps and a cinderblock shack. There was no antenna tower. Cray entered a repair garage. An adjoining office. A desk. A PC monitor and a computer of the obsolete digital hard-drive variety. He opened desk drawers and slid them shut. Somewhere between this place and Mogadishu the Pistone fellow had ditched the antenna lenses. Ungaroni probably had the discs—a billion dollars worth of information. It was just a matter of time before Paco made contact. He would want a cut. The visage of Constancia Ocho hovered in Cray's mental screen. And then that of Pistone. Ocho had moved as the invisible hand behind the ProCon Industries. Only afterwards was he himself made aware of the exposed position he'd occupied, and of the extent to which he and others had been expendable. The lovely fortune he'd earned over five years disappeared, and he'd spent the next four years as a pauper and a fugitive. Ocho's image hovered in memory, a head of red hair crowning a hard and knowing smile. Their paths would re-cross. Soon.

In the Ristorante Sorrento in beautiful downtown Iddan, Cray stood Ishaak a sumptuous meal. Confirmed: the Pistone fellow had been to the garage twice, once on the 14 of the third month of 82, during the race of the thousand kilometers. Ishaak had occasion to remember the same big Italian man had returned a week later, on the 22nd? Yes, it was the 22nd, to rent a Citroen quarter ton, the same vehicle Cray himself saw under repair—there was no mistaking the stove-in rear end because it was Ishaak himself had backed it up into an oncoming refrigerator truck, the same one driven by the Lebanese Muhammad Habibi, he of the big mouth and the loud voice who delivered fruits and vegetables to the big market run by that Indian rascal Tanibranath on Italo Balbo Boulevard. Well, then, Cray mused. The woman had lied. What's more, there were Ishaak Briccone's photographs. They showed unmistakably the big Italian taking down the aluminum tower. That would have been a week after the demise of Castigné.

The little Somali fellow protested he was a Muslim and that he didn't drink but after a third he confided, Signora Caruso and the motor-cycle man *fécero l'amore*, which is to say, they had made love, but that had been later, at 1 PM in the back of the garage in the room where madame took her little sleep. Safe to say Ishaak would have said more had he been asked more, but if the English man knew about the item in the blanket wrapped in the tarp and hidden in the joists of the garage he didn't say, and he didn't offer, and Ishaak was not so tipsy as to be making gifts.

Early next morning Ishaak backed the Rover into the garage. He was most surprised to see *Madamma* Caruso had hired a mechanic, a very tall, bronze-bearded fellow with enormous shoulders. The new fellow was changing tires on the American Chevrolet pickup. He looked up and smiled as Ishaak descended the Rover. Then, from where he stood at the key rack Ishaak could see the English man through the small window to Madame Caruso's office. Their voices grew louder and Madame shrieked. Ishaak hid behind the truck but the Englishman saw him. "Come out of there."

"*Signore?*"

The Englishman made a grab for him but Ishaak was too quick. He would have made it to the street but the skinny European woman made no effort to hide the big gun she held in her hand.

Ishaak saw Madame Caruso leaning in the doorway to the office. She had blood on her face.

The Englishman seized Ishaak by the hair and said to him very slowly, "You saw him take it down. You know what I'm looking for."

Ishaak was made to climb to the overhead storage shelves. He descended slowly with the heavy wrapping and he handed it down. The Englishman and the European woman laid it out on the floor of the garage. There lay the EM hoops. "Good," says the Englishman. He turned to Madame Caruso. "And the discs?"

The new mechanic had engaged the European woman in conversation.

"Cray," she said. "This fellow has something."

The mechanic came forward. "Signore? Can we talk?"

The three conversed most intently for a minute or two in the office. They came out into the garage together. Ishaak hid behind the Rover and listened.

"How long ago was this?" says the Englishman.

Says the other, "It would have been my first day of employment here —the 3rd of the month."

"You say he gave you a small package."

"Oh, yes, *signore. Madamma* Caruso made the package. I was sent to mail it."

"To what destination?"

"I don't remember the specific address, you understand, but I do remember it was somewhere in Switzerland."

That afternoon, *Madamma* Caruso closed the garage for the day. She and the mechanic took a siesta. She registered surprise at his having appeared as out of nowhere. Who was he, anyhow? The big fellow quickly allayed her anxieties and parried her questions and they spent an astonishingly pleasant afternoon together. When she woke from a most profound and refreshing sleep, he was gone. More surprising, her broken nose, her loosened teeth and the bruises and contusions the Englishman had visited upon her were all healed. She sat up in the narrow little bed in the store room anent her office and wished he hadn't elected to leave quite so soon.

Two days later, Cray and Endicotte rendezvoused at the Hotel Genevre. The Colonel dressed in quasi military clothes—jodhpurs and a field coat replete with swagger stick. "You lost them at the morgue, you say."

"Sonofabitch hit me with a hypo." Endicotte replied. "Be a month before I sit down."

"In the ambulance."

"Right! Got the Clinique General logo bigger'n life."

"Well then," Cray mused. "We know who he is—Armand Cirilotte Bombaste, doctor of forensic pathology, director of the morgue. Come, Charles. They shouldn't be hard to trace."

****

Once more, Phoebus belched into the quiet of Borgia's dining room. Mental calendar said the date was July 07 of the year 2080. An Earthian year had nearly passed. Measured by immortality, it was so little time. Yet, in the arithmetic of events, so much had happened. As for the wager, surely, now, DiDi wouldn't…

In a corner of the softly lit room, an invisible someone snickered.

Ammon's Horn

BOOK TWO

Ammon's Horn

1. Experiment Perilous

October, 2080: Sunset Boulevard, Hollywood.

At Bunny's Retreat, Phoebus had reduced his beautiful bronze beard to a scruffy stubble, paunched his belly and shuffled his gait. He went by the name of Harry ("Bunghole") Peebles.

Peebles, a sallow-faced, baggy-eyed, knock-kneed wino, was pursuing disaster. Daily, he vacuumed the ankle-deep carpets, (three stories) scoured six bathrooms, swabbed commodes and bidets, washed dishware, emptied ashtrays, and collected, washed, ironed, sorted and re-distributed a half-ton (he swore!) of feminine laundry. By night he fetched and carried, a lackey to as crass and carping a platoon of bitching ladies of pleasure as ever called themselves acolytes to the god of love—an association he would have stoutly denied if anyone had asked him. Chagrin gnawed his gut, that an immortal, once worshipped through the land of civilized men should be reduced to fetching and carrying in a brothel—wasn't that a bit much, now? He was vacuuming the carpet in the drawing room—the Pussy Parlor is what the girls called it—and someone had left on the telecom unit. A talking head naseled the News:

'...sandbags and landfill are just not doing the job,' so says

Senator Clench Grinder of Virginia. 'The waters of the Atlantic are rising,' she insists, and she claims downtown Norfolk is in three feet of water,. The Administration calls global flooding 'a lot of menopausal hysteria,' and the demand for high-tech levies a lot of pork. Senator BobbyJean Crunchit of Highbourne, Colorado, Chair of the Committee on Appropriations, is said to be 'taking the request under consideration.' Hamilton Glib here, reporting from Presidential HQ, DC II, Sciatica, NY.

And still no word on the whereabouts of Anatoli Polichuk, world's most renowned scientist who disappeared from a hospital in Geneva two months ago. Police are questioning employees of Clinique General Beaulieu. Says Chief Inspector Philippe Apollinaire of the Geneva Prefect: 'Insofar as there's been no demand for ransom, isn't it just as likely the absent minded professor wandered off and got himself seduced? snicker-snicker-snicker'

Peebles mused. That was not precisely what Chief Inspector Philippe Appolinaire had said, but let it pass. Bunghole Peebles popped a forefinger at the TeleCom unit, UBS Channel 33. A grave econo-guru was saying:

…what was once the United States of America, the greatest power and the most influential economic force on Earth, is now reduced to twenty-nine pieces of quarreling real-estate, a collection of carping, querulous little remnants of their former glory . But the future…not all bleak. Quebec, Nova Scotia and Newfoundland, in their recent quest for union across the old border…

Phoebus half-heard. His mind was preoccupied with the pleasure he would take in eviscerating one Connie Ocho and in reducing one Kari Agapé to strip steak. Avid imagination chained them to opposite sides of a mountain peak and giant buzzards...or was eagles?...never mind...would tear out their...Peebles popped his forefinger once more. Int.Sport 54 yammered:

In international sports: Michiko Bludthurst of Brass Knob, Kansas wins the Snuff Derby...five dead and three wounded, she brought home the ESPI package hidden in a condom dispenser in the lobby of a laundromat in Pazardzhik, Bulgaria—and speaking of the unaccounted for whatever became of Motor Cycle champ il Benni the Piston? Rumors have it the mighty Benni was abducted by a beautiful blond and is being held in a villa in the South of France...protesting mightily we bet. Oh, ha and ha.

The parlor phone rang. "Phoebus?"
"Didi?"
"We need to talk."
"Indeed!"
"My place. Around six tomorrow?"
"My duties?"
"You're relieved. Be here at six."
"Indeed!"
Someone switched the telecom unit back to UBS and a talking-head's voice rose, key of B-urgent:

This just in from DC II, Sciatica, New York: U.S. Secretary of Religion, the Reverend B. Mordecai Bloodworthy of the United Temple of Righteous Ardor, announced today establishment of a National Church of Salvation American to be headquartered in Langley Field, Virginia on the site of the former HQ of CIA until such time as Congress appropriates funds for building a National

Temple. The Reverend, meanwhile, continues his Crusade in the name of Jesus Christ All-American-Worldwide whose goal is nothing less than the conversion of everybody. In his capacity as a Cabinet Officer, the Reverend Bloodworthy has convened a conclave of world religious leaders to meet in Albuquerque, New Mexico. on the second of October.

But Phoebus had switched off. The squabbles of denominational churches were just not his cup of tea.

That evening at the Oriental Institute, University of Chicago, Didi was saying: "Ocho was your responsibility!"

"I'd have controlled her if you hadn't undercut me."

"Oh, come now, Phoebus. You were so besotted with her bod you wouldn't have known…"

"Besotted? Besotted?"

"Yes, besotted," Didi insisted. "How else explain your letting her leverage half the entire world without your knowing, or wanting to know…"

"Didi! I…"

"Oh, shut up, you look stupid with your mouth hanging open. In any case, I didn't ask you here to argue. Look!" At Didi's pointed finger, the telecom sprang to light. The scene presented was the laboratory at Montreaux.

"Ah-hah!" says Phoebus. "And don't we know her!"

"Hush, now," says Didi. "Just watch. And listen."

****

Connie Ocho stood on the catwalk above the intricate web of laser cannon, condensors and gravity-field generators with her pretty little head near dwarfed by a massive set of earphones. From the control panel Wanda raised the wall of quantum hydrogen on the manifest stage. The barely visible screen of pure energy cut the lab from floor to ceiling as a tenuous curtain of light. From the Master Control booth, Laszlo phased in the electromagnetic field. Slowly, over a span of a half hour, a soft humming and whining rose higher and higher in pitch. Then the Heisenberg governor flashed Quantum State.

"Nuclear fields established." Laszlo's voice came dry and flat through the earphones."

"Weak force actuated," Wanda responded. "Strong force entering… now! Dimensional vertices will breach. Prepare phase-in gravitation."

The humming sound rose in pitch and became a whistle, then a scream, and then it rose beyond hearing. The laboratory went silent. For ten vanishing seconds they looked into another world hardly daring to accept what their senses reported—a space, an opening into light and air, a seemingly infinite landscape one would have been tempted to step into. Then it was gone.

House lights came on again. "Well?" Madame Ocho shouted from the catwalk. "What happened?"

"Fifth dimension achieved," Wanda called back.

"Z'at all I get?" Ocho barked.

"That's it for now." said Wanda. "We followed the Polichuk protocol the way he set it up. But just as the gravitational field takes proper shape, it shuts down."

Ocho came stamping down the metal stairs to the lab floor. "Then you gotta be doin' it wrong!" She was fairly shouting. "I ain't payin' you to sit around playin' games. I want the five-an'-dime, or whatever you call it. I've got contract for a commercial center, a industrial complex and five condo developments worth 15 billion. and I want results and I gotta have 'em now!"

She found herself looking up into Wanda's plain-to-pretty face. The big woman looked down at her with something of a snide smile. "Sorry 'bout that, Ma'am. You don't like the way we work, go get somebody else."

"There ain't anybody else!"

"That right?" Wanda Waltari said softly. "Then get off my back, hum?"

Ocho ground her jaw and swallowed hard. "Wut's goin' wrong?" she asked more gently.

"As I say, this is the old man's protocol. We programmed it to go just the way he says. And it did. Except…"

"What, 'except'?"

"Well, Madame, it's got to do with what they call Bibitty-Bau curvatures. Quantum bubble-brane theory says Universe is like the skin on a bubble. And there's many, many bubbles whose infinite generation evolves as SpaceTime.' And sometimes a littler bubble gets pressured between two bigger ones and after a while its not a sphere anymore. Right now, proto-gravitational fields in the expansions are pushing our 4-dim. into a banana. And the big bubble, like next door, Polichuk says, it's got ten phys.-dims. plus the ST. Which is why we're the one getting squooshed. Fifty or seventy-five years ago they were trying to explain our universe's acceleration of expansion and they posited something called 'the great attractor." Except they couldn't find it. When we opened into that dim. a while back, we opened our four dims. into a fifth, and maybe a sixth. You follow?"

"Good enough. Go on," says Ocho.

"Then there's dimensional integrity," says Wanda.

"Wut's 'at?"

"Well, Madame, you remember from your phys classes in college: energy is neither created nor destroyed."

"It gets converted."

"Right! Well, same thing with dimensional integrity. It's neither created nor destroyed, it's re-configured. Which means our little dimension will never lose its integral sum over constituency, but it might add its S-over-C to the next dim. over. Like to say, we just might get sucked right in."

"I saw it, dammit! I saw…"

"What? What did you see?"

"I saw another world! Bubbles or bullshit, that was terra firma, and a sky and sun and clouds, the works!"

"I don't know what you think you saw, Ma'am. But it's dangerous for us to mess with it."

"I make dangerous! You do what you're paid for!"

Wanda Waltari mused. "Maybe the old man's holding out on us. Strikes me the dim.-field equations are skewed. There's got to be a point of equilibrium somewhere. We'll sift it, see what we come up with. Meantime, why don't you see if you can find the old man."

"Oh, I'm on it. Got agents in every country and back alley on seven continents. The old fart's hiding real good. But we know for sure is he ain't dead."

"How d'you know."

Ocho consulted her clip-board computer. "We intercepted a E-Gramm, Polichuk A. to Huffding B. Point of transmission, someplace in the south of France."

****

"Well, Phoebus. Your wiggly-jiggly Miz Frankenstein prepares to send the world down-tubes. What now?"

Phoebus stared at the tele-screen. "She is obsessed with real-estate. Hum. The religionists?"

"Interesting set of rogues. What are they up to?"

Didi popped her finger at the telecom. Scene shifted to the sleeping quarters of one Mordecai Bloodworthy.

****

Dawn bleared over the hills of Eastern Alabama and the birds had barely tuned up when a telecom voice shrieked in his ear. It was near a full minute before Garybob Mordecai realized it was the Rabbi Marshal

Foreshock trying to say something over and above the shriek of his own voice. The Reverend tried once more:

> Hey, Marsh, cool down, fella. I cain't make out wut yer tryna…Wut? Wut's disappeared? Ah know I ain't but jes woke up, but sounds like yew tellin' me…Noo Mexi-coe? Yeah, man. We bought them parcels ten dollahs a acre, ten thousand acres south o' Santa Fe jes las' month. They wut? Naow yew jes listen here, Marsh. Strikes me yew been pullin' too hard on that there Morgan David. Real Estate, it gits bought and it gits sold and mebee even annexed and appropree-ated, but it don't disappear!

Garybob Mordecai set the phone down on his pillow and hustled off to relieve an insistent bladder. When he returned Rabbi Foreshock appeared to have become more agitated than ever:

> Yayus, Marsh, the Malay Federation, they bought the whole lot. The Congressional District used t' be Texas, New Mek-sickko, Arizona, and them. Lord f'give me, but didn' we make a bundle? Wut's at? Malarki's threatenin' war? Him and the Malay Fed? Yeah, I follow. I understand. Wut I don't unnerstan' is this 'dis-appear.' That don't make no sense at-tall! Okay, Marsh. I gotcha. I'm takin' the next flight outta Mobile. Meet yew in Santa Fe, the Quadrille Hotel. Right. Bah, naow, Marsh.

****

Didi threw Phoebus her "I-know-something-you-don't-know" smile and the scene changed once more.

****

November 7, 2085 Peyote Wells, New Mexico, (pop. 13,000). The sun cleared the horizon at 6 AM. Sea gulls swooped and cawed in the desert air. Deputy Sheriff Joe Garcia claimed he could smell the ocean air all the way from Tucson Harbor. Garcia eased the department's second-best cruiser out of County Works garage in follow up to a spousal abuse report in Barranquilla. The neighboring town lay 15 miles north on New Mexico 187, parallel the Rio Grande along Interstate 25, and five miles northwest on Muchogusto Road. Seven miles up 25, habit said he'd gone too far. Experience said he should have passed BrokeSaddle Rock, but it hadn't registered with his corner-of-the-eye. There had been nothing there looking back. He was a good trooper. Things oughta be like they oughta be. Odometer against his daily trip sheet said he'd pulled out registering 73,588.03 elapsed miles. Present reading, 73,595.68. Simple arithmetic said he'd gone 7.65 miles. He hadn't overshot the Rock by more than a mile. Garcia rehearsed local data: Brokesaddle Rock stood 670 feet above the table-flat surface of the desert. It had got there before the snakes and prairie dogs. From any direction it was visible for fifteen miles.

In the early morning light, the Sergeant stood leaning against the fender of his cruiser peering into the brightening morning. He was roughly half way between Peyote Wells and Muchogusto Road. The Rock had always been visible from either point. So, where was it? Rangefinder In his binocs put Peote Wells water tower at 2 miles. Should have been more like 7. What happened to the other five? Desert mesas and stretches of road don't just disappear. Or do they? 'Less he was going loco.

Standard procedure said when everything else fails, call in. And that's what he did. Punched the button for Dispatch, Peyote Wells. "Unit Three-Ought-Five to HQ, 773 Dispatch, Garcia here."

"Munoz, dispatch."

"Hey, Munoz, something mighty funny happenin' here I can't find Brokesaddle Rock. I mean I'm on Muchogusto on Route two-five."

"Yeah?"

"And I can't find Brokesaddle Rock."

"Whatcha mean you can't find it?

"I mean it ain't here!"

"What you been drinkin', amigo?

"I swear, Lieutenant, I ain't touched..." and that's when the frequency quit. Munoz was saying something about officers who drank on the job, and kind of laughing his way through when it all went dead. Not even a hum in the speaker. Just dead. And when Garcia looked up again, the water tower wasn't there either.

****

Phoebus regarded the fading scene with grave interest. "I begin to catch the drift of events here, dear sister. Perhaps I'd best take a hand."

"Yes. Perhaps you'd best. Anything particular in mind?"

Phoebus grinned wickedly. "We've already sent in the clowns. And they have done well. Perhaps it is time for a bit of your style of things."

"The Twins? Of course. A marvelous idea!"

****

Villa Bonchance, Val Bourgette, Pontarlier, la France:

In the kitchen of the Villa Bonchance the handsome, bearded majordomo looked down at the plump, plain-to-pretty cook. "Who are you?" says she in pleasant surprise. She had paused in filling the dishwasher, and he in preparing a tray of aperitif.

"You don't remember?" says he.

"I never forget," says she. "I wondered if you had."

"Dear ChiChi. It was Brussels, in '59."

"No, dear," says she. "It was Amsterdam, in '61."

"And you were *maitrésse de salon*, a *soiree* for the *literati*," says he.

"I was madame of a *maison de plaisir*," says she, "an orgy for the Spanish ambassador, and my name was, and is, Berti."

"Just testing your recollection. You are as beautiful as ever, you know."

"And you're just as fullashit as you were."

"What are you doing here?" says he.

"Keeping an eye on an old friend," says she. "You?"

"Keeping the world from crumbling. It's much the same thing."

"The Polichuk?" says she.

"Among others," says he.

"Need help?" says she.

"All I can muster," says he.

"You're on," says she.

****

In the dining hall, Doctor Bombaste regarded his guests at the long table. To his right was seated Doctor Kirsten Lagerquist, a very tall and quite beautiful woman, and an engagingly homely little man who gave his name as Paco. To his left, the subject of their experiment, the big athletic fellow, an American—Italian, originally, but that was neither here not there. Doctor Tisibon sat at the far end. Bombaste waited until they'd arrived at sweets and aperitif and when everyone was more or less at ease he raised an eyebrow and Tisibon introduced the evening's thesis. He was at pains to describe his theory of *la connaisance*. He addressed his remarks to Kirsten, out of professional courtesy perhaps, and to the athletic gentleman. "And such," he was saying, "is what we attempted to effect…"

Doctor Lagerquist interjected: "But what have you done?"

"Rather to ask, what have we accomplished?" Tisibon corrected. "*En premier*, the objective…as says my colleague, we have isolated the mental process. We have transferred from brain to machine via trigital photonic process. Isolated, and transferred."

"Never this has been done before." Bombaste emitted a profound sigh, as out of a supplication for patience. "So, pardon, if you will, we have little anticipation of the difficulties. But, Polichuk, he was physically infirm. He might not have survived long enough, so there was the gentleman calls himself van Horn. We enlisted his assistance."

"And?" Kirsten sat bolt upright. The amazed young man, sitting opposite her, smiled in benign contentment, if not childish amusement.

"And," Bombaste continued, this time with some hint of defense, "there comes at this point what we will charitably refer to as the interference." Here he glared at Paco. "As a result there is transferred instead the mind of Aram Gregorian."

"And?" Kirsten insisted.

"And what we did not anticipate...we transferred also that of the Van Horn." Having delivered himself of this peroration, Bombaste threw up his hands and pursed his lips and raised his brows in an ineffably Gallic gesture of resignation.

"You have created a monster! " Kirsten hissed in amazement.

"Ah?" said Tisibon. "May I suggest you ask him."

At which point there intruded one whom the guests might have taken for Bombaste's majordomo, but if that is what he was no one was more surprised than the good doctor himself. In one afternoon, he had acquired a major d'. and, to his amazement, a round, rubicund woman in his kitchen who announced she was his cook, though who had arranged for their hire was beyond him. His colleague Tisibon was quite incapable of such practical enterprise. The tall bearded fellow leaned over Bombaste's shoulder and whispered into his ear. Bombaste's guests might have taken the doctor's response to be reaction to the message, which response would not have been entirely misplaced. He had half turned in his chair. From his seated position he strained to get a good look at the chap. That one stood attentive, awaiting further instructions. "Tell him..." Bombaste hesitated. "Show him in."

A minute of silence passed. The broad doors to the dining hall closed on the majordomo. A minute later, they opened once more and the major d' announced: "Colonel Cyprian Moore."

The new arrival stood for a time and took in the full import of what he saw. To those regarding him, this was a man of some fifty years, six-feet tall, rather full of figure and dressed in breeches, boots, field coat and a jaunty cap. At his hip he wore a holstered sidearm. "Madame? Gentlemen?" says that one. "I beg pardon for this intrusion,"

Bombaste formally introduced those seated about the table. "Please," says he, "join us."

If anyone at that table was apt to be struck speechless it would have been Kirsten for the gentleman who took a chair before her was none other than the same person she had seen in Le Brassus at the video shoot, and again in that hour in which Benni Pistone was struck down. Colonel Moore accepted a glass of wine. Kirsten studied him intently, but the Colonel seemed unable to take his eyes from the smiling visage of the young man who once had been Benni Pistone.

Paco Ungaroni regarded the Colonel with a look of anger and displeasure. Colonel Moore returned that one's glower with a wry smile. There was idle if congenial chatter. Then, the forthright Bombaste spoke up. "To what do we owe the pleasure of this visit, Colonel?"

"Thank you Doctor," says the Colonel. "But I don't expect you'll view my intrusion with pleasure. At risk of appearing gauche, I have secured your grounds. My four associates and I are armed and they have instructions—no one is to leave, nor to enter." The portly Colonel was looking directly at Pistone. "You see," says the Colonel, "to be most candid, I am a thief. On a considerable scale. I had been prepared to steal a fortune of monumental proportions. Prepared. Yes. But I was thwarted. Because there was another party…" and here he looked intently at Paco Ungaroni, "…another party who out of spite, if you will, or in retaliation, that party intervened."

"Yes?" says Tisibon. "What has this to do with us?"

"Oh, my dear Doctor," says the Colonel with a hearty guffaw. "It has everything to do with you. You have reserved it for me—the key to that fortune."

Bombaste spoke up. "You refer to an individual who went by the name of Bennino Pistone, I take it."

"None other."

"In that case, Monsieur you are disappointed again. That psycho-neurological entity is no more."

The Colonel expressed some skepticism. "You are going to tell me that is not Pistone."

"Let me demonstrate," says Bombaste. He turned to the Pistone entity. "Tell us, sir. Who are you?"

The young man looked away with some diffidence, then his gaze fell upon Kirsten and in a soft voice consonant with his statement he said, "I am Aram Gregorian."

A stunned silence befell those seated at the table. Kirsten regarded the speaker with a gentle smile.

Said the one claiming to be Gregorian. "Do not be alarmed. No real harm has befallen Doctor Polichuk. At our last 'contact,' shall I say? he was well, if a bit impatient."

"What kind of chicanery is this?" says the Major. "Do you think me a fool?"

"No, Colonel," Bombaste assured him. "Though one can appreciate your dismay. This is indeed Aram Gregorian. Yes, and it may well be, in addition, one who calls himself van Horn. And, if you permit, one Anatoli Polichuk. Mercifully, one at a time."

The Colonel regarded the Pistone entity with marked skepticism. "All of these in the body of Pistone?"

"Indeed," said Bombaste. "One might say our experiment exceeded expectations."

"Really," said the Colonel. "And Pistone?"

"You yourself saw to the demise of Pistone." All at the table turned to regard Kirsten Lagerquist. "I was there in Le Brassus. I saw what your man attempted."

"You saw?"

"I was seated no more than three meters from you."

The Colonel's gazed at her intently from across the table. "You're the lady in the other auto!"

"Yes. Thanks to you, the Pistone you seek may be no more."

"He went into coma, I hear."

"Yes. I am the physician attended him first. He suffered massive head injury—severe concussion. Now, thanks to these gentlemen and their heavy-handed methods, he is the shell of a body inhabited not by one psyche, but by three. Whatever you sought to accomplish, Colonel, I am afraid you have rendered it beyond your reach, or that of anyone."

"This is incredible!" The Colonel stared at Benni Pistone in disbelief. "Is this true, Doctor?"

"Oh, I am afraid so," said Bombaste. "Perhaps you will forgive us our zeal, but we, Tisibon and I, we had waited many years to acquire an adequate body with which to demonstrate the practical applications of our theory. Understandably, it had to be one fairly young and strong. And, necessarily, it must be irreversibly comatose. Our patience was rewarded. He almost, as the saying goes, fell into our lap." Bombaste continued with some pride. "We have, Tisibon and I, without subsidy from anyone, and at the cost of living like paupers, assembled our laboratory here in Pontarlier. Believe me, before we attempted to transfer the psychic entity that is Polichuk, we did everything possible to assure ourselves...how to put it? There was 'nobody home'." Tisibon stifled a giggle.

"Well, I don't believe a word of it," says the Colonel. "This is a clever little scenario designed to put me off. Well, Pistone? What've you to say? I will have my discs, you know, no matter what I have to do, and no matter to whom! Am I clear?"

At this point all seated at the table regarded Gregorian-Pistone, with amazement. He had sat up, and now he leaned across the table with alarm in his eyes. "Listen to me," he said. "You must listen! I have spoken with Polichuk…"

"You have what?" Bombaste shouted.

"It was 'on the way,' shall we say?" Gregorian-Pistone's eyes widened as though staring into a well of remembering. "He and the van Horn fellow, and I, we 'met,' so to speak. In 'passing,' if you will." The speaker smiled his bemusement. "In the TimeSpace of the mind."

"Bien!" Bombaste insisted. "And what did he say?"

Gregorian-Pistone gazed as into an abyss. "Something about our being in danger. He said there is a woman involved. He said she does not know what it is she does!" Here Gregorian-Pistone closed his eyes the better to see. "He spoke of someone named 'Wanda.' Said he explained to this 'Wanda,' because the other did not want to hear him, something about…'the instability of the geodesic of dimensional matrices.' Does that make sense? He said it is not revealed in the equations. Polichuk said something about the SpaceTimes being interdependent. That we 'share' them, whatever that may mean. Then he left me with this incredible, this incomprehensible picture of a net…"

"A net?" says Tisibon.

"Hush!" says Bombaste. "Please. Go on."

Gregorian-Pistone paused. He closed his eyes once more. "'Like the interstices of a net,' is what he said. Ten sides. Connected. One side common to each of others. Not to increase one but at the expense of the others because the universes are not infinite, they are expansive only within the totality. Like bubbles, he said. And something about…real estate? From the fifth dimension someone is going to make 'real-estate'? But, perhaps I mis-understood. He says to open one door is to close another. The Earth it will… vanish."

"Oh, come now, good people," says the Colonel. "Just how much am I expected to swallow?"

Gregorian-Pistone stared wide-eyed and unseeing at the Colonel. "Polichuk says to tell her," he was fairly shouting now, "tell Ocho she cannot have her 'real-estate'…she will destroy the world!"

"Who?" shouted the Colonel. "Did you say Ocho? Connie Ocho?"

"That was the name. Ocho. Do you know this person?"

To the amazement of all, the one calling himself Colonel Moore burst into laughter. "Oh, yes Doctor Gregorian, or whoever you purport to be." With a grim determination, he turned to Kirsten. "As you say, Doctor, you were the first to attend the stricken Pistone. I assure you, it was not our intention to injure him. What we pursued, if you will, was something he stole from us. Four computer discs. At your behest, Paco, he took them. Oh, come on, Paco. Don't protest, we have photographs of your big boy taking down the antenna. And additional photos of him and the Caruso woman, so please, don't belabor me with petty lies, eh? We've retrieved the antenna. But not the discs. The Caruso woman, I hardly think her clever enough. It is my belief you and Pistone planned to sell them back to me. Or to Ocho. Whichever made the better offer, eh? In any case, we know you flew direct from Somalia to Geneva. My man Charles was on your trail the moment you landed. And it was I who picked up your trail from Geneva to Le Brassus. Yes. We have searched Pistone's room, of course. And Paco's things. No, I believe Pistone had them on his person. Paco?" Paco glowered "Or, to reconstruct, a man lies in the street seriously injured. He knows who the parties are pursuing him. He realizes he may die at any moment, and—here is what I take to be a very reasonable conjecture—whom, does he see hovering over him in that fateful street? Why, a beautiful woman. And, apparently, a doctor. What does he do? He either tells her where the discs are hidden, or, assuming he has them on his person, he gives them to her, and with his last breath says to her, 'hide these.' Or, he manages to slip them to you, Paco. Well? Which was it?"

Kirsten returned the Colonel's query with a stony look. "I'm sure I don't know," she said.

At which point, as though on cue, the door to the kitchen opened and there stepped forth into the light of the dining hall a spare, tow-headed individual.

"Charles?" queried the Colonel.

"Been through her things," said the tow-head. "Zilch. Ditto the Macaroni." The Charles personage regarded Kirsten with an appreciative leer on his face.

"Enough!" the Colonel shouted. "I will have those discs and I will have them tonight! And if I have not made myself clear…Charles, see how persuasive you can be with the lady, hum?"

Charles stood behind Kirsten's chair. Just as she turned as though to stand, he took her arm, and then her hair, pulled her to her feet by the hair and held her at a rigid arm's length and made a fist, drew back his arm as though to strike, all this in seconds. The others at the table sat horrified and uncomprehending because the other had risen from his chair, had moved about the far end of the table and in seconds, faster than comprehension followed, he seized the outstretched arm of the one called Charles and quite pulled him about and he struck that same Charles fair in the nose.

Karen regained her balance, and her composure. She stood looking at him, at the swarthy face, at the unshaven cheeks and into the near wondering gaze of the boy who lived yet under the man's heavy features. She was flushed and drawing heavy breath. She reached for the chair to assure her balance and he reached out and drew her close once more, to comfort her, to…to what? She was at a loss to know because there crowded to her immediacy the question: Who? Which one?

"Stand away!" The Colonel stood the other side of the table. He'd drawn his weapon. "Enough of histrionics. I say, Charles? Are you alright?" The one called Charles had risen to his feet quite bloodied about the nose and in something of a rage. In American English he sputtered and cursed expletives and obscenities at the other and swore he would be avenged.

Paco was shouting across the table, "Benni! Benni!" and the Colonel was chiding Charles about putting himself to rights and something about asserting his manhood and not losing his grit over a bloody nose, during which minute or two the majordomo had unobtrusively re-entered the dining hall.

Alphonse stood in the light of the over-table Tiffany. He was very tall and very imposing. His voice carried an astonishing authority, soft and gentle as he might make it. He suggested that the Colonel was being ever so peremptory in his demands. The situation was, actually, of some delicacy. Further, he suggested, few things were so urgent that they would not look less so after a good night's sleep. In which regard, he had taken the liberty of preparing for each of the house's guests a room. Would they now, please, accompany him that he might show them to their night's accommodations.

Ammon's Horn

2. The Big LBO

Predidential Towers, Chicago.

Connie Ocho settled back into her enormous lazee-lounger with a CubaLibre and a cigarette and prepared for the next notch to her barrel. On the telecom, the talking head narrowed his eyes and set his jaw and summoned his finest *basso*:

> From the nation's capital, Peter Porter here bringing you live the proceedings of this extraordinary emergency session of the Board of Congressional Directors of the United States Incorporated at, DC II, Sciatica, in the beautiful Catskills of New York state. From the well of the chamber of the Executive, the combined Board and Directorate of Congress is being called into session by Chairman of the Federal Reserve, Chairman of the Department of the Treasury, President of the Securities and Exchange Commission and unerring leader and guide of our people in matters monetary and fiscal, the right honorable Morgan Ackerbee."

The Speaker of the Chamber intoned: "Mistah Acka-bee." Sustained applause. A little man with a shiny bald head and wearing enormous black-rimmed spectacles stepped up onto the podium. The microphone was adjusted for him. He began in a robust baritone:

> Ladies and Gentlemen of the Executive Congress, good people of the United States, Incorporated. Pursuant to the friendly buyout of the Federal Government under the benevolent auspices of BuyAmerica in 2029, the former states of the former United States were re-organized as Congressional Districts under the brilliant leadership of Mabel Leland Kamper of BuyAmerica, Hampshire-Holyoak Investments, South Hadley Falls, Massachusetts, and Wahneeta Buckettete of Oklahoma Fund, Drumbeat, Oklahoma. Under Kamper-Buckette, Plan One, power and authority of the former government devolved upon our present Congressional Executive. Under its authority our former fifty two states were reorganized into a set of twelve units, the Confederated Districts of the Incorporation, this re-organization much more in keeping with population distribution and each governed by its own central financial institutions responsible to Federal Commerce Commission and the Congressional Executive.

> Thus was our new nation created—the United States, Incorporated. By so doing did we generate maximum cash by selling off inessential and/or unproductive states. Nevada and South Dakota spring to mind. The idea was for the syndicate to then flip the core business back to the USI on a tax-free basis. A private tax ruling from the IRS was suggested as advisable. Corporate America was to be defined geographically as all of the former USA east of the Mississippi. It was suggested that under Kamper-Buckettet II we might minimize disruption of major-league sports, and also to keep the arches if we elect to

include St. Louis and Minneapolis in any agreement. In any case, we, the people of the United States, Incorporated would then be back to the status our country occupied on the eve of the Louisiana Purchase, though we did insist on owning Florida free and clear. All private property on the block remained that of its current owners, and those property owners were free to stay-put, or to sell out and move back east with the rest of us.

Asking price? A figure of 950 trillion was mentioned. This was two and a half times our GNP for the year 2030, a very attractive multiple for what had become museum piece property, most especially after the effects of the warming of our planet were no longer a question of debate, and in view of the loss of our former coastlines.

What did it get us? In view of the enormous debt run up by the previous administrations, under the former USA charter, we eliminated $500 billion a year in interest payments; we balanced the federal budget; without the national debt the Federal Reserve set domestic interest rates without worrying whether the Japanese or the Europeans would buy our Treasury Bonds because without deficit and without a national debt we didn't issue any.

In 2050 the friendly leveraged buy-out of our National Plat of Survey, Atlantic to Pacific, was begun. The sale of the State of North Dakota to the Maritime Commonwealth of Canada was completed in 2042. Such spin-offs continue. To date, this brings to four the number of poorly productive states being considered for lease or sale in the last seven months. To date, lease of the high and dry remains of former California-Arizona to the Indo-Malay Federation is all but complete. Outright sale of the State of New Mexico is even now being finalized with the Ministry of Finance in New Jakarta. Similar discussions weighing the sale of Nevada and Utah to the Consortium of Japan-Korea-Singapore are underway in Wichita. And on the buying side, if you will, Washington and Banque Toronto are at this very moment finalizing our purchase of the Maritime Provinces—Labrador, Nova Scotia and Newfoundland. The recent disturbance surrounding the Province of Quebec has been settled amicably and acquisition of that goodly Province by the USI is not precluded.

Today, under Kamper-Buckette II, discussions proceed in Toronto with an eye to the imminent formation of what will be called the Commonwealth of North America. To paraphrase the late, beloved Senator Mabel Kamper herself, there will be brought into play such truly choice properties as to make make further friendly buy-out of the United States Incorporated a particularly attractive instrument for the American people. In light of which, the Plan concedes, one might rather have owned Japan, Germany, or even Taiwan, except that those countries, alas, hold most of our debt. Hence, they have more logically become buyers rather than sellers. And, admittedly, such take-overs have been hard to sell politically. But, says the Plan, "the buy-out of the USI itself will be a politician's dream. Anent the joining of the USI with such productive units such as Manitoba and Saskatchewan, Americans will pay off their huge national debt, permanently fund social security, establish a universal and efficient Medicare, make prescription drugs plentiful and inexpensive and still permit us to enjoy a significant, if somewhat smaller, country."

And where does John Q. Public benefit from this? Consider: Each man, woman and child in the US will receive a $ 40,000 IRA account. The average citizen, 16 years old, will have an account worth $150,000 at the time of retirement, age 75. Our budget problems and the perennial problem of funding Social Security will be permanently solved.

Some economists and the carp-and-moan members of the press have said that these huge financial deals create no real economic value. They claim the market is being driven by the greed of corporate management, abetted by vested interests in the Directorate of Congress and a laissez-faire attitude in Whitehouse II. Such attitudes are themselves unproductive and offer no viable alternatives. Rather than criticize, won't we be better off helping our over-crowded and industrious neighbors use their strong currencies to invest in good old America, while we enable ourselves to put our own economic house in order? As a pragmatic and mercantile people who know both the price and the value of things, we have a rare opportunity to regain our economic momentum. Let us not permit such an historic moment slip away. A smaller, more focused America after shedding unproductive assets will emerge a more formidable competitor in the global marketplace.

"We're on the way, kid. Bank Toronto's gonna run the whole shootin' match." Connie lay back in her lounger. Her lips embraced a smile. Her eyes glazed. Fatigue weighted her eyelids. Good rum plied its magic and she drifted into that blend of memory and fantasy that is the absurdity of dreams. She was fourteen again, and her cousin Carmen, at sixteen, knew everything worth knowing and she laid it on. "Y'gotta yewmer yer hormones," her cousin Carmen used to say, "or head'em off at the pass, 'cos mutha naytcher she don't care how she jerks y'aroun'." Connie roused. It had to be hormones, and the warm summer evening. It had to be the view from twenty stories over Chicago and the cool breeze coming in off the Lake Michigan that made for the mood, the surge of half buried thoughts and moody memories. But why Carmen? She hadn't seen her elder cousin in fourteen years. From below, in the ribbon that was Lake Shore Drive, came a great honking and howling and Connie Ocho made out the unmistakable red and white lights of fire engines blinking and the gestalt that is memory playing on chance and on confused desire gave her back Carmen. "Tell Mister Cienfuegos this evening's meetin' is off." The child who was Constancia Ocho heard the words, and the woman she was becoming understood. She said nothing. She hung up the receiver of the telephone gently, quietly, as through a kind of prescience.

But Kari roused her to the light and cool of the salon. Connie Ocho and Kari Agapé listened intently to chairman Morgan Ackerbee's closing words.

"Consortium. Eastern Europe and Asia. And the Russki's. Everybody's gettn' on board. International. Means we're gonna run the whole works," said Connie brightly. "Krise," she chirped. "How big's 'at plat o' survey gonna be, hey?"

"Our people in the Hague are working on that now."

Kari Agapé sat back in the deep recesses of the divan. She sipped a cup of hot cocoa. "Connie?"

"Yeah?"

"We got trouble. The Malaysians, they've been on com. all day. Something about…"

"Hang on, kid. There's something new coming on."

A talking head addressed them dispassionately:

This just in, and believe me, folks, I'm not making this up: From Albuquerque, in what was the State of New Mexico: Answering to complaints from local law-enforcement in the area, State officials report survey teams dispatched to the southern regions of the state are mystified at their inability to locate certain towns along State Route 14 and on a line running north-northwest from Peyote Wells, just north of Las Cruces near the Mexican border to Lake Sumner and Santa Rosa in the central part of the state.

As we speak, authorities in Albuquerque are attempting communication with towns strung along US Route 40. Word has it there is no response from Alamogordo, the former US sci-tech proving grounds. They have not been able to raise the towns of Tularosa, Three Rivers, Oscura, Carizozo, Ancho, Corona, Duran and Santa Rosa. Towns farther north along US Route 40 are reporting widespread alarm. Rumor has it that this is a plot on the part of the Malaysian government in Jakarta to reduce the population in its newly acquired territories, a rumor Jakarta denies...

Hang on, folks. Word just in from Albuquerque. Oh, my gawd! It seems New Mexico State Police were in contact with local law enforcement in Tucumcari when communication was cut off. Efforts to re-establish contact have proven futile. The acting governor of the state has dispatched helicopters to the area. And that's all we have. Stay tuned for further developments.

"What d'y' make of that?" Connie Ocho asked.

"It's what I've been trying to tell you," said Tary. The Malaysians in San Diego, they're claiming their real estate is disappearing."

"Wha...?"

"That's what they say. Like we sold them a bad deal, or we're playing some kind of shell game. Connie, what's going on?"

"Don'know, kid. Unless it's got some connection with..."

Connie Ocho's eyes popped and she screamed, "Terreeee! Get me Geneva, pronto!"

****

Alone in her bed chamber, Didi des Dieux snapped her fingers and the Executive Chamber faded from the left half of her screen.

She snapped them again and Connie Ocho and Kari faded from the right. Didi drew a deep breath. She moved to the windows. The first morning light bathed the skyline of the great City of Chicago. "Didi, dear," says she to herself, "Phoebus claims to have her under control. But looks to me the human world is down-the-tubes—literally. Agreement or no, we'd better intervene before we lose room in which to maneuver. But, dear," says she to herself, "we do have a man in the field. Ah, yes," says herself to herself. "A man. And that may be the problem. Let's have a look-see at what's goin' down in Geneva town." She chuckled at her own wit. Didi was alone in her suite, which was fortunate. Any sensible on-looker might have thought she was losing her head to witness the magnificent 6-3 of Didi des Dieux pull her flimsy *nèglige* over head and vanish as the garment rose.

****

Meanwhile, back at the Villa Bonchance, Mackenzie van Horn wakened at 2 AM and within a sleepy minute realized he was in a strange place and that he did not know where to find the facilities. By dint of poking about in the vast, two-story house he found what he needed and as he stood fuzzy with sleep at the porcelain bowl the strangeness of the house bore in on him, and something like the following colloquy ensued between the Mackenzie and the van Horn:

"Mac? Yeah? Where the hell are you? Sheeit, man, I'm right here. No shit, Sherlock. Where's 'here'? Yeah, see what you mean. Like, who were those people at dinner? Hey, d' you dig the blonde? Oh, my gawd, wasn't she...? To die for, man! To die for! And go down smiling! Doesn't answer the question. What'd you get yourself into now? Well, I remember going to the *clinique*...the clin-neek...dig my crazy French. And I remember the little guy. Yeah! Polly-chuck. That's the one! And me makin' like a agent of the gumm-mint..." He dropped his voice two octaves. I am agent van Horn, representing her excellency Madame des Dieux of the University...oh, I was im-press-sive, I was! You see them cats step back? And then? The ruckus in the driveway...that little sonofabitch, Tizzybuns, got my gun! And the other one, Bumblast, drove the ambulance. I remember some at dinner. Lot's of talk, real scientific." Van Horn looked down at his endowment. Kry-so-my-tee! Ain't I some well-hung stud? Didn't ree-lize..."

By which point in the colloquy he had stepped away from the bowl and over to the sink. He stooped at the tap washing his hands and, by dint of years of habit, he splashed warm water on his face.

There were guest towels nearby to which he helped himself, and he rubbed his face and opened his eyes into the wide mirror before him. The face that looked back was not his own. Mackenzie van Horn turned about to look behind him. There was no one there. He turned back once more. The other fellow was still there. Van Horn blinked his eyes. As did the other. He assayed a grimace. Stuck out his tongue. The other answered in kind. Through an act of courage such as he'd never exhibited before, van Horn lifted his hand and, slowly, intently, he watched the other fellow do the same. They, van Horn and "this other guy," stood in a white tee-shirt. Each one had his right hand set upon the top of the head. Van horn stepped closer. He had never seen this face before. He stood stock still.

If...he broached the matter quire obliquely...if there was any connection, this other fellow also had curly hair, not iron grey, but rather deep chestnut brown. And this other fellow stood, not van Horn's five-seven. He had to be damned near six-one. And he wasn't the cute-round-masculine of a van Horn. This fellow was big jawed, and broken nosed, and fleshy lipped, and he was . . swarthy? Colloquy re-commenced:

"Mac? Who he? Don'know. Why's he? Whips me. Why're we? Yeah. He's..."

There had to be confusion, and then a great deal of disbelief that gave way but slowly to the inexorable fact that he was not asleep, but awake, not dreaming, but confronted with a waking reality. But this was a reality which in no way conformed to any he had known in his forty-two years. Then came a bit of terror, and a frantic struggle to explain. Yes. Which meant he went scrambling about in and amongst his wits to re-assemble, to remember...

"Mac, you dumb shit! Did you volunteer for this?"

Memory insisted. He had dozed off in the ambulance.

Then, voices. His own. And others. He had spoken with Anatoli, the phys-whiz. And somebody else was there. Like three guys in a dark room and nobody knows anybody else. "Are we dreaming, Mac? No, I don't ree-lee think so. Then I got a news flash, man. We ain't in the same bod we come in! Tizzybuns, and his fat friend. They had something to do with this." Van Horn assayed a look down at himself. He passed his hands over his chest and down to the firm washboard of his abs. In the mirror, he watched himself roll his massive shoulders, and flex magnificent biceps. He ran his hand down into his groin. "Woo-wheee! This ain't the bod my mamma gave me."

Now fully awake, and aware of the size and of the sheer muscularity of the body he inhabited, van Horn stepped from the brilliant light of the bath into the dim corridor. A thrill of mischievous excitement bubbled up in him. He had no intention of going back to his bed. Muffled voices rose from below and up the servant's staircase. Who might this be up and about at this hour. Van Horn strode easily. He was trying on his new body and so engrossed was he in the pleasure of it that he did not see the party standing at the head of the stairs until he was almost upon her and she spoke. As it was, he'd difficulty concentrating on what she said so taken was he with her powerful beauty hovering in moonlight.

"Van Horn."

"Yes, Ma'am! Reporting for duty, Ma'am!"

"There is work to do!"

"Then fill me in, Ma'am. I got a feeling some-thing big's going down. Or coming up?"

"Tell me—how do you feel?"

"I feel great! Matter of fact, never felt better."

"Then prepare for a shock. Something has gone wrong."

"Hah! Ain't a day of my life something hasn't gone wrong. An autobiography of errors. Charlie Endicotte, he says…"

"You are in Pistone's body."

"Yeah! Ain't this a bitch?"

"You, and perhaps the others as well."

"You will pardon the expression, Ma'am, but the world ain't gonna be big enough!"

"Enough clowning, van Horn. There is work to do."

"Clowning, Ma'am? Who's clowning? I just got me a six-foot, muscle-bound bod to work with. Show me the waaay!"

"Oh, gods, what have I to contend with? Listen, van Horn."

"I'm listening! I'm listening!"

"Ocho…"

"Who? Oh, yeah, the take-over arteest. Hey, lemme at'er!"

"She'll be in Switzerland, Tuesday the seventh."

"Yeah? Yeah?"

"The *Ecole d'Etude de la Science Physique*, just outside Montreaux."

"Yeah? I'll be there!"

"Now, here is what I want you to do."

"Hang on, Ma'am. I mean, with all due respect."

"Van Horn, be careful."

"Yes, Ma'am. But, what I wanna know is…hmmm…what's in it for me? I mean, I been through a lotta trouble. It ain't like every day a guy gets his brains shuffled…"

"There is nothing so serious that you won't be a fool and a rascal. Is that it?"

"It's like my daddy used to say, look to what side the bread is buttered."

"And?"

"What it comes down to is exclusive rights."

"I see."

"I mean, shucks Ma'am, I've been a five-seven runt all my life. Now I'm in this…this ma-cho bod, this hgnnnnn beautiful hunk of bone and muscle and maybeso I'm gonna have two or three guys looking at me so's I can't even pee in peace…"

"I'll do what I can, van Horn. But I make no firm promise."

"Yeah. And one other thing."

"Really!"

"Just one night."

"What makes you think you would survive it?"

"I might not, but hgmmmmm…what a way to go!"

Madame des Dieux bent close and whispered in his ear. What she said registered over and under and beyond her words and her nearness was a terrifying arousal. When she had spoken, she as suddenly vanished. Mack Van Horn stood in the darkness at the top of the stairs suddenly alone and perspiring and he wondered if he might not have dreamed it all. But, no. This enormous erection was very real! At the bottom of the stairs there was a door under which shone a bright sliver of light. The voices came to him now much more clearly. He pushed and entered.

But Mackenzie van Horn got shoved aside. It was Aram Gregorian took center psyche-stage, he who emerged the other side of the door into the stone and steel kitchen. The couple at the table turned to regard him— Paco Ungaroni, and Kirsten, the beautiful Doctor Lagerquist.

"Benni?" Paco Ungaroni looked up at him with hope and expectation in his homely face. "*Sei tu?*"

"Afraid not, sir. It is I, Aram Gregorian. May I?"

"Please." Kirsten Lagerquist drew a chair for him.

Paco regarded him unbelievingly. "Gregorian? You gonna tell me you not my Benni?" he said.

"Believe what you will." says Gregorian. "That is for you to decide." The well polished words were an anomaly emanating from this big, rough-cut figure. "Perhaps what I sought to demonstrate to Doctor Lagerquist in Upsala, with respect to the Ruiz fellow, and the Janssen woman, now becomes presented in terms of the outrageous. I can only ask you to put down your skeptical guard for a moment." Gregorian had fetched himself a cup and helped himself to coffee. "Yes, Paco, to answer your question: it is I, Gregorian."

"*Ma, ti dico che quest' é una cosa incredibile,*" says Paco.

"Hah," says Gregorian. "You should see it from my side! I am at once an object of wonder and a monstrosity, though I must say I'll have one magnificent monograph to write if I survive this. Meanwhile, I avoid mirrors. The shock is too much. And frankly, being athletic of body is not what it's cracked up to be. Let's face it, forty five years in that cramped little carapace my mother gave me—well, I got used to it, I guess. In any case, we had best do something about this situation before it's too late. As for your Benni, sir, the longer we wait the less likely he will ever be resurrected."

"What we can do?" Paco growled.

Gregorian stirred his coffee slowly. When he looked up, Kirsten was looking at him with a mixture of sympathy and clinical curiosity. Gregorian addressed his remarks to her. "Under optimal circumstances the original bodies in question might be sustained a month before neurological and physiological disintegration sets in. Given what I saw of the life-support apparati, I have little hope. As for the respective 're-placement of psyches,' I have had ample opportunity to study the situation—from the inside, as it were."

"Yes?" .

"An amazing phenomenon, I assure you." Gregorian ran his hand through Pistone's curly thatch. He sat back in his chair and addressed himself to Lagerquist almost as a teacher to a student. "Consider, Doctor, that what we describe as 'experience' is an accidental engram?"

"Accidental?"

"At your birth, what prediction could anyone have made of the woman the child was to be, beyond generalities? Little of course. In that sense, your 'self' began as an interaction of your psychical potentials with the social-cultural circumstances into which you were born—your particular mother and father, in that particular time and place. What I am saying is that the engram of experience, your self, or *Eigenweld*, becomes continuous, and co-extensive with the stimuli that help shape it, your unique *Mitweld*."

"You know Binswanger!" Kirsten fairly shouted. She chuckled with pleasure.

"The existential psychiatrist? As do you, apparently. Well then, as he says, each of us is unique for being an accident of his interaction with an arbitrary and contingent "world." It is that interaction constitutes experience. It creates in the process our 'self.' So says Binswanger. But then, this is elementary."

"Yes? And?"

"Pardon me for stressing the elementary and the obvious, but, you see, Doctor, the engram..." and here Gregorian turned his attention to Paco, as though to ensure that little man's understanding, "the *intaglio* if you will..."

"Ah, *si. Si capisce*."

"...the memory-engram becomes, develops, as a permanent and on-going inscription, if you permit. When the amnesiac has lost his memory, he has lost himself. It is largely this engram that constitutes the Aram

Gregorian who speaks to you now through that part of the human brain called the hippocampus major. He expresses his self to himself and to the world through the 'Horn of Ammon.' as it has been called."

"So, am I to understand that Pistone's brain harbors three such 'engrams'?" said Kirsten.

"Yes! Perhaps four. We're not sure of Pistone himself. The concussion was quite severe. But the amazing part, as the van Horn fellow and I have discovered, is that there is room for more! Popular cliche has it that a person in a lifetime uses only a fraction of his brain. Not entirely true. Nevertheless, the brain's capacity is far more than anyone has ever learned to employ. A person doesn't use all he has because he tends to be lazy, or because he lacks the stimulus, or the imagination."

"Very interesting, Doctor." says Kirsten. "The question is what's to be done?"

"Very simple. We must get this body and its residents back to the lab and initiate a re-transfer. The lives, and certainly the sanity, of four people are at stake. But we do have help of an extraordinary kind. I will explain that later."

Even as the sun broke the crust of darkness, Paco hurried to do as he was bid. Doctors Gregorian and Lagerquist conferred another half-hour and then they too went their respective ways. It occurred to Gregorian as he hustled in his preparations, this was the first time in their several years of acquaintance he had deigned to address her as 'Kirsten.' Something about inhabiting this big body was affecting him, no doubt.

****

Berti Huffding washed out the coffee urn and the last of the cups. This fellow calling himself Alphonse Apollinaire—a big brute of a man, good looking as all get-out—was as full of hot air as he was full of himself. She hadn't seen him in over ten years. Amsterdam, it had been. A problem having to do with the Spanish ambassador. International scandal. Alphonse was in the butler's pantry now, putting up the last of the day's silver and glass. He came up behind her. He put his hands very lightly upon her hips. He kissed the top of her head. Berti thrilled. As seasoned an old mare as she might be, she conceded, this big horse's ass had something special about him. His fine baritone hummed in her ear. "Dearest."

"Yes?"

"There is a man in our gardener's shed."

"Ah. The bloody nose."

"You might take him a pot of coffee." His arms encircled her generous waist. He whispered-blew in her ear. "When this circus is over and we've struck the tent. . ?"

Berti tittered. "We'll see, Alphonse. We'll see."

****

Armand Bombaste hadn't slept twenty minutes before Tisibon was at his side saying it was time, and they'd best hurry. Bombaste dressed quickly. In the kitchen, Berti handed him a cup of coffee. He swallowed a mouthful and was off to the garage.

Kirsten felt herself as one standing on the edge of a knife. To fall in either direction would be disaster, but the maid, Berti, the funny little woman with the knowing eyes and the taunting smile, had said, "Don't sleep! You will be sent for." And so Kirsten had re-packed her one grip. She sat on the bed in a dark bedroom and she waited. At quarter past three in the morning there came a soft knock on her door. Paco betrayed tension and anticipation written in his homely face. "Come," says he. "We go save Benni."

As for Colonel Moore: The tall majordomo had shown him his room. He turned down the bed. With that, Alphonse departed.

Colonel Moore removed his field coat. He intended to relax for no more than an hour. By George, he had cornered this gaggle of clowns. The discs would be his—and Ocho's funneled-off funds in the Chanticleer account. Sun-up in an hour, and they would be off.

At 12:45 AM the Colonel sat himself on the bed with one boot in his hand. He stared into the pale light of a moon squinting at the window. But then he heard a cock crow. Morning shattered its glory over the Alps. The cock sang again. The Colonel yawned and startled. His watch said quarter to five. A presumptuous sun glared at him through the venetian blinds. He re-placed his boot and prepared to rouse Endicotte. He stopped half way across the room. No need to chase your quarry if you know where he's going to be, eh? First, a quick look into the mirror, a cursory brush to one's thinning locks and that is when he spotted the discs lying right there on the bureau in their protective envelopes as though they had been placed there for him to find. Carefully, Cray let fall the discs into his palm. One. Two. Three. Four. Except that Four was not of the original sequence. Where was the original number Four? The activator. There was no directing the individual funds to their respective destinations without it. Had Endicotte made a copy? He hadn't mentioned. To activate, one needed an old PC. Peg was seeing to that. And the antenna would have to be re-established. Before Ocho made her final move. But, someone was pulling strings. Someone at whose behest he, Cray, was being made to dance. Alphonse the majordomo? Perhaps. One of Ocho's? What was his game? Whoever, and whatever, there was no way to know but to run this last disc. A quick look about the house confirmed suspicions. There was no one home. In the garage Charlie Endicotte lay supine atop the gardener's bench cocooned in a blanket and fast asleep. The ambulance was gone.

"Rouse yourself, Charles," the Colonel said. "We've traveling to do."

Charlie Endicotte yawned. "Where we going now?"

"I'm back to London. You're off to Somalia."

Ammon's Horn

3. Recon Patrol

The 'copter came out of the west with the brilliant light of a southwestern sun behind it. The chop-chop of the blades exploded over Joe Garcia's head and the huge machine set itself down on the far end of the Albertson's Supermart parking lot. A tall, rangy man dropped from the cockpit. A slighter figure descended from the rear and ducking into the furious dust they came running across the lot.

"Herb Carson, State Police." The tall fellow took Garcia's hand and squinted from behind his shades. The other man stepped forward clutching a closed, chin-to-heels, black, oilskin duster and a wide brimmed Stetson hat. "Breen," he said in an almost girlish voice. "I'm from the university."

"Well?" Garcia shouted. "Is it true?"

"Yeah," said Carson. "What's reported's accurate far's I can see. Albuquerque says problem's all the way south far's Guadalajara. Following a north-south swatch fifty miles wide either side of the line at longitude 105 to 107, everything inside that line is gone!"

"Gone?" says Garcia in disbelief.

"That's what they tell me," said Carson. "El Paso, like somebody wiped 'it off the Earth. The Mexicans are in a panic. El Carrizo, Coyame, Durango and Guadalajara, they're gone!" Carson lifted his helmet and

243

scratched. "Man, lemme tell you, this is crazy! Reports are coming in from the north. They're lookin' t' lose Albuquerque, too. This thing, whatever it is, it's makin' like t' go clear through the state."

"*Madre de dios!* Where's it gonna stop?"

"I just come from Albuquerque," Says Carson. "B'lieve me, they're scared shitless, it's like the whole state o' New Mexico's shrinkin'."

Garcia's eyes grew wide. He stared at an invisible mote in space. "I know, man. I know."

"Albuquerque says for you t' get on the horn," says Carson. "You and all law enforcement here to the border, get the word out—evacuate! Get everybody twunny miles east or west of a line running…"

"I can't! Peyote Wells and Las Cruces, they went about twunny minutes ago."

The pale little fellow called himself Breen stood listening intently. Garcia sized him up as one those intellectual types couldn't scratch his buns without a manual of procedures. Any minute now a gust of desert wind would lift him like dry mesquite. He was looking about at the empty town, "like a chick jus' come out the egg," Garcia would have said.

****

Federal District of Columbia II, Sciatica, New York: The President was worried because his Secretary of the Media looked worried, and when Miss Agapé was worried it meant he was going to have to make a speech. Or face the press and answer questions. That sort of thing always upset him terribly and he'd get hungry. He'd have to have one of the young lovelies from the typing pool up for lunch. But that made him sleepy so he and the young lady would take a nap and pretend it had all gone away.

And, on this particular morning Tari Agapé looked worried. She said it was something about New Mexico. And the Union of Pacific States or something or other. "Oh, yeah," says the President. "All them Japa-knees, or Java-knees, or Indo-knees, or somethin'."

And so they sent two of the girls from Interior to see that Mister President dressed properly in a morning coat, even if it was three in the afternoon, and there would be hundreds of reporters there and he was going to, "make a statement," Tari said. She had it all written out for him in big letters so he wouldn't have any trouble. "You just read it, she'd said, "and I'll take over from there." And so he read in a loud, clear tenor:

> Dis aftanoon, the twunny-secken of Nov, 2085, da ambassader from da Union of Pacific States delivered to Agatha Porterhouse Prybar, Sekar-tay-ree of State, a communique from Singapore stating in effect dat unless soitn conditions to be met by da US Inc., a state of war will be seriously considered as existing between our two countries.

The President paused to better understand the import of what he had just read. He looked anxiously over to where his Secretary of the Media sat. She smiled and gestured for him to continue, but he developed a frog in the throat and she continued for him:

> Conditions to be met are that the US Inc. make good the loss that the Union of Pacific States has sustained in the six weeks since inception of the Kamper-Buckettet plan which were sold to them as the former states of New Mexico, Colorado, Nevada, and Idaho. These losses are pursuant to the purported disappearance of large portions of territory, principally in New Mexico, but, it is alleged, there is no guarantee the disappearance will not continue in the other territories sold.

The President stood at Tari's elbow. Television cameras had him squinting into the lights and at the hundred or so members of the media before him. Mister President was heard to mutter quite audibly, "They accusin' us of a fuck'n shell game. 'At's wut it is."

There spread an excited murmur throughout the assembled reps. of the media. Secretary Tari Agapé continued:

> The United States Incorporated vehemently denies any wrong-doing. We urge our friends in the Union of Pacific States to sit with us and to discuss this matter as rational people.

Secretary Agapé motioned for a moment's time-out. Her photonic clipboard signaled emergency. She read:

> This from the Hexagon: Members of the armed forces of the Union of Pacific States are even now enforcing the borders between New Mexico and Texas and Kansas, between Colorado and Utah and Arizona, between Utah and Idaho and Wyoming, and between Nevada and California and Oregon and Idaho.

The President's mumbled once more, just loud and clear enough for the mike to register: "How come we got so many goddam borders?" The Secretary of the Media silenced the mike. A minute's earnest exchange took place between them. Kari continued:

> Ladies and Gentlemen. As you heard our beloved President say, a potential state of war exists between the Union of Pacific States and the United States, Incorporated . Even as we speak, the Hexagon has ordered an armored brigade to the Texas-New Mex. border, and a delegation from Singapore is meeting with our State Department...and, this just handed me...

Media reps. and the TC unit audience from Jersey to Las Vegas Shores saw Tari Agapé's face grow pale and her jaw drop.

"Ladies and gents, for whatever it's worth, her it is. Geodetic Survey says…" Tari scanned the clipboard and paraphrased:

Proceeding from New Mexico, southwards, we report the following towns and cities are no longer to be found—anyplace! El Paso is gone, and down Mexico way write off Ciudad Juarez. Then there's El Carrizo, and Coyame and Durango and Guadalajara…forget 'em. And, going north—Las Cruces and you might's well eliminate all the towns along the Rio Grande—matter of fact, if I read this right, the river's gone, too! Anyhow, everything between Las Cruces and up to but excepting Albuquerque. Whatever's doing this took a detour 'round Albuquerque, seems like. Then there's Santa Fe and all those little hick towns between Albuquerque and the Colorado state line. Hey, man, they're aaall gone! Not flooded out, mind. Just up and disappeared!

And while we're at it, here's a brief list of some of this country's more prominent people we haven't heard from in the last forty-eight hours: Senate majority leader Carl Snarl of Oklahoma was in Santa Fe at the time of its disappearance attending a conference on foreign affairs. And there's film star Shu'vawn McCuddle, and teevee personality Curtis Belch were skiing at Bosman Springs.

There were gasps of dismay from the Press Corps. Ms. Sec'tary's clipboard beeped and hummed frantically. Ms. Secretary read on:

Continuing with the geography. This also from Geodetic Survey, Colorado: Territory appears to be vanishing following a swatch of real-estate fifty-five miles either side of a line and adjacent to a line roughly following the 105th parallel and on up into the former state of Colorado.

That's what it says. And, if I read this right, you can write off Laramie and Sheridan and Bosman Springs and Bismarck. Whatever's doing this looks like it's heading northwards into Canada, and...yup, just in now. In Canada, the towns of Moosejaw and Regina in Saskatchewan are no longer responding to communication. All right, boys 'n girls, I want it quiet in here, I don't have to do this, you know! That's better. Our meteorological station at Cambridge Bay on Victoria Island no longer responds. And from Saskatoon, the Canadians have initiated an overflight survey. According to them, several of the Parry Islands just south of the Arctic Circle are no longer geography. Humm, are you listening, Rand McNally?

"Ms. Secretary!" The media was worried and anxious and demanding to be heard. "Ms. Secretary! " The Secretary's voice was nearly drowned in the hub-bub. "Ms. Secretary, we demand to know, what connection is there, if any, between the sale of the Western half of the United States and this incredible disappearance?"

The Secretary paused momentarily to think. "Okay, boys and girls! Shut it DOWN! This is a crisis of international scope. We will inform you about any new events as quickly as possible." An aide bustled up and handed the Secretary another sheet of paper. There was abrupt silence in the auditorium while she half-commented, half read-aloud:

Okay, guys. If I may...this just in from Moscow. It says here the phenomenon has apparently crossed the arctic circle and gone south over the North Pole. Our embassy in Moscow has issued a communique. According to Russian geodetic teams in the field…the big Island of Severnaja Zemlya in the far north Pacific is no more. Now the phenomenon seems to be taking a southerly direction roughly along a latitude of 105 and has in recent hours assumed a zig-zag course. From all indications, it has hit the Tamir Peninsula of extreme northern Siberia. It has claimed the town of Novorybnaja. More towns are predicted to fall victim following along the same zig-zag line. Residents of the biggish city of Irkutsk on Lake Baikal have been advised to evacuate as have residents of Ulan Bator in Mongolia.

Chaos and confusion reigned for a full ten minutes. At length, the Secretary regained control. The tumult subsided. Secretary Agapé continued:

Also says here our scientists at MIT and at Stanford are studying the situation. Best guess from the experts allows for some potentially massive force acting upon the Earth's surface. From all indications, it is causing the Earth to…shrink? That's what it says here. 'Causing the Earth to shrink! And I quote: 'Though from whence the force may be directed is as yet unknown Survey teams from the InterNational Geodetic Service are on their way now. Detectors will be placed at strategic points to determine the source of the force, and the 'destination' of the vanishing towns and populations.'

Tari's voice came on hard and stern in the mike. "C'mon. ladies and gents, let's not lose our cool. Keep it down to a dull roar…"

A voice burst forth from the taut tension of the room. A reporter stood and asked in a voice which betrayed the emotional edge to its control. "Ms. Secretary?"

"I recognize Cassie Aspersian from the Desmoines Debenture."

"Ms. Secretary, is there any truth to the rumor we are being victimized by forces from beyond the Earth?"

Ms. Secretary let fall a full half minute of silence before she answered, and then it was in a voice marvelous for its cool control. "Just lemme say this about that," she said. "Nobody's ruled it out."

****

Telly Malakas had long since left the auditorium. If there was anything he hated it was a crisis. They always upset him. And if he didn't find someway to relax his nerves, he was bound to suffer a headache severe enough to be medically designated a Force1 on the Migraine scale. But then, though he did not articulate this in explicit words, such crises— and they were always resolved one way or the other—such crises justified what his shrink agreed was a wonderful palliative—wonderful because it worked, and in therapeutic psychiatry whatever works is good science, or so says the psyche-shrink bible.

So the President was whisked back to the Presidential residence in the big Victorian house on Federal Street. He commoed on a closed link and made his order-request. The sweet voice on the other end said lunch was on her way up. For the next four hours, the President was incommunicado. After he had eaten lunch, he and she had a lovely snooze til the next crisis broke at 8 PM.

The communique said something about something in Siberia had vanished. Peripheral thought said he'd never liked the Russki's anyhow. And Siberia had to be damned cold!

"The whole thing?"

"Nosir," Secretary Agapé stood at the foot of the bed in what was generally agreed to be the New Lincoln bedroom. In deference to the heat of the afternoon, Secretary of the Media T. Agapé wore a light cotton blouse and brief cotton shorts (fashionably one-half size too small) and no undergarms. Mister President's lunch peered at her coyly from over the blanket.

Mister Prez. regarded his Secretary of the Media and peripheral thought said, by golly, he would have her for lunch some day soon. Lunch and Agapé smiled at one another knowingly.

"Nosir," Agapé was saying, "not all of it. Just a few towns in a fifty-mile zig-zag strip of real estate heading toward Novosibirsk."

Well," said the President in his best authoritative manner, "that's a relief. Wouldn't want them to lose the whole thing. Bad for...what's it bad for?"

"Our political image?"

"Yeah. That. Anything else?"

"Yessir, Mr. President. The Reverend Bloodworthy, and the Cardinal Vendetta, and the Rabbi Foreshock."

"Yeah? What about them?"

"Them too."

"Ah, yeah. Well, send the CIA, or th FBT, or somebody. Go find 'em..." President Malakas sat up the better to catch Poppyseed Avenue on PBS—he adored the puppets.

****

New York: 11 PM: Even as the Colonel had laced his boot in the Bernese Alps, Connie Ocho fidgeted aboard her private ballistique over New York harbor. Estimated Time of Arrival, Cointrin International, Geneva, 4 AM Swiss time. Kari Agapé sat in the seat opposite looking glassy eyed. In another ten minutes, she was fast asleep. Connie Ocho switched on the console in her seat arm and the flat voice of Enfotainer Felicia Freewind continued her report:

...in the Taymir Peninsula of Sy-beria, the town of Khatanga has van-ished. 'At's whut I said, kiddies. Van-as in -ished! And, movin' right along and south down the 105th meridian and as of midnight, New York time, the lovely town of Yes-see, the garden center Siberia, is a sometime thing. And, while we're at it, you remember Tun-goo-ska, don't you?—famous for its having been scorched by a meteor back in nineteen ought eight? Well, forget about it folks, it ain't no more. Pushing on, it says here, we can scratch Too-ra and Strell-kah from your plans for a Sy-berian spring hop and ditto Kah-chunga and Too-loon. This word just in: the fun city of Irr-kutsk is still on the air which is taking us close to the border of People's Republic of China and the folks in Bee-jing are getting antsy, we are given to bee-lieve. This just in. Scratch Irr-kutsk, folks. Springtime bacchanal cum orgy has been canceled as there's no *there* to get to anymore.

****

Connie Ocho switched off. A fax chattered in the console, half a page of encrypted text. She placed it in the scanner-decode. Text shone brightly on her screen.

Text:
From: Our man in Connecticut.
Re Memo: FBCIF Div.BBT
Intercepted interdept. memo reads:
Per Op. Tfthers: Confirm SL instrmt guts LatBnk,
Athns, KievTrst, WarsawBnk. per B1. Toronto. Divrsn
USAf CTn.
Subpna active CEO CP and ExO Ta. et al.
AG FN xpnds GJ to incld E-Shrink per Sbsm collude BJng.

Sino Fld FBCI confirms SBSM office cntct BJng RE Minstry.

Op. Tfethers expnd incld plot crnr E-wide RE.

40 agnts alert issue Sbpna C. Ocho T. Agapé, et al. end copy

Operation Tailfeathers, a crypt-euphemism for the opposition mounting against her. Those twits in the United Federation of Nations were miffed because she'd brought the mighty United States, Incorporated to its finan-political knees. Belatedly, they were getting self righteous about how she did it. Riga, Athens, Kiev—yes, she'd gutted their banks, and their national econs were largely in the hands of Subsume, UnLtd. So what? They would still be third rate beggars at a US-British table had it not been for her. And Toronto, what gripe did the Canadians have? She'd used Toronto as her funnel—her Chanticleer gambit had poured five trillion into the Canadian coffers and put Canada on the finan map, for krine-out-loud! An attorney general? A grand jury? Let'em try! And they were barking up the wrong ginko if they thought she needed the likes of the Chinese. But the vanishing real estate. That was troubling. "You shouldn't never mess up on your property," her uncle Miguel had always said. Property was "real." You could count on it. Not like in your "liquid assets," or your "book value."

Except Connie Ocho had a mind-scraping hunch she knew who-what was behind this "vanishing" real estate. Well, two hours to Geneva. She'd best get an hour's sleep. There would be heads to crack, asses to kick, and work to be done. She was asleep when the last fax came through:

From: Subsume CntrIntelgnce. Wtrbury, CT.

To: CP confidential:

Oppostn fielding undrcver agnt.

Unknown entity. Cvrname Mackenzie

Kari Agapé may not have been fully awake when she retrieved the fax, but her disciplined habits noted the gist of the text.

The name Mackenzie popped out. Mem of her stint in the Coast Guard retained the image of a charming, seductive little clown by that name. She would inform Madame P. of this Fax when she woke.

****

The moon was still full even as sunlight curdled the eastern sky. Bombaste had taken the wheel of the big ambulance. The bulk of the Pistone complex squeezed itself into the narrow passenger seat. Doctors Lagerquist and Tisibon and Paco Ungaroni made themselves comfy as possible in the van behind with the gurney and the oxygen tanks and paramedical paraphernalia. It took two minutes or so to back the big machine out of its garage and to negotiate the narrow drive to the main road below, during which time Bombaste knew a stage review in the proscenium of memory. In the course of that evening's after-dinner discourse, a penetrating exchange had taken place between four eyes, master and servant, which left no doubt who was in charge.

Alphonse, as he called himself, had restored peace and serenity to what had promised to be violence unleashed. Even the imperious Major Moore had holstered his weapon and had meekly followed the majordomo to his appointed quarters for the night. Alphonse saw the other house guests to their quarters, and he, Bombaste, had lain wide-eyed as the wondering child he'd once been, staring up into the image floating above him, into the eyes of the disembodied (?) visage of the one purporting to be his majordomo. Alphonse, or whatever he called himself, spelled it all out.

The import was most clear. He, Bombaste, was charged with transporting Tisibon and the others—specifically the Pistone physiology— to l'Ecole pour les Etudes de la Science Physique just outside Montreaux

254

which was clear the other side, south and west of Lake Léhman.

And so Bombaste did as he was bid and the others followed through, though they understood as much or as little as did he. Out of an unspoken urgency, one by one they had emerged in the waning moonlight, sleepy-eyed but willing, and had mounted the waiting ambulance.

Up front, it was Gregorian to the fore. "Where are we going?"

"Pardon, but who is it speaks now?" says Bombaste.

"It is I, Aram Gregorian."

"Ah," says Bombaste most cheerily. "Good morning, Doctor. How do you fare this beautiful morning?"

"How do I 'fare'?" Gregorian could not hide his irritation, nor his sense of irony. "If you have reference to this magnificent body, it fares very well. But then it has been well cared for."

"You are suggesting?" Bombaste assayed.

"I am suggesting, sir, that you and your colleague have more scientific ingenuity than you have common sense to guide you. Attend now," says Gregorian. He was speaking now in fluent French. "Time escapes us. We may not tarry. I have the unique opportunity to study the mind-brain problem from the inside, so to speak. Unique, I say. I, Aram Gregorian, study the neuro-physiological processes at first hand, those productive of the selves, respectively, of Pistone and Mackenzie, and that which is Anatoli Polichuk. As for the self that is Gregorian, I am, of course, as opaque as is anyone."

"Of course," says Bombaste. "To be expected."

"You are most obtuse, Doctor Bombaste. But it is to your better sense I now appeal. There is danger here. If my assessment of the situation is anywhere accurate, the delicate neuro-synaptic matrix keeping our respective psyches in separate quarters may very well collapse, as it were. The result may be the death of all three. Or an unremitting madness."

"How long do you think?"

"Judging from the friction between us, one must dominate at the expense of the others. The result—schizophrenia! Such as the world has never seen! As for the Polichuk, I cannot guarantee he will survive intact."

"Ah, yes, Doctor. It were best we return to Pontarlier as quickly as possible.

"I dare say."

Bombaste hit the accelerator, and the big machine surged ahead along the narrow mountain road. Thus it was they drove along in silence for some minutes. Then, to the surprise of Bombaste, the big fellow next to him began fiddling with the controls on the dash.

"Something?" says Bombaste.

"What day we are heffing?" says the other in a strangely husky, high pitched voice.

"This is Thursday, the seventeenth," says Bombaste.

"The seventeen. Yes, then it is best we hurry. That woman, she wants the real-estate, and for this she would risk...please, we must get to Montreaux."

At this point he had managed to punch in the radio. In good Suisse-Alemagne, radio Alsace proceeded apace with the world's latest installment on catastrophe:

...since the vanishing of the Mongolian capital at Ulan Bator late last night. A special delegation from Beijing arrived in New York to join this extraordinary session of the Security Council of the World Federation of Nations to address the problem of the vanishing real-estate. The council will hear expert testimony from scientists around the world attempting to explain what is happening to the Earth. Latest estimates have determined as much as fifteen percent of the globe of the Earth has disappeared and, it is estimated, well over fifty million people have simply ceased to exist.

Bombaste struck the steering wheel in exasperated amusement. "Are we really to take such stuff seriously?"

"What do I make of it?" said the Pistone physiology. "I make it the Wanda and the Laszlo, they have succeeded!"

Bombaste regarded the speaker with some alarm. "Ah, Docteur Polichuk!" he said. "You think there is a connection?"

"The fifth dimension! It shares with us the SpaceTime, you see. And so, it swallows mebee a piece of the SpaceTime of the earth!"

Bombaste let out a huge guffaw.

"The Earth!" the Polichuck insisted. "This very dimension of Universe. That is what I am trying to tell you. The woman, Ocho, she will destroy us all. Every-thing!"

"Mon dieu!" says Bombaste. "What shall we do?"

The big body sitting next to him straightened and asserted once more in Gregorian's voice, "In addition, we approach a critical confrontation of psyches. We must go back to Pontarlier."

Bombaste gave that a minute's thought and he said, "Pontarlier," Bombaste agreed. Yes. We go to back Pontarlier. We must save the *psychonomie, non*?"

A few minutes later the road directions indicated Vallorne to the west, forty K., and Montreaux to the North and east, 60 K.

Bombaste swung the wheel and the big machine swerved.

Tisibon put his head through the communicating window. *"Mon ami? We are going?"*

"We are going back to Pontarlier," says Bombaste. "There is coming *un' battail psychique!"*

"But we must to go to Montreaux," Polichuk insisted. "The universe is in peril!"

Bombaste appeared to ponder this a moment. "Ah, *mon capitan.* Before we save the minds of these good people, singularly and collectively, it is necessary we save the world, *bien?* We go on to

Montreaux!" Bombaste slammed on the brakes. The great machine skidded and swerved in the loose stone of the narrow road and a terrible jolt brought all to a halt. They sat in an uncertain silence and at something of an angle.

"Eh, *allor*? What have you done?" queried Tisibon. Bombaste restarted the engine. He shifted the transmission to its reverse gear. The huge vehicle roared and whined, it strained and shook, but it did not move.

Bombaste alighted from one side. Tisibon from the rear. They stood in the narrow country road appraising the damage. Kirsten was the first to approach, and then Paco. The right-front wheel had embedded itself in a run-off culvert.

"Ah, *sacre bleu*," says Tisibon. "Bombaste, what have you done? Comes the end of the world and we are stuck in a ditch!"

"*Allors*," says Bombaste. "One of us to man the wheel. The others to push."

"Push?" says Tisibon, with some incredulity.

"*Oui*. Push." With this Bombaste summoned Kirsten, and she and Paco placed themselves in the culvert and prepared to push the huge machine from its confinement. Bombaste mounted. The engine roared. "Push!" Bombaste could be heard shouting above the roar of the engine, the whine of the drive-train and the shoooshing of the rear wheels. But the vehicle did not budge.

From their dis-advantage in the culvert Kirsten and Paco and Tisibon were quickly covered with a fine, brown dust. They regarded Bombaste with some skepticism.

It was Paco who climbed back up into the roadway and who prepared to take over from Bombaste. Testily he drew open the door. "Come down," says he. "I am more experienced with motors. Let me try…"

But the words died in his throat, for advancing toward him from the van came the huge form of what had been Benni Pistone. He and Paco regarded one another. As though some subliminal message had been transmitted, Paco mounted into the driver's seat. The body of *il Benni* made its way carefully into the culvert. He waited until Paco shouted he was ready and gunned the engine, whereupon the Benni creature seized the front bumper of the ambulance and—lifted! The Engine roared and the huge machine shuddered a moment and, like unto some great and living beast, it lifted itself out of the culvert. The others stood in the roadway now. They regarded him with some surprise, if not skepticism. The door opened once more and Paco dismounted.

"*Bennino? Sei tu?*" Paco looked up at the younger man but that one sought the eyes of Kirsten Lagerquist and was silent. She, in turn, sought his gaze and there was as once before the nameless something passed between them, the wordless message they had read in one another's eyes on a brilliant afternoon when he'd carried her all naked and beautiful along the strand and over the sands of a beach on the Mediterranean sea.

****

Meanwhile, in Albuquerque, there were no cars in the Albertson's SuperMart parking lot. Garcia had a peek through the broad glass front and the huge supermarket was empty of people. Groceries sat piled on the checkout counters. A cash drawer stood open. The three men moved out onto Braveheart Drive bisecting the 'burb. The doors to small businesses swung in the wind, a few cars remained parked at the curb. At the intersection of Route 747 and Main Street, the traffic light changed to green.

Chief Carson hooked his thumbs into his belt and looked away. "Looks like folks here'bouts got the word. Nobody home. And from what they tell me, this place is likely t' be next."

Garcia peered down the deserted street. The dry wind of a late desert spring pressed his back. "Whole towns," he muttered. "They don't just disappear. I mean, it ain't natural!"

The big Anglo peered down at Garcia. "Everything's 'natural' if y' come t' understand it."

"Yeah?" Garcia ventured. "You understand this."

"Not worth a shit," Carson admitted. "That's why we got the perfesser here. Got any ideas, perfesser?"

Grunion Breen took off his spectacles and peered into his myopia. "Einstein postulated the curvature of space in the presence of sufficient mass."

"Yeah? Meanin' wut?" says Carson.

"Eddington, 1921, I believe. Verified. Solar eclipse. Light of five stars seen from Earth's perspective as behind the sun. During the eclipse their light was photographed. The light curved, around the mass of the sun."

"No shit?" says Garcia.

"So," says Carson. "Wut's that got t' do with this mess?"

Breen looked myopically up at Carson. "In my book, Dimensional Synergies, I postulate the separability of space from time."

"Meanin' wut?" says Carson.

"Breen placed his folded spectacles to his lips and he peered into the haze. "Common experience concludes two objects cannot occupy the same space at the same time."

"That's right!" says Carson.

"But two objects can occupy the same space at different times."

"Okay," says Carson. "I follow. So?"

"What this pre-supposes is the inseparability of space from time in the continuum of SpaceTime."

"SpaceTime. Um, okay," Carson conceded. "Go on."

"But if space can be bent in the presence of mass, as we have seen demonstrated, what's to say time may not also be bent?"

"Bent time?" Carson lifted his huge Stetson and scratched his head.

"That don't make no sense at-tall."

"Yeah," Garcia ventured. "I mean, how you gonna explain how come we lost Peyote Wells? I mean, goddamit, I got a report t' make inna mornin'. I mean how'm I gonna report to Peote Wells if Peyote Wells suddenly ain't there no more?"

"Perhaps you will," Breen mused. "In a different time."

They returned to the parking lot and remounted the chopper. From a thousand feet they looked down at the north village limits. Professor Breen consulted the computer display before him. "Gentlemen," he said. "This puts us at the periphery of the unnamed phenomenon. If as is hypothecated, this point in the continuum is to vanish next, we may have an opportunity to observe the effect. The authorities think to videotape the event, though I doubt the efficacy of that procedure, really."

Below them the town lay almost unreal in the glare of the late sun. Garcia watched Breen load and calibrate a large video camera at the starboard port. "Now what?" says Garcia.

"I have it set on slow take," says Breen. "There is nothing to do now but wait." So they, hovered, and they sat, and they waited. After a half-hour: "Oh, for cry-sake, lookah there!" Carson howled.

Garcia focused his binocs. At first he saw nothing but the scattering of small bungalows at the end of Mariposa Street vanishing into the prairie at the far edge of town. Then something moved. Garcia adjusted focus and a group of three marched down the middle of the street, a tall fellow in black up front, and another got up in some outlandish costume all red and white and wearing a pointy white thing on his head, and the third one wearing some kind of cape. The lot of them, Carson would testify later, "movin' right along like they was late for Sunday go-to-meetin' time, or somethin'."

"Who are they?" says Breen.

"Whipsashit ahtta me," said Carson. "They better get their asses ahhta there or they likely t' dis-appear! Better go have a word."

Carson set the coptor down in the main intersection. He alighted and approached the group of three just now entering the intersection. "Okay, just hold it right there. Who are ya and wutter'y' doin' here?" The fellow in black leading the group approached. "Who wants t'know?" he said undismayed.

"Carson, State Police."

"And I'm the Reverend G. Mordecai Bloodworthy, Secretree of Religion, the President's cabinet, Washington II DC. My colleagues are members of the secretariat."

"That right? Wut're you gentlemen doin' here? This town's off limits. It's likely t' disappear any minute."

"Disappear! That's what Foreshock said. Santa Fe. We were s'pposed t' meet. I can't explain…I mean, one minute we're at the airport waitin' for a cab take us into town, and next minute…there wasn't no town! We end up on the arse end of Noo-MEX-iko!"

"Santa Fe?" said Carson.

"It's gone!" said the Reverend.

"Garcia?" Chief Carson called. "Perfesser? Now, where in tarnation'd they…disappear to?"

Sergeant Garcia came running from across the street with Professor Breen scampering behind. Carson stared at them unbelievingly. They were drenched wet. "Chief Carson," Garcia wheezed panting. "You ain't gonna believe this."

"Wut! Wut!"

"It's rainin'! 'Cross the Street…it's comin' down buckets."

"No shit?"

"No shit! You tell 'em, perfesser."

"What the sergeant is saying is that it has already happened."

"Goddamit, will yew speak clear! Wut's happened?"

"The spatio-temporal discontinuity. It's sliced off the southern end of the town. Across the street, as it were…over there, you might say, is no longer there. Nor is it a part of *here,* or of *now.*"

Ammon's Horn

5. Siphon

AireSuisse Ballistique, orbital ballistic flight 907, departed Cointrin International, Geneva, 1 PM, Tuesday, November 30, 2085. Two hours later the anti-grav chute eased the passenger pod down into its cradle at Somali Field, Iddan, Autonomous State of Somalia, Federation of East Africa.

Charley Endicotte cabbed it to Iddan and to Garage Caruso. The Caruso woman suggested he could stick the antenna components where he pleased. Next AM, Charlie hired a truck and driver and two burly fellows who knew tools and such. The driver was a tiny, little fellow who knew precisely where Charlie wanted to go. Charlie had the uncomfortable feeling he'd be outdone in any test of chicaneries.

It was 2:35 PM London time when Cray got the email message, Iddan to London via satellite link. The shack was re-opened, the computer re-activated, the antenna re-erected and functional.

"All systems are go. Africa is up and operating."

****

From an office suite overlooking Nathan Phillips square, Peg Brewer

265

could see First National Toronto across the way and its UBADS antenna tower. The broadband scanprobe on her desk zeroed the selected range of signal frequencies. And, at 1 PM:

Brewer to Dover: "Chanticleer sings loud and clear."
Dover to Toronto: "We're ready for the lyrics."

****

In Dover, Cray set his commo receiver on the commode as he brushed his teeth. The obsolete digital PC announced in script and in a soft feminine voice given to an English precision:

Target account Chanticleer per FBCT.
Siphon virus surveillance.
Awaiting activation.
Access UBADS broadband originate Toronto.
Destination: Relay Colombo, Sri Lanka.

Cray finished his morning's toilette and chuckled to himself. Ocho's takeover of the world's banks continued. Brilliant, she was, even to surprising him with her imaginative grasp of the possible. "Why robba bank?" she'd once said to him. "Don't hafta if you own it." If he pegged her with any accuracy, she had a dozen or more anonymous fronts for her personal Chanticleer fortune, and it had to be enormous—or it would be until he siphoned it off. There fell to his most cherished fantasy a cameo scene wherein she stood before his desk, worn, tired, a shade disheveled. Just outside the door the law waited to take her. In a small voice she begged him, "Oh, Sebastian, darling, please! Help me! After all we've been to each other. .."

But the screen called him back to reality. Brewer had begun the big

Siphon. Cray chuckled to himself. "Big Siphon," indeed. It was the biggest bank heist in history, bar none.

Over his morning coffee Cray's PC continued its feminine croon:

Infection strategy proceeds.

The following accounts are now available:

Execute transfer via Toronto-Chanticleer account Fourbe-Olique, Couvrir, S.A. numero B73 0735 9915, Banque Lussembourg 573,000 Euro.

Execute transfer via Toronto-Chanticleer [3.3.74] to the account Fourbe-Oblique, Genevre, S. A. numero A99 41 990076 350,000 Euro].

Await activation.

"Excellent," Cray muttered. "Excellent."

Execute transfer via Toronto-Chanticleer [5.9.74] numero B88 87132, Probity Savings and Loan, Chickpea, Oklahoma, 1,357,94 dollars Americain. 1,048,7 Euro].

Execute transfer [5.17.74] Acconto Zbrissa-Scivola, Casa Risparmio S.M., numero AA 99 7602 3370. 3,537,000 Euro]. Subsume File Directory Override Siphon Yes. No.

Await activation.

Cray buttered a slice of toast and punched in a 1010 for confirm. Fifteen minutes to go. As fast as account Chanticleer funneled Ocho's funds from around the world through the Toronto transceiver, as quickly would the Siphon virus divert them, via the desert station in Somalia to the network interface unit atop the First Bank of Colombo north and east across the Indian Ocean, and from there to eleven pre-selected accounts—two anonymous holding companies in Switzerland and in Luxembourg, a charitable house in Oklahoma, an all but defunct trust in Italy, one dummy corporation in Rumania, three dead accounts right there in Canada, one persuasively legitimate front in New Delhi, and a self-effacing little mortgage company in Israel. Oh, yes, not to forget al Samaritan, the brokerage in Jericho, State of Palestine. The genius of it all, Cray rehearsed, was the random timing, a period of some thirty seven days over which one by one the funds, randomly sorted by the computer program, would be deposited in the various accounts, a little at a time so as not to attract attention unduly. Clever, yes?

Cray poured a second coffee and looked on with satisfaction. "What is it the old Venetians used to say? 'Vengeance is best savored cold.'" Operation Siphon continued, silent, efficient, unseen and unknown. An hour passed. The transmission continued. At 3:05 PM he might have been tempted to doze. The sheer weight of data was staggering, and the sums toted in the lower right hand corner of his screen approached fourteen billion. Cray puzzled. Why was Ocho pushing this all in one afternoon? Did she have problems and find it necessary to dump quickly? Perhaps the legitimate world was onto her? At 3:15—he would have reason to note the time and to remember it well—an interject broke mid-screen:

Account Epousseter-Couvrir, S.A. no. AB4 96120 7554,
  Banque Lussembourg 573,000 Euro.
Deposit to account denied. Over-load.

What? Cray was fully awake now. Denied? By whom? The interject continued:

Account Furbe-Oblique, Genevre, S. A. no. BBa 98735 992
  350,000 Euro.
Deposit to this account denied. Overload.

Cray jabbed the telecom furiously. "Peg! What are you doing?"

Brewer's voice came over the sat-link, calm and controlled, with but the slightest tremor.

"Nothing for me to do, friend. They're denying us."

"Denying? Who's denying?" Cray could have sworn she was chuckling through irony.

"She is, Cray. Ocho. She owns them. The phony fronts we bought into. They're part of her system. She owns the banks and the brokerages. They're all hers. We got no place to go!"

Only in that moment did it begin to penetrate, the common sense of what Peg Brewer had said. Then a surmise, an almost certainty.

Charlie Endicotte's brilliant sleeper had assumed the guise of an extant program in Toronto's directory, had become part of the installation procedure—like the color on the skin of an apple, Charlie said. Undetectable, Charlie said. It had lain dormant waiting for the signal to activate and to send financial goodies zipping at near light-speed across the globe.

But beyond even Charlie Endicotte's genius there must have waited a counter-snoop, an anti-viral device sensitive to any intrusion. Or, and here Cray tipped his hat to the enemy, perhaps the out-to-lunch and on-vacation addresses through which Charlie breached the firewall were themselves traps awaiting just such an intrusion as Siphon constituted. Perhaps, once detected, the anti-program alerted all the rest within the system and the intruder was, unbeknownst to himself, out in the open. How else explain the substitution of this odd item for the original activator?

Through his image-memory Cray saw the bearded figure of Alphonse, the major d'. As though in confirmation of his surmise, at 3:30 PM the counter-snoop surfaced on audio.

"Hello intruder. We've got your signal. We're tracing your address.

Want to save us a bit of time?"

"Hello yourself. Who are you?"

"CounterSnoop per Toronto, programs Vigilante and Median Finger."

"Toronto. Then you're Ocho's agent."

"That's right."

"You have a name?"

"Smith will do."

"Where'd we go wrong, Smith?"

"Well, for openers, your insider—the cleaning lady put the tap on our Matrix last September—she forgot to re-adjust the cerebro-computer-interface band to its original size. She's a hatsize six and he's an nine-ought-five. Regular operative assigned that console had to notice it right away. That was giveaway-one. So we went looking for more. The little transmitter, it's a beaut. Original design?"

"Yes, I believe it is."

"Which led us to your parallel-reader. Our sniffer sucked that right up and we're working on decrypt of your program. Couple hours we'll have it all scrubbed out of the works and we'll be at your door. Your friend here in Toronto's been a big help."

"Ah. You have Peg, have you? Well, then, 'bye."

Cray's screen went blank. The room was suddenly very quiet and very small. The activator disc. Someone had substituted. With trembling fingers Cray inserted disc 4. of Operation Siphon. The program switched to audio. A resonant male voice addressed him.

"Good day, Colonel. Alphonse here. Things have come a cropper, I'm afraid. Time to cut one's losses and run, eh? Unless there were some way to salvage something from the wreckage."

"I'm listening."

"Good. Then consider Ocho."

"Ocho. Go on."

"She ought to be stopped, you know."

"I see. And you want me to do it."

"I dare say, you helped launch her career, did you not?"

"Yes. I suppose I did."

"If you'd be so kind as to lend a hand. You know Switzerland, do you? A place south of Lake Léhman called Montreaux."

"Yes. I know it."

"She will be there in two hours. Meanwhile, the opposition closes in. I could stall them, I suppose, keep your Siphon in the works a day or so. Twenty, perhaps thirty billion, is not to sneeze at. "

"We'll need the original activator."

"Ungaroni…in the lining of his red racing jacket. If I slow things down a bit—say two days…"

"Make it three."

"Right ho."

"And fifty bil."

"I'll do what I can. Cheerie-bye, now."

The telecom signaled a call. Cray summoned up as much droll courage as he could muster. "Charles. I'm afraid we've been had, old boy. I'd suggest a meeting of the board. Geneva? Good. Til then."

****

From his godly vantage, Phoebus looked on as Cray-Moore laced his boots, buttoned his shirt, cinched his belt and zipped his fly. With care, he combed his thinning hair and his short beard and his eyebrows. The Major's broad behind disappeared beyond the bedroom door. Phoebus let the image of the room fade away. The god mused, "What is it they say? …'send a thief to thwart a malfactor,' or something like that."

****

271

Meanwhile, back at the Villa Bonchance, Berti Huffding was quite impressed with the big major d' and with what he could do—like make the telecom produce whatever he pleased, even to the extent of peeking in on real-live situations a thousand miles away. She thought back to the morning after the evening of the arrival of the good doctors and their guests—the same evening of the intrusion of that Colonel whatever-his-name and his nasty friend, Charles. She'd been up at dawn, had prepared coffee and brioche and, quietly, stealthily, she and Alphonse had gotten the three Doctors and their strange friends off in the big ambulance while the Colonel and his tow-head friend slept away the morning hours. At 10 AM, the Colonel and his friend took a coffee and completed their morning toilette. The Colonel and Alphonse conferred almost amiably, she thought, with Alphonse being keen to reassure, and the Colonel maintaining a skeptical smirk. Abruptly, Cray and Endicotte departed in their own tiny vehicle without the grace to express a modest thank-you.

Now she and Alphonse stood looking into the telecom. There was Doctor Tisibon! And Doctor Bombaste! And the lovely Doctor Lagerquist, and what in the world were they doing but trying to extricate the ambulance from where it had run arse-end-up in a ditch.

"Good Lord!" Berti exclaimed. Where are they?

"Where? Why in the Jura Mountains, about midway between le Brassus and Genevre."

"And the Colonel?"

"He knows they're going to the physics lab at Montreaux, so there is no need for him to chase them. They must meet once more, you see."

"Must? No, I don't see. What's the point?"

"The point, dear girl, is I've got to extricate the world from the silly mess I've contrived. I mean, before it all just…disappears. Yes. That would be terrible. No Earth. No people. What would be our use then? For whom would we be gods?"

"The world disappears," said Berti. "And you're gods. Sometimes you just don't make a lot of sense. But at other times…"

"Really? Well, just listen to this."

Berti had turned on the telecom for a bit of Mozart and the voices of the Blather/Robbins InfoTeam broke through with the news:

Blather here with news of Port Tucson, Arizona. Estimates put the amphibious landing at somewhere around ten-thou troops and armored equip. The reporter on the scene—unfortunately we can't get a video in there—says a carrier off Gila Bend Mountain…island…and our radar station at Independence, Mo. suggests possible air-activity, the Indo-Pacific Union probably re-activating the carrier George W. Bush sold to them by our own gov. back in 2065—take it away Kookie.

Robbins:

This just in from the Department of Defense: The National Guard is on alert along the US border from Port Memphis to Manitoba. Meanwhile, negotiations between the US Inc. and the Indo-Pacific Union seek to cool the situation over the vanishing real-estate which is now up and over the arctic and into Siberia. Says the Indo-Pacific ambassador to Sciatica, and we quote: 'This is a dirty Yankee trick: Sell the sandwich and steal the meat.' End of quote.

"Good gravy," says Berti Huffding, or something to that effect (they spoke a colloquial Danish). "Are we to take this seriously?"

"My, yes," says Alphonse. "Consider: The Earth will lose about ten percent of its mass. Which will decrease its gravitational contribution to the solar system. Mercury, and Mars will alter orbit. The moon will leave us—probably go barging into Venus, or something. The solar system will be up for grabs."

"My goodness!" says Berti. "Somebody ought to do something!"

"Indeed," says Alphonse. "Someone ought. I know I promised Didi I wouldn't, but, dash it all, this cannot be permitted to continue. Berti, pack my bags."

"Where are you going?"

"Why, to save the world, of course."

****

After their misadventure in the culvert at Cossoney, our friends made the return trip back to the environs of Genevre and by noon they skirted the city proper, proceeded south-and-east to the village of Montreaux. Against the chill of morning, Bombaste had insisted on throwing the vehicle's heater on full-blast. The interior of the cab became quite warm and van Horn, quite unused to the big bod he inhabited, became sleepy in spite of himself—a proclivity to which he was prone in any case. In this half doze, she came to him."

Van Horn!"

"What? Whoozat?"

"It is I."

"Ma'am!"

"Listen up, van Horn, You're going up against a tough cookie, understand? Connie Ocho is nobody's fool. Are you listening?"

"Ma'am!"

"She plays a dangerous game which may destroy the world. Are you listening?"

"Destroy the world. Yes Ma'am."

"I want you to stop her! Understand?"

"Stop her. Yes, Ma'am."

"When the time comes, permit Doctor Wanda Waltari to take over. She'll know what to do. Got that?"

"Wanda. Take over. Yes. Ma'am."

"Van Horn, you blow this one and I'll reduce you to under-the-bed dust bunnies in the funny farm. Got me?"

"Dust bunnies. Funny farm. Yes Ma'am."

Bombaste was nudging him. "Mon ami, perhaps you dream?"

"Dream. Yes Ma'am. Wha…Yeah. I guess I drifted off."

Van Horn directed Bombaste over an unprepossessing mountain track. It had to be the big broad's doing because he'd never been in these parts before, and yet, he "knew the territory." They arrived above the village, so to speak, at about 1 PM. The ambulance poked its huge nose down the narrow pass and van Horn pointed to the north, to the large stone building set athwart the entrance to a small valley. "That's the place," he said.

"You have been here before?" queried Tisibon.

"Nope. Never seen it in my life."

"Monsieur. If never before, then how to know?"

"I got put in charge, you see. Like I said back at the hospital, Madame des Dieux told me to take over. Gentlemen," he said in a bass-baritone of command and authority, "I have my orders. Oh, ain't I though? And how in hell did I get into this?"

The eyes of Tisibon met those of Bombaste in the rear-view mirror. Each made to the other a Gallic moue.

"OK, gentlemen," says van Horn. "Orders say down slope and to the right, and we make it into the village proper."

Bombaste guided the big machine carefully down the skiddish decline. Had he not been engrossed in planning his next shrewd move into this caper, or had Didi des Dieux been inclined to alert him, van Horn might have noticed the tiny Renault Petit Géant tucked away in a lay-by. Its two passengers watched the ambulance pass.

Ammon's Horn

Under van Horn's orders, Tisibon and Bombaste, Kirsten and Paco returned to town to have a bite of breakfast and to arrange for accommodations. In his magnificent bod, van Horn paused before the main entrance to the Institute while he, true thespian that he was, pulled back his shoulders, thrust out his chest and prepared for whatever role he might be called upon to fulfill. The thought wafted through his mind: "Might's well enjoy it while I got it."

5. Tactics

"So, troops. What's happening?" Unannounced, Connie Ocho strode onto the main floor of the Institute. Kari Agapé hovered behind. and a telecom camera crew of eight brought up the rear. Ocho cast a challenging eye about the cluttered lab. "Hey! Goddamit! Anybody home?" Laser cannon stared at her dumbly. Glass glittered. Reflected light ran in rivulets down the helical twists of borosilicate insulators. Somewhere a gas condensor burped and a radio control beep-beeped. An oscillator screen ran the same jagged hump of signal again and again like something possessed for being stupid. "Hey!" Ocho shouted.

Somewhere in the depths of the gymnasium-wide lab, a door slammed shut. A burly fellow in white lab coat entered the lab. He was intent on his clipboard computer and he looked over his granny-glasses with some surprise. "May I help you?"

"Who the hell're you?" Ocho exploded.

"Why," he answered in a mellow bass-baritone, "I am Doctor Mackenzie."

"Yeah? Who brought you aboard? Where's Wanda? What'd you do with the old man?"

"If I may respond to your inquiries one at a time, Madame. One: I was 'brought aboard,' so to speak, by the *Ecole* at the behest of Chief of Operations, Waltari."

"I might've known."

"Two: If by 'Wanda' Madame has reference to Doctor Waltari, she is presently in the annex conducting re-calibrations crucial to our work here. And if by the 'old man' Madame has reference to Doctor Polichuk…"

"Yeah, Buster. That's the one."

"Doctor Polichuk," he said, "is indisposed. We thought it best that he be returned to the Clinique for observation. His heart, you know." *How'm I doing, boss-lady?*

Ease up, Hollywood. Your act's getting thick. As I said, she's no fool.

But even as Didi des Dieux's words resounded in his mind, and as the snarling pussycat Ocho yammered at him, van Horn was conscious of a pair of great blue eyes regarding him from behind a condensor column. The blue eyes widened and became part of that complex of expressions referred to universally as a broad and beckoning, smile.

"And who, may I inquire, are you?" he challenged.

"I'm Ocho. I own this place. I run this show."

"Ah, Madame Ocho. A pleasure, I am sure."

"Yeah? Well, I'm not. Get Wanda in here right away. We got probs… BIG probs. Understand?"

"Yes, Madame. I understand." The big smile continued from behind the column, but now it wore a considerable body—appealing in its squat and square configuration. The warmth of the smile was something Van Horn understood. This had to be the Waltari. His tactics were clearly laid out. In what he considered to be his best performance to date, he communicated through the great brown eyes Benni Pistone had lent him. They sent her a message that said, "Oh yes, you fabulous creature, I want you. Ohmygawd but I do want you!" and there is no telling what might have happened right then and there if it had not been for the sudden emergence of another party.

She came in from the right, from out of the annex to the main lab, and what van Horn saw got cataloged through the inductively scientific habits he'd borrowed from Anatoli Polichuk, but in language reflective of the vernacular vulgate of Chicago and environs, to wit: *Another broad! Beautiful! Chrise is she stacked! Lookit them...Hey, Tiger, c'mere!* Such observations van Horn kept buried, of course, he being skilled enough an actor that what he and Wanda saw striding forth was taller than the Pistone body-hunk and to Waltari's experienced eye, a natural—i.e., *sans* artificial augmentations—auburn-haired beauty.

The redhead, being pre-menstrually estrogenically dominant, broadcast loud and clear in that subliminal frequency emanating from out the feminine circuitry of the limbic system, a message whose reception W. Waltari regarded at first to be mistaken. On a second thought, re-read and re-considered, it was accurate enough in its intent and instead, to Waltari's flexible proclivities, misdirected. If any interest was to insinuate itself 'neath the formidable threshold of her scientifically-impenetrable guard, it would not be a bosomy, broad-beamed auburn but more likely something described along the lines of the six-foot slab of sirloin. Even now she was doing a skillful *entrechat* between the auburn, herself and C. Ocho over whose head, figuratively and literally speaking, the afore-described, if silent, dialogues were taking place.

Thus, in the presence of—nay, say under the augmenting power of— a sudden surge of estrogen and other femigenic and hormonal agencies, Wanda Waltari read a message in the beefsteak's eyes that said, "Hey, babe, I'm on a gig so don't you be giving me away and I'll see you and explain myself soonest, you fabulous creature," all of which mutual gazing and pheromonic commentary was effected between Kari Agapé and M. van Horn and W. Waltari and quite over the head, so to speak, of the imperious and expostulating Ocho.

But C. Ocho had the floor and van Horn had the Pistone eagle-eye which read the security tag on the other party's broad bosom and so he swiveled about from where he had stood suffering C. Ocho's berating inquisition and he extended his right hand even as his left found her waist and his mellifluous baritone boomed, "Ah, Doctor Waltari. Doctor Mackenzie, at your disposal." He smiled.

She smiled. "Ah, yes," she said. *We've been expecting you. Damned straight, big guy. Don't know who you are*, says she subliminally, *and I don't know what you're up to but I do hope it's something nice.*

It was only after an intense ten seconds of such eye-language that Doctor Mackenzie became aware of yet another party standing there, a sandy-haired, surly fellow of anthropoidal demeanor whose security tag read T. Laszlo.

Laszlo a-hemmed. "Doctor? If I may. We are almost ready."

Wanda eased herself reluctantly from the strong arm encircling her waist. Her eyes took leave of the brown orbs riveting her own. "Yes," she said softly. "We must prepare."

At which point, as though on cue—though if cues were being given and taken van Horn suspected Madame des Dieux had something to do with it—van Horn once more permitted himself to be guided, though the unremitting gaze of the statuesque auburn was indeed difficult to relinquish. Van Horn might have bent to the temptation to do something stupid in her direction but that Ocho, jaw in high gear, took the glorious redhead by the elbow and stalked off.

"Aperture…" Doctor W. was saying.

"Aperture?" says van Horn with great academic interest. "Tell me about the aperture."

"The 5-dim." says she.

"Five and dime?" says he. "Ah, as in K-Mart."

"5-dim. as in fifth-dimension," says she, giggling at what she took to be his humor..

"Ah, to be sure," says he, at which point van Horn heard himself being very erudite in matters scientific. Having reluctantly relinquished W.

Waltari's ample waist and still feeling the pressure of her great bosom against his chest, to his own surprise he heard himself holding forth like a true professional on matters of the temporality of spatial extension, and the spatial interval of temporal incident, matters as arcane as an intellect has ever beaten its brow upon, and which he himself barely understood but to whose accuracy the subliminal presence of Aram Gregorian attested.

****

At the Café des Marmots our sleepy, surly and discouraged friends sat to one side, the eastward side, of the outdoor facility partaking of the excellent French coffee and consuming the establishment's marvelous brioche and croissants slathered in superb French butter. Colonel Moore (actually Sebastian Cray in disguise) sat diametrically opposed, on the westward side, awaiting the arrival of Charles Endicotte. They did not notice one another, at least not right off. But then Kirsten had made her way to the ladies' facilities and returning to their table she spotted the Colonel.

"They're here," she announced.

"Yes," said Bombaste. "They are here, and we know where they will be—wherever we choose to be."

"How d' you know this?" Kirsten inquired.

"That Alphonse fellow—my suddenly acquired majordomo. Seems to know everything, that one."

****

"Ah, Charles." Cray acknowledged his companion's arrival with little ceremony.

"Yo," Endicotte replied in kind. "They're sitting right over there. What's our move?"

"The fourth disc, it's in the lining of Paco's coat."

"Yeah? How d'you know?"

"Alphonse, the butler. He made a switch."

"Who..."

"Hup! I think they've spotted us."

The waiter brought coffee. Charlie Endicotte buried his nose in its fragrance and peered over the rim of his cup. Between the fat man directly to his right and the arse-end of a waiter clearing a table or three beyond, Endicotte made out la Lagerquist's incredible legs, and the squat figure of Paco Ungaroni jabbering into a cell phone. "Where's the big guy?" Endicotte inquired.

"Dropped him off at the lab. And la Ocho is there."

"So, Gen'rul, what's our next move?"

"We limit our target for now. Keep an eye on Paco." "Where's his coat? He's not wearing..."

"He's left it in the ambulance!"

"Now may be our best opportunity."

Endicotte drained his cup and was gone. He returned a few minutes later. "Well?" Cray inquired.

"Nothing," Endicotte replied. "And he's not wearing it. Where the hell'd he..." From where he sat Endicotte saw the group of four rise from their table. He was gifted a glimpse of la Lagerquist in sumptuous profile against the late morning sun. But beauty and desire were relegated to the hindmost and, in any case, Lagerquist did, as women will do at the oddest times in Endicotte's opinion, wander off without warning. Endicotte and Cray watched the portly Bombaste betray irritation and impatience. A cab waited at the curb. It was Bombaste paid the waiter as Tisibon mounted to the rear seat. In less than a minute, the cab roared off down the street heading east and south.

"Hup!" says Cray. "They're on the move. Come!"

Had impatience not prompted them to be off in such hurry, the occupants of the first cab, and those of the second, might have seen Kirsten Lagerquist re-appear under the parasol of the cafe just in time to witness the peremptory departure of that second cab. With some expression of impatience at the antics of the males of the species, she uttered appropriate Swedish epithets and it was only after some minutes of indecision that she became aware of the presence of someone directly behind her. Kirsten looked into the benign and smiling countenance of the Afro model from the photo-shoot, Didi Baguette.

There was no need to hurry, Didi assured her. Whatever anxieties may have churned within Kirsten's lovely bosom were calmed. She stowed her bag and they walked the beautiful mountain town and chatted, as women will do. Didi was full of news of Paris and men, of photo-assignments, and men, full of chit chat of this and that and of men. The two women did a perimetric tour of the town and admired the mountain view. By late afternoon, Didi Baguette was still chattering. Kirsten found herself back at the Cafe and in the middle of a very good *boeuf bourguignon* when his name came up.

"You mean Pistone?" Kirsten said.

"Benni Deee! That's the one. Yaaas, girl, who'd you think? 'So, anyhow,' she says t' me 'big's he is you'd think he'd be hung like a young horse, now wouldn't you...'" Didi lost herself in a prolonged snorfling giggle. "...and then he says t' her..."

In Kirsten's imaging mind, Benni Pistone rose once more against a brilliant sun from off the waters of the sea. She regarded Didi with surface awareness while memory and an unnamed urgency appraised the coarse creature before her. Doctor K. Lagerquist, world renowned neuro-physiologist examined the fine musculature, and the honed edge of Kirsten's educated sensibility scorned the broken nose and the scarred face, sneered at the tattooed forearm. An acquired sense of taste defended against sweat and hair and the sheer thickness of the man while social sensibility noted the fact of a needed shave. But then her critique dissolved under the remembered sensation of being lifted, of being carried, as a small child. Peripheral sensations noted the presence of others, terribly young and naked and beautiful, dozens of them gathering about as she was carried down the beach, but they too dissolved in the powerful sensation of her body pressed tightly against his own and, perhaps more than all else, she was held by the appeal in those brown eyes that never left her.

Didi had ordered drinks and had not ceased from chattering.

Kirsten was aware of herself responding—a 'yes,' a 'no,' a nod and a comment. What she heard, distant and now significant was the voice —"Doctor Lagerquist! Is it really you?" They were in the locker rooms and he was down on one knee before her, his hands dark against the white gauze with which he bound her foot and the words rumbled from his throat —"*Like you...I'm drownin'...*help me!"

Didi's big frame leaned across the table and his grey eyes sought Kirsten's own. "That's right. He's drowning. You must help him."

"What? I don't ..."

In Didi's grey eyes Kirsten was made to remember. She was the imperious Doctor Langerquist of near a year ago.

She stood in the labs of the *hospetalen* in Upsala, she to one side of the huge globe of cloudy liquid and Gregorian on the other. Something to do with trees. Mahogany, memory said. Somebody got hit on the head with a falling branch...in Greenland, yet. Gregorian's recorded voice described:

Subject: Jansson Helga, subject deceased 3:17 AM...psychic energy systems maintained...subject's brain continues production p300 waves...consciousness frequencies...

Kirsten gasped, "Benni! It is possible he may yet be..."

"May yet be made whole? Perhaps. You're the doctor. But, right now he's in danger, *cheri*, and it's the woman he needs."

"He spoke to me! I wanted him, even then. Why didn't I..."

"Don't really know. You might ask Binswanger."

"Bins…Oh, my God! Just who are you?"

"Just your run-of-the-mill breast-pocket guardian angel, dear lady, 'useful if a bit obtuse, always glad to be of use,' or some such thing."

"I think I'd best…"

"Yes, dear girl. He'll need all the help he can muster. Off with you, now."

Ammon's Horn

6. An Arrow Into the Air

In Washington DC II, Sciatica, at the White House, President Telly Malakas and his Secretary of the Media caught the one o'clock news.

Welcome to EarthWide News Tonight for this, the first of December, 2089. Despite citizens' best efforts, the City of Charleston, North Carolina, is no more. Final exodus from that old city has taken on the air of a major emergency in the last forty eight hours as the waters of the Atlantic have breached the levees from Beaufort in the north to the low lying marshlands of Georgetown. If this keeps up, says one observer, the Tugaloo and the Seneca Rivers rivers will soon disappear and the salt-marsh lowlands of that delta will be part of the Atlantic Ocean.

And, according to ABT News Summary International, New York, per 02.29.86: Our front-line correspondent reports armored units of the Indo-Malaysian Army moving across New Srivijaya, former New Mexico. Wichita Falls and Lubbock report mass evacuations of citizenry pouring east.

State Department says, 'Our forces are on the scene and

the situation is under control.' Well, now, folks. Whattaya make o' that?

President Malakas had them run the video a third time. He watched the screen intently. A simulation-imaged arrow traced the parabola. The missile assumed a beautiful arc from somewhere out of Sandia Pueblo. It reached its summit at 1000 feet over Paradise Hills and descended into the north-western suburbs of the City of Albuquerque. He waited almost breathless. The missile vanished. Where one would have anticipated an eruption of flame and smoke, there was nothing. "That's for real?" he said.

"Yes, Mister President. That is for real." Secretary of State Agatha Porterhouse Prybar stood behind the President's chair.

"They shot real ammo?"

"Yes, Mister President. One 140 millimeter crud missile. Hexagon says probably from an obsolete M-73 Schwartzkopf. We sold them a few hundred back in the nineties. The missile fell in the suburbs west of Albuquerque."

"That's stupid. I mean, they own it."

"Yes, Mister President. The former state of New Mexico is now New Srivijaya, an extension of the Indo-Malaysian Union of…"

"They why they shootn'?"

"Army Intelligence analysis says it was either an accident, or it was intended as a warning shot…"

"Warning shot? Who they warning?"

"The single shot may have been an accident, Mister President. Texas border is still 200 miles off."

"Texas." President Malakas fell pensive. "Lemme have my book," he said. In his high-school geography book Texas was the big one, left hand side toward the bottom. That's where they still had cowboys. It was blue. Near Mexico. Which was orange. And to the left of it was New Mexico. Which was green. Except it wasn't New Mexico. Not anymore.

Chairwoman of the NSA, Peggy Grosse Brusthalter said he was going to have to get himself a new geography book as his tattered version was at least fifty years out of date. The world had changed radically, she said, but Telly Malakas hung on to it. Some things change, but other things shouldn't—like his habit of mind carried over from childhood impressions —Napoleon, or somebody, annexing Italy.

Given to imagistic flashes, Telly Malakas pictured a little man wearing a funny sideways hat standing up to his waist in the Mediterranean sea. Italy floated nicely on the waves and the little man pushed it along and stuck it onto France. As for the threatened invasion of Texas, Peggy said the Indonesians were pissed because she said they said the US had sold them New Mexico and California and Arizona and was now using some dirty trick to take it all back. "How we doin' that?" Mister President asked.

"Damned if I know," said Madame Secretary. Fact of the matter was, however, that seconds after that missile-firing, Albuquerque had disappeared from the face of the Earth. Four hours ago. Mister President consulted his Rand McNally. Albuquerque was still there.

****

And it was still there when Supreme Commander of the Armed Forces of The Union of Indo-Malaysian States of the Pacific & Beyond, General Sir Samuel Hadiwijaja (*hah-dee-wee-yah-ya*) led an advance battalion of armored vehicles (the M73 was affectionately dubbed the Schwartzkopf Decapitator) up 1,340 feet over sea level to the kiddie park at the summit of Mount Taylor and had his 100 units deploy into parade formation. In doing so they took down ten acres of painfully acquired and lovingly transplanted pine trees (courtesy of the Alameda Chamber of Commerce) and thought to look down at the City of Albuquerque which the Supreme Commander would enter as a conquering hero, hoping mightily Operah Freewind of TellyNews InterNat. might be there to do an interview, and they would film it all, which he could then send to his Mamma in Sumatra. But it didn't work out as imagined (things seldom did) because the distance from Mt. Taylor to Albuquerque looking to be so close in the Reader's Digest Road Atlas and Vacation Guide turned out to be sixty-five miles.

In any case, he'd ordered the armored units into parade formation.

His adjutant Colonel Ibnu J. Mushtaque relayed the order and they filled the clear air of a New Mexico morning with diesel fumes and the horrendous grind and growl and whine of one hundred 50-ton vehicles (manufactured and assembled courtesy General Turbine, Flint, Michigan). At about the same time, some twit in B Company, having guided his AV the entire distance across the former states of California and Arizona, and half way across the former New Mexico with his tube elevated in firing position, realizing he was the only one out of 100 units so configured, and feeling he and his vehicle and crew might be considered conspicuous, compounded the error of his ways and swung his turret about 180 degrees. Somehow his gunner hit the trigger and loosed a 140 millimeter missile toward the suburbs of Albuquerque.

****

"Information is Clout." Some Greek philosopher had once said something like that. Connie Ocho was not really your standard reverential type person but she took her hat off to that observation, because, as she herself said, you had to keep an eye on the big screen, a finger on the hot pulse, and an ear to the wheel or some sonofabitch would sure as hell blindside you. Instinct, she'd called it. Like a good hound smelling the breeze. You had to know to read people. and situations, like when to buy and when to sell, and whom to trust and whom to skewer before you got it rammed up yours. Which is to say the smell of this situation was that of a rotten *parfum*.

The big guy who called himself Mackenzie had to be what her Uncle Miguel in East Chicago called a dirty sock in the rice pudding judging from the way he put out his hand to intro himself. Despite the hand, his eyes glommed Wanda like he was starving and she was lamb chops. Kari took one look at Wanda who sized up the big fella and lit up with a case of the hots. The big redhead was trustworthy right down to the finish line so long as there was no stack of macho beef to distract her, and from the vibes Connie intercepted in this thirty seconds of how-d'y-do foldyroll, Kari was making with the come-on and squeezing out the oozies. But Laszlo came stomping in and he gave the hunk a grim glom like to say who the hell're you, and that cooled the situation.

As for the hunk: "Van Horn! Mind the store!" The voice of Didi des Dieux ran in his mind.

"Oh, you here? I'm minding, Ma'am! I'm minding!"

"Then keep your hands in your pockets. You have the big piano-crate gal off balance, but the Laszlo character's got you pegged for phony. Better rouse Doctor Polichuk. You're going to need him."

"You sure you wanna do this, Ma'am?"

"Do it!"

"Yes, Ma'am."

Doctor Mackenzie and Wanda led the way with Madame Ocho close behind. Kari scampered to catch up and Laszlo trudged along looking sour and sullen. Madame des Dieux was there too, in a manner of speaking, keeping her thumb firmly on van Horn's inclinations. She just knew that B. Phoebus Apollon, or Alphonse, or whatever name he might be wearing, had skewed the probabilities of the game his way by infusing the Pistone bod with a hefty dose of pheromonic androgens which caused his masculinity to glow, as it were, and his auravibes to broadcast to the feminine receptivities of those closest. The upshot was a van Horn who was, in his own words, "on a rooool!" his wit acute, focus unerring, with all his Pistone physical resources at the ready. The group of six moved down the narrow defile permitted in the jungle of phys-sci apparati.

Wanda looked up at Doctor Mackenzie and she was saying:

"...because the equation describes the Bibitty-Bau as being parallel but not identical, you see, preserving the principle of instantaneity-but-not-simultaneity..."

"But of course," he said.

"...which would abrogate the parity of any particular dimensional in an infinite set of Feinman sums over histories..."

"But, of course," he said.

Wanda and Doctor Mackenzie moved around the perimeter of the laser-generator assemblage and onto the main stage of the lab. Above the manifest platform, a digital read-out said 01.13.43 "Come, Doctor" said Wanda. "We'd best hurry or we'll miss this opening."

"Opening? he said. "Of course, the opening."

"The interstitial paradimensional shift, you see. It presents 'our way' once in an inversely periodic cycle. The next one won't be along until AD 31."

"Aye Dee 31?" says Mackenzie genuinely confused.

"It is inverse, Doctor. This being the Year Geo 4.726 billion 509.375 million, Local Universe Time, or 2085 Modern Historical Era, the periodicity being reciprocally and mutually inverse by 1763.34 of our temporal years, we'll have to wait 74 years for another opportunity, and, inversely, that would be, conventionally speaking, in the year 106 AD, or 2148 Modern Era."

"But of course," says he.

"Or, we could opt for an interface of closer periodicity, which means having to re-calibrate all over again and that would take...forever?" She had bent to lift a recessed keyboard. He, gentleman that he was, had bent to help her and their cheeks brushed ever so lightly. "Forever," he repeated. They looked into one another's eyes. Her countenance had flushed to the most appealing rosy-red. Wanda stood almost nose to nose with him—this six-foot bod he stood in was something else! Nose-to-nose with this chunky broad, he worried he was taking what she said seriously and he couldn't help it. More alarming, he understood what she was saying!

"...like bubbles," she said.

"Yes," he heard himself saying. "I understand."

"Calibration control," she murmured into her lapel mike. "Quarkian stasis approaching. Coalescence in ten." Her eyes focused on his once more. "So we call bubble A, the Earth, *et al.*"

"Yes Ma'am, 'et all.'"

"And the Bibitty Bau..." They had drawn closer. Their noses touched.

"The Bibitty Bau?"

"That is the dimensional membrane, bubble B, sharing the surface area with the bubble A, being parallel but not identical, one possibility..."

He stilled her with a kiss. "Hmmm, *vive* the possibilities."

"Please. Be serious," says she, continuing, "...in an arbitrary selection from an infinite set of Feinman sums-over-histories."

"Whatever you say, Ma'am."

"Because if, as Einstein postulates, space has texture, and curves in the presence of mass..."

"...then, the Polichuk Conjecture says, time must have frequency."

"You know? How? It is not published."

"He told me."

"He?"

"Polichuk."

"Yes?"

"He's with me. Right now."

Wanda regarded him quizzically. She looked up over his shoulder. "Yes. And so is she."

Connie Ocho shouted from her vantage on the catwalk, "Okay,

loverbuns, knock it off! I want some work done here, and I want it done now! I ain't paying you people..." but her words were drowned in the sudden high pitched hum of hydrogen at 21 cm.

Van Horn stood amazed despite himself at the evanescent wall of light that rose from the manifest stage meters before them. It hovered and, if one could have said he could see it, it shimmied, and, somehow, in all who witnessed its emergence, it seemed to beckon, promising it would open to invite them.

Laszlo's voice boomed from the wall speakers. *"Coalescence begins at plus ten and holding."*

Wanda's eyes sought van Horn's own once more. "Because if time is part of SpaceTime, as such its frequency will shift as Space curves and distorts."

"Hmmmm , yeah. Gotta be. Gotta beee." And he kissed the end of her nose.

Wanda Waltari blushed red.

Laszlo boomed through the speaker: *"Control, ready for phase-in one?."*

"Wanda freed herself from his embrace. "Excuse me."

"Oh, must you?"

She did something at the control panel and the intensity of the hum increased. "Calibration," she said softly into her mike. "Initiate phase-in one, EM at Planck minus ten," she said, and then she was back in his arms. "Who?" she queried.

"What?" he said.

"Who is with you?"

"Oh, that. Waaal, y' see...I'm not alone. He's kinda looking over my shoulder, if y' know what I mean."

"Your shoulder?"

"Polichuk."

"Ah yes," she smiled. "You have read."

Laszlo's voice cut in over the speaker. *"Stasis established phase-one. Ready phase-two?"*

"No, calibration, we are not ready. Hold stasis," Wanda responded. She sought his eyes and avoided the quest of his lips.

"Lookin' good, people."

Ocho's amplified voice cut through the hum of the quarkian hum like jagged glass through tissue.

"Keep the damned thing open 'cause I'm gonna wanna get in there, hear? This is costing me mucho bucks and I don't want no screw-ups like last time."

Wanda's voice was like the crooning of a love song, the sensuous texture of her lisps rounded about and caressed her words and he would have—but she desisted and instead blurted out, "Polichuk says, time is the errant factor…"

"We live but once," he said. "Seize the hour of love, or it will, like a frightened bird, fly right out the goddam window."

"The Time differential lies either side of the adjacency. If A and B do not share Space, they cannot share Time. Perhaps B, is 'behind' A," she said.

"Oh, I love it when you do that—wrinkle your brow that way." In a bumptious mood, van Horn did a Rudee Valee imitation. He sang softly, comically:

Your time is my time,
your space is my space,
umbiddy um-bum de bum-bum.

Laszlo boomed, *"Control, We are about to lose stasis phase-one. Are you ready phase-two?"*

Wanda freed herself of his embrace once more.

Van Horn in the big body of Pistone stood behind her at the control board and watched intently her expert manipulation of EM phase controls. The humming grew higher in pitch, more intense. She had a concerned look about her. Van Horn reached to put an arm about her waist, but she avoided him.

"Phase-change is critical, you see. As we approach Plank-18, the hydrogen atoms are dissociated, they become naked protons. We make way for the phasing in of the EM forces, the atomic weak and the strong, to prepare for the final integration with gravitation. We approached it the first time, but…Calibration!" she announced into her lapel mike. "We are at Planck minus fifteen. Ready minus-five and counting."

"…*four…three…two…*" Laszlo boomed.

Van Horn stood a bit behind her facing the control console with his left hand on her buttock. He had his nose in the utterly entrancing aroma of her hair. He might have lost himself in the sheer pleasure of her physical presence had it not been for the marked tendency of the Pistone body to hyperopia which permitted those same eyes to penetrate the relative gloom at the edge of the manifest stage and to espy standing there a tall, sumptuous figure, a golden-haired person, a feminine personage who as he squinted those far-sighted eyes, and as he close-framed her twice-up, he discerned to be none other than the beautiful Kirsten Lagerquist. She was standing just beyond the prohibited periphery of the stage and she was regarding him with what he could interpret to be nothing short of outrage and anger.

"I have minus nine," Wanda announced into her mike."

"Z'at right?" van Horn chuckled into her ear. "Make mine a nine-plus, at least this chassis…" He might have pursued the naughty reference but the other, the Lagerquist, was now definitely glowering at him. He hadn't known anyone to hit him so hard with bad vibes since his childhood, or perhaps, his second wife Margo like the time she caught him…which is precisely the moment van Horn felt it beginning to happen. "No, man. Don't *do* that!" Polichuk had risen to psychic foreground.

"Excuse me, but, you see, that is Frieda, she is calling me…" "No, Doc.." says the van Horn "That's not Frieda. That's the Doc, Lagerquist. Name's Kirsten…Da, Frieda, my dollink. This is the Professor Doctor Waltari, you see, and we are working…"

"Who are you talking to?" Wanda turned from her position at the controls to regard him. "And why the funny accent?"

"Ach, Wanda, dollink. What he tries to tell you is that at the level of Planck-18, the dimensional geometry dictates if it is possible to be in the same place at a different time, it is alzo possible to be at the same time in a different place. At Planck minus 18 the equation says Space and Time are separable on the scale of differential dimensions. Da? Yes! Differential dimensions share the same Space with us, or the same Time, but not both."

Wanda Waltari had backed away now. She regarded the speaker with something of disbelief and anger. "Why do you choose this moment to play the clown? Can't you understand the procedure is critical…"

But the big fellow was looking back at her in a most curious manner, and as though correcting her, instructing her, and speaking in this atrocious accent.

"Becoss Time, you see, is the errant factor. The Time differential between the adjacent bubbles sharing the same b-brane, yes, the differential depends on the temporal frequency of that point in the Planck space, so percentage probability says what is there is in a different Time. You see? " Wanda turned to look in the direction in which he seemed to be directing his concern. "Da, dollink Frieda. I am coming. I have work. No, dollink. No hanky panky, I am working, you see."

"We are at Planck minus 17," Laszlo boomed. *"All personnel clear the staging area, please. Assume safety station behind the force field. Counting down…nine, eight, seven…"*

He had taken her by the elbow, as a gentleman assists a lady, and he continued his lecture in her ear: "This is the speculation Paluszka and Prime, the Czech and the English mathematico-phys genius the early 21st century. But the Grunyon Breen, he agrees with the Indian savant Buncom Bafa—I have the honor to study under Bafa, you know. His equations call for complete separation the Spatial and the Temporal factors, says space, a point occupies, but the Time..."

"Why are you doing this?"

"Ha? What I am doing?"

"This act. This imitation of the old man."

"*Ach*, no, dollink. No imitation. You see I..."

Wanda stared at the fellow in disbelief and in anger. His voice. His demeanor. He had changed so from the brash would-be seducer of minutes before. His words were the sophisticated rhetoric of the accomplished scientist. She was almost persuaded she heard Polichuk's voice emanating from this body. They stood behind the force-field barrier now. At any moment, Laszlo would phase in the gravitational energies. On the quantum level the differential energies binding and formulating this Universe-bubble would coalesce and become one. The four dimensions of this world would open into the five dimensions of the adjacent Universe. And then...

...*four*

...*three*

...*two*...

To the several persons standing transfixed before the manifest stage the absurd and unbelievable became the real. One moment they had stood squinting against the increasing intensity of the quantum-energy wall, and in the next moment the humming had ceased. The hard protonic light vanished. What appeared before them unframed and almost unreal was best described by Wanda herself as a hole in reality. Or, an opening into an alternative world.

In range of perspective going outward, there was a saguaro cactus at forefront, saluting them with its one arm raised. Moving outward the desert scene was confirmed, a vista of flat, featureless land but for mesquite and prairie weed. In the distance, grey and misty against the sky marched a range of low lying mountains. One noted that it was raining "in there." It might have crossed a witness' mind to wonder whether, given a shift in wind, the rain might not come to puddle the floor "out here."

"*Borjze moi*!" said the voice of Anatoli Polichuk. "We have achieved Planck-minus 18 stasis."

"Calibration," Wanda whispered into her mike.

"*Stasis achieved,*" Laszlo responded.

"Can you hold it?" Wanda whispered.

"*Stasis holding. All systems stable.*" Laszlo himself was whispering now. They were all whispering, as though to raise one's voice might cause this miracle to vanish.

"Now, ain't that a bitch!" Connie Ocho had come to stand at the edge of the stage. "Nice work, kids. We done it! Hey, Wanda, how much you figure's in there?"

"Madame? How much what?"

"Real estate, dummy. That's the whole point, ain't it? And don't gimme no shit about scientific progress and all that. Columbus didn't start out looking for no 'new world.' He was lookin' for marketable commodities —spices, and like that. What'd he get? Real estate. Two continents worth. Buy your spices at the supermart, but it's the property's the rock-bottom asset."

"Yes, ma'am. If you say so."

"What's the US Inc.? A whole lotta real estate. Them politicians, they been buyin' 'n sellin' paper money, lettn' the real asset goddahell, now they losin' it all makin' a fuckn' swamp. But out there…there's the next big plat, baby. Thousands o' square miles o' nuthn' but real estate ain't nobody gotta claim on. Me? I'm gonna be the next Columbus."

Connie Ocho stepped onto the manifest state and appeared to be making for the world-opening before her.

"Madame Ocho…please!"

"Who the hell're you?"

He'd stepped before her, a broad, hairy, dark and almost handsome young fellow in sweatshirt and jeans. But the voice didn't fit. "It is I, Polichuk, and I must warn you..."

"Peddle the comedy act somewhere else, buddy. And let go my arm!" With that, Connie Ocho freed herself of the grip on her elbow and marched forward. All who stood as witness held their respective and collective breaths.

One might liken the spectacle witnessed to what one does in viewing a video screen. There is the reality the viewer inhabits. It is unquestioned. It is "real." And there is the "world" of the screen. It, too, is "real" so long as the imagination grasps it as such. To those of scientific sophistication gathered before this "screen," the experience brooked of no technological manipulation of images. They knew themselves to be assessing two distinct, separate and equally "real" realities.

Connie Ocho continued to stand before the separation of these two realities. "Hey Kari!" she shouted. "You, Ah-gape! Come 'ere!"

From the relative gloom of the lab Karimina Agapé stepped forward, a large attache case in hand. The tall young woman tottered nervously on her heels and came to peer from "here" into "there," as through a hole in the space of the laboratory. "Oh, my goodness," Kari gasped.

"Get on the horn, Agapé. Get my office. Get me legal. Call Geneva EuroCom, tell'em I want a media battalion out here, pronto. Scare up the newspapers. You got your palm-unit with you? Good. Take this down, kid, script and audio. 'On this day, the 12th day December 2085, I, Constancia Ocho, CEO and President, Chair of the Board of Governors, Subsume Unlimited, being the first person to get to this place, whatever it is...hey Doc! Whattaya call this place? This the 5-dim?"

Laszlo had come to join them. He stood as amazed as the others. "What is she do-ing?" he gasped. "Doesn't she realize..."

Polichuk-Pistone called to her. "In my new calculation, what we experience is a parallel of the present TimeSpace of the here-now' with a past time 'there-then'…"

"Nevamind the lecture!" Ocho snapped. "Kari! Getcherass in here." And with that Constancia Ocho was seen to step across dimensions. She looked back at them, and she gestured for her cohort to advance.

Tentatively, Kari Agapé stepped forward. a large attaché case in hand. She assayed one long lovely leg over the invisible partition from the here to the there. In tight permed hair, in her tight, simple-little-black-shift (with a single strand of pearls), in heels and nylons, she was an anomaly against the unremitting judgement of the desert sky. Those on the "outside" watched her attempt a few steps in the sand. Her heeled pumps dug in and she staggered a bit, Had those on the outside been able to hear her, they'd have heard her, "My goodness," and her, "It's hot out here. Just like New Mexico. And it's raining!"

Those on the "outside" watched Kari set down her attache case at the base of a saguaro cactus. She extracted a digital-recorder. This she placed atop the case, mike and antennae deployed. Connie Ocho continued to assay the desert scene and she took the microphone.

To those watching, Ocho was a mime. She appeared to be shouting, but to them she made no sound. On her side of things, Ocho shouted into the mike, "3-2-1 and recording. C. Ocho here, dateline 12.12.85, regular time. To one and all concerned in the regular world, be it known this recording is by way of establishment of claim to all lands. territories, acres, plots…um…"

"Properties and grounds," Kari suggested.

"Properties and grounds…"

"Um…parcels, domains and tracts."

"Yeah, them too, in this newly discovered and unlisted property which nobody owns and has never been claimed, plotted, platted, listed, zoned, sold, owned, assessed, parceled, or built on. The…what the hell do we call it? Kari!"

"The…the…Commonwealth of…Connie?"

"Whaat?"

"Well, gee whiz, Miz. C. How'm I to know?"

"Okay. Go with Unincorporated Territories of the 5-dim. Got it?"

"We are recording, Ma'am."

"Call this claim number 01-001, said claim to begin at the edge of the river…what river is that? Tari?"

"I don't really know, Ma'am. But first. shouldn't we do a survey? I mean, we're going to have to register the plot, aren't we?"

"Right! Kari, get me New York! Get me legal! And my land office! Where's that damned PR team? Dj'you call the papers? Get some tee-vee out here! I can't make no claim I got nobody to claim to! I gotta have witnesses! You got that real-estate prospectus we got up? Lemme have it." Kari stepped back into "this world" and busied herself on her cell-phone.

Abruptly, a regulation Army six-by-six truck roared its way through the lab and over the dimensional barrier followed by a monstrous Armored Personnel Carrier, painted bright yellow and festooned with the figures of white daisies. The carrier came to a halt and like a monstrous beetle of old it proceeded to wave its antennae. A svelt and pretty little thing in old-fashioned Army khaki and a commo helmet dismounted and directed the lumbering machine with arm-signals. Witnesses on the "outside" stood fascinated at what they saw. It was, someone said later, like watching a television drama with the sound cut off. Once on the "other side," the little lovely in the commo helmet gave the truck driver instructions and the truck moved on into the desert. In seconds it was gone from sight.

Connie's fifteen-hundred dollar outfit was soaking through, her three-hundred dollar pumps were full of sand—she kicked them off—and the curly-bang-hug-the-ears coif she'd had done in Paris just a day before was a soppy mess. But she could not have cared less. She'd hung the mike about her neck and she pranced about in the wet sand and as the television cameras wound away she all but sang her spiel because there was not one but TWO worlds would attend her words, millions "out there" would catch her act on the evening news. CNN, Fox, EUROCOM.TC unit, PACIFINEWS, not to mention GlobalWeb and even the trashies like TC unit-Transom and WWK.Com, WorldWide-Keyhole would witness her claim to this New World of the Five-Dim., as she'd elected to call it, this virginal, because untouched, because never-before-inhabited-by-any-body world to which Subsume UnLtd., whose CEO was Connie Ocho, hereby laid claim. The whole kit and kaboodle. If she had created her own international and financial gridlock in the "old" world she was sure as hell going to sew this one up tight before all those real-estate hungry folks in the over-crowded world of twenty-five billion got wind of the fact that Subsume Unltd. had a whole new 'nother world to sell for development and the horizon was no limit!

"Vacant land," she sang from the text of Home Guide Plus Free Take One Visit Our Website www.subsumepubs.com the 115 page guide available FREE from any one of twelve-thousand three hundred fifteen Gemstone-Bosco Food-Drugs Supermarts scattered in towns and cities from coast to coast, an affiliate of BuySmart, Incorporated, subsidiary of Subsume, Unlimited. "Limitless possibilities here," Ocho sang from the book. "Look at this exciting land...hey, you!" she shouted at the camera crew. "Catch the landscape, asshole! Over there! Charming lots. Hundred acre plots...sub-dividable...ideal for highways....mid-size towns, shopping malls...multiplex theaters..."

Meanwhile, Wanda Waltari and Tibor Laszlo and the platoon of lab assistants looked on in amazement.

The big fellow, the swarthy athletic-looking type, had moved from amongst them and had mounted the stage. He crossed the dimensional barrier and elbowed his way through the TC unit camera crew. He came up behind the expostulating Connie Ocho.

"Madame? I can talk to you a minute, yes? Please?"

"F'krissake! You're in the take, goddamit! We got a telecast goin' here, fella..."

She'd seen this fellow somewhere before, of that Ocho was sure. But what struck her was the voice. And the accent. Misplaced. They didn't belong. This baboon sounded just like..."Reduced. Reduced." she sang. "Five-acre parcels. Valley View Estates has open space to offer. Great area plus beautiful country view. Perfect spot to build dream homes. Highway to connect valley and hilltop development. River plain ideal for..."

The huge swarthy fellow with the broken nose would not go away. He kept following her about and yammering in her ear. "Buncomb Bafa," he was saying, "...in 2013, yes, Bafa posits the theory says Time is the errant factor. Consider the Time differential between two adjacent dimensional bubbles...do not share Space, hence, they cannot share Time. Says Bafa. Yes? Why not? Because, you see..."

"Why not?" Ocho was glaring up into the fellow's ugly face. "Lemme tell you why not. Cuz you're standin' right inna way of the camera. See, schmuck? Now, getcher big, ugly ass outta here!" and with that she gave the big galoot a shove. "Okay, we got to edit that out! Got it? Okay. Picture this one, folks," Ocho continued to the camera. "Fourteen rooms right over there. Mid-level. Perfect for large family. English cottage style. Natural brick. State of the art kitchen. Three baths. Throw in woodtrim casements. Low-pitch roof. Three-car garage. "

The Army ten-wheeeler came barreling back and skidded to a halt nearby. A young lovely in fashionable sawed-offs and tank-top came running up with a large metal sign in hand. "May'um? May'um," says she. "I gotta talk t' yew, we found..." The sign read, "Route 183," and in smaller letters above the geo-figured logo, "State of New Mexico."

Ocho stared quizzically at the sign in her hands. Just then the baboon comedy-act came drifting back again and his Russky accent intruded. "But is Schlemielowitz, University Tel Aviv, 2015, says if is possible to be in the same point in space at a different time, why not at the same time in a different space? So..."

"So what's with this New Mex? I thought we was in the five-dim."

"It is what I explain, dear lady. This is the same New Mexico from 2085, but it is in different time, you see. As says the Schlemielowitz, the shift the dimensional interface…"

"Who are you?" Connie Ocho drew back her arm and sent the highway sign sailing like a frisbee. She stood her five-three before him. She took the front of his shirt in her right hand and sought to pull him down for a closer look. "We've met before, right? So. who?"

"Polichuk."

"Who you shittin', Mack?"

Van Horn elbowed aside the Polichuk psyche. The heavy presence of Didi des Dieux descended to him and his moxie bubbled to the fore. His velvet basso chimed in with a chuckle. "He ain't a-shittin' no-body, *Mem-Sahib*."

At which point, Aram Gregorian chimed in. "Ladies, gentlemen, we have no time for foolishness. We are about to expire. As psychic entities we're already disintegrating, can't you see…"

Van Horn protested, "Hey, Gregory, whatever your name is, who you shoving?"

"Nemmine the comedy act!" Ocho shouted. "Explain! How do I get me a fifth die-mension and come up with NewMex Highway 183 ?"

And the Polichuk entity: "Becoss, Madame, what you dis-cover here is a dis-placement of the state of New Mexico. We have made a short-circuit in the SpaceTime. The New Mexico of 2085 occupies the SpaceTime of the correlative SpaceTime that is Switzerland and so got put back in the dimensional parallel of 317. You understand?"

"Not worth a shit," says Ocho. "But, that's okay. Ain't nobody in 317, or whatever, gonna beat me to the claim. I'm still boss of the heap. Okay, crew! Let's make for them mountains over there. Get us some scenery. Do the voice-over later." Ocho stuck her head through the TimeSpace barrier as would an actor through a curtain. "Kari!," she shouted. "Hey Ah-gape, we're gonna need 30-second visuals, get the

305

agency on the horn…"

Van Horn came to psyche-foreground. What he experienced was himself—the communal bod, so to speak, standing ankle deep in wet sand. He surveyed the scene. It had ceased to rain and he felt the emerging sun steaming the curly head and the sweat pouring down his—Pistone's—face. The Ocho woman was standing three meters away doing some kind of real-estate spiel. The camera crew of five focused on her and the one Ocho called Kari had come to stand with them to one side.

Kari was a tall, tanned, long-legged auburn-haired, supple-bodied beauty. "Excuse me," she said. "May I?" She placed her right hand on his shoulder for balance and removed her left shoe.

Van Horn watched fascinated as she moved around him, She placed her left hand on his right shoulder and removed the other shoe. Then, in deference to the heat she doffed the bolero to her navy-blue shift. Her generous breasts strained at the sheer cotton. She turned and caught his eye. She was smiling broadly at him and he began to rise to the occasion. Ocho and cameras and desert scene faded and he saw Kari's pretty face flush red and her nipples rise against her thin chemise. Van Horn gasped. But then *her* voice intruded.

"Van Horn!"

"Yes Ma'am. Z'at you, Ma'am?"

"Van Horn, do I have your attention?" Madame des Dieux. Sometimes she reminded him of his eighth-grade English teacher. Kari's short skirt seemed to be growing even shorter.

"I'm listening Ma'am! I'm listening!"

"Whole cities," Ocho was shouting. "Krise. we'll make New York from scratch! The real-estate opportunities are ee-nor-muss…"

Abruptly, a chopping kind of sound hammered the air, and grew louder. Connie Ocho looked up and a helicopter crossed the horizon moving west to east. "Goddamit!" Ocho shouted. "Now who's gettn' inta the act?" The helicopter drew close enough for Ocho to make out the pilot and he seemed to be giving her a hearty thumbs-up.

"Paco! They've got him!" The voice shouted up and past van Horn's control. The big fellow, he who owned this body, Pistone, or whatever, was pushing his way up.

"Paco? What the hell's he doin' here?" Ocho snarled even as Kari Agapé raised her skirt and proceeded to remove her nylons. "My goodness," she was saying. "It's awful hot in here...out here...whatever." That lovely lady continued to smile at van Horn most winsomely while Madame des Dieux's presence drew even closer.

"Cray, and Endicotte. They have Paco. And the two Frenchmen."

Something new stirred in the big Pistone body. Van Horn ground his jaw. "Ma'am Dee-dyew, you crowdin' the act?"

"Somebody's got to pull the fat!"

Tary Agapé teetered on one foot in removing her nylons. Van Horn had slipped a muscular arm about her waist. She put an arm across his shoulders. He watched studiously as she thumbed the rim of her nylon stocking, right leg. But in that moment, and though he still held the psyche scene, his adopted physiology gave him a seething froth of anger. The gut tightened. The temp. rose. The upper lip curled and the teeth ground, "They hurt Paco and I'll break their fuckn'...wait up! I hardly know the guy. Why am I getting excited?"

"Move it, van Horn!" Madame des Dieux growled as his inner voice. "You're not on a holiday. Go earn your keep!"

"Krise, Ma'am," van Horn grumbled. "Sometimes you sound just like my first wife, Margie." To his own amazement, Mackenzie van Horn hiked his jeans and did what he imagined was meant by 'girding one's loins.' He gave the auburn beauty before him one last sigh of desire and took three strides forward. It might have boggled his mind if he'd had time to think of it, but once more the world was that of the of the labs in Vallorne. The veritable wall of glass and metal equipage loomed before him and he was looking into the big cherubic face of Wanda Waltari.

Something moved furtively in the jungle of glass. Van Horn could have sworn he saw, fleetingly, half hidden in the relative shadows of the lab and beyond this brunette piano crate, the face and figure of the one who called himself Major Moore.

****

"Be off with you now." With those words had Didi Baguette dismissed her. It may have been Kirsten's own sense of self possession was challenged. She had not been so spoken to since early childhood. But coming from Didi, or Chou-Chou, or whatever she called herself, the dismissal took on the air of not so much a dismissal or a directive as a guidance.

She had stood at the entrance to a huge, one story building of stone so covered with ivy it seemed to emerge as one with the greenery rising from the perspiring earth. It was a winery long abandoned until reclaimed and refurbished for its unencumbered floorspace. The doors were double, two eight-foot-wide panels of oak which, to her amazement, gave way at a slight push of her hand. Then came more to amaze. Out under the sun Nature had exhaled its abundance in wild and green profusion and in one stride one stepped into the abstract precisions of science, into its challenge to observed realities.

She had stood in a well-ordered wilderness of glass columns, cannons of light and artilleries of pure energy. She observed great black and shiny banks of instruments, extensions of the human hand into control and direction of the inhuman powers of the universe. This was not her science. It had nothing to do with the human mind. But then, she mused, to what abstractions had her own quest of that elusive entity lead her and her colleagues? She stood so musing for perhaps a minute. And then she heard it.

The voice. "Doctor Lagerquist?" The speaker was hidden

somewhere in a corner, behind a bank of instruments. He lay on his side on the floor and from where she stood she thought to discern the visage of one Claude Tisibon, familiar but for the absence of his spectacles. She approached him. He squinted up at her through his myopia. "If it would not be inconvenient..." he said. Only then did Kirsten discern the fact Tisibon was bound hand and foot.

****

Note: The party responsible for the errant firing of the 140 mm. missile into the suburbs of Albuquerque was discovered—a smoking 140 mm. tube is difficult to hide. He turned out to be a Sergeant Wahabe (wah-hah-bay) a member of the five-man crew of AV Unit 15, that vehicle commanded by none other than Major Ibnu Mushtaque (ib-noo moosh-tah-kay) battalion officer in charge of logistics and supply. Punitive action was called for. A court-martial in-the-field procedure was organized and all done according to the book with which in mind the sergeant lost a stripe and a month's pay.

As for the Major himself, one may conclude he fell victim to the General's propensity for that which was "fit" to the particular occasion. General Hadiwijaja was an avid reader of such English classical writers as Thomas Hardy and Charles Dickens and had come away from Amherst with an Anglo Saxon sense of the dramatic and the ironic, and with a fondness for "poetic justice" wherever he could find it. This in turn may explain why the General, being a pragmatic kind of fellow, up-braided and dressed-down his subordinate before a panel of his peers. Then, having consulted the Colonel's personnel file he discovered that Mushtaque, before having been called to fulfill his duty as a Major in the Reserves of the Armies of the Union of Indo-Malaysia of the Pacific States and Beyond, was a school teacher of pre-pubescent children back in Padang, Sumatra, grades 6 and 7, which may have led to the General's selection of "fit punishment," to wit: the Major would submit in writing (pen on paper) a statement to the effect that a.] he would never again permit any crew member to traverse the turret of his vehicle with a round in the breech; and b] that he would never delegate a firing order to anyone below the rank of lieutenant, this submission to be made in the Colonel's own hand to be repeated 5000 times and submitted to the Officer of the Day by sunset following.

Major Mushtaque did comply. So much is known. Infer we must that he labored dutifully a whole of that night of the 12th December and that his submission was proffered in fulfillment of his punishment on the morning of the 13th. From this scant information one must also infer this to have been in addition to, or in lieu of, more urgent matters.

Firstly, the weather had turned to rain quite contrary to general information indicating hot, dry weather for this latitude in this time of year. As Quartermaster General he had to see to the mustering of dry rations to the troops as a field kitchen was quite out of the question. Secondly, his daily Status Report states explicitly that as of their arrival on the flat summit of Mount Taylor the battalion would be incapable of reaching the border of the State of Texas before the battalion ran out of diesel fuel.

7. When in Rome

In the world so altered, our three men of the cloth clambered aboard the chopper as into something comforting for being familiar. Introductions proceeded all around. Then, Captain Carson called out over his shoulder and over the roar of the chopper. "Gentlemen," he said, "looks like we got caught in something mighty strange. Why don't you fill us in from where you see it."

"Well…" The Reverend Doctor Bloodworthy cleared his throat. "The Rabbi here thinks we're dead and maybe this here's Gehenna."

"Oh, yeah?" Carson scoffed.

"And the Cardinal here thinks we made it to Purgatory."

"Okay," Carson chuckled. "What's your take on it, Rev.?"

"Wal…" Bloodworthy pondered a moment. "I'd be tempted t' go 'long with either one of 'em, 'cept I never read no place in the Good Book the angel of the Lord went 'round flyin' a helicopter with a .38 on his hip."

"I 'spect you're right, Rev.," Carson growled. "I 'spect you're right. Wut this is all about's a screw-up. Somebody, one o' them scientific types, punched a wrong button, so this here's an accident was waitin' t' happen."

"Accident?" says the Reverend. "Mebbee so, Captain. But I don't b'lieve all accidents are…accidental."

"Meaning?"

"I see the hand of the Lord in this, Captain," the Reverend intoned most solemnly. "Else why does your 'accident' choose to include the leaders of three of the worlds five great religions? No, Captain, I believe the Lord intended for this to happen. The Cardinal and the Rabbi and I, we're agents of His mission. That's what I believe. "

"If you say so." Carson stifled a smirk.

"He is telling us it is time to end our sectarian and schismatic strife and to join forces in His name."

"Amen," said Victor Cardinal Vendetta.

"A possibility." said Marshall Foreshock. "We are, after all, the children of Abraham."

"One holy, Catholic and apostolic church..." Victor Cardinal Vendetta had bowed his head in prayer.

"Can that, Victor," said Bloodworthy. "If I'm right about what's happened, there won't be no more Catholic Church."

"What are you saying?" Vendetta snapped. "It was written as of the Council of Nicaea that the one, true and universal church under Jesus Christ..."

"Gentlemen! Gentlemen! Rabbi Foreshock protested. "If what you say is happening is happening, comes soon the true messiah, and your Catholic Church is..."

"Careful there, Rabbi. You're treadin' on delicate eggs here," Bloodworthy cautioned. "But I expect it won't be long before you see the light."

"I'm going to be converted? Is that what you're telling me?" Foreshock bridled.

"Ah, yes." Vendetta grinned. "What is it the Book says? On the last day comes the reunion of the body with the spirit and the conversion of the Jews."

"So, your union, it will read us out?" snarled Foreshock. "Five-thousand years of Hebraic history, it's *phhhht* nothing!"

"Marshall," Bloodworthy said placatingly. "We been offering you the way out of your error for over two-thousand of them five. You can't say we didn't try."

"Mordecai…" Marshall Foreshock's eyes had narrowed. His mouth was grim. "Mordecai, stick that up your…"

But at that moment the engine growled and its whine rose in pitch. Captain Carson took the big chopper to 1500 feet and turned north and east toward Albuquerque. The three religionists had fallen away from argument and into sulking. Sergeant Garcia and Professor Breen sat directly behind them with their noses pressed to the plexiglass ports on either side. There was little if anything to see but rain. A light fog had risen. Carson dropped to 750 feet and the Rio Grande shone in a struggling light. US Highway 40 bridged the river and they came to hover over small towns at the edge of the metropolis. "No, Captain," Breen was saying. I don't think one can speak of the 'edge' of it. You see, the discontinuity is not merely spatial, but temporal."

"Then how'd we get into it?" said Garcia.

"Difficult to say," said Breen. "I venture to say we didn't so much 'get into' it as become included. Somewhere—theory allows for an 'entry' of sorts. Our 'former' time becomes 'this' time, though the space involved remains constant."

"Somebody punched a button," Carson ventured.

"Something like that," said Breen. "My guess is there is a kind of quantum 'portal' has been opened somewhere, a doorway between 'then' and 'now'."

Carson screwed up his big, homely face with the effort of thought. "Okay, doc. Explain me this, then—'when' are we?"

"When?" Breen responded brightly. "Ah, ironically enough, I know precisely 'when' we are. The equations extrapolated from our temporal point of departure place us…" Breen peered furiously into his palm-computer. "It is 5:37 PM and counting, March 1, 317."

"Three-seven-teen?" Garcia squeaked. "Three-seventeen, what?"

"AD, of course." said Breen.

"Mebee so," Carson growled. "But that sure looks like good ol' twunny-first century Albuquerque t' me." They had descended to 150 feet. In the curtain of drizzle and fog they made out the houses and streets of a small suburban village. "That's gotta be Braveheart Drive," said Carson. "I know the place. Been there lotsa times. My cousin Angie lives near there."

"Hey," Garcia shouted. "I see couple o'cars goin' up and down the street. There's people!"

"Of course there will be people," Breen said. "We will not be the only ones caught in the discontinuity."

"No shit! perfesser." Carson was fairly shouting. "Looks like your dis-continuity scooped up all kindsa things. Looky there!"

Professor Breen and Sergeant Garcia peered from the starboard ports into the desert below. The chopper had moved westwards beyond the village over a flat expanse of desert floor incised with the wet gleam of US 40. They saw a small brick building—a former post office? And a farm house. Another farm house. Then a fuel depot—what had until recently been referred to as a "gas-station."

"See 'em?" Carson shouted.

"See what?" Garcia shouted back. He unlimbered his binocs. He saw desert and rock through the rain and fog. Then a broad, green-grey item took three of the four lanes of the highway. "What kinda a rig is that? I ain't never seen no sixteen-wheeler…"

"That ain't no sixteen-wheeler, Garcia."

"You're right. It's more like a—*madre de dios*—AAV! Here's another one! And another one! And them's tanks! There's a whole fuckn' army down there!"

****

314

The "army" to which Garcia had reference was actually no more than an advance party of ten M5-A7 Armored Artillery Vehicles—three recon, five light-fire and two in the HP, or "heavy-piece" mode carrying the 140 mm. artillery weapon. The young lieutenant in charge was under strict orders. a.] Find a fuel-depot of the kind dispensing diesel fuel; b.] commandeer said fuel-depot; c.] radio back to HQ the exact location of said fuel-depot. The orders were short and explicit in keeping with the universal assumption defining the limited capacities of any second lieutenant to maintain in mind any order given in more than ten sequential words, an assumption which Lieutenant Samuel Ishkandar mightily resented insofar as he of the entire unit spoke fluent and unaccented American. He was Indo-Malay born (Kuala Lumpur) but American reared. Sam Alexander had attended the L.B. Johnson Elementary School, Waco Texas; the John B. Connolly High School, Fort Worth, and two-years University of Texas at Austin working towards a degree in applied ergonomics and comfort engineering. He sure as hell spoke good American. If permitted to say so he would have told Colonel Mushtaque he knew these parts like his own back yard. So, it was with a sense of insult and injured pride that the lieutenant assembled his detail and put them on US Highway 40, Flagstaff to Albuquerque. They would detour north at Paseo del Volcan to Frontage Road where he was sure he just knew he thought he remembered an old-fashioned diesel truck stop at the juncture—or somewhere there 'bouts.

****

Out of habit born of training and hard experience, as in the recent Colombian fracas, Carson took his chopper in fast and low and at 50 feet with the sun behind him he had the AAV's in clear sight, ten vehicles, armed light to heavy and wearing the insignia of an active battalion. He made a pass and a tight turn for a second pass.

315

"Who are they?" Garcia queried. "Don't look like anything I've seen in these parts."

"Judging from the insignia, Indo-Malay army," Carson shouted over the din of his engine. "Legally, they own this part of the country, you know. The tee-vee says they're thinking about invading Texas. Krise, I don't think anybody took 'em all that serious."

"Then who's the other ones we just seen?"

"Gotta be the tee-vee."

"Captain?" The Reverend Bloodworthy struggled against the tilt and inertial pull of the helicopter. "What's happening?"

"Reverend, Looks like we just flushed us a contingent of the Indo-Malay army, prob'ly out of Fort Huachuca.

"Oh, dear Lord! The invasion!"

"Mebee, mebee not. This here looks like a recon detail. Main force's prob'ly back around the Fort." Carson put the chopper into a 30-degree forward tilt and prepared to make a second run. "These guys are armed heavy. Them are 140's looks like. Carson took them down to twenty-five feet, parallel to the column moving in the opposite direction. He had slowed to a crawl. From the bubble cockpit and through the ports Garcia and the others made out clearly the helmeted soldiers standing in the hatches. "Yeah," said Garcia. "That's who that's gotta be. Who'd of ever thought the New Mex'd get sold? To a bunch of…" Garcia's words died in his mouth. The rear of the 'copter exploded. In an instant smoke and acrid fumes filled the interior. "Krissamighty! They're firing! We're hit!" Carson shouted. "Going down! Everybody hang tight!"

8. Sam Spade

"When a man's partner is killed, he's supposed to do something about it…it happens. We're in the detective business. When one of your organization gets killed, it's bad business to let the killer get away with it. It's not the natural thing…" Memory of Bogart's image on screen stood tall and firm in his mind. Mackenzie van Horn was Bogart, he was Sam Spade, and for a time there Pistone's rage boiled under van Horn's role playing. Van Horn was acutely aware of the long strides these legs permitted him, of the huge clenched fists, of his keen eyes scanning the jungle of glass and pipe and cable. He drew back on the huge shoulders. He threw out the massive chest. The chunky brunette named Wanda called out a warning. He turned once, and smiled at her as though to bid her farewell, perhaps forever.

To one side, the left, he saw for an instant the doctor woman's blonde head. Gregorian would have emerged to cry out her name—Kirsten!—except that van Horn summoned all the strength of character he possessed, enough to submerge the Gregorian entity with the psychic equivalent of an elbow to the ribs. But it was obvious: Pistone had taken over. Madame des Dieux was calling the shots. He pivoted on his heel. He must rescue Paco. And the doctor woman, the deliriously, delicious…no!

He must keep his mind on Paco because van Horn understood. Paco was the key to inciting the Pistone entity, to summoning it's determination and its strength because Paco was his friend, his partner. "He was your partner and you're supposed to do something about it…"

Foreign words came bubbling up out of nowhere. "*Ei*, Paco, *'dove sei?"* Van Horn chuckled to himself. He was mumbling words in a language he didn't understand. This caper was getting goofier and goofier, but then he spotted movement.

The late afternoon sun hit the windows set high in this sub-grade cavern of a place. The light flared in the webwork of glass apparatus strung floor to ceiling and then flung itself once more in glittering shards across the room.

In that secondary explosion of light he saw…her! Unmistakably, the Lagerquist. The doctor type. The icicle Swede. Van Horn registered in a split second—she was bound and gagged. He caught the fear in her eyes and the fact her face was bruised and swollen about the left eye, all this from a distance of thirty feet and in a span of two seconds before she vanished in the web of glass, in the thick spattering of light. She was bait. He was expected to barge on in and chase the bait. They would be waiting for him, to ambush him, but he was too smart for such a simple-minded ploy. Van Horn chuckled to himself. Hey, man, he was goood! This kind of caper was right up his alley. He cut to the left in the direction he had seen her, but then to his right appeared a corridor of sorts, a tunnel of black steel boxes. He supposed condensors, energy piles, because cables and terminals. He was swift, but careful not to touch, to keep his keen eyes fixed on the next point of departure, the vantage that would take him behind them, where he guessed they crouched, waiting.

Then, they did it again. This time Paco. The sight was enough to enrage him. Paco…*che t'hanno fatto?* The strange words bubbled up again but van Horn understood their import because in the few seconds permitted he had seen Paco's face peering at him from between laser columns, saw the pain, the agony in that bruised and battered face.

"Benni!" Paco called out.

The rage boiled over. The van Horn part of him knew he'd lost control. "Hey!" he shouted. "What the hell's…" The big bod threw itself forward between two ten-foot high condensors, hopped over cables and shouldered its way through a nest of wicked looking wires and van Horn was dimly aware of the sparking and the arcing, felt the shock of current in his right arm, the blow of voltage in his upper back and the tongues of static electricity dancing about his head and before his eyes, but Paco was right there! before his outstretched hands, and he was about to reach his pitifully bound and battered friend when he saw his last light—a star of whiteness that turned blue and into whose depths he descended and the last words he heard were a snarling, "Okay, sumbitch. My turn."

****

Union rules mandated a lunch break. Ocho's TC unit crew disposed themselves as comfortably as possible in the vehicles and in the wet desert sand. Ocho puzzle-worried the road sign they'd found. And what the Polichuk comedy act had suggested sat in her craw like something undigested. In the relative comfort of the tarp-canopied six-by truck she consulted Guru, a private consultation program designed specifically to her needs. In the cramped interior of the APC jammed with electro-photonic equipment and to the scream of the mighty engine and the deafening rumble of steel tracks on concrete, the screen shone pearl-grey. The voice of her computer guru crooned.

Guru: Madame? You called?

Ocho: So, what's with New Mexico? I started off in Switzerland.

Guru: The distinction between Switzerland and New Mexico is insignificant, to say the least. From the perspective of Earth's history, you have retreated time-wise less than an eye-blink. Your present 'when' would

319

constitute the year 317 of the Christian era."

Ocho: No shit? What the hell am I gonna do with 317? I mean, I don't know nobody in 317.

Guru: Perhaps not, Madame, but the possibilities in politics and real-estate are, nonetheless, considerable.

Ocho: Yeah! Tell me about it!

Guru: Consider, Madame. The 5-dim. sweep has picked up the western half of the State of New Mexico, and, continuing northwards, it will come to include a zig-zag strip of geography including what are to be Colorado, Wyoming, Montana, plus Saskatchewan in Canada and a generous slice of the arctic. Tracing its route south once more, over the Arctic cap, it will claim portions of Siberia, Mongolia, China, Malaysia and Australia and a hefty slice of Antarctica. It is working its way up around the bottom of the globe and coming up through South America and Mexico.

Ocho: Wow! That's some plat. How much territory you figure?

Guru: The total in square miles, or kilometers if you please, is in the vicinity several tens of millions. Know you, Madame that there are included in the 'plat,' as you refer, considerable populations, including urban centers. Total population should approach upwards of a billion.

Ocho: Yeah? That's good! I gotta have somebody do the heavy lifting.

Guru: That, Madame, is the up-side.

Ocho: Awright, goddamit. Lemme have it all.

Guru: The infrastructure, madame.

Ocho: Infrastructure. What about it?

Guru: There isn't any. The dimensional separation is, as I suggested, arbitrary. In most cases, sources of energy—communications, electricity, natural gas, and what have you—have been 'left behind' as it were. As for the political situation. .

Ocho: Yeah? What about it?

Guru: To put it lightly, chaos impends.

Ocho: Up for grabs.

Guru: Indubitably.

Ocho: Okay, program. Let's turn this parade around. We're gonna need lots of ammo t' fight this war. Get my legal division on it. A few senators I bought, just for emergencies. Get hold of Spangler. Charlie's the best real estate attorney in Chicago. And get my media on it—GlobeCom's gotta be right there when I pull it all together and take it over.

Guru: Ah, Madame. Not possible. Not unless you find the precise portal through which you entered. Time will have 'moved on.' you see. And not possible if the laboratory has shut things down. Remember the plutonium batteries? Oh, yes, there is another errant variable operating.

Ocho: Wut? Wut?

Guru: CES. Remember?

Ocho: Should I?

Guru: *Consortium Energique de la Suisse.*

Ocho: My electric bill!

Guru: You did pay it, did you not?

Ocho: How the hell should I know? I got flunkies take care of that kinda thing.

Guru: Memory says your rapport with the CES was not the best, to say the least.

Ocho: They're gonna shut me down!

Guru: If they haven't already.

Ocho: Kee-ryst! What am I gonna do?

Guru: Panic is the first order of procedure.

Ocho: I'm doin' that! What's next?

Guru: Well, Madame, you could poke about in the sand and hope to find the portal. I don't foresee anything but the slightest chance of success. Or...

Ocho: Or?

Guru: Or, push on. The future lies ahead, and that sort of thing. Given the fluidity of the situation, chances are the dim.-sweep includes a few scientific types. They may be of help.

Ocho: Yeah. I guess.

Guru: Pardon, Madame. An urgent message via radar-recon. It seems we are not alone. A squad of ten vehicles of a military bearing has been spotted moving westwards on US 40 towards Albuquerque.

Ocho: Who you figure?

Guru: Judging from recent newscasts, there is said to be movement by the Indo-Malaysian army. Something about an invasion of Texas. My own quick look suggests an advance party.

Ocho: Yeah? Not in my 5-dim' they ain't! Hey, driver! Get this thing in gear! Let's see some more of my real-estate."

Connie Ocho assumed her command position in the turret once more. Almost inured to the incessant roar, she peered out from under the brim of her commo-helmet at what seemed limitless miles unwinding as a ribbon of highway.

****

Back at Villa Bonchance, Didi turned down the volume. Ocho's yammering was reduced to a comical pantomime. Phoebus sat in a corner of the salon and sulked. "You've taken over, haven't you, Didi."

"You had all but lost control, dear brother. I really had little choice. Extreme measures were called for. In any case," she was saying, "that will keep Connie busy for the nonce."

"Really," said Phoebus. "And what about Paco and Benni, and poor Kirsten?"

"Ah, Phoebus. You are the god of love. Surely we can arrange for that human errancy to 'conquer all.' A few simple cases of what the van Horn calls 'hot pants' has been quite efficacious thus far, I dare say. What is so amusing? Phoebus, I don't trust you when you go smirky and silent—not both at once."

"The Waltari woman," Phoebus chuckled. "I don't think she's allowed herself a modicum of the warm-wet-oozies since her first menstruum. It took her by surprise. She liked it." Apollo was grinning broadly.

"No doubt," said Didi. "But oozies or no, what are you going to do about the other one, the icebound Swede?"

"Ah, yes. The beautiful Kirsten. I just may have to thaw her out myself."

"Phoebus! Remember our agreement!"

"Yes, dear sister. I will play by the rules. I promise. Let's see, now. Ah, there she is." Phoebus did a parody of the voice and demeanor of an old-fashioned radio announcer of the nineteen-thirties and forties summarizing a thrice-weekly adventure series:

> In our last episode, the thieves had quite overcome our adventurers, but not, it seems, the intrepid Doctor Lagerquist, who upon arriving on the scene, assessed the situation with one look of her steely blue eyes, and she proceeded to free the good Doctor Tisibon.

"Your clowning aside," Didi crooned, "she does seem to have things well in hand."

Phoebus gave a broad smile. "Indeed," he said.

At that moment, Berti Huffding entered the salon. "Hey, good people," she said. "How d'you feel about a cuppa coffee?"

"Thank you, dear," said Didi. "May I opt for tea?"

"Indeed, Madame," Berti said. She caught sight of the screen. "Looks like our side's up to bat."

"Game scoreless in the ninth and our side on the ten-yard line,"

Phoebus announced.

"Let's have tea," Didi protested. "Then we'll lend a hand, if necessary."

"A hand," Phoebus mused. "Or perhaps a whole body. Or the appearance thereof. Hmm? Let me see now—what was the name I used on the Iraqui caper? That would have been back around 2005?"

"August, 2004. Operation Swift Sword. And the name was Peppercorn, or some such."

"Ah, Arthur Stringfellow Pepperdyne, to be sure."

****

In short order, Kirsten freed Claude Tisibon—that poor fellow had been summarily trussed like a festival goose and stuffed into a corner. Together they found Doctor Bombaste stuffed into a closet and not a little put out. The three then searched and found what the two *charogne* had done with poor Paco, and he, too, was freed. An impromptu conference ensued. It was agreed, four to one, with Tisibon abstaining in the absence of his specs, that as a first order of business the "anti-social-deviants," as Kirsten called them, were to be dispatched as economically as possible, and that the Pistone bod must be retrieved, and Paco Ungaroni, too.

****

As for the "anti-social deviants." The fortunes of war oft turn on a trifle, says some philosopher or other, an observation to which Cray might well have paid heed for the fact of the matter was they now had what they'd come for—Pistone, unconscious and helpless, and Paco Ungaroni no less, and all might have turned to their own good fortune had they not previously acted with a certain lack of foresight in a small matter. Or, rather, a small automobile.

Owe it to that frugal habit of mind attributed to the New England Yankee that Charles Endicotte had rented a vehicle large enough for himself and his companion. The Renault Petit Géant was the more economical in operation and in rental fee. Only now, when the chips were down and after the expenditure of considerable time and sweating effort did it become apparent that lifting the inert form of Pistone and the stuffing of his considerable bulk into the minuscule back seat of the Géant was simply not possible. This left them with the expedient of taking, instead, the great ambulance in which their adversaries had arrived. That taking would necessitate the ignition key, an item surmised to rest in the pockets of one C. Bombaste.

Charles Endicotte returned to the lab. He would have searched the pockets of the trussed and furious Bombaste but that individual had, somehow, freed himself, or been freed, for there was nothing left to indicate he'd been there but the rope with which he had been bound. It is at this point matters took a most curious turn. What has been described as one's "sixth sense" prompted Charles Endicotte to turn about to discern who it might be was staring at him. The shadows and the flickering sunlight reflected from the glass and steel implements of the lab deceived him, surely. That could not be who it appeared to be. Paco Ungaroni was out there, bound and gagged and slumped against a wheel of the ambulance. Then who was this?

A diminutive wraith of light and shadow danced between the steel and glass columns of the stasis-control end of the lab. It emerged in the form of Ungaroni

Then, as though to leave no doubt as to his identity, the figure stepped forward in full light and, grinning mischievously, held forth a short chain on which dangled a key. "*Ei, carogna*," he said, which is to translate loosely, "Hey, you sonofabitch." Then he raised a median finger, left hand, and vanished into the shadow works once more. Endicotte, enraged, took pursuit. "Cray!" he shouted into his cell phone. "The little daigo's loose!"

****

Sammy Blankenship ran the NorAmCo HPO15 Plus fuel depot corner of Paseo del Volcan and Frontage Road which was south of the suburb of Westgate and out on the western edge of anything. He was there 6 AM every morning, give or take ten minutes.

As a matter of habit, in what passed for a moment of meditation, Sammy would turn in the open door of the NorAmCo franchise and peer absently over the spare, dry yucca-dotted plains.

The sun greeted him as a glare in his eyes. The light was different now from what it had been when he was a youngster, since the great flooding. They said it was because the sun got reflected off salt water.

Sammy never ventured south enough to see for himself, but they said that what had been the southwestern portion of the state of New Mexico was now a shallow arm of the Gulf. What stood between Albuquerque at near 5,000 feet and open salt water were the Socorro Mountains to the west, and the Sacramentos south and east, and the fact the land elevation rose just a few tens of feet, enough to spare the north-eastern part of the state the flooding of what had once been the great state of New Mexico.

"Cause the Rio Grande Valley's under salt water now, y'see," the Reverend Ray Hidalgo explained. "Whole valley south of here," he said. "Most of ol' Mexico's gone, and Panama, and them."

So, the smell of salt water was Sammy's message now, mixed with the lingering perfume of flowering yucca.

"Strange are the ways of the Lord," the Reverend said.

"Mebbe so," Sammy conceded that. And the silence was his message. He stood and thought of all this. Then he turned and commenced his day's labors.

First regulars showed up around seven. Farmers, mainly. Locals.

326

Spring and fall, planting and harvest seasons, were heaviest. About now, late August, things were still quiet. Maybe a dozen locals and some out of town trade came in for a quick replacement of the Handy-Dandy cannisters of HPO15-Plus—mostly pick-ups, a few tractors and some cars. The law said you had to be licensed to dispense and Sammy had him the 5 by 7 holographic card with his photograph in the top right hand corner, laminated, framed and hung on the wall and it said Sammy Blankenship was certified and licensed to dispense HPO15 Plus and other volatile fuels by virtue of the three week-ends course he took in Santa Fe. That was because the HPO15 plus ethanol and a few other things that were under high pressure came out a vapor when you cut loose the valve. The pressure dropped to 120 psi when it hit the vehicle's combustion chamber. But it was still pressurized, and co-ro-sive and vola-tile and dangerous. Mister Oglethorpe—that's Herb Oglethorpe from over in Westgate—he owned the franchise. He also ran the real-estate office and he practiced law. He's the one put all the signs up around the place said: NO SMOKING.

What happened on the morning of the first of September is largely as Sammy saw it. If he survived it, that was only because he was terrified of firearms and when they came in all got up in camouflage uniforms and squinting at him from under helmets, Sammy figured, hopefully, they were part of a tee-vee thing making a movie, or something, but they had to be for-real because he couldn't make out a word they said so they were not from these parts, and not even Mexicans because Sammy didn't speak any Spanish except for a word here and there but he knew the lingo when he heard it and this wasn't it!

Then he saw the AK-53 slung over this one guy's back and Sammy figured maybe a hold up, except the business was 100 percent DebitCredit card and there was no cash on the premises, so there wouldn't have been anything to steal.

Then the one guy seemed to be the honcho he got on his cell phone and he got to talking that strange language and right about then Sammy

327

connected with the CNN NewsHour of the evening before. The news lady said something about soldiers, troops, something about the state of New Mexico having been sold barrel and breech to the Indo-Malay outfit. And something about parts of the state territory having "disappeared." So the Indo-Malays were going to send in troops from Arizona to which they'd bought the franchise, and which they were not supposed to do under the terms of the franchise, to enforce their sale. The CNN lady called it an invasion. Sammy pretty well followed his pa's opinion that most of the news you got off the teevee was serious hogwash and the rest was happy horseshit so Sammy hadn't paid it any mind. But then the AAV's came rumbling round the corner of Frontage Road. They came right into the depot, three of them, bigger than houses. Sammy recalled what the CNN lady said. So he figured, oh my God, that's what this had to be. An invasion.

Sammy got put off at first because the young fellow in camouflage fatigues—turns out his name was Sammy, too—he spoke as good American as Sammy did, more like a Texan, really, so they didn't have any trouble communicating, none at all. He was a lieutenant. He was in charge of this detail, he said. And he wanted fuel. Sammy—Blankenship, that is— he said no problem, just make with the DC card. He, Sammy, the lieutenant, that is, had only to shove his card into the slot at the ATM machine and punch in the number of cannisters required and the Handy-Dandies would come clinking down the rack.

That was the beginning of the problem. These people didn't have any DC cards, so there was no way they were going to get their Handy-Dandies. Nor could they release the valve on any one of the three pumps to avail themselves of a direct transfer, pressure pump to non-pressure tank. That got this lieutenant honcho type mad and he said to Sammy Blankenship that Sammy had better find a way to get some fuel going or he was going to have to bust open a pump. Sammy said he didn't advise that as the stuff was very volatile and might explode. And the lieutenant honcho said he never heard of diesel oil exploding that way. And Sammy Blankenship he said it wasn't diesel, it was HPO15 Plus."It's whut?" says the lieutenant.

"It's HPO15 Plus."

"Whut's that?" says the lieutenant.

"You ain't never heard of HPO15 Plus?" says Sammy Blankenship. "Been on the market going on ten years now."

"Whut is it?" says the lieutenant.

"Whut is it?" says Sammy Blankenship. "Why, it's hydrogen super pee-roxide, plus a skosh o' hydrazine and some ethanole and couple-three other things."

"Oh, shit!" says the lieutenant. "Where's your diesel?"

"Diesel?" says Sammy Blankenship. "Shucks, we ain't sold diesel in these parts since the big petro-leum bust of '47. Ain't nobody pumpin' oil out the ground no more. It's a poe-loo-tunt, y' know. You want diesel you gotta go t' Abilene. They still servicing them big umpteen wheelers. Leastways that's what I hear."

"Abilene, Texas?"

"Kansas," Sammy Blankenship corrected. From the look on the lieutenant's face Sammy Blankenship got the feeling the lieutenant didn't want to believe him.

While Sammy Blankenship and Lieutenant Sammy Alexander discussed these and other arcane matters, one of the troopers was busy at the pumps. The pump would not pump. And the directions—what he took to be directions—were printed atop the dispenser gauge in English, a language with which he had scant acquaintance. He was a sergeant. A veteran of three campaigns. He was ingenious in the deployment of field-expediency. FE procedures said use the simplest means to cut to the core of a problem. In this case the most direct approach was by way of a hammer. Which he was to find, eventually. And which he was to use.

Which accounts for three of the AAV's. The other seven were

deployed about the east-to-west approaches to the suburb of Westgate, north and south along Unsser Boulevard, east-west along Sage Road, then back up along 114th Street and back up to US 40. One might say they surrounded the City of Albuquerque about as well as a kitten surrounds the sofa she's sleeping on. The invasion took place at around seven in the morning when townsfolk were getting up and about their daily business and most apt to be surly and annoyed to be told their town was henceforth commandeered by a group of strange looking men in camouflage fatigues the likes of which none of the townsfolk had ever seen before outside digital-video shows and to whom they paid as little mind as possible, most of them having better things to do..

As noted, the AAV's had set up a perimeter defense about the eastern approaches to the town, expectations being any counterforce would come roaring in from the direction of Texas, up route 40, and/or 25 and smack-dab through the center of Albuquerque. In which event their on-board radar-recon would alert them in ample time to respond. And so the seven massive vehicles sat, one in the parking lot at Santiago's Gemstone-Bosco Food and Drugs, and one in the playground of the John Marshall Washington Elementary School. One of them took position at the top of the hill in the town park, and the others at the junctions of Sage Road and the Boulevard and at what they took to be main street and the four main avenues feeding into the downtown business district. Meanwhile, orders also said "constant recon." And they said "preserve fuel." In light of which orders the AAV's sat like great hunched pussycats, silent but for the gutteral purr of auxiliary engines powering the generators which fed the on-board radar.

24. Out of this World

From the APC turret twelve feet above ground Connie Ocho had to be the first to see the chopper lying like a huge grasshopper with its face in the mud of the Rio Grande and its sorely blasted arse-end in the air, the whole apparition smoldering and long past the cares of this world. Ocho's driver squawked something over the intercom and the massive vehicle slowed, and stopped. There was someone standing in the middle of the road gesturing, ordering them to stop. Connie Ocho dismounted.

The closer Ocho got, the taller he appeared to be and the more imposing. So she did what she always did when threatened—she lengthened her stride, widened her hips, threw out her chest, thrust her jaw and prepared to be as nasty as she knew how to be, which was considerable. He looked down at her as she looked up. He had the sun at his back and it was in her eyes so she had to squint upwards even as she prepared to bully, bitch and generally badger this Anglo looking clown into submission. "Howdy," he said. "Herb Carson, State Police." The voice was soft and deep and gentle. "Good of you to stop. We got some folks here got banged up a bit."

"What happened?" Ocho ventured.

"We got shot down."

"Shot down? Who…"

"Indo-Malay recon. Young fellas have got to be a might nervous on the trigger. Took my tail pylon clean off."

"Indo-Malay? What're they doing here?"

"Hey, it's their playground, Ma'am."

"What're you talking about? This is the five-dim."

"That's whut the perfesser tells me. But this part o' New Mex. 'n everything in it got picked up, I 'spect."

"No way, ho-zay! I paid good money to get this 5-dim. thing moving and I've got first dibs on it."

"You did?"

"That's right, buster. Me, Connie Ocho, CEO of Subsume UnLtd., president of FirstBank Toronto and chairman of the board of General Inclusion."

"Wall I'll be shucked. 'Scuse my language, Ma'am, but I think you better come over and talk to the perfesser. You tell him whut you done, let him explain whut kinda mess we're in."

Ocho stepped to one side and put the late morning sun fully on this fellow. Then she saw the kerchief wrapped round his head half hidden by his Stetson. It was blood soaked. "You've been hurt!"

"Nasty bump's all this is. But if y' don't mind, Ma'am, Sergeant Garcia's in a bad way. And the Reverend. If you got a medic aboard your carrier…"

****

Sammy Blankenship had a few surprises yet to come. The armed AAV's took up pert'near all the space on the depot's concrete slab, but then came an APC tall as a barn and painted white with yellow flowers. In a few minutes up come five three-quarter ton vans sprouting antennas, logo says GlobalNTC unit and pretty soon you got soldiers running around all over the place, and people with teevee cameras chasing after them and Sammy was afraid one of the soldiers might get ticked and unlimber a rifle, all but this one, a sergeant judging by his three-up and three-swinging, kept chasing Sammy Blankenship around hollering at him, "Diesel! Diesel!" and Sammy's trying to get it through the sergeant's thick skull, "There ain't no diesel!"

Sammy's little office got turned into a dispensary because there were four people banged up some and a doc got busy antisepting and bandaging. Turns out one of the people hurt, the tall skinny guy with the Adam's apple needed a shave talked like he was from Alabama or Arkansas, one of them, he was a preacher. The lady in charge of the APC, she and the lieutenant got to arguing something awful and Sammy Blankenship was afraid somebody would hit somebody. But then the little guy in the duster came in, the bald eagle with the thick glasses, and he starts in explaining things and everybody kind of cooled down.

"Whut kind of 'event' you got in mind?" Carson asked. In a kind of mutual acknowledgement, the others returned to the subject at hand. "I mean, we oughta kinda watch for it so's we'll know."

Breen considered a moment. "Hard to say, but for a *gedanken* example, say someone fired a gun 'there and then.' At just the right moment. Say the bullet left the barrel in time for the discontinuity to shear the arc of incidence."

"Or a 40 millimeter shell," Lieutenant Alexander suggested. "We fired one by accident. Never did hear the shell go off. Matter of fact, it was vectored for impact right about…here."

"Lieutenant," Carson scoffed nervously, "you just made my day."

"Discontinuity," Breen was saying. He struggled for a metaphor, an image, something to give the abstraction substance. "Like a piece of cake," he said. "You cut a wedge. The cake has a space in it now. The wedge is whole, but it's…separate."

"I follow," said Carson."

"Now, we don't know," Breen continued. "Whether the discontinuity is permanent. There have got to be a million events initiated 'over there,' so to speak, whose arc of incidence stretches over time, and over space."

"'Arc of incidence,'" Carson repeated. "Like it started to happen 'over there' and it might finish over 'here.'"

"That's exactly right," said Breen. "And one way or another, we'll know about them. And that will mean the portal between 'there-then,' and 'here-now' is closed.

"No way to go back? ventured Garcia.

"No way to go back," Breen affirmed.

"You're sayin' I'm gonna be stuck here?" Ocho said. Something like worry penetrated her usual defiance, so that in her macho-chic garb, she suddenly looked child-like and pathetic. "Like I'm never gonna make it back?"

"That may well be the case," Said Breen.

"Horseshit!" Ocho shouted. "I'm the one opened this thing up, and I'm the one says when it shuts down. Route 185 and Muchogusto Road. Along the Rio Grande. That's where I come in, and that's where I'm goin' out. Hey, whatta you think? I ain't got nuthn' in here. Not 'less'n I operate from out there. Got nuth'n and I ain't nobody without the money. And the power. That's what it's all about, now ain't it? Blather! Hey, numbnuts! Let's put this circus on the road. Hear me? We're headin' back! Where is everybody? Where's my crew? Where'd everybody go?"

The door slammed behind her. Through the glass front the men watched her march onto the apron and the summoning of her troops.

****

The Reverend Bloodworthy had suffered a fractured humerus. The doc splinted and bandaged his arm, and his patient sat in some pain and discomfort for a while. But he got bored listening to Professor Breen explain about dimension and portals, and time and space, and something called "branes." All well and good, says the Reverend to himself. These scientifical types could explain anything they put their minds to and still come up empty because they left out of it the author of it all, the Engineer of the Universe. Mordecai Garybob Bloodworthy excused himself quietly and slipped out the door.

He betook himself across Frontage Road into the open desert. He climbed a low-lying table-top and fell to his knees facing an early afternoon sun. "Lord?" he said.

"Son?" came the answer.

"Guide me. oh Lord."

"Where do you want to go, child?"

"Wal, Lord, seems like we in a new situation now. The scientist people have ripped off piece of the world. The good Christian folk come with it are gonna need the light and the way and the word. I was all set to become the Secretary of Religion in the old world, you know. Like t' say, your right-hand man in the field. But I guess you had other plans. I'm seeing your hand in this Lord, picking me up with this 5-dim. thing, the way you did. Like you had me in mind for a special mission."

"Did you, now?"

" 'And I shall be sent into the cities of men, unto those who are deaf to the word of the Lord, and I shall open their ears that they may hear. I shall unseal their lips that they may speak, and their hearts that they may know His ways are the ways of the light, and the way, and the truth.' "

"My, my, Mordecai. Sounds to me like you got yourself all primed and pointed and ready to go."

"Yes, oh Lord. You have but to show me the way."

"Have I now? Well, you're right in saying you've ruined part of my world. But then, you've been doing that since Eden."

"Lord?"

"I've kept an eye on you and your end of things. Seems you humans don't need me when it comes to creating problems for yourselves."

"Thy will be done, oh Lord."

"Really?" Like to say if it goes wrong and you end up hurting, it was my will. Then it's up to me to pull your chestnuts from the fire."

"I didn't mean it that way, Lord, honest. It's just that given the ways things are goin', what with this tearing' up the world and all, I figgered you had t' have a hand in it. Not just for the punishment of it, though Lord knows we deserve plenty o' that, but mebee the opportunity, if y' know what I mean."

"Opportunity?"

"Yea, Lord. Like t' say for two thousand years we been tryin' t' open people's eyes to the light and the way. Been a mean fight every inch, day in and day out. And the competition, it just don't lay down and quit, y' know. But now—oooo-weee! A new world! A fresh start. Fella happens t' be on the scene, why it's like God Hisself gettin' him in on the ground floor, offerin' him a ex-clusive franchise, if y' know what I mean."

"Exclusive franchise, you say."

"Well, Lord, ain't it?"

"Well, son, the light is one you won't see, and the way is whatever you prefer. As for the truth, your memory remakes it and your history rewrites itself. Now, honestly, tell me I'm wrong, Mordecai."

"No, Lord. You're right. Miserable sinners are we all. You have but to show me the way, Lord, for thy will is my will. and thy work is my work, forever unto the judgement day, Amen!"

"Haven't heard a word I said, have you? Well, then. Have a look for yourself. Here comes your resolution. Bah, naow, Mort."

What could the Lord have meant? There was no one about, except a tiny woman in a commo helmet just now coming around the bend. "Afternoon, Ma'am."

"Who the hell're you? That's right, you were with the chopper."

"I'm kind of an emissary of the Lord, y' might say. And you kinda strike me as somebody's got big trouble."

"Outta my way, buster. I got no time for no sermon."

"Listen t' me, Con-stan-see-ya…"

"How d'you know my name?"

"Shucks ma'am. The whole world knows Con-stan-sya Oh-cho. Mos' pow'ful woman inna worl'."

"Yeah?"

"Like I say, ah'm a kinda emissary. Come t' open y' eyes, make y' see what you been lookin' at."

"Yeah? Like what?"

"Like this right here's a meetin' o' the powers o' the earth, and the powers of His kingdom. Well, ain't it? You wanna be the boss o' the whole shoot'n' match. And yew gonna be. Yes, Ma'am, I got it on the bes' authority, yew gonna be jus' that."

"Is'at a fact? Well, you're right about one thing. Troubles I got. Plenty. I'm the one paid for all this y'know. I made it possible. The opening of the 5-dim., 'n all that."

"Yes. I know."

"A whole new world, that's what I'm offerin'em. And whatta I get for it? Investigations. Indictments. Like I was some kina crook, or somethin'. Top o' that, there's a invasion, the Indonesians, and them. I mean, I ain't had the place surveyed and I got a fuckn' war on my hands arready—you should pardon my French."

"Is there no justice?"

"And just when we get the portal open, they're tellin' me it's gonna shut down and I gotta wait seventy four years for it t' open again. Hey, I'm gonna be damned old! Well, I ain't gonna stand around with my thumb in it, Mac, lemme tell ya. I mean, how'm I supposed t' give'em this whole new world they shut the damned thing down on me."

"Indeed. The ways of the world are nefarious."

"I mean, my money, my banks, they're all over there! Now my

crew's run off on me like they was on vacation, or somethin'. I mean, I gotta get back, like right away!"

"Let us pray for guidance. Oh, Lord. Thou hast dipped into thy bag of wonders and offered us a whole new world."

"Better ask for a driver. My girl's off gettin' laid in a sand dune, or somethin'. How'd you happen t' get aboard, Rev.?"

"Chance, my dear. Sheer chance. Or, as I prefer to see it, the hand of the Lord Hisself has guided me."

"Yeah? T'what?"

"Me, and Him. We have a understandin', y' see. This new world, it's gonna need guidance. Jus' like folks need t'be told what t' do with their money, their stocks 'n bonds and like that there, and they need the gummint t' keep things organized, so they gonna need spiritual guidance keep'em on the straight 'n narrow."

"And you're gonna be right there to provide it, right? Like the pope o' the world."

"As I say, me and Him, we have a understandin'."

"Yeah. Gotta have somebody keep the slobs in line."

"If the Lord sees His way t' honor me…"

"Okay, Rev., I gotcha. You keep 'em guilty and scared, I'll keep 'em poor and hustlin'. But what we gotta do is keep the portal open. I gotta have access from there to here. Let it leak! Me, I'm still gonna be top o' the heap. C'mon, Reverend. We gotta keep the goddam thing from shuttn' down!"

"Praise the Lord…"

"…and time is money. You command, I'll drive. Let's put this show on the road!" Connie Ocho unlimbered her bullhorn and her voice rebounded against the still desert air. "Awright, people. Now hear this. We're headin' back, y' hear? Anybody goin' back with me assemble front of the depot in five minutes, and hustle your ass we ain't got no time t' waste!"

338

Out on the depot apron there was a stir of activity. Voices broke the late morning stillness. Engines revved and the unmistakable roar of the APC engine split the air. A fearful silence fell on the little depot office.

Cardinal Vendetta began to pray. "Almighty and eternal God, the very earth trembles in thy glance…"

And while those in the office pondered the consequences of this strangest of events, Sammy Blankenship was having his own problems. The Sergeant, whose name he never did get, kept insisting there had to be a way to get diesel fuel to issue from the nozzle of this HPO15 dispenser. In his native language he allowed as how he'd already screwed up having been the one to fire a 140 round accidentally for which screw-up he'd had his arse reamed, and this time he had his orders and he would be damned if he didn't find a way to carry them out or the next reaming might be permanent! Sammy might have attempted to wrest the nozzle from the sergeant's hand if the sergeant hadn't been bigger than he, and if he hadn't in addition to his inherent ferocity an AK5 strapped to his back.

It wasn't until the little Specialist 2C re-emerged with a hammer that Sammy Blankenship permitted himself a pure and unmitigated panic.

****

"How did you get loose?" Cray shouted into the shadows of the lab. Kirsten's flickering figure teased him from amid the glass and steel columns. "

"Come and discover," she shouted back, and she actually laughed before she vanished.

"The little daigo is loose." Endicotte's voice in the cell phone echoed in Cray's mind. But Ungaroni had been there. Sitting on the ground, bound and semi conscious. And now the Lagerquist woman appeared like some mischievous sprite and teased him, and led him on, and vanished again. Sebastian Cray paused a moment. He had a splitter of a migraine coming on. Pain gripped his stomach and promised him a wakened ulcer. He was perspiring premonitory anxiety. Control was slipping from his grasp. Worse, there was something about this situation had become quite suddenly, unreal!

"I say. Are you looking for someone?"

Cray wheeled about. He stood looking up into a gaunt and very Anglo-Celtic face and into eyes shrewd beyond their myopic pretense at simplicity. "Who the bloody hell are you?" Cray demanded.

"Pepperdine is the name. Arthur Stringfellow Pepperdine, laboratory supervisor, don't y'see. Now then, if it's the big, Nordic blonde you're after, she's off in that di-rection. How-evah, if it's the little fellow with the improbable nose, he went in that di-rection, I believe."

Pepperdine Stringfellow smiled down at Cray.

Cray returned the smile with a glower. "You're having me on, aren't you? You're one of them!"

"Having you on?" the other protested. "Why, sir, what possible reason…and who, might I ask, are 'them'?" At the crash of breaking glass Cray wheeled about. Endicotte in the shadows was cautioning silence and beckoning with his free hand. When Cray turned about once more, the Pepperdine fellow was gone.

"What's going down?" Endicotte spoke through a rasp of frustration and anger.

"I don't know how they're doing it, Charles, but we're being mousetrapped, I fear."

"What're we gonna do?"

"We chance it, or, we cut and run."

"Be a shame give it up after we come all this way."

"Are you game. Charles?"

"Go for it."

"Good show. You bear right. I'll go this way. Circle about. Meet you up front."

****

Tisibon was without his specs. Bombaste was preoccupied nursing his outrage at having been treated like common package of goods and he'd not had his blood-pressure medication.

It fell to Kirsten to discern the prepostrosity of the situation. It was at Doctor Pepperdine's direction that Kirsten had initiated the game of cat and mouse amongst the laser columns. She was to lead on the Endicotte fellow, Pepperdyne suggested, and Paco Ungaroni would lead on the Major, except that Paco wasn't really there. It had to occur to one wedded to hard facts as was Kirsten Lagerquist that an illusional trick was being played here, or, alternatively, something was being perpetrated that had nothing to do with "facts" as she knew them.

So went the game for some twenty minutes during which time the proper Doctor Lagerquist fell into a kind of sober assessment. Where was she? In Switzerland. What was she doing here? How had she come to play cat and mouse with these dangerous characters in a winery-cum physics lab in Switzerland when, properly, she belonged in the laboratories and offices of the Hospital in Upsala? It was all in the name of "love." How preposterous. How unforgivably romantic. That she should have pursued a figment of her hormonal imagination half way across Europe. But then the image of Pistone rose before her eyes. She stood once more in the unblinking sun of the Cote d'Azure. She was being carried, bodily and stark naked by a total stranger down the strand amid a large crowd of youngsters equally naked who at first cleared a passage, who gaped in awed silence and who then burst into an unrestrained whoop of approval and applause. How utterly preposterous. Unforgivable. But it had happened. She had wanted to die! Yes. Bury that fact as she might, it was true. She would have given up her life to unbearable anxiety. To despair.

She stood hidden behind the huge glass columns of six laser cannon.

Out there stood the stage of the 5-dim. demonstration on which the cannons' terrible light was focused. In time of the mind and in the scenario of imagination she visited once more those few moments of shock and of joy, she nursed the unreality of those minutes by the sea, and he was smiling at her. His face was close to her own, and he carried her, their bodies pressed together so close, and he was smiling. She would have thrust away the image as something silly, something, unforgivably banal, unworthy of herself but then someone seized her about the neck.

Something cold and hard was pressed to her ear. "Okay, luv," Endicotte said in a mock Cockney accent. "Tell'em we've done wiv fun'n gymes. Oi wants the lit'le dygoe, and oi wants 'im naow or oil blow yer friggn 'ead orf, mind." He kept his hold and he pushed her, forced her out onto the stage.

Wanda looked up at them. As did Doctor Pepperdine, and Laszlo. These spectators turned away from the desert scenario and with equal equanimity they regarded the appearance of the one called himself Major Moore.

That one strode across the stage, gun in hand and full of command as is one whose patience has run out. "All right," says he. "I want the Ungaroni fellow. I want him here, and now, or I will not speak for the consequences. Do you hear me?"

"You need not shout, you know," said Wanda. "The gentleman you seek is right there." She pointed to the desert scene.

Moore and Endicotte gaped.

Assuredly, that was Paco. And there was Kari Agapé. She and the little Italian stood in the bright sunlight of a desert scenario. The clouds of a recent rain shower parted and Kari stood prim and patient, if in slight dishabille. Paco slouched, hands in pockets, as though waiting for something to happen and quite oblivious to those standing in the laboratory without. Kari and Paco gave every appearance of two people waiting at a roadside stop, perhaps for the bus to appear.

"Ungaroni!" Cray shouted. "Come out or I will kill the woman!"

"No need to shout, sir," Wanda said. "He can't hear you. He is in another world, you see."

"Another world?" Cray repeated. "Another of your devilish tricks, more like. I know a holographic projection when I see one. Ungaroni," he shouted again. "One minute, and the woman dies."

Those present turned as one to watch Ungaroni. He continued to slouch and to shuffle about on the hard asphalt of the highway. He kicked at a stone, and looked upwards into the clearing sky very much like one killing time, as they say, waiting for an appointed minute when something agreed upon was to happen.

Kari removed her shoes. She poured sand from one of those black pumps and she regarded the other shoe with some irritation and distaste.

It may have been as Wanda suggested, that Paco Ungaroni and Kari Agapé could not hear Moore's outcry.

However, those on the outside could see into that alternative world much as one might see a performance on an enormous television screen. What they saw was a speck on the bright horizon that slowly took on form. It was the APC. Ocho was returning. Paco Ungaroni and Kari Agapé came to attention now. They moved to one side of the roadway and, indeed, they acted in every respect like eager passengers waiting to board a bus. Paco vanished for a moment, "off stage," as it were. He re-emerged with a red zipper jacket clutched in his left hand. If one could have made out the logo on the back he might have read something about a Racing Association.

"No! Bloody hell! I won't have it!" Cray shouted. "I see through this now."

What happened next took them all by surprise, not least of all Major Moore, who was really Sebastian Cray. That portly gentleman in field jacket and jodhpurs was seen to dash across the manifest stage with an alacrity few would have credited him and in so crossing he knocked poor Laszlo quite off his feet. Nor did he hesitate at the dimensional boundary, but he bounded across as though he had every assurance of what he was about.

Those in witness stood helpless as he dashed down the intervening ten meters of Route 40. The APC kept coming. Paco and Kari waited. Only at the last moment did they turn to acknowledge his approach. Cray seized Paco's jacket. Paco snatched it back. Cray struck poor Paco in the face with his fist and knocked him off his feet. Then he must have heard the rumble and roar of the APC because he stopped and stared at the steel-treaded monster even now approaching, lurid and absurd in its flowered motif.

The acting vehicle commander peered down from the topmost turret hatch. It was the Reverend BillyBob Mordecai Bloodworthy looking nothing short of comic-ridiculous in a commo helmet. From the driver's hatch someone else in a similar helmet shouted out: "Cray? Z'at you?"

"What? Who? Connie? What the deuce…"

"I got a bone t' pick with you, Mack ."

"Have you, now? And I have a score or two to settle with you. Come down!"

"Ain't got time t' stand around talkin', Cray. That portal's liable t'close any seckin' now".

"I know a scam when I see one, Ocho, and I must say you've gone to elaborate lengths this time."

"Geddadathere, schmuck!"

"See here, Ocho. I've had enough of your chicaneries…"

So they stood, she tucked into the body of the steel beast and peering out; he below in the breeches and garb of an English gentleman at hounds looking up. The enormous mechanized monster rumbled and mumbled as though impatient to be on. Cray stood at its very front, gripping the downslope edge of the vehicle and he shouted over the din of the engine, something about debts due him, and chicaneries and about "having been hung out to dry."

Connie Ocho answered in kind, but then, to those on the "outside," as it were, watching this silent mummery, she seemed to change. Cray shouted, but she stared -- outward. As though she were seeing what neither he nor any one else was given to see. She was conjuring a tall slender gentleman with a fine Roman nose and intense black eyes hidden behind great green sun glasses, threatening the untested appetites of a fourteen-year-old, and the words 'myopic owl' surfaced in memory. She was recalling what the TC woman said that night about Miguel Fuentes and the collision with the fire truck in East Chicago. An accident, they said. That's what it was. It was really nobody's fault. "It was nobody's fault," Connie muttered. "Uncle Miguel? Carmen? I love you..."

At which point there occurred in the distant horizon of that desert scene two explosions which arrested everyone's attention. The first made itself known to our spectators on the "outside" as a great if silent burst of light. The second, no more than seconds later, was not to be ignored. It's light seemed to occupy a point in the distance which would put it in the south western suburbs of the metropolis of Albuquerque. To those on the "inside" the sound was more in keeping with what one might associate with a bomb, or an artillery shell. Light and sound were followed by a billowing cloud of smoke.

In the laboratory there was silence. No one seemed capable of saying a word.

After a long interlude, Kari Agapé emerged from the desert scenario with a bloody-nosed Paco in tow.

Tary, winsomely disheveled and wind blown stood on the bare demonstration stage in her tight skirt and her sheer underslip. Her auburn hair was endearingly tosseled and she carried one shoe in her hand. She smiled at them. "My goodness," Kari said matter-of-factly, as might an actress address a soliloquy to a theater audience, "my goodness, but it's so warm in there." And she tittered.

But attention returned front stage. The massive vehicle moved. It's engine rumbled louder and its steel track creaked and shrieked and slowly it moved forward. Cray who stood directly in its path was persuaded to step back. And then to step again. "Uncle Miguel," Ocho was saying. "Uncle Miguel, there ain't gonna be no meeting...Uncle Miguel." In a matter of ten seconds, Cray had stepped back in a bit of alarm, and stepped again as though he still expected the monster to stop. They hadn't settled their dispute, but the vehicle increased its forward motion and he turned about and might have stepped aside to let it pass but that it made a sudden thrust and he was forced to retreat, to step lively, as it were, and what those on the outside saw last was the vehicle in forward motion, gathering speed and Cray running before it, toward them, on the outside, as it were, the huge iron thing suddenly looming at the very portal and Cray pursued, admitting at last that it might very well run him down. He was, someone later remarked, not unlike an actor in the cinema, or on the television in an action close-up, fleeing for his very life but the onlookers were never to know whether it ran him down or not because at that precise moment the laser cannons went dark and the entire scenario shut down. Our spectators were left for some moments staring rather dumbly at the empty manifest stage.

"The arc of incidence," Wanda said, as to everyone, and to no one, "An action has got to move through Space and over Time. But Time got sheared, you see." Then a curious look crossed her features, as of a realization delayed and only now arrived. "Laszlo," she queried. "You did pay the electricity assessment, did you not?"

They continued to stare at the bare manifest stage, but then their revery was shattered by the sudden emergence on that very stage of the one called himself Pepperdine. "I say," says that one. He regarded them all with a quizzical smile. "Good show, wot?"

Only Charles Endicotte permitted himself a "sheeeesh!" of amazement before he pushed Kirsten away and he himself vanished into the shadows of the lab. Had the others not been preoccupied with resigning themselves to what had transpired they might have heard the slamming of the freight-door entry and then the puttering of the little engine of the Petit Géant vanishing into the lowering day.

Ammon's Horn

Post-Script

The desert sun torched Benni's face and the sweat poured into his eyes. At Bahado, he had left the dry riverbed of the Jube and struck out into open country. The roar of the Harley and the merciless light framed his world. If not for Paco, he wouldn't have taken it on, but Paco said he had to because his life depended on it—whose life—Paco's life? Or his own? He didn't quite understand. The smart-mouth bitch in the magazine office said he lacked *acutezza*. He was stupid. Had to be. Nobody but '*no stupido*' rode off across the open desert if he didn't have to, but he had to, because Paco said…

"*Il'y'a de derober un' bil-yón!*" Castigné shook his fingers at the enormity of it, grinned like a kid getting away with something—*un' millión d'un millión!* Mind's eye gave Castigné a cynical face in a huge head and a barrel body on match-stick legs but he, Pistone, couldn't be remembering because Castigné had been dead when he got there! And anyhow, what he was remembering was all wrong. The cinderblock shack was the other way, up near Baidebo. He was standing in the middle of that dim little room staring at a faded calendar on the wall, It said July, 1935. A picture of Mussolini all jaw and gesture—*Il Duce ha Sempre Raggione!* —"the leader is always right!" and Castigné slouched in the chair behind

349

him was already beginning to stink so that couldn't have been, but if so why was he—how could he be—remembering?

This other one, the con, the short *Americano* with the pot-belly and the curly hair, always smiling that one, through his teeth, and he says, "Paco says you got to hide the discs. The Caruso woman won't do. They're onto her. And the little black thief's been bought and sold—took your picture taking the antenna down. Once they get their hands on the discs you and Paco, you're dangerous. The one they call Cray, he'll order you hit, both of you. I mean, that's the way it's done, man, in the detective biz, y'know?"

And there is himself objecting, shouting, "*Ei, scimunito!* You silly asshole! How could you be telling me this if you were not there. The computer deal in Somalia, that's before you ever got into the act."

"That's OK, Benni-guy," says the *Americano*, "I'm with you now, right here, and that means I'm part of the deal—whatever it is, whenever it was. You 'n me, we can dream it up any way we want it to be—you 'n me, and Doc. G., and the little Ruski doc. Like one big happy—hallucination! Hah! Yeah, ain't this a gas? Say, man. I do like this bod!"

Which is where he proved her wrong—the French bitch at the magazine—because he'd outsmarted the smart guys. By the time Cray or his buddy got to Bakool, il Benni was gone and the discs were safe in a postal storage box in Geneva. He'd mailed them right under the noses of the Somali bandits when his fuel inject filter clogged for real this time just ten kiloms out of Iddan and he's trying to blow the sand out, and the sun's baking his brains twice over. These scruffy-looking desert cockroaches stuck a rifle in his ear and said they wanted money while making like to steal his 'bike—eight of them to one of him—and he's not so sure they won't put a bullet in him and leave him no more than a puddle of scarlet piss in the sand.

That's when the remembering took a different turn from what he thought he remembered that it really happened. In this version, van Horn came into it with a grin, a bag o'bullshit and one very big AK-52 to suggest the *banditi* take a hike. Van Horn says there's no telling if Cray hasn't got agents in Iddan just waiting for him to show up with those discs, so why not let himself, the Dutch trader, Mik-hai-all van Hor-nen-dahl, import-export out of Amsterdam, handle the deal. Cray and them don't know van Hor-nen-dahl and he takes the discs and mails them to Geneva. The next time he sees the package of discs, Paco is shoving them into the pocket of his red Association racing jacket like a pack of his goddam smokes. Suddenly, he continues remembering aloud:

But how can that be? Never knew no van Horn until that night he was looking in the mirror in the bathroom the villa Bonchance belongs to them two French clowns and he's stroking his dong like he never seen one before. I think this phony sonofabitch is playing with my mind! He's making things up like he wants them they should'a been, like you remake a movie you don't like how it ended. Gets me talking to myself out loud, like, just so's I can keep track of me. Whose bod is this anyhow? I think I'm goin' outta my head!

The other one, the Doctor Gregorian, at least he's got enough class he ain't playing games, all he's got's a hard-on for the big blonde. She keeps starin' at me like she's got the hots... for me? Only seen her once, f'chrissake, at Le Brassus, we was shootin' a TeleCom video for the magazine, they stick her on the bike with me, sits behind with her arms round me I thought she was gonna crack my ribs, I swear, breathin' in my ear, making like she's riding a case o' the hots. Figgered her for some middle age broad ain't been laid and I'd of...but they got her outta there, ready for next shot so I never got no chance t' talk t' her.

Gregorian. That's who it was. He's talkin' t'me inside my

own head, I mean it's like I thought I went nutso in spades havin' another guy inside my head, then twice, three times over nutso -skizzy, there's two more! Them docs—the French clowns, Tizzibono and Bombasto, or whatever—they talk like I was dead! I mean, I'm layin' there, can't move, can't talk, and they're talkin' like I was cold meat, f'chrissake. The Gregorian guy, he says hey, Benni, let's get outta here before these characters do us some more damage, and that's when we done it, picked up and moved outta that lab scene middle o' the night, get us a 'burger 'n coffee. Dig that—get *us* a burger.

San Tro-pay, get the Somali sand outta my craw. Lotsa sun, water, naked broads, the whole works an' I'm out inna deep water just foolin' around 'cause I like water, lotsa clean, cool water after all that fuckn' sand an' I'm under water fishin' up clams jus' f' fun and I see this body, big body, tre-menduss, nothin' like the skinny little tittybump kids onne beach, I see her comin' down inna water, big nekkid and beautiful an' like to drown, and I grabs her and we're huggin' real close. She coughs up lotsa water, cut her foot so I'm holdin' her up, helpin' her walk, n'en I'm carryin' her downa beach an' she's lookin' at me like she wantsa eat me alive, an' I come up and it's the goddam Gregorian jumps inna the act. 'Kirsten!' he says. 'Is it really you?'

Then I remember where I seen her was when I'm layin' flat on my back inna street in that hick town tourist trap in Le Brassus and that crazy fucker chases me down with a car, hits me clean off my bike and I remember, I'm layin' there, can't move, and it's her, an' she's talkin' t' me, sayin' my name, an' the las' thing I remember is I reconnize who she is from the video shoot and she's cryin', f' chrissake, 'n then I guess I passed out, an' nex' thing it's Gregorian takin' over the show.

F'while there I think I'm back onna beach. The light. Right in my eyes. But I'm back in some kina hospital place. One o' them two loony Francos says somethin' about fortunate accidents, like somebody clobbered me—I gotta super lump back o' my head and bannages all around, an' I know it's the same place we started, 'cause that's gotta be the van Horn sittin' up onna gurney over there, and that's gotta be the Gregorian over there, and this guy here, he's gotta be really me, the Pistone. I'm doin' the seein' 'cause I reconnize what I'm lookin', who I'm lookin' at. It's her! She's bendin' down close, smilin' the way she knows how, y' know, like my uncle Nick usta say, 'with the whole face,' and she's sayin' t' me, real quiet like, 'Benni? Benni, is it you?' An' I sez t' her, 'Yeah, babe, it's me. An' y' know what? I ain't drownin' no more', and she comes down and she kisses me, real good, and she sez somethin' about bintswaggers, or somethin' an' I ast her, later, what's bintswaggers? and she laughs an' she sez it's nuthn', jus' a doc she usta know…

****

There was a cab waiting for van Horn next morning, and then a private *ballistique* at Cointrin, Geneva, non-stop to O'Hare, Chicago. Two hours later he was in the chancellor's mansion on University Avenue. A stone-faced maid admitted him and escorted him into Madame's boudoir and quietly closed the door.

Mack van Horn stood a trifle travel weary before the huge mirror in her boudoir. He patted his broad paunch with some satisfaction and ran his fingers through the thick thatch of curls on his broad head. He smiled at his reflection with some satisfaction. "Ah, 'tis a fine and handsome lad, y'are," he said in a brogue. "But couldn't y' mother ha' given y' another five inches t' be standin' in?" Then he chuckled at his own self-conscious wit.

A mind's moment took him back to Tisibon's lab. He was bidding Kirsten adieu (a kiss to the cheek) and the doctors. He shook Benni's hand. "Been good knowing us," he said. Everyone had a good laugh at that one. Then the memory-reverie shattered. As out of nowhere, Didi des Dieux appeared behind him. He turned and smiled at her, diffidently, almost expectantly. "Good morning, Ma'am," he said. "Agent van Horn reporting."

She lay back on a chaise lounge. She was wearing a gauzy film of a thing through whose layers he might, if he'd dared be obvious, see the sumptuous components of her incomparable bod. "You did well, van Horn," she said.

"I did, didn't I?" he said. He swallowed hard.

"It all worked out as we'd hoped," she said. "Now, little man, time for one's reward, hum?" Van Horn approached the lounge. He felt the perspiration trickle down his back. His throat went dry, and for some reason he could not shape into words, he was afraid.

"You know who I am, don't you dear?" she murmured.

He didn't remember having done so but somehow he was undressed and hairy-naked. He lay with her. She held him. She brushed his lips with her own.

"Who...you...are?" he squeaked. "Yes, Ma'am. I figured...no ordinary..."

"That's right, Mackenzie. I am no ordinary woman. But then, you are no ordinary man, are you?"

"Me, Ma'am?" van Horn protested. "Oh, shucks. I'm just a plain old..." A sudden light of knowledge descended on van Horn. By that light, he choked and trembled, but capable of a facetious streak to the end, he clowned, "So, tell me, little girl, what's your name?"

"We will make love now, Mackenzie." Fear made him small. He looked up into her eyes from between the cleavage of her breasts.

She opened to him that incredible body. "We will make love, and I will take you with me to another world."

"Ma'am?"

"I will keep you, and we will make love—forever."

"Forever, Ma'am? Excuse me, but that's a mighty long time."

"You said it yourself, Mackenzie. That you might not survive it. Remember?"

"Yes, Ma'am. I remember. But I was just…I mean, I…I…I…"

****

Kirsten Lagerquist and Benni Pistone were married in Benni's hometown of Chieti in the green and beautiful Italian Abruzzi. Biographical history records Kirsten learned to enjoy pasta and vino and that she put on weight and learned to speak the local Italian dialect like a native. It says they were deliriously happy for several years and that they produced two fine, if outsized, children. The record says Kirsten rose to directorship of the Institute at Upsala and that with her collaboration Aram Gregorian and Claude Tisibon perfected the Psyche-Transferential process of Virtual Immortality for which they shared a Nobel Prize.

As for Benni, he regained his international cross-country championship in 2086 and, having bested the best in the world's most demanding contests, he went on to create new challenges. It was he who established the Trans-Alpine Supreme Cross Country Motorcycle Race, Obervald to Monthey, roughly 150 kilometers through and across the Bernese Alps.

His old rival Paul Giradoux witnessed Benni's fall into a crevasse in the Fiescher glacier. Scientists calculate il Benni will emerge at head of the valley in exactly 342 years. given the present rate of glacial retreat, on a Wednesday afternoon at between 1:30 PM and nightfall. We expect he will be mounted and as avid as ever to cross the finish line.

Kirsten is not known to have married again, though those who knew her best said she lived out her life and raised her children as a woman quite happy and fulfilled.

As for Anatoli Polichuk, record says his psyche was successfully transferred to a younger body and that in this new if pseudonymous identity he lived on for many more years. A search of the vital stats. of that time gives his fourth wife's name as a Huffding, B., of Amsterdam. As to his having made any further contributions in physics, the supernet is mute.

As for the 5-dim. phenomenon: COSE, the Congressional Office of Scientific Explanations, concludes the alleged dimensional aperture does not fit Standard Model of Everything, hence, it could not have been achieved. WGW (We Got It Wrapped) theory says "Hermosillo" and "Siberia" and such are holdovers from the ancient Aztec-Esquimaux mythology. Maybe so, but we sure do miss ol' Albakurkee. COSE says the inundation of territory from New York to Miami Beach was a natural aberration not likely to have happened the first time and statistically unlikely to happen again.

As for Mackenzie van Horn, he died peacefully—in his sleep it is presumed—cause of death indeterminate. Post-mortem examination suggests he succumbed to what an anonymous wag has called "terminal pleasure," this judging from the permanent erection which no post-mortem artistry was able to eliminate, and from the equally ineradicable smile on his face, either of which may or may not have had anything to do with the feminine underpants (courtesy Victoria's Secret, size 10) found clutched in his hand.

~FINIS~

Outhouse Express. Weatherwatch, EA.COM.: Shandeken-in-the-Catskills, New York, 05.14.89:

Howdy, NetNerds, Maud Pritchet here from atop Slide

Mountain with your news and weather on the Everywhere and Anytime Broadband comin' t' you via AM, FM, TV, Cell, Ipod, Blueberry, Cockleburr or whatever electro-photonic ghizzy suits ya. And, if you're payin' attention, providin' you with a satellite view of what used t' be the Hudson Highlands and the Breakneck, and Cold Springs, courtesy RovingEye Transmit.

From about 3000 feet we're lookin' down at the placid waters of post-flood and cat-ass-stro-fee. Lookin'south and east, there's what used to be Hudson River valley. Before the Atlantic filled her up, that is. And the East River back-flowed. And the Long Island Sound over-flowed. And they swamped the New York Island. Can't see it from here. but they tell me it kinda took little old New York City by surprise.

Ain't had the heart to do it myself, but them that's done it by boat tell me Times Square's thirty feet under. Empire State building's still there. Top stories sticking up out the water. Bridges are gone. The Brooklyn. And the George Washington. Remember the Verrazano Narrows? They're tellin' us the Statue of Liberty's up over her nipples. Ain't naught but water now. All the way west and north, Schenectady to Peeksakill and down the Jersey Shore. Whole of what used t' be the south-east bottom of the state is one big lake.

Folks up here in the highlands are singin' the blues. Hey, Chestertown, where are you? And, like, I remember Plattsburg. Things are gettin' crowded, lemme tell you. I mean, little places like Elizabethtown and Witherbee lookin' more like war camps than the neat little old towns they yewsta was.

Sanitation's gettn t' be problem, too. All that water, like the poet says, and damned little of it drinkable. Sewarage? Gettn to be hazard. How does a party lift the lid on the bowl and not pee in his neighbor's chowder? Got folks askin' when's the water gonna retreat? Hey, Cholly, it's got to have somplace to retreat to. Got no idea where that might be. Or when.

And now, brought to you by FloatnSpit, the makers of floatation collars, waterwings, scubatubes, and like that.

A look on the Corporate front. Official voice of the Federated Republic of the US Inc. says the Auto-no-mouse state of Nebraska has struck water! That's what it says here. Water! As in fresh and drinkable. No more'n 650 feet down. Says here 'geological types affirm the water to be a tail end of what they used t'call the Oh-gah-lah-lah aqui-fer extending south across what was the state of Kansas and into old Oklahoma and all the way down to the New Mex.' Them Nebraskans are claimin' ex-clusive rights, would you believe. But the Auto-no-mouse state of Kansas says the aquifer crosses the old state line and they're digging like t' save their lives, which, come down to it, what with they got thirty years' drought, and like that, most likely they are.

Reps in Oklahona, as in Auto-no-mous State of, their senator here in in Sciatica, DC, says the aquifer was first dug in Chicopee, OK., back in the nineteen-ought-thirties and, by golly, precedent and the history books give them prior claim t' that water, he sez.

Cimarron Times is makin' noise like mebee the two Auto-no-mouse states gonna re-mobilize the old national guard and they're lookin' t' hire the Indo-Malays in New Sree-vee-ja-yaa—that's the former New Mex—for help.

I mean, what with them Indos havin' all them tanks and artillery and like that looks like mebee we're headin' into a war. Been a while, ain't it? As says the philosopher, 'Sheee-it, man, things are gettn' back to normal.'

Ammon's Horn

About the Author

Born on the banks of the Detroit River in an orange crate house next to a pot-belly stove in the cold spring of 1930,Guerrino Amati (G. Amati) worked his way through a BA English from Wayne State University and, later, after a stint in the US Army, an MA from the University of Chicago. Associate Editor for Popular Mechanics Magazine in the early sixties, he taught English grammar, rhetoric, literature, logic in City Colleges of Chicago from 1962 to 1995. Amati began writing in 1982, happily ensconced with his wife in an old farm house in rural Crete, just south of Chicago. He has written three novels and eight short stories. With five children—two daughters, three sons—this "old man is trying like Hell to get someone to publish his ironic, sardonic take on this most absurd of species."

If you enjoyed *Ammon's Horn* consider these other fine Books from Savant Books and Publications:

A Whale's Tale by Daniel S. Janik
Tropic of California by R. Page Kaufman
The Village Curtain by Tony Tame
Dare to Love in Oz by William Maltese
The Interzone by Tatsuyuki Kobayashi
Today I am a Man by Larry Rodness
The Bahrain Conspiracy by Bentley Gates
Called Home by Gloria Schumann
Kanaka Blues by Mike Farris
First Breath edited by Z. M. Oliver
Poor Rich by Jean Blasiar
The Jumper Chronicles by W. C. Peever
William Maltese's Flicker by William Maltese
My Unborn Child by Orest Stocco
Last Song of the Whales by Four Arrows
Perilous Panacea by Ronald Klueh
Falling but Fulfilled by Zachary M. Oliver
Manifest Intent by Mike Farris
Mythical Voyage by Robin Ymer
Hello, Norma Jean by Sue Dolleris
Richer by Jean Blasair
Charlie No Face by David Seaburn
Number One Bestseller by Brian Morley
My Two Wives and Three Husbands by S. Stanley Gordon
In Dire Straits by Jim Currie
Wretched Land by Mila Komarnisky
Chan Kim by Ilan Herman
Who's Killing All The Lawyers? by A. G. Hayes

Scheduled for Release in 2011:

Wavelengths edited by Z. M. Oliver
In the Himalayan Nights by Anoop Chandola
Blood Money by Scott Mastro
Random Views of Asia from the Mid-Pacific by William Sharp
Almost Paradise by Laurie Hanan

http://www.savantbooksandpublications.com

www.ingramcontent.com/pod-product-compliance
Lightning Source LLC
Chambersburg PA
CBHW051446260626
47162CB00001B/280